DREAMING
IN THE
SHADOWS

Ross Caligiuri

23/50

Ross Caligiuri
3530 E Sutton Dr
Phoenix, AZ 85032
DreamingInTheShadows@gmail.com

Ordering Information:

Quantity sales. Special discounts are available on quantity purchases by corporations, associations, and others. For details, contact the publisher at the address above.

Orders by U.S. trade bookstores and wholesalers. Please contact distribution at: (651) 341-2269 or email DreamingInTheShadows@gmail.com

Library of Congress Control Number: 2017902221
Ross Caligiuri,Phoenix,ARIZONA

Publisher's Cataloging-in-Publication data
Caligiuri, Ross.
Dreaming in the Shadows / Ross Caligiuri
978-0-9985841-0-2 (pbk.) — 978-0-9985841-1-9 (ebook)
1. Young Adult — Science Fiction —Visionary and Metaphysical.
2. Dystopian —Third Person.

The text of this book is set in 11-point Calibri

Visit us on the Web! DreamingInTheShadows.com

Printed in the United States of America
First Edition
10 9 8 7 6 5 4 3 2 1

CHAPTER 1

As her feet beat the concrete ground beneath them, her chest began to ache. It had been a long time since she had run at a full sprint. She was, quite literally, running for her life, and leaving everything she had known before behind. Regardless of her past experiences, here she was, blindly following a girl, who was virtually a stranger, because she had promised to lead Eleanor to safety.

The two girls continued to move at full speed, and Eleanor thought about the note she had left on the kitchen counter for the man she loved and had shared a life with over the past three years, Deryn. Saying goodbye to his face would have been too emotional for her. She knew he would have begged her to stay, or to come with her, and neither of those things were an option.

Eleanor had scribbled out the letter for Deryn in the early morning hours, while he slept in their warm bed. He remained sleeping until their house filled with the sound from the old speakers that hung in every room. Mandatory laws demanded that every home be wired to receive the daily, city-wide, morning announcements from their leader Dr. Secora. His voice infiltrated the entire sector as he spoke from his office, located on the top floor of Obsidia, the main building in the center of Constance.

Eleanor had secretly removed the letter from her pocket, and placed it discreetly onto the counter, before the two of them left their small house to start their days. For Deryn, the day had begun just as any other. For Eleanor, it signaled the end of the life she had grown to know.

Her vision was flooded with the recent memory of her mother's trembling lips, and her father's tightened shoulders. Her parents had stood at the front door of their house, as they watched their daughter begin to walk away for the last time. Her younger brother, Will, fumbled for words that his developing mind could not yet form.

The necklace that hung down past her collarbone, hit against her skin with every step she took. Her father had given it to her as he said his final goodbye, and had informed her that the pendant originally belonged to an estranged, older sister that Eleanor never knew existed.

Her father had turned his face away before she could plead for more answers. Representing an older sister that her father had implied suffered through a similar isolated fate, the necklace brought comfort of the unknown to Eleanor. She left her family behind, moments before she met the strange girl that now guided her towards her new future.

The city sector of Arrant, where she had spent her whole life, looked much different to Eleanor as she dashed through the back alleys. From the main streets, on the other side of the tall buildings, the everyday bustlings of the citizens were in full effect. Their daily routines had always turned a blind eye to the reality of a situation like Eleanor was in.

At this moment, most people trapped inside the high concrete walls of this sector, were starting their work break. They were finding a nice place to sit and eat their lunches. It was necessary to seek shelter from the dust that was constantly emitted from the labor building that Eleanor's sector was known for. If you had the skills and income in Arrant, it was easy to run a small business. Unfortunately, most of the inhabitants there were destined to work their lives away, stuck inside the gloomy factory. Some of the athletic types could apply to work for the Agency. They were promised a life of luxury, and in some cases, even travel. The applicants that left the walls of Arrant however, never came back.

As she said her goodbyes, members of the Agency had shown up at Eleanor's parents house looking for her. They had demanded that her parents turn her over to them. Her father had blocked the doorway, allowing time for Eleanor to escape.

Eleanor ran as fast as she could, but the agents were quickly closing in on her. Thinking fast, she sidestepped into an alleyway between two buildings, attempting to throw them off of her trail.

Suddenly, a hand reached out and covered Eleanor's mouth. She screamed, and the noise was muffled by the stranger's hand. Before Eleanor could fight off her attacker, a soft voice spoke out to her.

"You need to come with me if you want to survive," the girl didn't wait for an answer, and immediately set off running.

Eleanor weighed her options and in a split second decided it was better to follow the strange girl. She had a feeling in her gut that it was the right move to make. She hoped that wherever this girl was leading her would provide her with more answers to the wildly confusing situation she found herself in.

Eleanor's only clue about her new world came from her parents. She had an older sister that had suffered the same detached existence that Eleanor was now faced with. The reason her parents had kept such a secret was unknown to her.

Eleanor had heard talk of the rebellion that existed inside the city of Constance before. Most of the information she gathered was considered an old fairy tale by the general public. There were a few stories here and there about people angered by their present living conditions, who had demanded that the center of Constance be held responsible for it. However, information was never passed between the five different sectors that formed the entire city. Over the years the tales of the rebellion had become children's bedtime stories, and people did not take them seriously.

The unfamiliar girl who guided her path, seemed at ease. As if the concept of escaping the Agency was nothing new to her. Eleanor wondered how long the girl had been a part of the rebellion. Considering the excellent physical condition the girl was in, and her impressive stamina, it seemed she'd been involved for quite some time. No one in Arrant lived a life physically demanding enough to need to run for that amount of time. No one that wasn't set on becoming an agent, at least.

Eleanor's arms and legs began to burn and she desperately wanted a moment to catch her breath. The alleyways and buildings of Arrant sped past her vision. She had lived her whole life inside of this sector, but she no longer had her bearings about her and couldn't even make an educated guess as to what her location was.

The girl turned around, and after noticing the fact that Eleanor was losing steam said, "Why don't we take a break here for a second."

"Yeah, sure. If you think it's safe enough." Eleanor responded, trying to seem nonchalant, even though she was incredibly relieved at the suggestion.

Eleanor slumped against the wall of one of Arrant's gray brick buildings. They were in an alley, still hidden from the main road. The girl walked over and pulled a jar of water out of her bag.

Now that they had finally stopped, Eleanor had a chance to get a good look at the girl. She was slim, with long legs. Her dark tanned skin was in stark contrast to her bright green eyes. Tight, curled blonde hair hung down most of her back, held by a thin string that worked its way across the top of her forehead.

"Here. You should drink this." The girl handed the jar of water to Eleanor. She tried her best to contain her ravenous thirst and accept the offering with grace.

"Try and save some for later. We still have a long way to go. I can only assume that some of those agents will be making their way here soon enough." The girl watched Eleanor as she took a drink that had lasted the entire time she spoke.

"Thank you," Eleanor managed to get out between gulps of water and gasps for air. "Where are we headed, anyway?"

"For now, don't try and overthink things. We have everything set up for you. All you need to do is keep up with me." The girl tried to smile encouragingly at Eleanor, but it came across as sympathetic pity nonetheless.

"Those agents that showed up at my parents' house, what exactly do they want from me?" Eleanor asked, her voice shaking.

"They were there because of what you are. They were after me too, but that was for things that happened awhile ago," the girl replied.

"I've heard others talk about people like me that have the same dream, night after night," Eleanor said. "They say it's some kind of a warning signal. Does all of this have anything to do with that?"

The girl looked her square in the eyes, and in a comforting voice replied, "Hold out a little longer, if you can. I promise you will get all the answers you need." She placed a hand reassuringly on Eleanor's shoulder as she continued talking.

"While we are resting here, you should know that the first step when going into hiding will be to choose a new name for yourself. The life you left back there on your parent's front porch is gone. It's time to leave it behind for good. So, what will it be?"

Eleanor slouched further into the wall, taking a moment to think. Emotions washed over her again as she thought of her family and Deryn. The thought of leaving them behind made it difficult to concentrate. She decided, in order to remind herself of her past life, she needed to incorporate her past self within her new name.

"Nora," Eleanor announced. Saying it out loud was painful—she knew her old life was now completely gone with those two syllables being said aloud.

"I like it. It's very pretty. Nora. Okay then Nora we should get moving. One more long sprint and we should be at the wall. Think you can handle that?" The girl took off before she could respond. Nora scrambled to her feet and started to race after her.

"Wait! You didn't tell me your name!" Nora called out. The girl made a sharp turn around a corner.

"Phoenix!" The girl yelled back to Nora before she disappeared from view.

CHAPTER 2

Phoenix stopped running as the two of them reached the tall concrete wall that separated Arrant from the sector to the west. The wall ran across as far as Nora could see. Savoring what could be her last moment inside of Arrant, she looked to the north, towards the center of the city. Obsidia, where Dr. Secora lived, was a prominent fixture in the sky, locked away inside the walled-off portion of the center of the city. From her schooling days, Nora recalled learning how the city was split into five different sectors. Each was a small wedge that centered around a large circle in the middle, which was where the large, high-rise building was located.

From what she remembered, the center, circular portion of Constance was where the Agency operated from. Directly south of the center was where her sector, Arrant, was located. Arrant was known for producing the building material used to wall off the entire city—both the inner walls used to separate each sector, as well as the outer wall to protect the whole area from the outside world.

To the west of the wall, where she and Phoenix currently rested, was the sector known as Blear. The area was used to purify water and provide it to the entire city. School children learned about these other sectors, but were never shown photographs of its citizens or landscape.

If the two girls had gone to the east instead, they would have ran into the equally large wall that separated Arrant from Fallow. Here, she learned, was the area of Constance dedicated to procuring fresh food for the city. From Fallow, you could continue counter-clockwise around the circular city to Sonant. All of Constance's history was recorded and stored there.

Lastly, located between Sonant and Blear, in the northwest, was the sector known as Jejung. Completing the entire circle around the center of Constance, Jejung was identified as the prison sector. This was a place that had tall tales about it, stories of bad children being shipped off there, to live out their days. Besides the horror stories used to intimidate children to behave, the citizens of Arrant had little information about Jejung.

Her eyes fell from Obsidia in the center of Constance and she noticed that Phoenix was struggling to locate something in the large wall.

"It has to be here somewhere," she grunted out loud. Phoenix frantically ran her hands across the surface of the wall, pushing into a brick every so often. Nora joined in and mimicked her actions.

"What are we searching for?" she asked Phoenix, who was clearly frustrated at the situation.

"We have a hidden way to travel through the wall between Arrant and Blear. It's around here somewhere. This was how I was able to get to you in the first place." She sighed impatiently. "This is my first time coming here alone. I thought I would recognize the disguised brick by now, but this whole wall looks the same to me!"

Nora could feel the intense disappointment Phoenix had in herself at the moment. Without knowing what to look for, she continued to randomly press on bricks in the wall. Suddenly, one of the larger concrete blocks pushed in slightly. Phoenix looked over at her surprisingly.

"Finally!" Phoenix exclaimed. "Thanks for the extra set of hands." She moved over to Nora and began to push the large brick completely through the wall. "I'll go through first, then you need to follow me immediately after I signal that it's clear."

Nora watched as her guide disappeared through the gray wall. Uncertainty crept into her mind as Phoenix's arm poked back through the wall, and signaled to Nora that it was her turn. Squeezing her body, she was able to squirm through the newly made opening. Once on the other side, she brushed the dust off of her clothes, and saw that Phoenix had already begun replacing the brick, making the wall whole again. She turned to face the new, unknown sector as Phoenix began to walk away from the wall.

"You'll need to put these on," Phoenix said as she tossed a small pile of clothing at Nora.

Phoenix quickly began to remove her top layer of clothing—a disguise to safeguard her travels through Arrant—and revealed a starkly different ensemble that was completely foreign to Nora.

Hidden under a layer of dull gray and purple, the chosen color scheme of the Arrant clothing designers, the girl wore a long shirt that was a lighter shade of red and had a tie around the mid-section. Her shoes weren't the ordinary style Nora had seen her whole life either. These were much higher on the ankle and didn't have any laces. Her eyes drifted up, and she noticed a necklace made out of rope that hung around the girl's throat. Anyone living in Arrant that chose to wear something like that would have been ridiculed. Silver was by far the accessory of choice there. It's a good thing the girl had attempted to cover it with a bland, gray scarf while in Arrant. The whole outfit was stunning to Nora's innocent eyes.

Nora couldn't help but take in her new surroundings as she quickly pulled the new clothing over her Arrant outfit. Blear was much different than she imagined. Arrant was a dusty gray region full of concrete, while Blear had a very lively feel to it. Once they had walked a few blocks in, Nora noticed a huge, bluish-gray body of water in the center of the sector. She paused for a moment and took in the view.

The buildings around her were made of mostly wood, which gave Blear the complete opposite look of the gray-bricked Arrant landscape. Everything here had a fresh coat of paint on it, and made the sector feel vibrant and clean.

The people walking around Blear seemed to prefer the color blue. Most of the men wore knee-length pants, and lightweight shirts. Some of the women wore bathing suits, loosely concealed under thin, long, opaque jackets. All of them looked ready to enter into the water at a moment's notice. They all walked at a leisurely pace and seemed to be in good spirits. Nora immediately felt jealous of these citizens. This must be why they kept the sectors separated from each other, Nora mused. If they didn't, she was sure that everyone in Constance would have wanted to live here instead.

Metal piping ran around the entire area, flowing into the various buildings from the enormous water source. A single, huge pipe ran right through the center of the sector. Suspended high in the air, the long tube passed over the water and into the wall that separated Blear from the center of Constance. Nora wondered if she would ever get the chance to see inside the center area, reminding herself of the Agency and why it would probably be better if she never did.

As they walked, Phoenix seemed to be on high alert for any sign of the agents, though she had not seen one since she watched Nora's parents' house, back in Arrant. Nora's excitement over seeing another sector seemed to ease Phoenix's suspicions slightly.

"Look at those vehicles out there on the water!" Nora had grabbed onto Phoenix's blue threaded jacket unable to contain her excitement. "I never thought I would ever see so much water in my entire life. Let alone people swimming and driving in it."

Nora's excitement radiated off her. It was good for her to have a moment of distraction, to take her mind off the recent events.

"Have you ever been in the water?" Nora asked Phoenix.

"I wish," she replied dully, showing a side of her Nora hadn't seen yet. "There never seems to be any time to enjoy the things around us anymore."

"Well then, how about you and I, right now, make a promise to each other. After we meet with your leaders, we will come back here and get in," Nora said with sincerity.

"If there is time before I have to go and find the next recruit, we will come back here. Don't get your hopes up, though. I haven't been able to make time for anything like that since I joined the rebellion," Phoenix informed her briskly, returning to the girl Nora had come to know over the last few hours.

"Okay, but if it works out, and you still don't want to go, I'll throw you into the water myself, if I have to."

Phoenix smiled and grabbed Nora's arm playfully. "Come on crazy girl, we are close. Our destination is in that building over there."

The two of them climbed through a few windows of the abandoned buildings and eventually found themselves on the rooftop of one of the larger units, six stories up in the air. It was a relief to be out of sight, and not having to worry about getting caught. But when she looked over the edge of the building, Nora felt her chest tighten. The people down below looked incredibly small from the high vantage point.

"Be careful here," Phoenix told her. "We have to walk along this plank from here to that roof over there." She pointed to her left.

"Would now be a good time to tell you I'm not a fan of heights?" Nora's whole body was tense. "I've spent my life avoiding them at all costs."

"Your life has just begun Nora, embrace the new you! Don't worry so much about avoiding things," Phoenix said as she walked over the frail boards to show Nora it was perfectly safe. The display did little to ease her mind.

"Take a deep breath and then move," Phoenix guided Nora. "Don't look down, just trust me. This isn't how you die."

Nora took one last gulp of air and started to walk the board, high up between the two buildings. The plank creaked under her feet and Nora's heart sped up.

"You're halfway across," Phoenix encouraged her. "Just stay focused and keep looking into my eyes."

A few more steps and Nora had made it safely to the other side. She fell to her knees, struggling to catch her breath.

"We are going to have to work on that part I guess." Phoenix smiled at Nora as she walked over to a big steel door on the rooftop. "Ready or not, here we are."

The sunlight behind them was just starting to fade as Phoenix closed the door. Nora found herself in a dark stairwell. The paint on the walls had started to chip off, and the amount of dust on the sides of the floor made it clear how sparsely trafficked it was.

Overhead flickering lights illuminated the walls' light blue shade. She wondered what the original purpose of the building had been.

Down a few more flights of stairs, Phoenix seemed to have given up on worrying about the possibilities of an agent following them. Her body language helped Nora to relax as well.

When they had reached a landing in the stairwell marked with the number three, Phoenix opened another big steel door. A man stood in the entryway, a rifle aimed at the two girls. Nora inhaled sharply, she'd never been near a gun before.

"Hello there, Miss Phoenix," the man with the rifle said. Upon recognizing Phoenix he lowered his weapon. "Oh, and you brought a friend with you this time. Alright Miss Phoenix, you know the drill."

She stepped aside and ushered Nora forward. The man with the gun brought out a small wand and started to scan her entire body with it.

"No need to worry miss. Every new person gets to meet Mr. Wand on their first visit. What's your name?" He asked.

"Nora. What are you scanning for?"

"Well, Miss Nora, you are about to find out in a second here. Let's see." The man with the gun pushed a few buttons on the wand. "Miss Nora, my name is Jack, and you are cutting it really close. You better head on up to the Dream Machine immediately." He looked over to Phoenix.

"Six hours?" He asked her. "You guys must have found this one just in time. You'd better hurry. No time for your typical five-hour tour of the building with this one."

"Shut up, Jack," Phoenix said as she playfully pushed him out of the way. "Come on Nora, he's right. We don't have much time."

The two of them went down the hallway, and left Jack standing at the door, a smile on his face. The hallway was very dark and she placed her hand on Phoenix's back, continuing to follow her blindly into the darkness.

Nora's eyes began to adjust to the light source that came from up ahead. They entered a large open room covered with the same

9

chipped blue paint. The room consisted of three stories, and they'd entered at the middle level. The level below them was an area packed with tables and several people walking around.

Phoenix and Nora climbed up the outer staircase to reach the top of the large room and then made their way over to a door located at the end of the long platform.

"Here we go," Phoenix said, turning back to Nora. "Try not to let this room scare you."

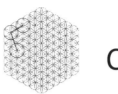# CHAPTER 3

Phoenix marched into the room first, and Nora hesitated for a few moments, took a deep breath to brace herself, and then walked in.

The room inside was large, open, and had a curved ceiling. Most of the room was dark, except for the large machine in the center and a few consoles that blinked around it. The floor was made of old tile, which gave the room a slight chill.

Phoenix stood by two men near the large machine in the center. She motioned for Nora to come over and meet them.

"Hello," Nora said simply to the two men. She looked at both of them, her attention immediately drawn to the one on the right.

"Hello, Nora. We have been waiting for you," the man on the left said. "My name is Otto, and this is Bray." Nora reached out for Bray's hand. His handshake was firm yet gentle at the same time.

"Hello, Nora. I'm Bray. We are going to save your life now," he said in a deep, calm voice which attracted Nora to him even more. Bray's eyes seemed to be pure black, as was his hair and the clothing he wore. She noticed markings on his skin that crept up part of his neck. Nora assumed these were tattoos, even though she had never seen a tattoo in real life before.

Nora looked over to Otto. He had rather unique features, with long dark hair matted together in large clumps. The sides of his hair were short and gray. There were small holes in his lips and eyebrows with bits of metal in them which drew her attention. The two of the men looked like they must have been from the same sector, although Nora had no idea which one.

She immediately felt out of place in the Blear clothing Phoenix had given to her and wished she was still wearing something that represented her own sector more. Bray was still looking at her, but when she turned towards him, he quickly averted his eyes.

"Welcome to our, and soon to be your, new home," Otto said. "We have rules here, but first, we must take care of you. Sit down here." He ushered her toward the large machine in the center of the room, which glowed like a beacon under the single light from above. "This is our very own Dream Machine."

Nora hesitated to follow his directions. She had not received answers to most of her questions, and now was expected to blindly follow the orders of two men she did not know. Before she could protest, Bray attempted to ease her worries.

"You've been having a reoccurring dream involving your own death, right?"

"Yes," Nora replied, unsure of the intention of his question.

"You have been brought here, to us, so we can fix that." He paused to smile at her. "Do you trust me?"

"Do I have a choice?" As Nora replied, Bray placed a hand on her lower back, ushering her towards the Dream Machine.

Without questioning him, Nora sat down on the flimsy looking chair. He instructed her to extend her legs onto the small wooden box in front of her. She was nervous, but tried to appear brave. Aside from the light that shined down on the Dream Machine, there was nothing new or beautiful about the equipment. The wooden chair she sat in was old and weathered. There were places for your arms to rest and a stained, old wooden box for your feet. The wood, on both pieces, was old and cracked, and had a dark, reddish brown color. The areas where the padding of the chair used to be had darkened, visibly showing that it had been worn down by all of the other bodies that had sat in the same position. She wondered exactly how many other bodies had been there before her.

The entire floor that surrounded the Dream Machine was made out of rusting metal. The bolts and rivets that held it together had started to wear, and some of the metal casing had begun to bend and fan out. The one thing this chair had going for it was that the rusted metal matched the chair's faded brown color.

Above the chair hung a single lightbulb. Next to that, a type of helmet with colorful wires coming out of it rested on a stationary arm. The cables were the only part of the whole contraption that looked new. Nora's eyes followed the trail of wires from the helmet, down the arched arm that held it up, and onto the chair itself. From there the cables reached out to where she would place her arms. On each armrest were small belts with a metallic disk attached to them, and the wires ran down to the floor from there. Bray instructed Nora to place her wrist on the small disk as he strapped the thin belts around her forearm.

Otto lowered the arm with the helmet on it while Nora followed the cables from her arms to another cold metal disk that pressed against her back. There was also a third set of disks that had similar belts attached to them.

"Lift your shirt up so the disk can make direct contact with your back," Otto instructed, "Then pull up your pants so your calves touch the ones down there too."

Nora did as she was told, but felt self conscious at having her stomach bared to everyone in the room. She had never been very confident about her small-framed body. Otto reached around her and pulled the strap connected to the larger disk behind her. His hands grazed Nora's mid-section as he worked. The combination of the cold disk and the new stranger being so close to her exposed stomach made a chill run up her spine.

Bray walked over to one of the consoles and started pushing buttons, which caused the Dream Machine to come to life with a whirring sound. Nora continued to visually follow the wire lines from her feet out onto the floor. From there the cables spread out, and reached over to three separate consoles.

"This one is for vitals," Phoenix informed Nora, anticipating her question. "This console over here is for us to be able to join in your subconscious with you and guide you safely through your death vision." She walked over to where Bray was standing. "And this last one is so we can record exactly what you are seeing."

Although Nora's immediate questions had been answered, the information did very little to ease her anxiety. With the bright light from above, Nora couldn't make out anything beyond the consoles. The room felt infinite in size, as if they were all on an island in a deep, dark, corner of space.

Otto lowered the helmet onto Nora's head and told her to relax. The screech of the arm as it bended down added to her uneasiness.

"Ready?" Otto asked Bray.

He looked up from his console before responding. "Logging in. Okay, we are all set. Going live in 3...2...1—"

Before the last word could form in Bray's mouth Nora was overcome with a rush of blackness. It was a nothingness so deep she thought that she may have stopped breathing. She tried to remain calm. As the time crept by, she attempted to think of her family and Deryn. For some reason she was unable to form proper thoughts. It was as if the recollection was always just out of her mind's reach, somehow hiding from her within the darkness. When she tried to speak, no words came out. Whatever this was, it seemed to be taking too long and Nora began to feel flustered.

13

Almost as instantly as her dismay set in, a light appeared far away from where she was located. At least Nora thought it was a light. It was small, like a pinprick in a black curtain. The glowing dot slowly crept closer to Nora's eyes. She felt herself reach out for it, but the darkness was so intense she couldn't see her own body. She could only focus on how slowly the speck moved.

The light leapt forward without warning, and suddenly consumed Nora's view. The blackness all around her had instantly transformed to a bright white. Nora felt herself squint, but this did nothing to affect what she could see. She could feel that she had eyes, but her eyelids seemed to have no function in this new world.

A small line appeared in the distance and stretched across her whole field of vision. She couldn't put her finger on what color it was, perhaps it was a color she'd never seen before and her brain simply didn't know how to categorize it. The streak grew thicker, and then burst outward, stretching all around her.

Colors began to fly past her. She saw orbs of light shuffle wildly across her eyes. Despite how intense this all was, she remained calm. One of the orbs headed right towards her. Nora attempted to turn and flinch away from it, but it was futile. The orb smacked right into her. She felt as if she had stumbled backwards.

"We are in," she heard someone say. "Nora, can you hear us?"

"Yes. I can hear you. Where are you, and where am I?" she asked, her voice shaking.

"We are right here with you."

"I can't see you. What is happening to me?" Nora felt the confusion taking over her again.

"Just open your eyes."

Nora realized that the voice belonged to Phoenix. She opened her eyes, and to her surprise, Phoenix was standing directly in front of her. Bray and Otto stood behind her. The room they were in had a dark green floor, resembling a floating island, that reflected a darker purple color. The same purple hue filled the sky above her that was covered with millions of shooting stars.

"Where am I?" Nora asked the three of them.

Phoenix was the first to respond. "This is the control room inside of the Dream Machine. One of the rebels here designed this platform to help calm the minds of the newly Defected. From here we are able to access the different areas of your subconsciousness."

"Nora," Bray began, "I want you to try and focus. We need you to show us the vision you have been seeing in your dreams."

"Sure. Wait, how do I do that?" Nora felt foolish for having to ask.

"Let the Dream Machine do the work. Just relax your mind and take us there." Phoenix chimed in.

Nora thought deep and hard about the nightmare she had been having repeatedly over the last three months. She focused her mind and attempted to recall every detail she had memorized.

The scene came into view around her. It surrounded the four of them and replaced the purple and green world of the shooting stars. The recognizable images from Nora's dream rose from nothing and enveloped the world around her. The location was familiar to her, although this time things felt different. Everything felt more real than it usually did in the dream.

The sky was dark, and there was a crisp, cool breeze in the air. The old, stretched out trees that covered most of the area came into her view. She had never seen anything that even vaguely resembled them in the real world.

The ground was damp, and covered with dead leaves and small weeds. She knew the trees were brown and the leaves above her were green, though the nighttime light cast a blueish hue over everything.

"Okay, Nora," Otto called out to her. "Focus on whatever usually happens in your vision. Don't try and manipulate anything. Relax and let the dream be your guide."

Nora tried to understand what Otto was saying, and started to walk towards her right. In her nightmare she had always gone right. Every time. This time would be no different. She pushed through the trees and slid in between a few that had grown close together. The further she went, the less she felt attached to any of it. Her mind merged with whoever controlled her dreaming body. All Nora could do was watch as her body moved along its predictable route inside of the dream.

Walking into the woods, as she always had, the loud sound of running footsteps became audible. She stopped moving and turned to look over her left shoulder. She heard someone yelling at another person to get up, and to keep moving. It was dark around her, but Nora could still see the mass of people as they ran through the wooded area only a few yards ahead of where she stood.

Nothing had ever completely come into focus in her dream over the last few months. This time Nora could clearly see the people's faces as they ran by. A young boy locked eyes with her as he raced by, his light hair catching the wind as he moved. She continued to watch him as he travelled across the landscape.

On cue, a scarred female face appeared before Nora. Though Nora didn't know the woman in real life, she was a familiar face to her in the dream world. Every time she had this dream, the woman yelled something at Nora that she was never able to understand. The sound of waves crashing against a shoreline replaced her voice. The woman grabbed Nora by the arm and pointed her finger ahead of herself, and then took off running in the direction in which she had pointed.

Nora's body moved to catch up with the running woman. She had no choice as her limbs still moved on their own. This was a strange feeling to her, being pulled and pushed at the same time, while not actually telling herself to move.

In her dreams, her actions had always been dictated by her mind's influence over the world it had created. During sleep Nora felt as if she was watching a movie play out from the comfort of hiding behind her own eyes. Inside the Dream Machine, things felt different. The world that had developed around her felt all too real. She could feel the wind blowing through her long black hair, and her clothes hanging loosely from her skin. Instead of watching her body move, she could feel it move. It seemed like her mind was inside of a puppet that was connected to a marionette's strings.

The two of them neared the edge of the wooded area, and the woman squatted down, motioning for Nora to join her. The woman spoke to her, but no words ever seemed to form. Only white noise filled Nora's ears. A wrinkled brow covered the woman's scarred face, and her forehead was deeply furrowed. The woman yelled something again, shaking Nora's shoulders as she pleaded for something that Nora couldn't comprehend. The woman then got up and left her, running hard and fast across the open field.

This event signaled the part of the dream Nora hated the most. She felt herself get up and start to run after the woman. She was still visible up ahead, and waved her arm for Nora to catch up. A bright light suddenly beamed down from above, and shone on Nora from behind. A thumping sound pulsed high in the sky above her. The light made Nora freeze in place, as fear took over her whole body. The woman yelled out to her one last time as Nora felt a huge push from behind her, which caused her to fall hard onto her knees. When Nora looked down she saw blood spilling out from her chest from the fresh bullet wound.

The scarred woman in front of her was still yelling, trying to urge Nora to get up. She began to move towards Nora's bleeding body. Before she got too close, a gray mustached man in brown clothing suddenly appeared from behind her, grabbed the woman around her chest, and then dragged her away. Nora watched the whole scene helplessly.

At that point, Nora's surroundings returned to the purple and green, shooting star landscape. She breathed in with relief as the grueling scene faded from her eyes.

"Okay. Good job Nora. I know that can be difficult. We have it recorded now," Otto said to her. "Now it's time for the part you won't like so much. We are going to run it again. This time one of us is going to assist you. It's going to feel strange, but do your best not to fight against us."

The scene came into view around her again—the trees, the leafy ground, and the dark sky all just as they were before. This time however, Nora turned and saw that Otto was standing behind her.

"Just try and relax. I'm going to stay right here with you. I am going to attempt to move your body out of harm's way at the last possible moment. Then you will be set on your new path."

His words still made little sense to Nora. She hoped they all knew what they were doing, and had no choice but to trust them. Regardless of the outcome, she welcomed Otto's attempt to save her in the dream, desperately not wanting to feel herself die again. Everything started the same as before. She went to the right, the footsteps sounded, the scarred woman appeared, and yelled and pleaded with Nora, she followed the woman again, and the light shone down from above, just as it always had.

"I can't. She won't let go," Otto's voice struggled. "Nora, you have to relax. Don't fight it!" he urged her.

As he yelled his instructions at her, Nora couldn't feel herself doing anything other than going along with the dream. Before she could try to stop her body's movements, the pain and blood came. Nora felt her body fall limp onto the ground.

Her surroundings returned to the control room, still inside of the Dream Machine. Otto appeared shaken up and paced back and forth. "Nora, it is very important that you let me help you. I could feel you pushing me away. I'm not sure how you did it, but we are going to have to go again. Don't resist me this time."

Nora's mind was quickly thrust back into the dream. Things progressed identically as before. The trees, the damp ground, the footsteps, the furrowed brow of the scarred woman. This time Otto moved her body as the light from above began to shine. She panicked, and reached out wildly in an attempt to grab on to anything around her.

She grabbed onto Otto's arm, and then Nora's view point suddenly shifted. When she looked down at her body she saw Otto's torso and legs, clad in his dark clothing. She looked around, confused, and then caught sight of her own body, her own eyes looking right back at her. Her brain was unable to comprehend what had happened. She felt the pain of the wound, and the warmth of sticky blood. As she fell to the ground, somehow inside of Otto's body, she saw her own self standing over her, watching in shock.

Before Nora had a chance to figure out what had happened, the four of them were back inside the purple and green control room. Otto was gesturing wildly and shouting at Bray.

"What was that?!" Otto screamed at Bray as though this was somehow his fault. "I'm done with this. I'm out of here. I don't ever want to feel anything like that again."

Bray attempted to calm him down. "Relax, Otto. Somehow the two of you switched bodies inside of the Dream Machine. Be thankful nothing more serious had happened to the both of you."

"Nothing more serious?!" The rage in Otto's voice was in full force. "You try watching yourself get shot through the back while you stand helpless inside of a stranger's body. I'm done with this. You save her if you want to. I'm not trying that again." Otto immediately vanished from the control room.

"I'll go get him," Phoenix said before she was gone too, and left Bray and Nora alone.

Nora looked over at Bray, puzzled. He walked over to her, and Nora felt small compared to him.

"We are going to keep trying," Bray said, and sighed. "Just so you know, nothing like that has ever happened to any of us while inside of the Dream Machine. I'll be honest with you, whatever you did probably scared the life out of Otto."

CHAPTER 4

Having been left alone by Phoenix and Otto, Bray and Nora's vision drifted back into Nora's dream. As the wooded world reappeared, Bray stood directly behind her.

He spoke to the back of her head, "Try and stay calm okay? I am going to be right behind you the whole time. I'll try to pull you away from that gun shot at the last possible moment, so that I can get you onto your new track."

Nora simply nodded in response, and concentrated on the events that would soon unfold. Within only a few moments, the action commenced—the bodies went running past her across the expansive, wooded field. She felt Bray place his hand on her right shoulder as the woman's scarred face came into her view again.

The woman quickly fled from where the three of them stood, and as always, Nora's body followed, with Bray directly behind her. The entire time they ran he kept his hand firmly on her shoulder.

When they caught up to the woman at the usual spot, Nora knelt down next to her. She could feel the weight of Bray kneeling behind her, which caused her body to tilt backwards, in an almost gravitational pull towards him. The woman's mouth began to move, and the sounds of nothing and everything escaped her lungs all at once. Nora only wished she could hear what the woman was attempting to communicate.

"Should I get up and run with her again this time?" Nora asked Bray, without turning to face him.

"Yes, you should." His hand gave her shoulder an almost-imperceptible squeeze. "Our best bet is to remove you from the situation at the last possible moment. This way we don't throw anything else off balance."

His last sentence piqued Nora's curiosity, but she had no time to ponder it since the scarred woman had already stood up, and taken off running into the open field again. Nora allowed herself to go with the magnetic pull of the dream, and therefore followed the woman. Once they'd reached the designated spot, Nora did her best to remain calm and focused as the light from above flooded her from behind. The shadow of her body on the ground before her increased exponentially in size in an instant, and stretched far out ahead of her.

The next step in the progression of things would be the gunshot, and she was well aware of that. The pain of the bullet as it ripped through her flesh would overwhelm her, to the point that the entire world would no longer exist. The past and future would no longer matter, all that would be real in that moment would be the tunnel the bullet drove through her back and out the front of her chest, and the immense world of that pain. Closing her eyes, Nora braced herself for the experience, but suddenly her body was hurled to the left, and she landed hard on the damp ground. Gathering herself quickly, she looked down to inspect her chest for the hemorrhaging of blood—a disturbing sight that she'd grown so used to seeing.

But this time nothing was there. Disoriented, Nora looked wildly around the open field, trying to find the answer to a question she didn't know how to ask. Her vision alternated rapidly between the dark field and the kitchen of her parents' house. She felt her mind grasp at the thin strings that once connected her to both worlds, feeling the fabric of her existence there unwinding, like a loose thread being pulled from the quilt of its reality.

She glanced up as the scarred woman, who at this point would have already been running back to her, froze in place. The woman opened her mouth to shout at Nora, but instead of a voice she heard the sound of a rushing stream. Nora wished, now more than ever, to be able to hear the woman, but the dream began to fade away. Suddenly she and Bray were back on the main platform, stars shooting themselves relentlessly across the bright purple sky that hung overhead.

She shivered as an uncontrollable wave of weakness came over her. A flood of chills and pain brought Nora down to her knees. She wrapped her arms tightly around herself, attempting to ward off the influx of convulsions that pressed her body further towards the green, sparkled ground. It felt as though she was being torn apart from the inside out. Slowly the contractions faded, allowing Nora to regain control of herself.

Bray stared at Nora with wide eyes. He furrowed his eyebrows, deep in thought, and the two corners of his mouth curled in opposite directions—unsure what emotion to be feeling. She had not witnessed this expression on any other face before.

"What?" Nora asked him. The look on his face was starting to make her uncomfortable. "Did it work?"

Bray shook his head. At first Nora thought he was telling her that their attempt had failed and they would need to run through the whole dream again. But the continued insistence of him shaking his head made it clear it was due to sheer disbelief.

"How did you do that?" Bray asked her, stunned.

Nora shrugged her shoulders, confused, "How did I do what? Weren't you the one who pushed me away from the bullet?"

When he responded, Bray intently locked his eyes with hers, and at that moment she was acutely aware of the intense attraction she felt towards him. "I didn't get the chance to do anything Nora. I just watched as you shifted the placement of your body, all on your own."

Nora was still unable to grasp what had happened, "Does it matter that I did it myself, as long as I'm on the new track now? Wouldn't that be as good as you pushing me out of the way?"

Bray bent down and placed both of his hands on her shoulders. "You don't understand, Nora. No one has ever been able to move themselves in their own vision."

Nora reached her hands up to place on top of his, and in a soft voice replied, "I don't get it, I didn't do anything!"

"Well, whatever the cause of it is, I've never seen it before. We've done this with dozens of people, and every single time, one of us had to help the Defected change their path. In all of our history here, no one has ever done what you did."

"Maybe I just got lucky," she rationalized, starting to feel uncomfortable. "Well, what do we do now?"

Bray shook his head a few more times, as though shaking off the residual disbelief, and then stood up briskly, "I guess it's time for your tour of the building. Phoenix should be waiting for you—if she was able to calm Otto down, that is."

Bray straightened his posture, sensing Nora's desire to leave the Dream Machine. The brightly colored landscape of the main platform then faded back into the black nothingness they had both come from. When she opened her eyes, Nora saw she was back in the room with the dim light that hung overhead. Her body was still seated in the broken down chair, with her feet propped up on the wooden box. Bray was several yards away from her at one of the consoles, collecting the new data.

She removed the straps from her wrists and ankles, and then the largest one around her stomach. Immediately self-conscious again, she tugged her shirt down to cover her midsection. Once she had freed herself completely, she made her way over to the console that Bray occupied.

"Are you coming with?" she asked him, hopefully.

He answered without looking up at her, "No, sorry." He pushed a few buttons on the console in front of him. "After something as big as this, I have to check all the new data and make sure we were able to capture what happened. I'm sure Otto and the others will be curious to see your results."

It felt extremely odd to Nora to hear someone talk about a recent experience as 'data,' but she shrugged the feeling off. "Okay," she said, "Well I hope I get the chance to see you again."

Finally Bray looked up at her and smiled, "You can count on it."

# CHAPTER 5

As Nora stood in the doorway, on her way out of the Dream Machine room, she looked down over the railing, to the floors below. She shivered as she began to descend the steep stairwell—headed towards the ground floor in the hopes of finding food. On her way down, Phoenix appeared from one of the corridors.

"Hey. How did it go in there, were the two of you able to finish?"

"Yeah," Nora replied, still trying to figure out exactly what had happened inside of the Dream Machine. "I guess it took longer than Otto had expected it would." She then inquired as to Otto's whereabouts and why he'd reacted the way he had.

"Don't worry about him," Phoenix said with a dismissive wave of her hand, "He's grumpy most of the time, but he can be nice when he wants to be. Anyway, I think it's time for the grand tour of your new home." Phoenix reached out and grabbed Nora's hand.

"Lead the way, Miss Phoenix," Nora teased, lowering the pitch of her voice in her best impression of Jack.

"Well I'm glad to see the Dream Machine didn't affect your mood. Most people come out feeling disorientated, as if they left a part of themselves inside of the machine."

"I'll be alright. I do feel a little light headed, and sort of disconnected from reality, but that could just be because I haven't eaten in a while. I'm starving." She glanced over at Phoenix. "But I'll worry about food later, let's get this tour started."

The two of them set off down the stairwell. Phoenix took time to show Nora all the different sections of the rebel base along the way. Nora was impressed with how much had been done to retrofit the place, although they had neglected to attend to any sort of cosmetic remodeling. Water stains were on all of the walls, and old blue paint seemed to cover everything.

"Over here are the beds and sleeping quarters," Phoenix said as she gestured at the area they'd just reached. "Guys are on the left and girls are on the right. We keep genders separated so that we don't lose focus on our task at hand. As fun as romance can be, I'm told it is too distracting." Phoenix explained.

"Where do those doors lead?" Nora asked, pointing down the hallway.

"Some of the higher ranking rebels get their own rooms. It's one of the benefits that comes with devoting your life towards bringing down the Agency," Phoenix answered succinctly.

"I'm guessing two of those rooms are for Otto and Bray," Nora commented.

"That is correct," she confirmed.

Phoenix then showed Nora how each bunking space had its own bathroom area, and that Phoenix herself was staying in female unit D-A, which consisted of four beds. Nora peeked her head inside the sleeping area for a moment, and caught a glimpse of two beds on one side of the room and two on the other. The two halves of the room were separated by a narrow path, only wide enough for one person to walk through at a time.

"You know," Phoenix began. "There is an open bunk in my unit—in case you would feel more comfortable staying near me for the time being." Phoenix leaned against the wall outside of the entrance to the room.

"I haven't been to a sleepover in years," Nora said with a laugh. She looked at Phoenix with a twinkle in her eyes, "I suppose I'll take my chances with you."

There was something about Phoenix that Nora was really beginning to like. She couldn't put her finger on exactly what it was, but Phoenix had such a confident, capable aura about her that Nora was able to easily trust her wellbeing in Phoenix's hands.

They continued on with the tour until Phoenix stopped at another corridor one floor down. When she swung the door open Nora saw that the entire perimeter of the room was lined with screens and consoles. In the center was a circular map of the entire city of Constance. A small path led around the room, forming a square around the center table.

"This is what we call the War Room. It's where we can track some of the agents, like the ones that were chasing after you earlier. If we're lucky, we can actually gather intel about things that are going on inside of the city." Phoenix paused for a moment, and motioned towards a smaller console in the far right corner of the room, "Also, this is how we found you."

"This console is able to find the Defected like you who are nearing their vision courses. Unfortunately, as of right now, we only get a twelve-hour window to locate them. Some of the Defected put out a stronger signal than others for us to pick up on." Phoenix's eyes dropped to the ground. "We are making every effort to extend that small time frame as well as get people to the Dream Machine faster. As their death timeline approaches, it becomes more and more difficult to pull them away from their original fate paths. I'm afraid little progress has been made so far—we just don't have the right information yet."

Phoenix turned and made her way out of the room, signaling to Nora that this part of the tour had ended. Nora's thoughts lingered on the War Room even after they left. There was so much new information to process, and she found herself fascinated by it all.

As they made their final descent towards the ground floor, Nora couldn't help but wonder what the bigger picture was. She was hoping more answers would come to her organically, because she didn't want to force the information out of Phoenix. Since she was a new rebel recruit, she tried to maintain a level of respect and deference to everyone else.

They entered into the large room that made up the ground floor. Large wooden tables were set up in the center, and steel pans filled with food were stationed around the edge of the room. Members of the rebellion stood in line, waiting for their turn to load their trays up with food.

The floor was filthy—covered in dirt and a thick layer of dust that was constantly getting kicked up each time the line edged forward. It seemed like everything around her was in need of a good scrub down. Phoenix guided Nora towards the front of the food line. Thankfully, Nora observed that at least the serving trays appeared to be clean.

"Hey. No cutting in line, Phoenix!" a guy yelled as they passed him.

"Relax, Trim. This is Nora, she just came out of the Dream Machine. She needs to eat." Phoenix informed him.

He bowed his head apologetically at Nora, and smiled as he lifted his face back up to look at her.

Phoenix leaned in towards Nora as they continued to make their way to the front, "Trim has been here for a little over a year," Phoenix began. "The girl standing next to him is Bretta. Apparently they're an item now. She has only been here for a few months, she was the newest of the Defected until today, when you showed up," Phoenix informed Nora.

As Nora glanced over at the couple, she noticed they were holding hands. Trim stood a whole foot taller than Bretta. His dark hair was slicked back, and reached past his shoulders. He was dressed in black clothes, similar to the rest of the rebels. The majority of his exposed skin, besides his face, was covered in tattoos from what she could see.

Bretta was slim and appeared to be younger than Trim. It was hard for Nora to guess their exact ages, but Trim was clearly several years older than Bretta.

The thing that caught Nora's attention the most was Bretta's hair. It was dark, but when she moved and the light hit her hair, you could see a distinct purple hue. Her hair was stick straight and flowed far past her waistline. Her appearance prompted Nora to pose a question to Phoenix.

"Do people living in the other sectors have different-colored hair? In Arrant you only see people with black and blonde hair, like yours and mine."

Phoenix burst out laughing at Nora's naïve question. "Bretta wasn't born with purple hair. Here, in this rebel base, people are free. They are encouraged to live life the way they deem fit. Because of that, some of the rebels like to express their individuality externally as well. That's why you'll notice many of them have tattoos and metal rods sticking out of their skin. Another common form of expression is dyeing your hair different colors. I'd recently been wearing mine pink, but I decided to get rid of it. I wanted to keep some of who I used to be alive. Also, the less we stand out, the easier it is for us to travel between the sectors. People like Bretta and Otto have to take the back alleys and hide in the shadows."

Nora thought about what color she might choose, if she were to change her hair color. Green was a nice, fun color, she mused. But after a moment of picturing herself with neon green hair, she shook her head. She preferred Phoenix's idea of maintaining some piece of who you used to be. Maybe one day she would change it, but for now she'd stick with what she had.

The food was not very different than what Nora was used to eating, which was a relief. She hadn't been sure what to expect. The large pans were filled with various types of steamed and fried rice, stewed beef, baked fish, chicken drenched in gravy, pastas, and boiled vegetables. Near the end of the buffet were large bins of white bread, fresh salads, and platters of various types of fruit. Nora didn't pay much mind to what she scooped onto her plate, she just took a little bit of everything.

Phoenix waited at the end of the food line for Nora to catch up, and then they carried their trays of food over to an empty table near the back of the room. As Nora passed the other tables, most people didn't pay her any special attention at all. Every once in a while someone would glance up at her, and she would flash them a small, polite smile, unsure of how to behave.

The two girls sat across from each other at an exceptionally large table. There was at least five feet of space between them. Nora swept her hand across the surface of the table, clearing off as much of the dirt and dust as possible. Though she tried to be discreet about it, Phoenix picked up on her concerns.

"You get used to it. At least the plates and the clothes are clean."

Nora forced a smile onto her face, and looked down at her clothes, suddenly remembering that she was dressed in clothing from Blear. The Arrant apparel that she'd worn all her life was hidden underneath.

Phoenix noticed this as well and said, "You'll get used to that too, eventually." She raised a forkful of chicken to her mouth. "When we get done eating, I'll show you the closet in our sleeping unit. You can find something you feel more comfortable wearing."

"Thanks," Nora said gratefully. She let out a sigh after she swallowed her first bite of the food. She was surprised at how good it was. Mass-produced buffet food didn't tend to be of such high quality.

"How long have you been with the rebellion?" she asked Phoenix as they ate.

"It's been almost two years since I left Fallow. Time seems to go by faster the longer I'm here. There is always something that needs to be done."

"Two years? You don't look like you could be much older than I am. You must have been really young when you became Defected."

Sorrow flashed in Phoenix's eyes before she responded. "Yeah, I was young. I was ready though. When your time comes, you don't really have a choice in the matter, anyway."

"Did you know anything about the rebellion before you joined them?" Nora asked.

"Nope. Not a thing." Phoenix stirred her food with her fork. "That's how it is for all of us, one day your living your normal life, then suddenly the world turns upside down. A whole new world materializes,

27

one which you never even knew existed. At that point you can either welcome it or..." Phoenix's voice trailed off, and she stared down at her food.

"Or what?" Nora asked urgently.

Phoenix sighed before she continued, "Or you can wait for a few of those agents to show up at your doorstep. Trust me, they don't give you a choice. And once they find you, they scoop you up and ship you off, out of your sector."

"Where do they take you?" Nora pressed. She felt bad for asking so many questions in succession, but her curiosity was getting the best of her.

Phoenix didn't seem to mind the onslaught of questions though, or at least she didn't give off any sign of annoyance. "If you are lucky, you go to the prison in Jejung."

"I was told that is where the criminals of Constance go," Nora said. Her face grew serious and she asked in a hushed whisper, "You're telling me they send all of the Defected to the prison?"

"You don't have to whisper, Nora. Everyone here knows about that already," Phoenix replied, her mouth half full of food. She swallowed before continuing. "We all made a choice, and here we are in Blear, spending our lives in this dirty building. But it sure beats the alternative."

"Have you ever seen the prison?" Nora asked.

"No one here has. Everything we know is information that has been passed down over the years from the higher-ranking rebels."

Realizing her constant barrage of questions was starting to get rude, Nora took time to think before asking one final question, "What happens if you aren't lucky?"

"They take you into the center of the city first. I'm sure you've been curious all your life about the tall building, Obsidia, that sits in the center of all the sectors."

Nora nodded, thinking back through some of her memories, and how Obsidia had always risen above Arrant, day in and day out.

"You guys don't know what happens inside of there?" Nora asked, forgetting about her resolve to cease the interrogation.

"Nope." Phoenix sounded just as frustrated as Nora felt. "We think they have a way of manipulating your memories to make you forget. Both Bray and I can attest to that. Obsidia stays lit up at night, right? So whatever happens in there obviously needs constant power, even after the rest of the city's lights-out curfew."

She was about to ask Phoenix yet another question when Trim and Bretta approached their table. Trim had his plate piled half-a-foot high with food, whereas Bretta had only a modest helping of rice and stewed beef, with a few carrots on the side.

"Do you care if we join the two of you?" he asked.

Phoenix put her hand up, stopping Trim from sitting down. "Only if you promise us that you two are not here to make out. I mean, I've seen enough of that between you guys to last me a lifetime, and we are trying to eat here after all."

Nora suppressed a laugh, not wanting to seem rude to her new acquaintances, but Trim and Bretta took the insult in stride and burst out laughing.

"You know we can't promise you that," Bretta remarked with a smile as the two of them sat down. She took a seat next to Nora, and Trim sat down beside Phoenix.

Trim cleared his throat before he spoke again, as he turned his plate in front of him on the table, as though strategizing about which angle was best to attack it from. "So Nora, has Phoenix filled you in on all the news that's been going on around here since your little Dream Machine incident?"

The way he phrased the comment caused Nora to swallow hard, nervous that she may have done something wrong earlier. "No. We just now finished up with my tour of the building."

As Trim chewed a large mouthful of food, Bretta chimed in, "Well, unfortunately for you, there isn't much time before our next big move."

"Next big move?" Nora asked her.

"Sounds like we are moving out bright and early tomorrow. Trim and I, you and Phoenix, Bray, Otto, Jack, and Cady. Otto ordered it about an hour ago."

Nora was stunned. "Why would he want me to go on a mission with you guys? I haven't even been here a full day!" she exclaimed.

Bretta shrugged her shoulders. "I only know what I've been told, and as I'm sure you'll soon figure out, most of these guys don't tell me anything. Trim says it has to do with my uncanny ability to put my entire foot in my mouth," she said as she winked at Trim.

Nora wondered what could be so important that would require her to leave the rebel base so soon. She thought about why Otto would even consider bringing along someone as new as her to a mission out on the field.

Nora glanced over at Phoenix, in an attempt to assess the situation. "Maybe he wants to take us for a swim in the water out there."

Phoenix raised one of her eyebrows as she chuckled, "Oh, I highly doubt that."

CHAPTER 6

"Go ahead and set your stuff down here," Phoenix said as she gestured towards the empty bed next to her. "I'll grab you some bedding from the closet."

"Thanks," Nora said, and then set her pack down on the bare bed.

Phoenix walked towards the closet in the back of the room, and then lit a flame in the small lantern that was mounted on the wall. Within a couple minutes, the bright overhead lights shut off, casting shadows that fell around her, signaling the city-wide curfew was now in place.

The room was smaller than it had appeared from her brief inspection earlier on the tour. There was barely enough room to walk between the two beds on each side, and only a slightly larger pathway through the center of the room. A mirror and sink stood in one corner, and a closet in the other. Phoenix retrieved a stack of bedding from the closet and handed it to Nora.

Nora made up her bed and placed one blanket on top of the cot. She set the second, thinner blanket, at the foot of the bed, in case it got colder in the middle of the night. The sheets were a dull gray color, which reminded Nora of Arrant.

She started to daydream about what was going on in her old sector. By now, she figured, Deryn would have found the note she had left him on the counter. She wondered how he would feel as he read the letter alone in their old bedroom. At that point it was past curfew, so the lights would have been turned out, and he'd probably be sitting on the edge of their bed, reading the note by candlelight. Nora leaned back into the cot and began to absentmindedly finger her necklace. She drew in a deep breath, closed her eyes, and tried to stay positive.

Just then, Bretta walked into the room, and let the door slam shut behind her, which stirred Nora from her depressing revery. Nora opened her eyes and left her sad thoughts of Deryn behind in the darkness. She watched Bretta walk over to the sink in the corner and turn the water on. Bretta caught Nora's gaze in the reflection of the mirror.

"There you are Nora. Trim and I were wondering which room you ended up in." Bretta smiled and looked over at Phoenix. "I wouldn't have guessed that Phoenix would want another person in here. Makes it harder for her to sneak off to Otto's room in the middle of the night."

"Hey, now." Phoenix looked up from the bag she was shuffling through while she sat on her bed.

"Oh yes, how could we all forget about the biggest crush in this dusty place?" Bretta noticed the confused look on Nora's face. "She didn't tell you, huh?" She smiled before continuing, "Yup, our little Phoenix here is just over the moon for Otto!"

Phoenix stood up, and dropped her bag on the ground. "I am no such thing. I just, I don't mind being around him is all," she said, with a defensive shrug.

Bretta turned to Nora with a look of clear disbelief and then bursted out laughing, causing even Phoenix to laugh at herself for what she had said. Nora laughed along with them, enjoying the distraction.

"Don't worry," Bretta said to Nora, "If you're sleeping here with us, you'll hear all the new gossip about Phoenix's love life," she had a mischievous twinkle in her eyes.

"Well Nora, maybe your arrival will take the gossip spotlight off of me," Phoenix said lightheartedly.

Nora wanted to play along, but talking about boys made her heart heavy—knowing she had left the one she loved behind without saying goodbye. The other girls noticed the somber look in Nora's eyes as she thought yet again of Deryn.

Bretta tried to ease the situation, "From what I hear Nora, Bray is going to be your escort all day long tomorrow. I can't say I would mind that fate!"

"Bretta!" Phoenix admonished jokingly, "What about Trim?"

"What about Trim? I'm allowed to look at the menu without ordering." A massive laugh formed in her abdomen before she could finish her own explanation.

Nora felt herself drifting off from the conversation, and her eyes grew heavy. A smile crept over her face, as she thought about spending the whole day with Bray. Her attraction to him, so soon after leaving Deryn behind, filled her heart with guilt. Her mind flooded with the allure of Bray mixed with the love she had for a man that existed in a world she could no longer be a part of.

Nora saw visions of her and Bray in the Dream Machine room—the fantasy crept into her sleepy mind and began to play itself out in detail. The blue, chipped-paint world developed around her and replaced the lonely cot she was resting on. Every emotion she had felt, only moments ago, was washed away by the powerful stream of imagery that seemed to force itself into her tired thoughts. Soon she was wholly within that imaginary world, which to her heart felt eerily realistic.

She watched as the two of them stood close together. Nora reached out and grabbed Bray by his hands. She felt the warmth from his face as he leaned in towards her. As he kissed her on the lips, Nora's mind gave in to the oncoming dream and she fell asleep.

* * *

"Rise and shine, sunshine."

Nora forced her eyes open at the sound of Bretta's extremely chipper voice the next morning. Bretta stood directly over her, nudging her shoulder gently. Bretta was already showered, completely dressed, and made up. Nora groaned and closed her eyes, not ready to leave the comfort of the cot just yet.

Oblivious, Bretta continued talking in a loud, boisterous voice. "That's right ladies and gentlemen, Bobby, tell the beautiful Nora what she's won!" She turned from one side to the other, as if looking at imaginary audience members, and her voice grew even louder. "You've been selected to tag along on today's gorgeous, early morning, all-inclusive mission!" Bretta hung over Nora with a big smile on her face, waiting for Nora to respond.

Nora was too tired to play along. She rubbed her eyes with one of her hands, sat up, and looked at Bretta, trying to figure out what was happening around her. Phoenix was still laying in the bed next to her, holding her pillow tight over her head.

"Not a morning person?" Bretta asked Nora. "That's okay, neither is this bag of bones over here." She lifted her foot up and playfully kicked Phoenix, who continued to ignore her. Realizing that neither of the girls were up for her antics that morning, she put her hands on her hips.

"Oh well. I'll go bug Trim. Get up and get ready. I left my make-up out on the sink if you want to fix... well, this," Bretta waved her hands around Nora's face. "I'll meet you two at the lockers in a bit."

With that, Bretta left the room. They continued to hear her chipper voice greeting the other rebels as she bounced down the hallway. Phoenix rolled over and looked at Nora, removing the pillow from her face. She smiled at Nora, squinting her eyes to adjust them to the brightness of the room.

"Thank the heavens there isn't two of her in this unit," she said to Nora. "Although she's right, we should get ready. You are coming along today and you are going to want to make sure you are wide awake in case things get a little crazy out there. I didn't want to tell you last night, I figured you had enough on your mind already and I wanted you to get a good night's rest. When we are out in the sectors, there is always a good chance the Agency will make an unexpected appearance."

"Well, thanks for being considerate," Nora replied, relieved that Phoenix had chosen not to weigh her down with more anxiety-causing information last night. She rolled onto her back and stretched before letting out a sigh. Yesterday had been so physically and emotionally exhausting that Nora could have easily continued sleeping for many hours more.

The two of them got up and headed down the hallway toward their unit's bathroom. Nora felt the urgent energy of everyone getting ready for the day ahead. Even though she was running low on time, she desperately wanted to take a shower, so she figured she'd make it a quick one. She pulled back one of the curtains and turned on the water, testing the temperature with her hand. Nora started to remove the clothes she had worn the day before and consequently slept in. At the sink, Phoenix only washed her face and brushed her teeth before heading back to the sleeping unit.

"Don't take too long," Phoenix called out to Nora as she left the bathroom.

As the shower head poured water over her she felt like the stress and overwhelming emotions from the previous day were being washed away. She leaned her arm against the cold, tiled wall, and gently rested her head atop her forearm, letting the warm water run down her back. Her head was spinning, so she focused on the sound the water made as it hit the floor of the shower stall.

After a few more minutes she turned off the running water, and stepped out to towel herself off. She retrieved her clothes from the pile she'd left them in on the floor, and put them back on. Getting dressed in the dirty clothes made her feel like the shower hadn't accomplished anything. She opened the door to the hallway and made her way back to the sleeping unit, walking briskly.

Phoenix was at the sink and mirror, in the back corner, peering at herself. In the corner of her eye she caught sight of Nora as she entered the room.

"Oh, no no no," Phoenix chastised, "You can't wear that. We are going into Fallow today. The agents would spot you in a second wearing that, it's clearly clothing from here in Blear. Go pick something else out from the closet—the clothes are separated by sector."

Nora opened the small closet and saw all of the clothes folded and neatly stacked. By her count, there were enough clothes crammed into the small closet to dress the entire group of rebels. Nora wondered if this was standard procedure across the board, or if it was only like this in the girls' sleeping units.

Nora was weary of taking something that Phoenix had possibly already picked out for herself, so she was hesitant to grab anything yet. She shuffled through the stacks, lifted and separated the items, and eventually found a long white dress that had a small red stripe running down the middle of it. She'd never worn a dress before, and it was more revealing than any other outfit she'd previously put on. It barely reached her knees, had thin spaghetti straps, and a low-cut sweetheart neckline. Nora regretted even trying the clothing on, immediately feeling vulnerable and self-conscious.

"Let me see," Phoenix called out, motioning with her hands for Nora to spin around and model the outfit for her.

Feeling embarrassed, she crossed her arms over her chest, trying to cover herself up. She hated being so exposed, and at the moment she felt both emotionally and physically unprotected. When she caught a glimpse of herself in the mirror, she was a little startled. It was a huge departure from what she'd typically wear.

Growing up in Arrant, the women concealed much of their bodies. Light jackets were always worn, since the sun never broke through the dust-covered sky for long enough to warm the sector properly. As a result she'd grown accustomed to choosing warmth over style. Nora sighed as she looked in the mirror, beginning to understand how her previous life in Arrant had resulted in extremely poor body image. She relaxed and let her hands hang down at her side.

"You look great!" Phoenix exclaimed with a smile. "Look at that body! I wish I had your legs." The way Phoenix spoke to her made Nora feel slightly less self-conscious.

"Come over here Nora, let me show you something you Arrant girls are missing out on."

Phoenix grabbed a handful of brushes and some pencils off of the sink. Nora could already guess what it all was, after seeing how some of the other female rebels in the base looked. The vast majority of the women in Arrant had never worn make-up. A rare few would simulate the effects of make-up with homemade concoctions, but even then it was never more dramatic than a little rouge on their cheeks. Since Nora was trying to be openminded and welcoming to the new changes in her life, she didn't object when Phoenix told her to close her eyes and hold still. Phoenix then ran one of the pencils across the base of her eyelid.

After that, Phoenix took a small brush, dipped it into a small pot of black powder, and then swept it across Nora's eyelids. Nora tried to remain as still as possible, although she couldn't help but flinch a few times. Phoenix grabbed Nora's jaw with her free hand to hold her face in place.

"It's fun to use. Try to be careful and not use too much if you do this yourself next time. There is a fine line." She stopped and then took a step back to admire her work. "There," she said, beaming proudly, "Take a look."

When she looked into the mirror, Nora barely recognized herself. She took a moment to take in the new face Phoenix had just given her, and turned her head to see herself from different angles.

"Go ahead and grab a jacket and pants from the Arrant pile and put them in your bag. You'll need to put them on later, before we head out into the sectors. There is a pair of Fallow appropriate boots at the bottom of the closet for you," Phoenix informed her.

As she quickly shoved the Arrant clothing into her pack, Phoenix got up and grabbed her own bag. "Come on, we better get going." Nora took a deep breath and followed Phoenix out of the room. When they were halfway down the hallway, Nora stopped.

"Hang on, I forgot something," she said, and then ran back into their room to grab a scarf from the closet. She wasn't sure if she was quite ready to face the world with so much extra skin showing, and wanted to have something to cover herself up with, just in case.

CHAPTER 7

After a quick breakfast, Nora followed Phoenix into an area that had been omitted from the tour the day before. Dark blue lockers lined both sides of the room and a door was located at the back of it. There was a row of wooden benches in the middle of the room and bright overhead lights. She caught sight of weapons in a few of the open lockers. There were dozens of people crammed into the small space, and Nora recognized a few faces.

Trim sat on the bench next to Bretta—the couple looked like they were about to make out at any moment. Phoenix had already made her way over to Otto a couple lockers away, and the two were laughing. Jack stood near the door, rifle in hand, talking to a small mousy girl. She was the youngest looking one of them all.

Bray was digging through a locker near the back of the room. Nora navigated her way around the benches and people and approached him. When she reached him he was in the midst of strapping a rifle across his back.

"I guess we're stuck together today," Nora said, with a hint of a smile on her lips. "Do I choose any locker I want? And what does a girl have to do to get a weapon around here?" She was trying to sound calm and flirty, but she had never even seen a weapon up close, let alone held one.

Bray reached over in front of Nora and opened a locker. "How about this one?" He asked, as he gestured to the empty locker. "And we'll work on that weapon thing."

Nora laughed and stood back, noticing that Bray was wearing Arrant clothing. She had to admit that she liked seeing him in the clothing of the world she'd grown up in. For a moment she daydreamed about living a life with Bray back in Arrant, the two of them existing in a normal world together.

Phoenix approached the two of them, and interrupted Nora's fantasy. She had a rifle strapped to her back and a belt that held two more guns on her hips. She pulled on an Arrant jacket and effectively concealed all of the weapons.

Phoenix noticed Nora looking at the guns. Pointing to the rifle she said, "Long," then to the hand guns on her hips, "Quick," and finally to a knife that stuck out of her boot, "Short. That's all you really need to know about weapons." She finished with a smile and Bray laughed at her.

"I hope you haven't listened to too much of what comes out of this one." Bray winked at Phoenix. "Well, Nora. Which of the weapons looks the most natural to you? We have a few extra rifles and small hand guns, and plenty of knives."

"I don't really feel comfortable with any of them," Nora replied honestly.

"Rifle it is. Don't worry, just keep it pointed away from the rest of us and that pretty face of yours."

Her heart skipped a beat with Bray's compliment. She silently thanked Phoenix for that morning's makeover.

"Alright, everyone." Otto had climbed up to stand on top of a bench in the middle of the room and had begun to address the crowd. "Let's get ready to roll out of here. We are going to be moving back through Blear and into Arrant. From there we will cross the sector and enter Fallow. It's going to be a long walk. We don't anticipate any movement from the Agency, but as we have all learned, anything can happen out there. Take your time and double check your bags. Make sure you have your clothing for Fallow on underneath your Arrant layer. If you don't, we will leave you at the wall."

Nora spun to look at Phoenix who had already anticipated her next question. "Don't worry, you don't have to change out here. Take your bag and head through that door over there, you definitely can't wear that dress into Arrant."

Nora entered the small room as instructed and shut the door behind her. The space was extremely small, allowing only enough room for Nora to stand and change. The dress, which reached only down to her knees, left her exposed to the cold air in the room, which was being pumped in through a vent on the wall. As cold shivers ran across her body, she quickly pulled on a pair of gray pants, tucking the long dress into the waistline. The boots she had grabbed from the closet went halfway up her shins, and fit snugly under the long pants.

She returned to the bench where Bray and Phoenix were waiting, opened her bag, and placed the dull gray jacket over her shoulders. "Okay, what's next?" she asked them.

Bray removed the long rifle from Nora's locker and handed it to her. "Combat training," he said with a smirk.

Nora's hands reached out and grabbed the cold steel barrel from him. Bray turned her around and placed his arms around her shoulders, helping her to hold the rifle against her underarm, as he pressed his chest against her back. He spoke in a low voice into her ear.

"See that tip at the end of the barrel?" he asked, forcing Nora to squint down the length of the weapon. When she nodded he continued. "Place that between the two pegs here, and squeeze the trigger."

His exhalation against her ear and neck caused Nora to tilt her head slightly. Her cold skin welcomed the warmth of his body. She tried to stay focused on the lesson as his breath grazed her collarbone.

"Place the strap around your torso, and let the rifle hang behind you, underneath your jacket." His hands worked the thin strap over her shoulder, lifting the back of her coat so the weapon could fall into place.

Nora turned around to face him, quickly noticing how close he still stood to her. His dark eyes looked down into her own. Bray reached past her into a nearby locker and retrieved a small knife.

"For now, why don't you hang onto this knife. Keep it somewhere on your body that is quickly accessible." He patted his hands on her waist which caused Nora's heart to flutter and her body to freeze in place. "I suggest your hips, or down in your boot like Phoenix. None of us expect you to have to use your weapons today, but if the circumstance presents itself, it's better that you understand how to defend yourself. Until then, keep them concealed."

Nora nodded and bent down to slide the knife into her boot as Bray backed away from her. She felt a sudden uneasiness when he left her side, made worse by the feeling of the knife's hard handle against her shin, and the weight of the rifle on her back.

After their final check, the rebel group exited the base and entered into direct sunlight. Nora blinked a few times, trying to adjust her eyes to the bright sun that poured down over Blear. The change in light reminded her of Arrant's dust-filled sky. Her eyes had spent a lifetime accustomed to the drabness that constantly hung overhead.

"Won't these Arrant clothes give us away out here?" Nora asked Phoenix.

"Shhh. No. We are only crossing the alley here. We won't be exposed again until we get to the wall," Phoenix responded.

Nora decided to just fall in line and not get too caught up in the specifics. After all, Otto seemed to have it all under control. He moved at a brisk pace as he crossed the small alleyway between the rebel base and the building next to it.

The entire group quickly dipped across the alley, following his lead. As they traversed between the buildings Nora caught sight of the giant body of water in the middle of the sector again. Immediately she felt an almost irresistible pull towards it. She turned away from the water, in an attempt to ignore its allure.

As her eyes readjusted to the darkened room inside of the second building, Nora felt the dust in the air settle on her exposed skin. An awful, pungent smell caught her off guard, causing her to stop momentarily and cover her nose. She continued on, breathing through her mouth as infrequently as she could, to avoid inhaling too much of the smell. The building was clearly filled with a rampantly growing mold. The damp air and walls provided a perfect breeding ground for it.

Jack and the small mousy girl, further ahead of Nora, turned on their flashlights. They quickly moved behind poles that stretched high above them. Nora followed one of the poles with her eyes, all the way up to the top floor of the tall building. The ceiling reached high above her, and she caught sight of windows as she let her gaze drop back down.

"Clear. Anything on your side, Cady?" Jack called out from his position in front.

"Clear here," Nora heard Cady, the small girl, call out. Her voice was as mousy as her appearance. The rebel group picked up the pace and moved through the rest of the room quickly. Nora was thankful for the increased speed, hoping they would get out of there as soon as possible. Jack and Cady approached a staircase and began to climb. Hurrying to catch up, Nora stepped through the door that led her to the stairwell as well. She started to ascend them hastily, being ushered from behind by Phoenix. Otto and Bray gathered at the top of the staircase, cautiously opening the door together.

By the time Nora climbed the last steps and walked out onto the rooftop, Otto and Bray were looking out over the edge of the tall building. They nodded at each other and took a few steps back. Before Nora could grasp what was happening the boys sprinted and jumped from the rooftop. Her heart stopped as the boys were in mid air, and did not resume its beating until they had landed safely on the roof of the adjacent building.

Walking to the edge of the rooftop, Nora gauged the gap to be around seven feet. The second rooftop was lower, which would make the long jump easier. As she anticipated falling she began to shake with nervousness.

She backed up a few feet, and took a deep breath. Nora tried to ready herself, but her body felt frozen with fear. Frustrated, she closed her eyes and tried to picture the gap she had seen, imagining it to be smaller and less overwhelming than it actually was. She opened her eyes with a start as Phoenix grabbed her hand.

"Here, this might help," Phoenix said, and then began running for the edge of the building, forcing Nora to keep up by tightening her grip on her hand. Before she knew it, Nora had jumped into the air, half on her own accord and half from the force of Phoenix pulling her along.

Phoenix landed on both feet and slid to a stop. Nora however, landed on one foot and one knee, stopping too abruptly, and falling over. She quickly jumped up and dusted herself off, too embarrassed to look up at the rest of the rebels. When she finally did raise her head, Bray was looking at her with a smile. Nora let out a small laugh and smiled back at him, brushing her black hair out of her eyes.

"You will get better at it," Bray reassured her. "Phoenix almost broke her arm the first time. That is probably why she held on to you so tightly." He laughed as Phoenix lightly punched his shoulder.

The group entered the next building through a steel door on the roof. Descending the stairs towards the ground floor, Jack and Cady immediately moved towards the front side of the building that faced the main street of Blear. The inside had huge floor-to-ceiling windows, which Jack and Cady had ducked down behind, cautiously peeking above the sill.

The rest of rebels found something to hide behind as well and waited. Jack lifted his arm into the air, and then after pausing, brought it back down quickly, signaling the go-ahead to the others. The group crept across the giant room, heading straight outside through a small wooden door. As her eyes adjusted once more, Nora realized they were facing the giant concrete wall that separated her from her old home.

CHAPTER 8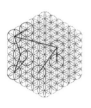

Otto searched for the loose, gray brick that was hidden in the wall. Nora stared at Otto as he deftly worked his hands over the various blocks, impressed with the ways the rebellion had of getting through the different sectors of Constance. Somehow the secret portals had managed to stay hidden. Nora was amazed the rebels had been able to sneak from building to building, sector to sector, and between the walls for so long. As Otto located and then pressed the hidden brick all the way through into Arrant, she wondered how she had never noticed them moving around inside of her sector before. She guessed it was mostly due to the fact that if you didn't know to look for something, you could miss what's right in front of your eyes.

They all silently waited for him to finish clearing the path. Without saying a word, Otto motioned with his hands for them to come forward. He placed a finger in front of his lips, to signal the group to stay quiet, and then pressed his palm down towards the ground, which meant to stay low. Finally he swept his arm out in front of him, ushering each rebel through the hole into Arrant. Nora's body tensed up and her palms grew sweaty as the reality struck her—she was going home.

"Okay, let's split up," Otto said out loud as Nora pushed her way through the small opening. "Trim and Bretta, you are with me, we will head around Arrant from the south—staying hidden from the public eye. Jack and Cady, circle around from the north. Keep your eyes peeled for any sign of the Agency near the center of Constance. Bray, Phoenix, and Nora, you three are going through the middle. You will be out on the streets, so make sure that you don't draw unwanted attention to yourselves. We will all reconvene at the next wall."

As she marveled at the way the rebel group listened to every command Otto made, Nora admired how precise and calculated his directions seemed. She squatted next to Phoenix as Trim, Bretta, and Otto took off, crossed a small alleyway, and disappeared around the corner of a building. Jack and Cady moved in the opposite direction—keeping the wall to the left of them.

"Once we get out of the alley, stay calm and act natural," Bray instructed Nora. "Remember, act like we are just everyday citizens of Arrant. Phoenix and I will protect you if anything goes wrong. Keep your rifle hidden unless one of us tells you otherwise."

Bray's presence had a certain effect that made Nora feel safe and comfortable—at least as safe and comfortable as she possibly could be in that situation. He moved in front of the girls and started to walk through the alley towards the main road ahead. Nora saw the muscles in his back tense as he made his way.

"Try not to fall in love with him," Phoenix whispered jokingly to Nora. Nora attempted to roll her eyes dismissively, but her blushing cheeks gave her away. Phoenix picked up on the guilty look. "I'm guessing, by that expression on your face, it's too late already?"

"Is it that obvious?" Nora asked, her cheeks growing increasingly warm and a bead of sweat forming on her temple. Nora wasn't quite sure why she felt so embarrassed about her feelings towards Bray being revealed.

"Not to him probably. Guys are pretty dense about that stuff. Plus I've spent a lot more time with you." Phoenix smiled, trying to put Nora at ease.

Although only a day had passed since she left Arrant, to Nora it had felt like an eternity. Her clothing and gestures mimicked the old Eleanor, and her heart was weighed down with guilt because she was merely doing an impersonation of her former self. She reminded herself that her whole life had been spent here, and hoped her natural body language would help convince the other citizens of Arrant that she was only out enjoying another day in the dust-covered sector.

As they walked, Nora contemplated how funny fate could be. Had she never remembered her dreams, there was a chance the Agency never would have shown up looking for her. That meant that she could have spent the previous night in her own bed. She would be just waking up now and making breakfast with Deryn, waiting for the morning announcements from Dr. Secora to begin.

As she took her last step into the main street, Nora realized that though she had changed so much over the last day, the world around her had remained the same. Familiar faces walked around the town, many of them men heading towards the factory to start their workday. Nora hoped Deryn wasn't among them as she passed by. She wondered if she should have told Phoenix and Bray about him.

Sensing Nora's growing anxiety, Phoenix stayed close to her. "Don't worry. We are just out for a walk before we start our day. Nothing unusual is going on. We're just a small group of friends enjoying the morning and each other's company. We only have a couple more blocks to go, then we go east, through a residential area. After that, we will be at the wall. It will go by fast."

The shops and restaurants of the sector were just opening for business. Nora felt more like a tourist than a life-long citizen of the area—one day in Blear and she already felt like an outsider. She contemplated dying her hair purple so she would have to stay hidden in the back streets like Bretta.

Walking next to each other, the three of them tried to blend in with the regular citizens. Her body tensed up each time they passed a local, but they were all too busy doing their own daily routine to even give her a second look.

Still, each passerby made Nora's heart skip a beat. She tried not to make eye contact with anyone, worried that word had gotten out about her running from the Agency and joining the rebellion. She knew that was a crazy thought to have as she herself, while living in Arrant, had never been aware of anyone becoming Defected. That kind of information remained hidden from the locals.

When the three of them turned onto one of the residential streets, the houses around her came into view, and Nora began to sweat, her anxiety level suddenly skyrocketing. Her heart started to race and it felt like it might leap right out of her chest.

"Oh please, any street but this one," Nora begged Bray.

"This street is our only direct route to the wall from here. We don't have much of a choice."

"This is the street my parents live on." Nora pointed further down the road, "It's a little up ahead, with the dirty white fence in front of it."

Through the dusty air she was able to make out a small crowd gathered in front of her parents' house. Bray motioned for her and Phoenix to stay low and move slower, his eyes adjusting to the dust and catching sight of the crowd as well. The three of them silently moved to the right side of the road, ducking behind a large bush.

Bray's head fell as he realized it was the Agency that was gathered around the home. Two agents emerged from the house, holding Nora's father by his arms, walking him down the stairs into the street. Seconds later, her mother was escorted out as well, her younger brother, Will in her arms. They guided her down the front steps and out into the street. The agents gathered around her family, blocking them from Nora's view.

Altogether there was a group of over a dozen agents. She'd had no idea that there were that many of them in Arrant. The Agency must have found out about her desertion. Her chest tightened, knowing the agents were interrogating her parents as to her whereabouts. Nora gasped and her mouth grew uncomfortably dry.

"That's my family," she whispered to Bray and Phoenix. "What do you think they'll do to them?"

"The center of Constance must have alerted the local agents," Bray told Nora, "Looks like we got to you first. You should be thankful. Don't worry, they will release your family once they realize your parents don't know where you are."

Nora sighed, as she watched her mom being led further into the street. Nora's eyes widened, as she caught sight of someone standing in the street next to her father. As her vision focused onto Deryn she clasped her hands together so tightly that her knuckles grew white. "I have to get closer. I need to hear what he is saying."

Without waiting for permission from Bray, Nora moved closer to the house, darting to hide behind another group of bushes. One of the agents began to speak in a booming voice.

"Dalt and Annie Rose, you are being summoned to the court house of Arrant in an ongoing effort to keep Sector 5 safe and secure from all rebel militias. Please proceed immediately. Thank you for your cooperation."

Her parents went along with the agents, without any hesitation or resistance. They were surrounded on either side by agents, in addition to the agents that led them and the several more that brought up the rear of the group. Deryn remained standing still on the sidewalk, watching them make their way down the road.

Hoping that they might have some answers, Nora glanced over at Bray and Phoenix, who had joined her, but before she could whisper a question she heard one of the remaining agents start to speak.

"Recruits, on my orders," one of the agents called out. Clearly he was the one in charge. "Stay at the Rose homestead and keep watch. Usually within a twenty-four hour period, the Defected will return to familiar surroundings. Stay sharp until further notice."

The agent in charge then made his way to follow Nora's family and the other agents as they marched towards the courthouse. They had walked off too far for Nora to hear anybody anymore, but she saw the head agent yell out a command to the agents towards the back of the group, and they immediately withdrew their rifles and pointed them at her parents' backs.

As the crowd cleared Nora noticed that Deryn was still standing there, and did not seem to have moved an inch. She wished that he would have gone with her parents. Instead, her heart grew heavy watching him stand in place, talking with the few agents that remained.

Deryn shook hands with a couple of them, which shocked her. She wasn't quite sure what to make of that gesture, and her mind began to race. As the questions in her head continued to form, Nora was no longer content hiding behind the bush, watching from a distance. She stood up and made a running dash to get closer to the house. She found a hiding spot behind a large oak tree.

When the group of men had all turned to face away from her she was able to make her way over to the fence that lined the house. Pressing her ear between the cracks in the dirty white fence, she could hear the conversation between the agents and Deryn.

"Well, for me it was my girlfriend. The love of my life," she heard Deryn say. "I came home from work and she was gone. I had heard from her parents that she had become Defected, and decided that I needed to do my part in order to bring her home safely. I hope eventually that she will come to her senses and realize that we are all here to help her."

"Deryn, we are glad you have decided to join the Agency," one of the other men said.

A hand appeared on her shoulder—Bray had joined her and was crouched down beside Nora. Phoenix had stayed a few yards back to ensure their safety from any agents that could sneak up behind them. Nora felt a pull towards Deryn. She wanted so badly to run over to him, and tell him that she was okay. That she was sorry, and needed to stay away for her own safety. To tell him of all the dreams she had over the last three months, and how she was faced with life or death. That she hated leaving him behind.

Despite knowing better, Nora began to stand up. Before she'd even reached the top of the fence, Bray had pulled her back down forcibly, and was huddled over her, keeping her pinned to the ground. His arms wrapped around her shoulders from behind. His chest was pressed so firmly against her back that she could feel his heart racing.

Anger burned inside of her and she struggled to escape Bray's clutch. Bray began to rock her slightly, back and forth, as he shushed her. His chest rose and fell against her back as he breathed deeply. Her body went limp as she stopped resisting and the anger was instantly replaced with an onset of tears. She began to shake uncontrollably as more tears welled up in her eyes. She turned around to face Bray, and he looked down at her with an understanding expression.

"I know," he said softly. Nora, still trapped in the cage his limbs made around her, stopped holding back the tears and let them pour out, soaking the front of his shirt. After the wave of crying subsided, she looked up at him again. Their faces were so close that the warmth of his breath dried the damp trails the tears had left behind on her cheeks. She closed her eyes, and then as if she was being pulled by some kind of gravity, her mouth met Bray's. His lips were half parted, and he immediately leaned in, kissing her back. She pulled her lips from his and pulled slightly back, shocked at what had just happened, and that Bray had not even resisted.

They kissed again, a firmer and more fervent kiss. When she opened her eyes she felt slightly dizzy and disoriented. Bray's arms loosened their grip on her, and once she had her bearings again she darted off to hide alone behind a tree.

Bray finally opened his eyes, long after she had escaped his embrace, still living in the moment of the passionate kiss. He blinked, trying to understand what was happening around him. Phoenix shook her head at him with a crooked smile on her face.

"I'll go get her. You stay here," Phoenix told him with a sigh in her voice, motioning for him to sit back down. She raised herself up to a crouched position and dusted off the dirt from her knees. She stayed crouched down as she moved, not wanting to draw attention to herself since the agents were still standing in front of the house. Bray leaned back onto his hands, the soil compacting beneath the weight of his palms—it felt like the wind had been knocked out of him. For a minute he forgot all about the nearby agents, the mission, and the danger of the situation at hand. He forgot about his fellow rebels and the fact that he had enough firearms strapped to his body to wipe out a small village. For a minute the rest of the world disappeared, and nothing existed except for the racing thrill in his heart. He felt as though he could still feel Nora in his arms—her phantom presence was unmistakable to him. Letting out a deep breath, he looked up at the heavy gray sky, and watched as a beam of sunshine sliced through the distant horizon.

CHAPTER 9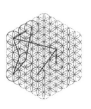

Bray caught up to Nora and Phoenix a block away. He walked at a leisurely pace behind them, trying to allow Phoenix time to console Nora, who was still teary eyed.

Phoenix walked beside Nora with one arm around her waist. Bray knew instinctually that Nora had a relationship with the man who had betrayed her and joined the Agency. In a moment of desperation and despair, she had turned to Bray to find comfort. He kept a lengthy distance from the girls as he waited for the situation to stabilize.

"Tell me about what your life was like here in Arrant," Phoenix prompted Nora. "What did you do around here when you were growing up?"

Nora forced a smile, she knew that Phoenix was trying to distract her from what had just happened. She decided to humor her—it couldn't hurt to recall a few memories that stayed cemented in the streets of Arrant.

As she drew a slow breath she gazed at her surroundings. There were too many memories that had occurred on these dust-covered roads and she found it hard to pick only one.

She could have told Phoenix about how she used to run around this row of houses with one of her childhood friends. About how, one night, when she was out later than usual, an agent had stopped her and asked why she was out so late unchaperoned. He then proceeded to escort her back home in time for the city-wide curfew.

She could have spoken about the time she had fallen down, and had hurt her leg so badly that her father had to carry her home in his arms. It was difficult for Nora to remember that her whole life, up until the last twenty-four hours, had been spent in Arrant. Her knees felt weak as the reality of her present situation set in. She couldn't choose just one single memory to tell Phoenix, because it would not do justice to portray how beautiful her former life was.

"I couldn't possibly pick just one," she managed to get out before the entirety of the life she had so recently left behind came flooding back. "If I think of a particularly good memory during our walk,

I'll be sure to share it with you," she said as she flashed Phoenix a grateful smile.

Realizing that Bray, Phoenix, and the rest of the rebels had probably gone through similar traumas and felt similar emotions, Nora knew she was in the company of people who could truly empathize with her, and this made her feel better.

All of the rebels were impassioned, to a nearly obsessive degree, towards their goal to bring down the Agency's oppressive force in Constance. They had each been forced to sacrifice their entire lives, and it was time for them to reap the rewards for those sacrifices.

Witnessing how strong Phoenix and Bray were mentally and emotionally gave Nora the hope that she too would grow to be like them one day. This gave her the courage to keep moving forward with her new life. The life she had in Arrant was gone, and no amount of mourning it would be able to bring it back. Instead she decided to be grateful for the life she'd been given by the rebels, as it was far better than the alternative. She could focus on the possibilities of what could be.

As the three of them walked on—Bray still trailing behind the girls—Nora occasionally commented on certain houses they passed, not sure if it was for Phoenix's benefit or her own comfort. It seemed as though every house on the block had a memory attached to it. Nora tried her best to keep the stories light. She pointed out the house where she'd had her first kiss with a neighborhood boy, a blond-haired kid who had the most perfectly white and straight teeth she'd ever seen. When they reached an old house at the end of the block Nora pointed to the airy porch and mentioned that an old lady used to sit out there every evening at dusk on her rocking chair, and sing the same old, beautiful song. Nora used to make it a point to pass by the house on her way home, if it was possible, so that she could hear the song at the end of the day.

Phoenix's ears perked up at the mention of this. Art and culture inside of the sectors was a subject that rarely came up in conversations between the rebels. Phoenix asked Nora if she could sing the song for her.

"I'm not much of a singer," Nora exclaimed, her cheeks warming slightly from embarrassment.

"Oh I don't care, I've always wanted to hear music from another sector. Now, out with it," Phoenix demanded in a teasing voice.

Nora's gaze dropped, feeling uncomfortable at the prospect of having to sing.

"Fine if you won't sing it, I'll share my favorite song from Fallow, when I was growing up." Phoenix cleared her throat.

"Sleep little bird, the night has come,
spare me your cares for a while.
Gone with the breeze, your worries are free,
so let your dreams run wild."

Nora looked over at Phoenix with shock. She couldn't believe what she'd just heard.

"Is that a song all people from Fallow know?" Nora asked her.

"Yes, we are all taught this song when we are children. We use it as a bedtime song for the children, to help sooth them to sleep," Phoenix replied, stopping to look at Nora. "Why?"

Excited, Nora rushed over her words to explain her curiosity, "We have a very similar song. I mean the words are different, but the melody is exactly the same. Do you think all the people of Constance know this melody?"

Phoenix just laughed at Nora's excited response. "I'm sure it is a very common melody throughout the entire city, it's not very complex compared to many of the other popular songs of Fallow."

Nora shook her head emphatically, not believing the coincidence had no significance. "The lyrics in Arrant have the same meaning. Our song begins like this—" Nora lifted her head, hoping the angle would improve her singing voice.

"The sun has gone—"

"Good morning citizens of Constance," the nearby speakers, hung from a street post, interrupted her. "As always, may your day be filled with gratitude for the life Constance has provided."

The overpowering voice belonged to Dr. Secora, the leader of the entire city and Agency. "As our time here continues to move forward, we are reminded of those left in the past. Thanks to the efforts of hardworking men and women like yourselves, we are all able to endure and survive. Be thankful tonight for the life you have been given inside of these walls. Before these walls our world teetered on the brink of extinction. Constance is vigilant. Constance is pure," his voice faded from the speakers.

Nora tilted her head, "Do you guys know why they walled off the city in the first—"

As quickly as Nora had started talking she was interrupted again, when Bray grabbed her and Phoenix forcefully and threw them up against the concrete wall.

"Ow!" Nora exclaimed.

"Shh!" Bray whispered as he placed his hand over Nora's mouth to silence her. "I saw agents up ahead." He peered cautiously around the wall. Nora struggled to catch her breath from under his hand. "We are going to have to sneak through here before they spot us. Let's move quietly, until we get to the other side of the street," Bray darted out in front of them, releasing the girls, and peeked around the corner again. When Nora reached Bray's side and caught sight of what he saw she gasped.

Seven agents were gathered in the middle of the street. One stood in front of the other six, addressing them quietly. Nora tilted her head in an effort to hear what he was saying, but she couldn't make anything out. She waited as the Commanding Agent ended his speech. The group of agents split up: one pair of agents headed down the block, turning around before coming back up the next block. Another pair of agents made the same movements, but they were positioned further away, down the main road. Nora's heart jumped as the last pair of agents started heading directly towards their location against the wall. The Commanding Agent paced down the main road on his own, and the wandering agents reported back to him after every block.

"Quick, in here," Bray directed Nora and Phoenix, motioning towards a small door that was across the alley from where they stood.

The three of them sprinted towards the door, keeping their heads low. Bray arrived first, ramming his shoulder hard into the door, forcing it open, and then let Nora and Phoenix pass through first. Once inside they were able to see out onto the main road through small windows. Nora breathed a sigh of relief when she saw that the place was empty. It appeared to be an abandoned shop. She stared out the window at the Commanding Agent—he passed directly in front of the small store.

"We are going to have to run, okay?" Bray said, looking pointedly at Nora. "They have us surrounded. Luckily we are only four blocks from the wall. If we can get past him, we can lose them near the factory."

Nora had seen the factory every day of her life, up until a day ago. Bray and Phoenix would benefit from her knowledge of the area. "If I remember correctly, there is a door to the factory that the city always keeps unlocked. They use it for deliveries and shipments in and out of the building."

"Great. Can you show us where it is?" Bray had a hopeful look in his eyes. Nora nodded, hoping she wouldn't disappoint her fellow rebels with her first chance to actually contribute. "On my count, we move,"

Bray commanded. He paused, still crouched down on the small building's floor. "1...2...Now!"

The three of them burst through the front door of the small business, onto the main road. Immediately Nora heard a voice call out. The Commanding Agent stared Nora dead in the eyes, and the hairs on the back of her neck stood up. The Commanding Agent started to run towards them, and began to close in on them fast.

"I've got eyes on them!" he bellowed out over his shoulders to the other agents. "East. Heading back into residential," he managed to get out in between his short gasps for air. He was moving at full speed.

Nora turned away from the oncoming agent and focused her attention forward. She felt a hand push against her back as Bray prompted her to take the lead.

"Get us out of here!" he yelled behind Nora. She could hear the panic in his voice.

Nora ran as fast as her untrained body would allow. Her lungs burned as she made a right turn onto another residential street. Facing down, she tried to block out everything around her, and concentrated solely on the rhythm of her feet hitting the ground. She let out a focused breath and took a left turn. Nora pushed on as they ran straight down two more blocks, turned right, and then took another left. She was heading towards the factory, but taking an indirect path in an attempt to throw the agents off their trail.

Taking one final turn, the factory came into view. It stood taller than the houses in Arrant, and had a very plain, squared-off frame. The dull gray pipes on the roof spewed dust into the sky above them. She raced around a corner and quickly wedged her small body through a crack in the fence that surrounded the factory.

"The door is just up ahead," she called out without turning around.

When they reached the factory Nora stopped and crouched down against the small, rusted railing that led up the concrete steps to the door. "Now what?" she managed to get out. Bray looked up at her, panting almost as heavily as she was. "Do you think we lost them?" she asked.

"I don't see any of them anymore," Bray replied as his body began to relax. "I don't trust it enough to sit here and wait it out though. I'm sure they will be onto us soon. There aren't a lot of options for us to hide around here. We need to keep moving, Hopefully the door is still unlocked."

Nora shook her head, feeling useless to Bray and Phoenix now. She let out one last giant breath and felt her heart begin to slow its pace. "I don't know where to go. I've never been inside the factory before."

Bray sighed and she felt the weight of the world pressing down on her shoulders. Nora stood up and joined him and Phoenix in front of the door to the factory. It was the moment of truth. The three of them exchanged an anxious look as Bray placed a hand on the door's metal handle and turned it. It opened and a cool breeze emerged and swept over their faces. One by one they walked into the dark factory, with no idea what their next move would be.

CHAPTER 10

Once they were inside the factory, the heavy, metal door creaked as it slowly began to close. After a full minute the door to the outside world finally slammed shut, and they were plunged into total darkness. If it had been a weekday the factory would have been full of workers, all trying to earn a meager living. Factory workers were made up of those who didn't have any other particularly useful skill. But since it was the weekend, most of them were home with their families.

The large building was cold and the air was significantly denser with dust than the streets of Arrant. Even Nora wasn't comfortable breathing in, despite the fact that she had grown up with the dusty pollution in Arrant. She placed a hand over her nose and mouth in a poor attempt to filter the air. The small hairs on her arm stood up from the cold temperature.

They had entered onto a small railed platform that was built high above the main floor. The ground level was full of old metal machines that were used to manufacture all of the building materials that Arrant was known for providing the rest of the city with.

Bray surmised that they could follow the small railway to the center of the room and turn towards the left at the four-way junction, which would lead them to the back of the building. From there, Bray hoped that they could find a way that would lead them back outside, to the wall where the rest of the rebels would be waiting for them. He knew they would be worried and wondering why it was taking them so long.

The three of them continued on forward, cautiously navigating the narrow catwalk, being hyper vigilant, so as not to make a misstep which would result in plummeting to the concrete floor below. In between carefully calculated steps, Nora visually searched the building's interior, straining her eyes to see through the dust and darkness. The factory ceilings were so high up that she was unable to see them. There were many hanging bulbs that would have been shining brightly had it been a workday. The metal walkway they were on hovered directly over the machines below them.

Nora had always known that the workers of Arrant made building supplies inside of the factory. It was common knowledge in Arrant, that once a week, the main wall between Arrant and the center of Constance would open, and a small group from the Agency would enter the sector. They would walk through town to the factory, where they would collect the production from that week's labor. The agents loaded up a large metal hovering cart with the heavy building materials. It had the capacity to bear several tons of weight and still float effortlessly across the ground, with minimal assistance. It needed only two people to navigate it in the right direction, back towards the opening in the wall. Four small, spinning exhaust vents pivoted around the base, which caused dust to expel outwards in every direction from below it. Once the dirt-encrusted hovering cart—its flatbed loaded up with construction supplies—disappeared beyond the wall into the center of Constance, the wall would be closed up immediately behind it.

Nora broke the silence that had taken over since the three of them had entered the factory. "Where do all the building materials end up?" she asked Phoenix, unsure if even Phoenix would know the answer. "I know once a week the Agency shows up and carts the materials towards the center of Constance. Once the wall is closed behind them, no one in Arrant seems to have any idea where it goes. Did the material ever show up in Fallow?"

Phoenix looked shocked that Nora, nor the rest of Arrant, had been told what the material they produced day in and day out was used for. "It is mostly used for the prison in Jejung now. The prisoner count grows everyday and the inmates are put to work, using the materials in order to expand the structure. Pretty sick if you ask me, being forced to build your own cage."

It had never occurred to Nora that the prison in Jejung would need to be expanded, or that was where the materials were shipped off to. "That is where we will end up if the agents catch us, right?"

"You can bet your life on it," Phoenix responded tersely.

Suddenly Nora caught sight of a small sliver of light reflecting off the ground below them. She visually followed the trail of light to a door on the main floor. A single foot then stepped into the room, blocking the light source and the sliver vanished.

"The rebels must have come in here," a man's voice spoke. "We checked the surrounding streets and there was no sign that they had gone another way."

Bray motioned for Nora to come closer to where he was standing. She squatted down low and moved towards him, carefully holding her rifle against her body, to prevent herself from accidentally making any noise.

"I think we should move," Bray whispered to her. "It's only a matter of time before they look up here and see us."

They sat motionless, watching the agents below them begin to creep further onto the main floor. The agents spread out and began to search the aisles between the large machines—the beams from their flashlights dancing across the concrete floor.

"You two, stay here and guard the door," the Commanding Agent called out. "I don't want anyone to get in or out of this building. You two move upstairs and check in those small offices that surround the main room. I'm going to head towards the back. It's possible they have already taken off."

The agents separated themselves into smaller groups, following the Commanding Agent's orders without question.

Knowing that the two men who had been ordered upstairs would eventually cross onto the metal catwalk, Nora swallowed hard and whispered, "Yes, we definitely need to move."

At the small juncture in the center of the room, which had paths going in all four directions, they turned left and began to head towards the back of the room. Carefully placing their feet as quietly as possible, they crossed above two of the agents who were searching the ground floor. Nora tried not to even breathe as she crossed over them.

The two agents upstairs were loud and clumsy. From the sounds that emerged it was clear they were constantly bumping into things. There was an exit located directly below them, but they couldn't make it there now. Instead, the three of them inched their way further down the railway towards the back wall.

"We are almost there, but the Commanding Agent is directly below us. Since there is only the one door on the back wall, we'll have to go right past him." Bray pointed in the general direction of the door. He stopped walking and looked around the room. After a moment of contemplation he said, "I have an idea."

Bray grasped his rifle with both hands and then disconnected the lower portion of it. He fiddled with the detached piece until he was able to shake out a few bullets. With great precision he threw the bullets one at a time, as hard as he could, towards the side door the three of them had entered from.

The bullets made a loud clatter as they struck the metal door, along with the surrounding railings. As they fell to the main floor, the bullets continued to make noise, striking staircases and hanging beams. In the cavernous factory each metallic plink rung out as clear as a bell.

In surprised voices, the agents yelled out, and took off running towards the location of the noise. The commanding agent raced over as well, and once he was a safe distance away from them Bray said, "Let's go now," his tone hushed and urgent.

Staying close to Bray and Phoenix, Nora pressed her body against Phoenix's back. The three of them, as one single unit, made their way down the metal stairs as quietly as they could, running as soon as their feet hit the ground floor. They moved towards the door, sprinting from one large machine to the next, so that they would remain hidden from view. Bray looked at the girls and held his breath as he slowly opened the door. Nora winced and prayed that it would open silently. Once he'd opened the door wide enough they were able to catch sight of the wall directly outside of the doorway, and knew Fallow lay on the other side. Luckily, because of how high the wall was, as well as where the sun was positioned at that particular moment, no direct light poured in through the opening. Only a small, faint light entered.

They all squeezed through the door, not wanting to open it any further than they had too. Once they had made it outside they saw Otto and the rest of the rebels leaning against the wall waiting for them.

CHAPTER 11

"What took you so long Bray?!" Otto demanded as the trio jogged towards the rest of the rebels. "We've been waiting for you to catch up. The charges to blow open the wall are set. Hurry up and get changed into your Fallow clothing."

As he changed clothes, Bray explained to Otto that the agents had stumbled onto their location near the main road, and that they were currently inside the factory, so they needed to hurry now more than ever. The agents may have been momentarily thrown off, but they were smart, and would figure out what had happened pretty fast.

Nora opened her bag and took out the clothing she'd picked to blend in with the citizens of Fallow. As she removed the Arrant disguise she revealed the dress she still had on underneath. She liked having one consistent layer of clothing on beneath all of the various disguise outfits. The dress was her authentic layer, the layer that expressed her personality and who she wanted to be. So even when covered up by the drab Arrant fabric, she knew that her true self still remained hidden beneath.

Nora wondered if Phoenix would have the same reaction as she'd had, once Phoenix was thrust back into her original sector. She wondered if there was a man there that would elicit the same heartache in Phoenix as Deryn had for her. She decided that if Phoenix experienced the same thing that Nora had back near her parents' house, she would be as good a friend as Phoenix had been to her. She'd help her bear the emotional burden, and do her best to take her mind off it.

"Why do we need the explosives this time for the wall?" Nora asked Otto as he impatiently waited for her to put the last item of clothing on. Bray and Phoenix had already finished changing. "Is there no hidden hole in this wall?" she continued.

Otto shook his head. "Not here. We haven't been to Fallow since the rebellion began." Nora looked over at him in confusion, his statement was hard for her to believe. Seeing her reaction he went on to explain. "We were ordered not to make contact with the rebels in Fallow until everything was in place. When that time came, they would either come to us in Blear, or we would go to them in Fallow. That is the only knowledge of the their rebellion that we have. We don't even know if the rebel base in Fallow still exists. All of our information has been passed down to us, for so long now, that nothing can be taken to be a definite fact anymore." He paused and looked up at Nora. "The only certain information we have to go on, is a name."

"That's it?!" Nora was shocked at the lack of information the rebel group had. "This whole rebellion has been going on for all this time, and you don't even know if there are more of us on the other side of this wall?"

"That's it," Otto confirmed. "Sometimes you just have to take a leap of faith."

"Well, why now?" Nora asked Otto bluntly, afraid of the answer. "Why wait all of these years and decide now, to go into Fallow. What has changed?" Nora demanded. The pitch of her voice rose with anxiety, wanting to know the answer before risking her life any further.

"I'll explain after we get out of here, the agents that were following you could be here any second." Nora wasn't satisfied with Otto's answer, but rationalized that getting away from the Agency was the most important matter right now. She quickly stuffed her Arrant clothes into her bag. Otto glanced at the other rebels. "I'm going to blow the charges now. Get down behind me," he instructed.

Otto pressed a button on a small, black device, and moments later an explosion rang out. The sound was loud enough that anyone nearby would have heard it. As the dust cleared from the blast, the slam of a metal door sounded in the distance.

Nora's heart stopped as an agent emerged, and looked directly at them. The agent yelled out seconds before a gunshot sounded from behind her head. As the agent's body fell to the dirt, a cloud of dust rose up around him. The rest of the agents came running through the doorway, past the fallen man, and headed straight for the rebels. The small group of agents quickly spread out and began to take cover behind the large piles of damaged building materials the factory workers had discarded, to protect themselves against the oncoming gunfire from the rebels.

Panic stricken, Nora whirled around to face the wall. Her heart sunk when she saw that the explosive Otto had set off had only loosened a single brick. Otto began to kick at the blocks that surrounded the small hole, but none of them budged, despite the intense force of his well placed blows. Bray raced over to Otto's side and began to shove his entire weight into the cement wall blocks. Otto continued to kick with as much force as he could muster, but even with their two efforts combined, they barely made any progress.

"Damn!" Otto cried out. The agents were fast approaching. Otto tried in vain to worm his way through the hole in the wall. "It's too small, we won't make it through!" He turned towards Nora. "It's too late to turn back now. Those agents will report our whereabouts to Dr. Secora, and that we were trying to get into Fallow. Nora get over here next to me!" he ordered.

Immediately Nora dropped her bag, and dove towards the ground next to him. He grabbed her shoulders, "We need you to squeeze through this hole," he said hurriedly. "You have a shot at fitting. But you need to hurry."

Nora was hesitant, nervous at the thought of such responsibility, but didn't want to make a habit out of questioning Otto's orders. Despite the rush of fear, she began to climb through. Suddenly realizing something, she whipped her head to face the men behind her. "Wait! What about Cady? She's small too. Can't she go through instead of me?" Nora turned to see Cady, her rifle aimed at the approaching agents.

Otto shook his head, "Cady's an expert shooter and we need her help to fend off the agents. Regardless, it has to be you Nora. You need to trust me on that. We have to get you through and then defend ourselves against these agents. Then you'll have the chance to make it to the rebellion on the other side. Now, move!" Otto barked. Nora had never seen Otto this stressed before. He sat on the ground directly behind her, his teeth clenched.

Nora sucked her breath in, and leaned all the way back. As Otto and Bray lifted her body off the ground and started sliding her through the opening she gazed up at them with wide, terrified eyes. The rough edges of the opening scratched her exposed skin and ripped through her dress. She turned her head to the right, in order to fit the rest of the way through. The last thing she saw before she was on the other side was the herd of agents racing towards them, their feet raising up a cloud of dust in their wake.

Trim and Bretta stood up and began firing their rifles at the oncoming agents, forcing them to dodge behind a wall for cover. Their advancement towards the rebels was momentarily paused.

"They are going to try and come around our sides and flank us!" Bretta yelled out to Otto. "Finish what you are doing and let's get out of here!"

Nora, safely on the other side, peered through the hole back into Arrant. Otto and Bray were still sitting on the ground, gasping for air.

Bretta and Trim's legs shook as they fired their rifles in the general direction the agents had been coming from. Phoenix was next to Cady and Jack, on the other side of Bray and Otto, keeping watch for the agents' impending assault.

Gunfire continued to ring out from the Arrant side of the wall, and Nora curled up on the ground and pulled her knees towards her chest, her back pressed firmly against the wall she had just passed through. She waited for a sign that one of her fellow rebels would climb through and join her so that she wouldn't be all on her own. When she turned to look into the hole again she was able to see Phoenix's body from the waist down. From the way Phoenix's legs were moving, Nora could tell she'd begun firing at the agents as well.

The urge to climb back through the wall and rejoin them was overwhelming, and she reached over to the hole and placed one of her arms inside. Grabbing at the edge of the opening, she began to shove her upper body back into it. A hand reached out and grabbed hers, and pushed her back towards the Fallow side of the wall. Then, she caught sight of Bray's face through the hole, and she flushed with a warm relief, assuming he was joining her.

She leaned her head into the opening, until her face was only a few inches away from his. They were both crammed into the tight space between the two sectors. "You need to back out," Bray began, his voice tense. "Replace the brick in the wall. I don't think the agents saw you get through."

More gunfire sounded from behind Bray's head, and Nora's throat tightened again as she tried to swallow. The idea of being abandoned and alone in a foreign sector of the city made it hard to breathe.

"I don't want to go alone!" Nora cried out to Bray. Right then, in that small space that existed between the two sectors, she felt so close to him, despite the fact that there was a nearly impenetrable wall that separated them. Every breath he exhaled warmed her face. What he was suggesting now, for her to seal up that wall, made a chill run through her.

"Nora you have to," he implored. "You need to reach the other rebels inside of Fallow and tell them what happened. You need to find a woman named Lace, okay?"

"I'm not ready for this," she cried out in desperation. " I'm not ready to say goodbye to you!"

"Don't worry Nora, this is not goodbye. We will see each other again, I promise you." She could hear the sincerity in Bray's voice. "Come and find us once you've talked with Lace," Bray said. "To answer your question from earlier Nora, you are the reason we are here. You are what has changed. You are why we needed to meet with the Fallow rebellion now."

As the reality of his words began to sink in, he squeezed as far through the hole as was possible, and gave her a brief yet intense kiss on the lips.

Bray retreated back to the other side and Nora sat back, stunned. As she heard the gunfire and yelling continue in Arrant, she could do nothing but stare at the concrete wall. She could no longer see anyone through the opening, and was only able to catch the occasional shadow that cast itself into the opening, spilling over onto the Fallow terrain. With as much strength as she could muster, Nora heaved the huge brick up, and back into the wall. Pushing her full weight against it, she was able to shove it back in entirely. Once the opening was closed off, she could no longer hear the yelling or the gunfire. She had sealed herself off, and could now only hear the sound of her abandoned, racing heartbeat.

CHAPTER 12

Nora sat with her back against the wall. The weight of loneliness in such a foreign place made her limbs feel incredibly heavy. As she waited for her heartbeat to slow, she tried to calm herself, by imagining that Bray and the rest of the rebels had gotten away. She closed her eyes and pictured them all, running through the streets of Arrant, until they were able to take refuge in an empty building. They are safe, she told herself. They will make it back to Blear.

Absentmindedly she ran her fingers over the small necklace her father had given her, that she still wore around her neck. Over the past couple days the necklace had become something of a calming device. She thought of her parents' determination to hide her, and imagined what her sister must have gone through to stay alive.

Nora contemplated how strong she was going to need to be in order to survive this transition. As the necklace slipped between her fingers, she wondered if her sister had ever made it to a safe place. She could only hope that she wasn't rotting away in the Jejung prison—within the walls her very own sector's residents had helped build.

Visuals of what she imagined the inside of the prison to look like flashed through her mind. Although she could fathom what the interior of the complex would look like, she couldn't imagine what her life would be like there. She thought back to her childhood, and how she, along with the other Arrant children, were disciplined—the threat of being shipped off to that prison was always looming over their heads. Jejung had always seemed surreal to Nora, as though it were a dungeon from some old fairytale. Swallowing hard, Nora released the necklace from her grasp, let it fall back onto her chest, and stood up.

For the first time, Nora looked out at the Fallow landscape. Lush, brown soil squished under her feet, and a few yards ahead the wet soil turned into a dried out, yellowish grass. After that, expansive fields stretched out to the horizon—the golden crops reached high into the sky and swayed in the wind. The undulating sight was hypnotic.

Arrant always had a dim, gray feel to it. Her entire life she had existed beneath its cloud-filled sky, seeing everything through dusty air.

It was only upon revisiting Arrant, after having been outside its walls, that she realized how depressing everything looked there by contrast. Blear was a landscape filled with vibrant greens, gleaming streets, and shops bustling with life—all centered around an azure-colored lake.

Nora felt overwhelmed from all the recent traveling, and at how vastly different each sector was. As she looked around Fallow it was clear that this was the most beautiful sector she'd seen by far. The crops, which stood straight up, never grew closer than fifteen yards to the wall. Between the two was a thin layer of dried out grass. To her left, the wall continued up a hill towards the center of Constance, and led all the way up to Obsidia.

Nora decided to walk alongside the wall, up the hill, for a while. The wind felt good against her skin, and her forearms grew goosebumps due to the slight chill. The trendy Fallow outfit she wore consisted of knee-high boots and a dress. As the skirt of the dress billowed in the wind, Nora relished in the liberating sensation her garments made her feel. It was obvious why Phoenix chose to wear this type of apparel every day. She only hoped she looked half as good as Phoenix did.

The wind blew at Nora's back as she continued up the small hill towards the center of Constance. With her hands in her pockets to warm them, she felt a small rope inside. When she inspected it further she recognized it as the same kind of accessory she'd seen Phoenix wearing the first day she'd met her. She tied the rope around her forehead and pinned back her long, black hair.

After some time had passed, her calf muscles began to ache from the hill's incline, so she wandered over to the golden crops, where the ground was flat.

When she approached the edge of the field, she could see that the crops reached high above her head. She made her way a few yards in. The crop was so dense with overgrowth that it made it difficult to see very far ahead. It was much darker inside the crop, since the wheat stalks blocked much of the sunlight from reaching her, and the air was still. The atmosphere within the field was starting to make her feel claustrophobic. As her boots crunched over the fallen wheat kernels, it dawned on her that she had no way to orient herself. Everything around her looked identical, and she began to realize that if she continued on much farther, she might be irretrievably lost within the belly of this wild and rolling wheat field. To her left a creature stirred in the rust-colored stems. Terrified, she stopped in her tracks with her eyes open wide, suddenly feeling hyper vigilant. She held her breath and waited for further movement from this mysterious creature. A few moments later something rustled in the stems again, this time closer to her. Immediately, she spun on her heels and fled back through to where she had entered from, not bothering to even protect her face from the numerous stalks that whipped against her cheeks as she raced past. Once she'd made it back out, she breathed in deeply, taking in as much oxygen as her lungs allowed.

She made her way back towards the hill. She'd have to continue along the wall and deal with the exertion of the hike—traveling through the field was clearly not an option.

Her calf muscles tired out again quickly on the trek up, but she soldiered on. She dug into the soft dirt with the heels of her boots, and took slow, deliberate strides. Suddenly realizing how parched she was, she reached down to her waist to retrieve her water, but realized she didn't have her bag strapped to her. She had left it on the ground next to the wall back in Arrant. Her arms twitched as panic and frustration set in—she needed to move along quicker and find something to drink soon. Nora doubled her pace up the hill, fueled with the adrenaline of her survivor's instinct.

When she'd reached the top of the hill, her body covered in sweat, a small wooden house come into view. It blended in somewhat with the land around it. The little building was made from wood and had not been painted. The raw brown of the walls and roof was a very close shade to the dirt field that surrounded it.

Crouching down towards the ground, Nora waited and watched the house for any signs of life. After several minutes had passed and nothing moved, she stood up and made her way to survey the backside of the property.

She hid behind a large mass of compressed golden stalks near the wooden home. Allowing a few minutes to pass, she stood again and moved towards a smaller wooden structure located in the rear of the property, which stood alone in the short, dead grass, about fifteen yards from the house. She scanned her surroundings until she spotted her next hiding place—a round stone structure, about three feet in diameter, was positioned nearly halfway between herself and the house. It was constructed of neat stone rows with a wooden arch on top of it, from which a thick rope hung and disappeared into the opening of the stone structure.

Taking one last breath in, Nora scrambled over to the stone structure and crouched down behind it, hiding herself from view. After another few minutes of surveillance, she began to get up to head towards her next hideout. She reached her fingers to the edge of the structure to pull herself up. When she placed her hand at the top of the rocks she felt something cold and damp.

Curiosity took over and Nora stood straight up, forgetting to be discreet, and bent over to peer down into the opening. Her eyes widened when she saw that a bucket was attached to the end of the rope, and below that was a small pool of still water, a little further underground. Nora stuck her arm in and tried to reach down to scoop up a handful of the water but it was too far away. She reached up, grabbed the rope, and lowered the bucket down into the water below. As the liquid filled the pail it grew heavy and she had to dig her heels into the dirt to haul the bucket back up. It bounced off the sides of the inner stone wall a couple times, spilling some of the water, but she was eventually able to get it out.

She set the bucket to rest on the lip of the stones and then sat beneath it. Nora tipped the pail towards her, and began to gulp down the cold water, spilling a good portion of it onto herself and the ground around her. The water soothed her aching throat as it slid down into her stomach. Knowing that she didn't have a jar or container of any kind, so that she could take the water with her, Nora sat on her knees and drank down as much of the water as she could. Once the worst of her thirst was satisfied, she remembered to continue to keep an eye on the house to make sure no one would discover her.

The water soaked through the front of her dress, cooling her warm skin. She took one last giant gulp. Since there had been no sign of activity from the house she decided it was safe enough to venture over to it. It stood two-stories tall and blocked off most of the breeze.

When she reached the side of the home, Nora reached out a hand and ran her fingers over the splitting wood. The door had not been shut tightly, and the slight opening allowed a sliver of the house's interior to be visible to her.

She lightly pushed on the door, and it swung open, creaking loudly. Wincing at the noise, she stopped to listen for any signs of activity within the home, but there was none. To the right of the entrance was a small kitchen. As she made her hesitant way further into the house a sudden breeze pushed against the door and it creaked loudly again as it shut. She silently admonished herself for being careless and not closing the door herself. Moving carefully Nora worked her way through the small kitchen. The cupboards were made from the same dark wood as the house's exterior. There was a little sink in the corner, near one of the windows Nora had been watching earlier. Quietly, she walked around the flat wooden bench in the kitchen and into another room that had two couches and a small table. The furniture was dirty and stained, showing no signs that anyone had been around long enough to clean it in quite a while. Beginning to feel safe that she was, indeed, alone in the home, she returned to the kitchen, and opened the nearest cupboard.

Realizing how hungry she had become after quenching her thirst, Nora reached into the cupboard and found a package of crackers and some chocolate cookies. She ate the majority of the bland crackers, and took a handful of cookies, before replacing the packages.

A sharp sound behind her caused Nora to whirl around, the cookies flying from her hands onto the other side of the kitchen. Panicked, she looked over to the door, hoping it had just swung open again from the wind. When she felt a firm hand on her shoulder she yelled out in surprise.

She turned to see an older man standing behind her. A trimmed, dark brown beard circled around his mouth, and his lips were dry and cracked. Raising her arms in a helpless attempt at self defense, Nora's neck tingled. She felt a small prick as something punctured into her skin from the hand that pressed on her shoulder.

The air left Nora's lungs as she looked into the older man's green eyes. His tanned face began to blur and she felt her knees buckling as they threatened to give out. Her eyelids grew even heavier as her whole body gave into the pressing weight. Collapsing to the wooden floor, the man's dirty work boots was the last sight Nora saw before losing consciousness.

CHAPTER 13

A layer of dry film had crusted over Nora's eyelids while she was unconscious, and as she struggled to crack open her eyes she winced in pain. Her mouth, equally dry, made it clear that she was dehydrated, and that she must have been unconscious for quite some time. She tried in vain to sit up, but could not manage to find the strength to raise her upper body. Whatever chemical used to knock her out still wreaked havoc on her, and had left her in a weakened state. She was able to move her fingers, but wasn't able to lift her arms much. Pain shot through her lower back as she tried to lift her right arm. She was only able to raise it a few inches off the bed she was laying on.

As she focused her disoriented gaze on her surroundings, Nora was blinded by an intense white light. She managed to lift her heavy head off of the bed, and pressed her chin into her chest. Squinting, she saw two white walls that converged at an angle directly in front of her. Tilting her head back she saw the ceiling above her was the same bright white. When she rotated her head to the left, a sharp pain shot out through her neck's stiffened muscles, and she saw that another white wall ran parallel to the bed she was laying on. She shook her head, in an attempt to remove the effects of the chemicals from her system. When she was able to focus a little bit more, she noticed that the wall directly across from her had a small window. The only thing visible through the small opening was yet another white wall, which made it difficult for her to even recognize the window was there.

Her senses slowly came back, and eventually she was able to swing her legs off of the bed and set her feet down onto the white, cold, floor. After several gut wrenching attempts, she managed to get herself seated in an upright position, and then scooted herself forward until she was seated at the edge of the bed. Looking at the completely white floor, her vision swam with dizziness, and she had to look away. Although her surroundings were unfamiliar, and her situation was obviously precarious, she wasn't panicking, strangely enough. Everything seemed to blend into itself. The bed frame, although metal, was painted the same shade of white, and a pair of white slippers were on the floor next to the bed. The bedsheets too were white and she'd been resting her head atop a white pillow. Fearful of making any noise and attracting the attention of whoever had put her in the all-white room, Nora began to wonder where she was.

She looked down again at her body—the red dress she had been wearing had been replaced by a white one. P5A041 was sewn with purple thread into the top left corner of the fabric. A chill ran up her spine, and when she reached around to the back of the garment she found that it did not close all the way, the entire length of her body was exposed. She attempted to rearrange the clothing so that she was covered up. It continued to pull apart every time she let go, leaving her exposed, and this contributed to her rising feeling of vulnerability. When she stood up the open-backed dress reached just above her knees. Nora sighed and then, not willing to walk around with her entire backside exposed, decided to turn the dress around so that the opening was in the front. This way she was able to clasp it shut with her hands as she moved around the room.

She began to search the all-white room for something she could use in an attempt to tie the front of the dress closed. When she didn't find anything suitable, she grabbed the pillowcase from the bed. After considerable effort, she was able to rip the pillowcase to form a long strip of fabric. She wrapped it around her waist and tied the remaining fabric around her stomach, securing the open gap.

Nora began to pace back and forth across the room. The area wasn't very large, but the all-white aspect made it seem somehow infinite. After she walked the circumference of the room, she estimated that it was about twice as wide as it was long. She made her way over towards the only window in the room. When she peered through it all she could see was another white wall. Pressing her face against the window and turning from left to right, she determined that it was not another room, but rather some sort of hallway. There were no signs of any other life, which made her feel extremely trapped and isolated in her white prison.

As she continued to pace through the room she thought of all the other rebels she had met during her short time in Blear. Bray weighed on her mind most of all. She hoped that they all had made it out of Arrant and safely back to Blear. Nora envisioned them all sitting down inside the base, laughing and enjoying each other's company.

Pressure began to build in Nora's chest as she realized her new rebel friends would have no way of knowing that she had been taken and placed in this unforgivingly white cell. She fell down to her knees, and clenched her teeth. Her palms began to sweat as a sense of claustrophobia set in. She had no idea where she was, so even if she somehow managed to get in contact with the other rebels and tell them what had happened to her, she couldn't tell them where to find her now. Nervous beads of sweat grew along her forehead as she attempted to logically deduce her whereabouts. She had to figure out where she was, how she'd gotten here, and how long she'd been locked up for.

As the reality of how dangerous her situation was began to set in, she instinctively reached up to her chest to grab her necklace and calm herself down, but it wasn't there. Her eyes immediately filled with tears at the absence of her most precious treasure—the only thing she had retained from her old life. Filled with sudden anger she leapt up and aggressively ran towards the wall, crashing into it with all the force she could manage.

Surprisingly, the impact was soft and she simply bounced off and fell back onto the ground. Shocked, she lightly punched the wall. It was not a hard wall at all, but rather appeared to be cushioned slightly. She began to comb the wall's surface, punching different spots and pressing her weight into them.

A few strikes later, she noticed that the wall to her left felt different—it was lighter, as if it were made of a different material. Nora pressed her body into it with all her weight. It definitely had much more give and sunk further in than the other areas she had investigated. Nora began to repeatedly push on the small section with all of her weight. Every time she pushed into it, she felt the wall give a little before resuming its normal position in the white room. After she'd thoroughly exhausted herself, she collapsed and rested her head on the wall, aggravated that this new information she'd discovered proved to be useless.

"The drug he used should wear off soon, and then we can ask her. For now, all we have is the brain scan to go off of." Nora lifted her head up off the wall in surprise, as a woman's voice from the other side became audible. She pressed her ear and cheek against the wall even harder, trying to make out the woman's words.

"We need to prep Room 504," the woman continued, and then uttered a few more words that Nora couldn't quite hear. Nora strained her neck as she pressed her right ear against the wall as firmly as she could. "As soon as the subject is awake, I want to run a full test on her, and compare the results against the brain scan we took when she arrived."

Nora closed her eyes, and when she heard no one speak on the other side of the wall for several moments she grew fearful that she'd been left completely isolated from the outside world yet again. Just when she was starting to assume the worst, a second voice spoke.

"This could be the answer to what we have been working towards for all these years." This time the deep voice belonged to a man. A sense of optimism and urgency came through when he spoke. "I'll begin to prepare the lab for us," he continued. "When the subject is awake, I'll meet you there."

Before Nora had time to process this new information, the woman began to speak again. "I can't believe how close we are cutting this one. If she had been brought here a few hours later, this all would have been another lost cause. I'll call down for someone to come up here and escort the subject to you once everything is ready."

Nora kept her ear pressed against the wall for several more minutes, in hopes of hearing more voices, but was met only with silence. Remnants of the chemicals in her system made her feel suddenly lightheaded, so she made her way back over to the bed.

She sat very still, and stared blankly out at the room as she replayed the conversation she'd just heard over in her head, trying to make sense of it all. In particular, she wondered why they had scanned her brain, and what they could possibly be looking for.

Thinking back to what Bray had said to her the last time she saw him, before she'd had to seal up the wall between them, she laid back down on the white bed. She let her mind linger for a while on the moment he'd kissed her through the wall. Nora still couldn't make sense as to why he'd told her that she was what had changed in the rebellion. Whatever his reasoning was, it must have been good enough for him and Otto to shove her through the wall alone and instruct her to find the second rebel group hidden in Fallow. The only good outcome from her current situation could be that the voices she'd heard belonged to members of the Fallow rebellion group, but she had no way of knowing if that were the case.

A wave of calmness washed over her as she replayed her and Bray's kiss yet again. Her whole life, walls had held so much power over her. She hated the sight of a wall, because she longed to see what was beyond it. But the wall she'd kissed Bray inside of, that wall was different from all the rest, because they'd blown a hole right through it, temporarily joining the two separate worlds. For a brief period of time, when they leaned their faces into the opening, they existed in unchartered territory—neither in Arrant nor Fallow, but rather in the nameless place they had created in between. For thirty seconds Bray and Nora were the two sole citizens of this territory. With the gray brick crumbling around them, with gunfire sounding on one side of the wall, and golden stalks of wheat soundlessly swaying in the distance on the other, their lips met. They kissed each other with a kind of sad hunger, not knowing if it would be the last. Nora closed her eyes and allowed the memory to wash over her, and then without realizing it, she fell asleep.

Some time later, Nora was jarred awake by a heavy clunking noise, coupled with a metallic jingling sound. She sat up with a start, realizing she had dozed off, and wondered how long she had been asleep for. It could have been anywhere from minutes, to hours, to days for all she knew. Wiping the sleep from her eyes, Nora stood up from the bed and walked back over to the wall she'd been able to eavesdrop through earlier.

Placing her ear against the cold padding again, she strained to hear any sign of the world outside of her white prison. The metallic sounds that had woken her grew louder, and before she had time to react, the wall swung open, and shoved her back onto the floor. Scrambling to get her bearings and prepare for whatever was about to happen, she moved quickly away from the opening and back towards the bed.

A man had entered through the opening, into Nora's private blank cell, and was now coming towards her. He towered over Nora, and moved with confidence and precision. He was dressed in thin white pants and a matching white shirt which had R4F041 embroidered on the left side in red. The most striking thing about him, by far, was his imposing, dense brown beard. It was groomed meticulously and kept short along the sides of his face, but tumbled down wildly from his chin—curled in multiple directions, like the roots of an ancient tree. Deeply etched wrinkles around his eyes indicated that he must have been around her parents' age. She tried to study his expression for any sign of malicious intent, but couldn't get a read on him.

Too afraid to move, Nora stood still and waited for the man to speak, but he never did. She was only just barely able to catch a glimpse of his thin lips through the thick beard. As the bearded man got closer to Nora, she raised her arms in defense. He grabbed both of her flailing limbs with a strong grasp, and no matter how much she struggled to break free she couldn't. The bearded man effortlessly turned her around, held her down firmly, and then pinned her arms behind her back. She felt cold metal cuffs being placed around her wrists, and heard them click as they locked.

The bearded man spun Nora back around, placed a hand on her lower back, and pushed her towards the opening in the white wall. She dug her heels into the floor and tried to resist with as much strength as she could muster, but the floor was so slick that she couldn't get any traction, and just slid helplessly toward the doorway. Realizing the futility of that approach, she quickly changed tactics, and let her body go completely limp, forcing the man to drag her dead weight across the room.

"What are you doing to me? Let go of me!" Nora pleaded with her captor. She attempted to turn around to look him in the eyes, but his grip on her was too tight. "Please, tell me where I am! Who are you?"

The bearded man said nothing in response to Nora's incessant questioning, he simply continued to shove her into the hallway outside of the room. Turning to the right, Nora passed by the window that looked into the room she'd been confined in. The hallway ahead of them split up into three different paths, and he led her towards the one on the right. As he escorted her down the hallway she continued to give him as much trouble and resistance as she could manage, while attempting to keep an observant eye on her surroundings. The whiteness of everything, however, made it difficult for her eyes to focus.

As they continued down the hallway they passed a small window on the right-hand side. When she went by it she peered in. The room inside was identical to the one Nora had just been removed from. Disoriented, she started to wonder if she was being led in circles. Looking at everything they passed, Nora realized with a heavy heart, that the area had been set up to detain more people. When she looked down the hallway she saw four more windows on the right side that were identical to the one that looked into her cell.

Instead of passing by those windows, the bearded man jerked her to the left, and they headed down a different white hallway. They finally came to a stop at the end of it, before a purple door that was labelled "Test Lab 504." Nora clenched her fists in frightened anticipation, terrified of what might be on the other side.

CHAPTER 14

The bearded man pressed his palm onto a small device next to the opening, and the purple door slid open. As Nora had expected, the room was all white. She'd grown so used to the lack of color at this point, that seeing anything besides white would probably have been pretty jarring.

The wall across from her featured several dark screens, with various images moving across them. More displays were located on her right, attached to three consoles. There were two people who sat at the consoles, pushing buttons, and conferring with each other. They looked up at her briefly when she entered the room. Nora couldn't quite decipher what the images displayed on the screens were, but she could only assume they related to the large machine stationed in the center of the room. She recognized it immediately—it was a fancy version of the Dream Machine from the rebel base in Blear. All of the familiar parts and components were there, but this one was clean and had a smooth, glossy glow to it. Nora noticed how the machine reflected the overhead lights over the rest of the room.

Making her way over to the machine, she caught sight of a helmet, similar to the one that had been placed on her head when she'd been strapped into the Dream Machine. This helmet, however consisted of a clear plastic shell, as opposed to the rusty bowl of Blear's machine. The wires coming from the helmet had been gathered into a tight bundle that fed into thick, white plastic tubing. The tube of wires attached to a movable arm, which allowed the helmet to move, and was affixed to the chair below.

Metal disks were embedded into the arm rest of the chair. These were free of rust, and much cleaner than the ones from her last encounter with a Dream Machine. There were no wires visible as the white tube ran into the back of the chair and kept them hidden from view. She felt along the padding with her fingertips, and felt where the disks would meet her calves. From the chair came three white tubes, stuffed with more wires, which split out to the three consoles.

A calmness swept over her as she was reminded of being introduced to Bray, the last time she had been in the presence of such a machine.

"You may leave us now," the woman who sat at the console said to the bearded man, breaking the silence in the room.

Her bearded escort bowed his head at the woman and then made his way back to the door they'd entered from. He pressed his palm on the device at the side of the door, and it noiselessly slid open to allow him to exit the room.

"Hello, Eleanor," the man seated beside the woman greeted her with an uncharacteristically deep voice. She recognized both of their vocal tones immediately—these were the people she'd overheard through the wall of her cell. "It is good to see you up and walking around. Please feel free to familiarize yourself with the Subconscious Impression Replacement Transport, or more simply SIRT, as everyone here refers to it now. It will not hurt you."

Pretending to continue to inspect the Dream Machine, Nora scrambled to come up with a plan. She felt she needed to protect some information about herself from these strangers. Sliding her hands across the white padding of the chair and over the metal disk near the bottom, Nora glanced up to see if they were buying her act of ignorance with regard to the machine.

"I am Dr. Edmonds," the man continued, bowing slightly in her direction. "And this is Dr. Willow," he said, gesturing to the woman. "We are both lead scientists here."

Nora made eye contact with each of them separately before she returned the small bowing gesture. She remained silent though, still not ready to speak, fearing she might reveal something she would later wish she had kept secret from her captors. Both of them wore long white shirts that buttoned in the front, and each had small purple lettering on the left chest area, which read: P5A001 and P5A002.

"We are excited to be working with you today," Dr. Edmonds said. "You are a very unique girl." Still bent over the Dream Machine in her guise of inspecting it, she didn't see his expression when he said this, but she could sense the smile in his voice. He continued talking, despite the fact that Nora was not acknowledging anything he said. "We would like you to lay down on the SIRT, whenever you feel comfortable."

Finally breaking her silence, Nora asked, "Why am I here?" She wanted to keep asking all of the questions burning inside of her brain, but managed to restrain herself and let her first inquiry hang in the air.

Dr. Willow stepped away from her console and made her way towards Nora. "Eleanor, you were brought here, as many people in your same predicament are. However, most people like you are not brought to Dr. Edmonds and my level of the building for testing. You have been brought here, directly to us and for a particular reason."

Sensing the same hesitance in Dr. Willow's voice that Nora herself had used to restrain from giving away too much information, she nodded and thought of what would be her next question.

"Where am I?" Nora decided this was as good of a follow-up as any.

Again, her question resulted in Dr. Willow taking another step towards Nora. She cleared her throat, and then answered Nora's inquiry with a question of her own. "Well, Eleanor. Where do you think you are?"

Instinctively, Nora's eyebrows furrowed with frustration, realizing they were playing the exact same game she was—they were keeping as much information as possible to themselves. She decided that all she could do was continue to go along with it, and feign ignorance as best as she could.

"Arrant?" she asked, purposefully imbuing her voice with a tone she hoped came across as clueless and naïve.

"Now Eleanor, you know that isn't true," Dr. Edmonds chimed in, shaking his head. "You were found in Sector 4 before they brought you to us."

Nora forced herself to remain calm. "Okay, well then if I'm not in Arrant, and I'm not in Fallow, where am I?"

Dr. Willow sighed, obviously nearing the end of her patience with the charade. "Eleanor, you were found alone in Sector 4. No one around here is quite sure how you managed to leave your own sector. You were brought to Obsidia, like all the other Defected the Agency finds throughout the city."

The way that Willow so plainly put it shocked Nora, as much as she had assumed that she was not in the hands of the Fallow rebels, she'd still been praying desperately that she'd not been taken to the center of Constance. With Dr. Willow's last statement her worst fear was confirmed. She scanned the room again, focusing intently on anything that could help her.

"What do you want with me?" she asked softly, her voice breaking with emotion.

At that point Dr. Edmonds interjected, in an attempt to diffuse the situation. He seemed to choose his words carefully, "You are here because we found an abnormality in your brain scan. We administer the tests to all of the Defected that are brought to us. The results of your examination has created quite an intriguing puzzle for myself and Dr. Willow."

She remembered, yet again, the last thing Bray had said to her—that she was the change they had been waiting for. She thought of the rebel base inside of Blear and her time with Otto and Bray inside of the Dream Machine there. It seemed like everyone knew something about Nora that they weren't sharing with her. Still, she knew she had to continue to play along with the game, and keep her mouth shut. She nodded at the two scientists and flashed them a fake smile. She had to protect Bray and the rest of her new rebellion friends, and the more information these two were able to get out of her, or even the slightest slip of the tongue, could cause irreversible harm to the Blear rebel group.

Dr. Willow continued to move incrementally closer to where Nora was standing near the Dream Machine. "We would like you to climb up on the SIRT for us Eleanor. Then Dr. Edmonds and I are going to run some tests. Do you think that would be okay with you?"

Knowing that the two scientists were up to more than they were letting on, Nora continued her dumb act, "Do I just climb up on it and sit?" trying to act as though she'd never seen a machine like it before.

Dr. Edmonds turned his back to Nora, averting his eyes, "You are going to have to turn your gown back around—the way it was originally placed on you."

Nora looked down, having forgotten that she'd rearranged her clothing. She tried to steady her voice as she spoke. "I would rather not, if you don't mind. I don't feel comfortable with the dress facing the other way."

Dr. Edmonds seemed to lose his temper when she said this, "You can either turn the gown around the way it's meant to be worn, or we can remove it for you," he said, his voice raised. "I'll leave that decision to you."

Deciding that obliging with his request was a better alternative to having no clothing on her body at all, Nora slid her arms out of the shirt's sleeves and began to wiggle around to bring the opening to the back. Though she resented having to do this, she did acknowledge the fact that Dr. Edmonds had been respectful enough to turn away and give her a bit of privacy.

Dr. Willow helped Nora secure the garment, and likewise averted her eyes. Nora flashed her a small, grateful smile when they were done. Dr. Willow responded with a friendly wink, and this helped calm Nora down considerably.

"Alright now, go ahead and climb up onto the SIRT please," Dr. Willow gently instructed her.

Climbing into the upright bed of the large Dream Machine, Nora kept the opening of her shirt closed behind her with one hand, as she hoisted herself up with the other. It was rather difficult to get into it, and had clearly not been designed with the ease of smaller-framed, more modest people in mind. Once she had successfully mounted the machine, she turned over and began to fit herself into the contours of it.

For the second time in her life Nora found herself being strapped into a Dream Machine, only this time she was in Test Lab 504, inside Obsidia—the immaculate, all-white building in the center of Constance.

CHAPTER 15

Once Nora was into the proper position in the Dream Machine, Dr. Willow began to rearrange her dressing gown. "We need the transfer disks to make full contact with your skin Eleanor," Dr. Willow said, as she pulled the fabric out from under Nora. "You may keep the gown draped over the front of yourself, but your back, arms, and legs need to be exposed." The metal disks and padding felt cold against Nora's skin.

"Once we get everything in order, we will lower that helmet down onto your head," Dr. Willow informed Nora, gesturing above her.

Nora glanced up at the helmet, remembering at the last second to feign ignorance about the equipment. Luckily neither scientist seemed to notice her slip-up.

"I'm all set to go over here," Dr. Edmonds called out from his seat at the console.

"One more sequence to run over here, and I am ready to go too," Dr. Willow responded, as she lowered the helmet down gently onto Nora's head. "Just try and relax now," she said to Nora. "This first part can get a little intense. Try and remember that we are here in the room with you."

Dr. Willow walked over to the consoles, where Dr. Edmonds was already staring intently at the screen before him. He looked over to Nora as Dr. Willow started the countdown.

"We are going live in 3...2...1—" Dr. Willow announced.

The machine was activated, and Nora felt the familiar slip from reality that she had experienced before. There was an immediate nothingness, followed by a white pinhole of light which grew larger as it moved towards her. Or perhaps it was she who grew smaller towards it, it was impossible to tell exactly what was happening in those moments. Then there was the flash of colors, as small, multi-colored orbs began to fly through her field of vision.

Suddenly, all the movement ceased, and Nora looked out into a dark, and seemingly infinite room. Although her surroundings appeared completely black, she knew there had to be some source of light, since she was able to see her body when she looked down.

She was dressed in her generic Arrant-style of clothing. It looked so gray and plain to her, now that she'd seen a wide variety of outfits from some of the other sectors of the city. Nora waited for something to happen as she looked out at her dark surroundings.

"I don't get it, all the data confirms that the SIRT is working properly," Dr. Willow's voice startled Nora—she'd thought she was there in the dream state alone.

"I'm lost in all the blackness," she heard Dr. Edmonds call out to Dr. Willow. "I'm not even sure I made it through with you."

"I'm lost too," Dr. Willow responded, sounding disoriented. "Eleanor, Eleanor, can you hear us?"

Hesitant to be of any assistance to them, she paused for a long time before finally responding, "Yes, I can hear you. I'm in here too," she said.

"Where is here?" Dr. Edmonds asked.

"I don't know," Nora replied. "Everything is totally black except for my body, aren't you guys supposed to be—" Nora cut herself off, realizing she'd been about to give away important information. She prayed the scientists were too distracted to realize what she had almost said.

"Eleanor, I am going to attempt something," Dr. Edmonds' voice called out loudly, "Okay, do you see anything now?"

Just then, a single tree from the woods in her dream became visible. It appeared to be a few yards away from where she stood. The trees from her dream were very unique, so there was no mistaking it.

"Yes I see... a tree," Nora said, choosing her words as carefully as possible.

"Okay great, can you move towards it?" Dr. Edmonds asked, sounding excited.

Nora walked over to the tree and placed her hand at the base of it. Though she had felt it before, it still shocked her how realistic the tree felt to her touch. The tree seemed to pulse and vibrate as she pressed harder against it, and it felt almost as though her hand was able to sink into it slightly, as she leaned into it more. She experienced a very strange sensation as she made contact with the tree—it was as if she could feel how the tree felt. She shook her head, feeling ridiculous. Trees don't have feelings, she admonished herself. As her palm rested on the base of the trunk, the blood that flowed through her body began to pulse in rhythm with it. She was struck with a sudden clarity as every fiber of her being became one with the tree. This tree, she realized, had been created from her own mental imagery and placed into this world through her connection with the Dream Machine. Suddenly, the tree disappeared.

"What happened?! What was that?!" Dr. Willow exclaimed, panic stricken. "Eleanor, what are you seeing?"

"The tree vanished," Nora replied bluntly. She was beginning to feel frustrated, so she took a deep breath.

At that point the darkness began to fade away, and before she knew it she found herself back in the white lab, laying on the Dream Machine. She opened her eyes and sat up, and saw the two scientists staring at her in shock.

"Did you..." Dr. Willow began, directing her question towards Dr. Edmonds. There was a hint of fear in her voice.

"No, I didn't, did you?" Dr. Edmonds replied slowly, as he shook his head in confusion.

Dr. Willow shook her head as well in response. After a moment of contemplation, she turned to observe Nora, "Did she?"

The two scientists continued to stare at Nora for several more seconds in silence. Dr. Edmonds broke the silence by clearing his throat. "Okay. Eleanor, that will be all for today. We are going to have to run this data through our consoles now." Dr. Edmonds looked back down to his console screen and started pushing a series of buttons. His eyes were wide as he took in all the new information that ran continually across the screen.

Dr. Willow reached forward and pushed a button on her console. A young male voice came through the small speaker, "Yes Dr. Willow?"

"Patient P5A041 needs to be escorted back to her room now. Thank you," Dr. Willow replied. A minute later the door to the lab slid open and the bearded man walked through.

With his assistance Nora removed the helmet and climbed down from the Dream Machine. The two scientists were in a frenzy, scrambling around the lab. A hint of a smile came to Nora's face as she saw them attempting to make sense of what they had just witnessed. Nora knew that what she had just done inside of the Dream Machine, while the scientists watched, was far from ordinary.

The bearded man reached out for Nora's shoulders, turned her around, and cuffed her hands behind her back. He then escorted her out of the lab and back into the long, white hallway. Nora tried hard to focus on her surroundings, and to remember the path they had taken from her cell to the test lab. Her mind was racing with the recent events that had transpired. She wasn't quite sure of what to make of it all just yet—

all she knew for sure was that she couldn't wait to get into the Dream Machine again.

When she was back in her room, and the bearded man had shut the wall behind him, she sighed, resigning herself to the indefinite period of isolation she had returned to. She walked over to her bed and curled up on it, pulling her knees in tightly to her chest. Though the events of the day had worn her out, she wasn't quite ready to give into the magnetic pull of sleep. She began to daydream and recalled her brief time inside of Fallow. She thought about the cool breeze she'd felt there—how the air was crisp and smelled like grass. The memory of the vast, open landscape was a welcome relief, and starkly contrasted her current environment.

Reaching out her hand, it was as though she could actually feel the tips of the golden stalks of wheat brush against the pads of her fingertips. The crops tickled the palms of her hands, and the breeze brushed back her dark hair. The sun that shone in the clear blue sky above warmed her cheeks and she turned her face up towards it.

Then, Nora's thoughts turned to Deryn. She tried to remember her happier memories with him back in Arrant, before she had to give up her life and become one of the Defected. One evening in particular came to mind, when he'd just come home from a hard day of working in the factory and they'd both curled up in bed together. She reached out and touched his face, feeling the roughness of his beard stubble as she navigated the contours of his jawline. Breathing in deeply, she inhaled the scent of his dirty blonde hair, and sweat-soaked uniform.

As she drifted further into the space between dreams and reality, the scene in her head was replaced with images of a small room, surrounded by brown, dirt walls. She saw herself laying on a bed under a single light that had colored wires sprawling out from it. Bray sat on a chair across the room from her. She could see the violent rise and fall of his chest, as though his breathing were labored, and heard a guttural cry escape him before he whispered her name under his breath.

"Nora, where ARE you?" she heard him say to the open room. "It's been too long. Where did you go?"

Watching Bray in that state flooded her with emotion. Finally he stood up, sat on the edge of the cot, and leaned in to kiss her lips. "Please Bray, you have to come find me," she pleaded.

Bray suddenly leapt up off the bed and turned to look directly at her. "Nora?!" he exclaimed in disbelief. He rubbed his eyes and blinked several times, as though he couldn't believe what he was seeing. "What... how... where?" Bray stuttered. His hands reached out for Nora again just as she felt herself helplessly giving in to sleep. Before Bray was able to reach her, the scene faded away, and the undertow of sleep pulled her down into its hazy, warm world.

CHAPTER 16

For a moment after she woke up, Nora forgot that she was being confined in the center of Constance. But as she peeled her eyes open and rolled over to her side, her all-white, grim reality came into view once again.

Though her environment was unstimulating, she could at least focus on her growing desire to return to the lab and be hooked up to the Dream Machine again. Nora had decided that her best tactic was to sit patiently and simply wait for the opportunity to arise. Even though it had not been very long since her visit to the lab, she'd already grown impatient. Her hands fidgeted and she tapped her white slippers on the ground, with no idea how much longer she'd have to wait.

Getting up from the bed, she made her way over to the window in the opposing wall. She pressed her forehead against the window, and visually inspected every square inch that was visible from her limited perspective. The view started to make Nora feel as if the world around her was shrinking, and she began to pace back and forth alongside the wall. Her steps were fueled by anxiety—it felt as though her mind was starting to slip away from her, and this was a disorienting and unsettling sensation.

Part of what contributed to this was not having a grasp on how much time had passed since she'd arrived. All she knew was that she had slept twice so far and had been escorted to the lab once, but she had no way of knowing how much time had elapsed during her first or second period of sleep.

As a sudden burst of panic bubbled up in her, she slammed her palms against the window—with the hopes that it would catch someone's attention—but nobody came to check on her.

Her thoughts turned to her parents. She hoped they had returned home safely. The thought of her actions causing harm to them, or to Deryn, or to anyone around her at all for that matter, made her stomach hurt.

She wondered how something as beautiful as changing your own destiny could have such ugly consequences. First it was her parents and Deryn, then because of her, Otto, Bray, Phoenix, Jack, Cady, Trim, Bretta, and the rest of the Blear rebels had been placed in harm's way. Of course, she too was included on the list of lives she had risked with her actions. Everyone on this list was put there because of a single decision that Nora herself had made. Everything around her had changed so drastically, and it had all happened so fast.

She contemplated going back into the lab and letting herself be pulled along the original fate string she had felt back in Blear, the first time she was hooked up to the Dream Machine. She could return everything back to normal, and just live out her remaining days in the Jejung prison. It might not be the worst fate in the world, she reasoned. Maybe the older sister Nora's parents had told her about would be there, and could help her acclimate to the prison life style.

Instinctively she lifted her hand up to her neck, only to be reminded that her necklace was no longer there. It seemed silly to her now, that she had placed so much hope and desire into one little object. She felt like the life around her had changed for the worse. After she met Phoenix in that alleyway, back in Arrant, she'd gotten a glimpse of what a new life could be like. She'd gotten a small taste of the freedom and independence the Blear rebels had, and saw that happiness, romance, and friendships were all still possibilities in this brand new world.

Nora dreamed of being back at the wall with Bray and Otto, refusing to go through the hole created by the flawed explosion. In her fantasy she cried out to the two of them, insisting that she should stay and choose safety over the faint possibility of a heroic outcome. Her emotions quickly began to rise up in her, until she couldn't control herself anymore.

"Let me out of here!" Nora cried, as she yelled and banged on the window with all her might. "I can't be in here any longer! I'm going crazy! Please! Somebody, get me out of here!"

When her voice grew hoarse she shut her eyes and slumped against the wall in defeat. In an effort to fight against the overwhelming pull towards resignation, she began to daydream, imagining her successful escape from the horrible white cell. She mentally traced the path she had taken from her cell to the test lab a few hallways over. Near the door to the lab, she visualized the bearded man standing, as he waited for the scientists to give him orders to retrieve Nora and escort her back to the room marked 504. She envisioned the bearded man being able to hear the cacophony that she created in her cell, and silently begged him to come and check on her.

As her fantasy continued, she saw the purple lab door slide open and the bearded man enter through it. She saw Dr. Edmonds give him the go ahead, and saw the bearded man simply nod in response, before walking back out the lab. The pleasant daydream began to calm her down, and Nora's heart stopped racing. With every fiber of her being, Nora willed her fantasy to become a reality.

After exhausting herself from her emotional outburst and intense visualizations, Nora returned to the crumpled, white linen sheets of her bed. She entered a nearly catatonic state, not thinking of much of anything at all. A long period of time passed, and then she heard the unmistakeable sounds of her cell wall about to be slid open. She leapt up in anticipation, and watched as the wall moved to reveal the bearded man standing at the opening. He peered into her cell, and she studied his face, trying to figure out whether or not she was still dreaming.

She shut her eyes tightly for a few moments, and then reopened them, blinking repeatedly. It was difficult to discern reality from her imagination, because in her daydreams things always felt so real. After she gave a concerted effort at deciphering the nature of her current situation she gave up, and shrugged her shoulders. She smiled when she realized that she felt a rush of happiness and relief, regardless of the fact that she didn't know if the bearded man actually stood before her, or if it were purely her imagination.

In order to avoid another physical confrontation, Nora preemptively turned her back to the bearded man, and brought her hands behind her. He walked over to her, cuffed her, and then turned her around to face the exit, just the same as before. His hand pressed into her back—with the same firm touch she had come to expect—and he proceeded to guide her into the long white hallway.

Again, the bearded man said nothing as the two of them walked. Nora peeked into every single window they passed, but nothing had changed since her last trip through the labyrinth of hallways. If she paused too long before a window, the bearded man would prod her along with a push.

Now that she had more information as to her geographical whereabouts, Nora tried to examine her surroundings through a different lens. She was inside of Obsidia—that much she knew. She felt an urgency to figure out an escape plan, since she was certain that after the scientists were done with her, they'd be shipping her off to somewhere much more difficult to escape from. If she ceased to be useful to them, she'd most likely be sent to the high-security Jejung prison—if she was lucky. If she wasn't so lucky, she'd be sent to her death.

Nora was startled out of her obsessive, mental note-taking at the sight of several scientists coming down the hallway. Not a single one of them met her eye when they passed her, nor did they seem surprised to witness a young lady such as herself being led down the hall, restrained, by the bearded man. They treated the whole situation as though it were business as usual, and Nora supposed that around here, it was.

The bearded man pressed the heel of his palm into her side, indicating that he wanted her to turn to the left. She was quickly learning the non-verbal language of this oddly quiet man—different touches meant different things. After they turned into the final hallway, Nora caught sight of the test lab, the same she'd been brought to the last time. She had been fairly certain they were going to the same place, since the route had felt familiar, but the numbering on the sign near the purple door was unmistakeable. The bearded man again placed his hand on the pad beside the opening, and held it there for a few seconds until the door slid open. After he guided her through the entrance, the scientists nodded him away. He left, as wordlessly as he had entered, and the door slid shut behind him. Nora stood there, still near the lab's entrance, unsure of what to do.

Nothing appeared any different in the lab from the last time, with the exception of an additional woman being present. The new woman didn't look up at Nora, but instead stayed focused on the console in front of her, on the right side of the lab.

Dr. Willow saw Nora's curiosity in the new woman. "Hello again, Eleanor. I hope you slept well after our meeting yesterday," Dr. Willow said. Nora silently tucked away the information regarding how much time had elapsed since she'd last been in the test lab. "Dr. Edmonds you know already, and this is Brielle. She will be sitting in and observing your testing with us today," Dr. Willow said with a smile.

Hearing her name mentioned, Brielle stood up, and immediately Nora noticed that she was dressed differently than Dr. Willow and Dr. Edmonds. She didn't wear the same long shirt that buttoned in the front, but rather wore a form-fitting white shirt, with an extremely high collar, and sleeves that reached all the way to her wrists. The tight garment revealed Brielle's thin frame, and she wore her blond hair pulled tightly back into a bun, which accentuated her facial features. She had high cheekbones, that gave her face an angular appearance, and light eyebrows that starkly contrasted her dark brown eyes. She had a narrow, sharply angled nose, and unnaturally red lips. Nora realized the reason for Brielle's striking appearance was due to the use of makeup. This reminded her of Phoenix and the rest of the rebels back in Blear, and she felt a pang of emotion as she made the connection.

Brielle greeted her, "Hello Eleanor, today I will be assisting Dr. Willow and Dr. Edmonds. We are going to try and figure out what went wrong with the programing that was installed during your testing yesterday. The two of them have been working all through the night and we are ready to try again. Are you okay with this?" Brielle's voice was soft, yet still somehow authoritative.

"Yes, we can try the test again," Nora replied eagerly. She was much too excited to feel the rush of being hooked up to the Dream Machine again to give much thought to her response.

Brielle nodded and smiled at Nora, "Okay, go ahead and climb up on the SIRT, just like last time. And um..." she paused and let out a light chuckle, "Don't forget to turn your gown around again."

Brielle's tone and the way she phrased things made Nora wonder if Brielle had been told about her clothing being backwards, and her resistance the day before.

Climbing onto the Dream Machine again, Nora used one hand to grab onto the padded seat and her other to hold her clothing together in the back. Though she moved awkwardly, she was able to successfully mount the machine without exposing herself to anyone else in the room. The familiar chill of the equipment caused her to shiver as she pushed aside her clothing so that the metal disks could have direct contact with her skin.

As the scientists went through the operating procedures, in preparation for starting up the program, she tried to relax and prepare herself. Once everything was ready, Dr. Willow began the countdown. The moment before she hit zero, the blackness engulfed Nora.

Nora found herself in that empty, dark room again. This time, however, she could see Dr. Willow, Dr. Edmonds, and Brielle staring back at her a few feet from where she stood.

Brielle turned to Dr. Willow. "I was under the impression that the two of you had straightened this out already," Brielle asked, confused. "Why hasn't Eleanor's subconscious impression loaded into the SIRT yet?"

Dr. Willow and Dr. Edmonds exchanged a concerned look, but neither scientist answered Brielle. At that moment, Nora knew exactly what she needed to do to keep the three of them from questioning her abilities any further.

She took in a deep breath, forced her mind to relax, and then let the vision of the strange, wooded trees fill her mind.

One by one, the trees appeared before the four of them. After the trees were distinctly visible, the ground below their feet came into view. Dead leaves then piled up around their ankles, and they all felt the leaves' crunchy, slightly ticklish presence. The sky was slowly imbued with a faint blueish hue. Lastly, a shadow was cast down behind each person's figure, and behind each tree—the moon of Nora's subconscious world had risen.

Brielle let out a breath that she must have been holding for a while. She turned to the scientists. "Okay good, you two had me worried for a moment. Please continue on with your testing while I observe from here."

Dr. Willow and Dr. Edmonds made their way over to where Nora stood. "We are going to stay right behind you Eleanor," Dr. Willow informed Nora. "Just let the world take over your mind and body, try your best to stay focused on what you are seeing and feeling."

Nora pretended to barely understand Dr. Willow's request. But of course, being that this was actually her third time being hooked up to a Dream Machine, she secretly felt like a seasoned professional now. Nora had already learned a lot about what she was capable of while inside her own subconscious world, due to Bray's approach at guiding her through the process.

When the ground began to shake, and the rumble of footsteps became audible, Nora prepared for what was coming next—it was about to happen. She feigned a look of fear and shock as the stampede of people ran in the distance, wanting to pretend that it was her first time seeing the vision of her death. The light-haired boy locked eyes with her as he sped by, indicating all the familiar pieces of the dream were in place.

The scarred woman appeared near Nora, when the sound of the footsteps began to fade away, just as she had done every time before. The woman stopped running as she came face to face with Nora. Her eyes were still filled with alarm, and her jaw was still set in determination.

The woman opened her mouth to speak, and Nora gasped. Instead of the distorted sound of waves that had come from the woman's mouth countless time before, Nora heard the clear sound of her voice. "I don't know who they are, but they're coming for us. We need to get out of here, now!" The scarred woman yelled into Nora's ear.

Feeling more excitement than usual rush over her, Nora turned to follow the woman further into the woods. Her mind raced as she focused on the voice that had never been intelligible to her before, and felt a rush of excitement as she replayed the woman's words in her head.

Nora followed the woman to their usual spot at the edge of the wooded area, and crouched down beside her. She leaned in as the scarred woman spoke to her again. "Something has changed," the woman said urgently.

Before Nora could process what she was saying, the woman went on. "They are getting stronger, we need to get you out of here. On my mark... ready?.. RUN!"

Nora felt flooded with a mix of wild emotions at this unexpected turn of events. She stood dumbfounded for a few moments, but then got up and ran after the woman who was already many yards ahead, trying desperately to catch up to her.

The bright light from above began to shine and encircled Nora. As she watched her silhouette form on the ground in front of her, Nora's hands rose up to her face as she remembered the reality of where she stood inside of this dream world. The woman turned around and yelled at Nora. "Go back Nora. You have to go back. Go back and warn the others!"

Feeling her mind race with all of this new information, Nora felt overwhelmed. She turned her head and saw that Dr. Willow and Dr. Edmonds stood, watching her, a few feet behind her in the open field. Feeling utterly helpless, Nora reached out towards them with both of her arms, terrified. She knew that her death in this subconscious realm was imminent.

As she braced herself for the gut-wrenching pain, her viewpoint changed. It took her a moment before she realized that she was watching herself from a small distance, being torn apart from something above. As she heard the thumping sound in the sky above her, Nora watched her own body as it fell to the ground. And then, right on schedule, the nothingness of the empty, black room returned.

Brielle and Dr. Willow stood close by Nora in the room. Dr. Edmonds was on the ground, to her right, wheezing as he gasped for breath. Nora, too, felt it difficult to breathe.

Brielle broke the silence and spoke first. "What in the world is going on!?" she exclaimed. "Dr. Edmonds please respond immediately!" She sounded extremely excited.

With his legs shaking, he struggled to stand upright and face them all. "I... I'm not sure," he said. He dusted off his long, white, buttoned shirt, slowly, as if attempting to collect his thoughts. "It's as if..." he began, but then his voice faltered. "Eleanor!?" he called out, in a demanding tone.

He ran over and grabbed her shoulders, "What have you done? It couldn't have happened that way... could it?" he asked in shock.

The look of desperation in his eyes as he tilted his head made it clear that she'd have to explain what had just happened to the three of them. She swallowed hard, realizing she may have just put herself in great danger by what she'd done.

"Yes Dr. Edmonds," Nora started. "You and I switched places during my vision it seems. I'm not sure how, but as far as I can tell, that is what happened."

Thinking back to her first experience hooked up to a Dream Machine, Nora remembered how she had accomplished the exact same feat with Otto. Nora decided it was still a good idea for her to keep her prior experiences a secret from the rest of them.

"I think we have found exactly what we have been looking for after all these years of failure," Dr. Edmonds said to Dr. Willow, his voice breaking with emotion. He turned towards Nora. "Eleanor, thank you!" he exclaimed, and then, to Nora's surprise, hugged her.

At that point the darkness began to fade away, or perhaps the brightness from the white lab just took over and drowned that darkness out. It was possible that the black room was always present, and that the various environments around Nora just kept her from seeing it.

Sensing the glow of light from the lab's overhead bulbs through her eyelids, Nora opened her eyes to see Dr. Edmonds hunched over, tears in his eyes.

He stood back up and immediately started pushing all kinds of buttons on his console.

Walking over to the wall, Brielle removed a small, white communication device. "Yes, immediately, we will wait for you before going again," Brielle spoke into it, and then replaced it on the hook. Brielle walked over to where Dr. Willow and Dr. Edmonds now sat at their consoles, quietly talking with each other. Dr. Edmonds was shaking his head and staring at the ground. He looked up at the sound of Brielle's voice. "Start pulling up all the data on your consoles from the most recent test," she ordered. She then paused to look Dr. Edmonds up and down. "And please, collect yourself. He is on his way down to the lab right now."

A lump formed in Nora's throat as the door to the lab slid open minutes later, and an older man entered. Nora noted how tall he was, and what a commanding presence he had. His dominant stature made Nora cringe, and it felt suddenly as though every nerve ending in her body was electrically charged. Without having to be told, Nora knew exactly who this man with the dark, piercing eyes was.

"Hello Eleanor, I'm Dr. Secora," the man said. Trying desperately to contain the whirlwind of intense emotions within her, Nora sat quietly next to the man responsible for everything that had happened to her over the last few days.

"I hear you are quite the talented little girl," Dr. Secora continued. The condescending way the word little rolled across his tongue made Nora's face scrunch in disgust.

"Let's have a look at your earlier test results inside the SIRT shall we?" Dr. Secora headed over to the consoles and sat down with Dr. Willow and Dr. Edmonds. Brielle explained to him their most recent experience inside of Nora's subconsciousness.

Dr. Secora glanced at the computer screens as he rifled through a stack of papers. He asked the two scientists a few questions, but neither had much useful information to answer him with. Nora could see the frustration growing in his expression.

Dr. Secora turned towards Brielle, still looking for an answer. "Hello, Father," she said, to Nora's surprise.

He nodded and smiled in response to his daughter's words, "Brielle, what is your opinion of Eleanor so far?"

Brielle straightened her posture, making it obvious that Dr. Secora intimidated her. "Eleanor has shown unpredictable mental strength, both in our conscious world and in her subconsciousness." The words came out sounding somewhat rehearsed, as though Brielle had started forming her response the moment after she called for Dr. Secora. "I believe we have a rare opportunity with her, Father," she added, her words this time sounding more natural.

Dr. Secora raised one of his eyebrows, "You do, huh? What would this new opportunity for us entail?"

Brielle straightened her posture once again as she answered, "I believe we should run Program 7." As the words left Brielle's lips, Dr. Secora's eyes lit up in a way that made Nora's blood run cold.

"Brilliant as usual, Brielle," Dr. Secora replied, a sinister smile creeping onto his face. He turned towards Dr. Willow and Dr. Edmonds, "Doctors, please install Program 7 into the SIRT."

CHAPTER 17

Both Dr. Willow and Dr. Edmonds stared blankly in response to Dr. Secora's demands. Dr. Edmonds was the first to speak up, "Please, Dr. Secora, you must understand that Program 7 is untested. We just don't have the data to ensure the safety of our subject."

His defiance enraged Dr. Secora, who grabbed Dr. Edmonds by the throat, "I wasn't asking you," he screamed, his face less than an inch from Dr. Edmonds. "Never make the mistake of questioning my authority again!" He shoved Dr. Edmonds, causing him to crash into his console. "Now," Dr. Secora continued, straightening his collar, "Run Program 7!"

Before she realized what was happening, Dr. Edmonds pressed a button and Nora was plunged into the darkness, without any warning or countdown to ready her. She sat in her usual nothingness, rattled from how abrupt it all had been, and had no choice but to wait for the consoles to load up. Though she didn't know quite what to expect, she wasn't particularly at ease anticipating whatever would be coming next, given what she had just overheard them say about Program 7.

Soon she was able to catch sight of the familiar white pinhole of light in the background. A wave of white proceeded to take over Nora's vision, as it always did, which was followed by the various colors and orbs. Once everything faded away, she was left in a black, infinitely dark room again. But this time something felt different.

It took her a few moments before she could begin to focus, at which point she noticed a small cluster of white dots, and then a few red dots in the far distance below her feet. As she continued to observe them, she realized they were multiplying.

"Eleanor, what do you see?" Dr. Willow asked her. Though she could clearly hear Dr. Willow speaking to her, she couldn't see her.

"It's hard for me to focus on much," Nora replied, "but I can make out a few red and white dots far off in the distance. They are all really far away from where I am now," Nora replied. Her fear of being attacked by Dr. Secora made her answer the question honestly.

"Okay, good. Please Eleanor, I want you to focus on the red dots that you can see. Watch closely for any variations and then report any changes you observe," Dr. Willow spoke in a professional tone, and the warmth that was usually in her voice when talking to Nora had disappeared.

Relaxing her mind, Nora chose one red dot to focus on, and the distance between her and the dot seemed to diminish. She still had difficulty understanding how things moved in her subconscious world though, so she couldn't discern whether she was moving towards the dot, or if the dot was moving towards her. As the red dot grew in size, Nora observed it changing shape—it went from being a small pinhole of light, to the shadowy red outline of a human body. The deep red color that surrounded the body danced in the darkness—its movements resembled the fluidity of water, yet had the flickering energy of a flame. When the shadow was still enough, the figure of a small-statured female was visible.

She continued to follow the red shadow's transformation, and more things became visible in her environment. A large, gray circle formed around the woman's red shadow. Nora recognized the shape instantly—from the time she was in elementary school that shape had been used to represent the city of Constance in all geography and history classes. It was divided into five wedge-shaped pieces of equal size, and there were numerous red and white shadows that pulsed in all of the sectors, including the smaller circle in the center. All of the shadows seemed to belong to humans.

Though she couldn't be sure, Nora assumed she was staring down on the whole city of Constance. All five of the sectors were present and the outline of Obsidia in the center of Constance was distinctly visible.

Now that she'd gotten a better grasp on what she was looking at, she felt ready to report to the scientists. "Dr. Willow, when I focused on one of the red dots, it drifted closer to me, and now I'm pretty sure I'm looking down on the whole city of Constance. It's completely filled with white and red shadow people."

"Very good Eleanor," Dr. Willow praised, a hint of warmth returning to her voice. "That means that Program 7 is working as intended. Now we would like you to focus further on the red shadow, as you call it."

Turning back towards the red, flickering silhouette of the woman, it grew closer to her. Nora's vision shifted until she stood next to the shadowy woman, on level ground. Nora reached out to touch her, and the woman turned to Nora. Behind the waves that pulsed through the moving red shadow, Nora was able to vaguely make out the woman's face. Once she focused in even more, she picked up a confused expression on the woman's face, and realized that the woman was clutching a small child while looking directly into her eyes. At that moment, the woman faded away, and Nora's entire subconscious world shifted in front of her eyes again.

A city street materialized around her, and Nora immediately recognized it, due to the painted buildings and the crystal blue lake at the end of the road—she was in Blear. It felt as though she then melded her own thoughts with the red shadow woman's consciousness, and then Nora allowed the woman to guide her way. Nora's body moved on its own, just like the first time she had entered her own subconscious world with Otto and Bray.

A loud noise sounded from behind her, and as the red shadowed woman looked back to locate the source of the noise, Nora's viewpoint was turned towards it as well. Two people ran out of an alleyway to her left—they looked like they were members of the rebellion, though Nora didn't recognize them. She heard the loud noise again, and this time Nora realized that it had come from a nearby gun. As the bullet drove directly into her right leg, Nora and the shadowy red woman fell to the ground as one entity—their collective body shielding the child from the impending danger of another shot. The two rebels removed the small boy from the woman's grasp before running out of view.

"Pull her out, stop the program!" Dr. Willow cried out. "It's killing her!"

Back in the lab, Nora's body lay motionless, still hooked up to the dream machine, as blood trickled from her nose and mouth. "You're killing her!" Dr. Willow cried again.

Dr. Secora rushed over to the console where Dr. Edmonds sat stunned. Dr. Edmonds couldn't believe what he'd just seen and he was frozen out of fear. Pressing various buttons in a complicated sequence, Dr. Secora shut down the SIRT.

He called out in a confounded voice to the two shocked scientists, "Take Eleanor back to her cell and let her rest. Begin reworking the coding of Program 7 immediately. Eleanor is going back in to find that immoral woman, first thing in the morning!"

CHAPTER 18

When Nora woke up she was back in her white cell. As strange as it used to feel to her before, there was an odd comfort in her surroundings now, that she couldn't quite put her finger on. Her head spun, and she was unclear as to how she had gotten back there. The last thing she remembered was being on the street in Blear, and the red shadowed women, and...

Nora's eyes widened as she remembered the recent events. She had been shot in her right leg while she occupied the red, flickering silhouette of the woman's subconsciousness. After the gunshot, however, everything had gone completely dark.

She sat up quickly and pressed her fingers into her thigh to inspect the wound. Instantly, a horrible pain shot through her. She fumbled with her clothing and opened her gown by pulling apart the slit in front. A grapefruit-sized bruise was present on her upper leg. How did that get there? she wondered. There must have been a connection between the red shadowed woman and herself during their mental bonding inside of her subconsciousness while Program 7 ran. Somehow she must have adopted the woman's role during the gunfight that had erupted in Blear. Nora wondered if that were even possible. Program 7 must have been designed as a quicker method of finding and correcting the Defected, in order to most efficiently ensure their destinies.

Laying back down, Nora found it difficult to keep her eyes shut. Every time she closed them, the white and red dots of the shadow people appeared across the inside of her eyelids. Program 7's effects lingered within her. Nora shook her head in an attempt to rid herself of the shadowy visions. She decided she'd try things on her own, without the scientists, Brielle, and Dr. Secora watching over her every move. She closed her eyes again, and did not open them. The red and white dots remained, but there were fewer of them than there was when Program 7 had been running. Focusing on one single red dot, it then moved to the forefront. She observed as the red silhouette walked briskly, and turned the corners of the gray-walled world that it moved within. As the shadow approached Nora's location it stopped a short distance from her. Unexpectedly, just at that moment, Nora's cell wall opened.

The bearded man appeared, as wordlessly as ever, clearly ready to escort her back to Test Lab 504. She leapt out of bed, her heart racing, as everything clicked into place in her head. It all came to her at once, like a wave that washed over her. The bearded man was the red, pulsing shadow that Nora had just seen in her subconscious world. Apparently she didn't need the assistance of the Dream Machine, or Program 7 to see the secret he had kept from her.

"You have to get me out of here," Nora exclaimed to the bearded man as he walked over to her. "If you take me back to that lab, you will be sealing the fate of all of us."

The bearded man did not answer as he approached Nora. He looked her dead in the eyes, then looked down to the ground. When he brought his eyes to meet hers once again, he motioned for her to turn around and face the white wall behind her. She complied, desperately wanting to get through to him. She turned around and put her arms behind her back, as she always did. The bearded man grabbed her wrists and fastened the handcuffs on her. This time, however, he did not securely tighten them.

"I am more like you than you will ever realize," he lowered his head to be near her and spoke in a hushed tone into her ear. Though she had assumed his voice would be somewhat gruff, given his physical appearance, it was even raspier than she had imagined. Despite the rough sound of his words, there was a tenderness to them. "Today you will need to forget about the rest of Constance and focus all of your energy into fighting for your own life." Before Nora had time to think about what he'd said, he stood up and cleared his throat, indicating that their brief exchange was now over. He forcibly turned her around and directed her into the hallway.

As they moved along Nora felt something dangling down from the metal cuffs. Whatever was there certainly had not been present any of the other times she'd been restrained. She twisted her wrists around in an attempt to feel the small object better. Finally she was able to graze her fingertips across the surface of it. As she fingered it, the meaning behind the bearded man's words became unmistakably clear— the object entangled in her handcuffs was the necklace that had belonged to her sister.

Nora's eyes darted around the white hallways for any sign of another life. Her mind flooded with questions about the bearded man. She replayed his words over and over in her head. She now knew he was

Defected, just like her and her rebel friends, and she wondered why he had chosen today to finally speak to her.

As they stopped in the middle of the hallway and approached the first window to one of the empty white rooms, Nora tried to turn and face the bearded man. The sheer strength he had over her small body kept her firmly in place, facing ahead. Nora dug her heels into the floor, refusing to walk further towards the lab. She needed answers from the bearded man, and this might be the only opportunity she'd have. He decreased the pressure on her lower back and then bent down to speak in her ear once again.

"You need to keep walking," he whispered. "If the others sense we've communicated whatsoever, they will kill us both." He resumed his normal degree of pressure on her back. "I've been watching your results and I know what you are capable of. You need to trust your instincts. Try and focus on me, so that you can enter into my subconsciousness. I won't resist you. As you do so I'll continue to guide you towards the lab, so that if anyone is observing us through the surveillance cameras they won't get suspicious."

She instantly understood the plan, and closed her eyes, feeling her mind drift upward, away from where her body resided in the real world, just as she had done back in her white cell before the bearded man had appeared. In her mind, Nora could easily make out both of their red shadows against a dark gray floor. Looking down on herself was an odd, and disorienting feeling to her. Nora focused on the bearded man's shadow that stood behind her own. Slowly, his red glow enveloped her whole view, and she could feel herself entering his conscious world.

Her view shifted from the gray outlined realm into the bearded man's reality. Inside of his conscious mind, Nora could feel the bearded man's oversized hand, as if it were her own. She could feel the fabric of the white gown the hand pressed against, the warmth of the body beneath it, and the hard spinal ridges buried beneath a thin layer of flesh. Her heart fluttered as she realized she was actually inside the bearded man's mind, and she knew it wasn't her imagination this time. In this moment, she marveled at how small her body seemed, from the perspective of the bearded man. She tried to focus on what needed to be done before the two of them reached the sliding purple door to the lab.

Nora closed the bearded man's eyes inside of the hallway, and entered into his subconsciousness. A memory of the bearded man waking up for his day flooded her vision. She could feel his presence inside of his own mind alongside hers. Together they dove further into the recesses of his mind.

His life's memories were projected for her, in an all-encompassing way—she not only could see things, she could smell, touch, hear, and feel them. And perhaps most surprisingly, she actually experienced the very emotions he had felt during the events. The first memory that appeared was that of a beautiful woman, and two small children running around happily in a yard behind a small wooden house. The woman had extremely curly, long, blonde hair that flew wildly in all directions as she ran, and her laugh sounded like a silver bell being rung. The children—a boy and a girl—screamed gleefully as she chased them. The grass was a vibrant, bright green, and a bit overgrown. A sprinkler went off every now and then, each time spraying an iridescent sheen of water across the yard. Nora watched all this from the back porch of the brown house, and felt the contented warmth that filled the bearded man's heart as the scene unfolded. Time seemed to move at a faster pace inside of his subconscious world, even more so than what Nora had been exposed to inside of the Dream Machine and Program 7. It was as if Nora was watching a highlighted reel of the bearded man's life.

It was only another moment before the bearded man brought Nora into a different memory. She watched from behind his eyes as he placed his palm on the entry pad beside the purple entrance into the room labeled 504. He then calmly stepped into the empty test lab. After walking over to one of the consoles and pressing a sequence of buttons, he hoisted himself up onto the Dream Machine and closed his eyes.

Not wasting any time or allowing Nora to gather all of the new information he provided her with, he brought her to a final memory inside of his Defected mind. When she looked down she saw a large pair of hands, that she quickly recognized belonged to the bearded man. Feeling the muscles in his hands move as if they were her own, together the bearded man and her retrieved a small piece of paper from a drawer, grabbed a pencil from the table in front of them, and began to write. When they were done writing, Nora saw two phrases.

THEY ARE COMING FOR YOU
ESCAPE TODAY

Relaxing her focus, Nora let herself float out of his mind and into the space above where the bearded man and herself walked the white hallway. She located her own red shadow standing in front of his as they walked the dark gray outlined floor and re-entered her own mind. An intensely refreshing feeling overwhelmed Nora, like how it felt returning back to her bed after a long day of work. A slight tremor shook through her entire body.

Nora felt the bearded man's hand squeeze her lower back and then release its grip slowly, signaling to her that he understood she had left his mind and entered back into her own body. Instinctively she smiled, and said, "Thank you," without turning around or stopping, and trying not to even move her lips. She watched as he placed his hand on the pad next to the lab's purple door, and she took a deep breath as it slid open.

CHAPTER 19

Once Dr. Willow signaled to the bearded man that he could leave, Nora felt the tightness of his grip on her lessen, but he kept his hands on her a moment longer than he needed to, as if attempting to give her one last signal. She appreciated his effort, but it was unnecessary—she intuitively knew what had to be done. After undoing her restraints he left the room so swiftly that by the time she'd turned around the door was already sliding shut behind him. She hoped that would not be the last time she would ever encounter the bearded man.

When she'd arrived, Dr. Willow and Dr. Edmonds were at their usual consoles, pressing away on small buttons and checking various wires to make sure things were connected properly. Dr. Willow looked over at Nora, "Hello, again Eleanor," she said with a smile. "How is your leg feeling this morning? I hope that awful bruise didn't cause you too much discomfort while you were resting." The kindness she had constantly shown towards Nora made her suddenly feel overcome with sadness, knowing what she had to do over the course of their next testing session.

"Where is Brielle and Dr. Secora?" Nora asked her. She'd assumed they'd be present for the next attempt with Program 7.

"It seems there has been a situation near the Blear wall. Brielle was sent to monitor things there and report back to Dr. Secora with a full report later today," Dr. Willow responded nonchalantly. It was somewhat shocking to Nora that Dr. Willow was volunteering so much seemingly-privileged information.

"I'm sure you know the drill by now," Dr. Willow continued. "Go ahead and fix your gown and hop up onto the SIRT please. Today is going to be a very exciting day for all of us," she beamed, and her eyes lit up with obvious excitement.

As Nora nodded she mentally made one final decision. Though making this decision eased her sorrow somewhat, it also made what was to come all the more real. She lowered her head and walked over towards the Dream Machine in the middle of the white lab, knowing it would be for the last time.

Nora glanced over at the two scientists, who were both immersed in the duties of setting up the program on their consoles. Neither one paid any attention to Nora and continued on with their backs towards her. Deftly, Nora unclenched her fist, where she had hidden the necklace, undid the clasp, and then placed it around her neck. She then climbed up onto the machine's white padding and laid down, her heart racing at the prospect of being caught.

Hearing the scientists verbally running through their usual checklist with each other, Nora tried to tune out their voices and closed her eyes. She had to force herself to focus, because what she was about to do would require her complete concentration, and all the energy she could muster.

"All systems check out and are completely operational," Dr. Willow said to Dr. Edmonds. She shot a quick, distracted look over to Nora, "Subject is ready," she affirmed.

"Loading Program 7 into the SIRT now," Dr. Edmonds replied. "We are going live in 3...2...1..."

This time, Nora went through the usual introductory stages faster than normal, too impatient for how long the startup normally took. The moment she saw the white pinhole of light, she dove towards it. Without holding anything back, Nora let herself fall into the white void, as the light engulfed her. All of the colors and orbs moved by her at a fast pace.

Nora arrived at the black, empty room with record speed. Dr. Willow and Dr. Edmonds were nearby, as she'd expected. They both cast a confused look at each other, wondering why Program 7 had failed to load, yet again.

"I'm checking on it now," Dr. Edmonds called out.

Nora knew that timing for this was crucial—if she was a second off it wouldn't work. She took a breath, waited for a moment, and then counted down from three. As she reached the end of her countdown, the floor below them lit up with red and white shadows, surrounded by the dark gray outline of the city of Constance. Dr. Edmonds looked up at Dr. Willow and smiled—Program 7 had finally loaded.

Dr. Willow glanced over at Nora, "Eleanor, we would like you to remain focused again today. We are going to attempt the same test as we did yesterday. Hopefully we'll get better results this time."

"Okay," Nora said simply. She wanted to play along and appear as agreeable as possible.

Nora dove into the white and red dots below their feet, with her full focus. She watched as the gray outline of the city grew closer and as the different colored specks slowly developed into shadowed outlines of the people they represented. Dr. Willow and Dr. Edmonds struggled to keep up with Nora as she found exactly what she was looking for and her vision zoomed in towards it.

"Eleanor," Dr. Edmonds called out with apprehension in his voice. "We will have to ask you to slow down some. We are having a hard time mapping your trajectory."

Pretending not to hear his orders, Nora sidled up beside the two white shadows she had chosen as her targets. One red, pulsing shadow stretched out near them. Nora's now hyper-intense focus allowed her to move with great swiftness inside of Program 7. Her plane of view shifted rapidly, and the shadows—which had just been below her feet—now stood directly before her. Nora moved towards one of the white shadows and without any hesitation, entered it.

As the white silhouette and Nora became one, the conscious world of the shadow's owner became visible. From the white shadow's perspective, Nora could see herself, a few feet away, laying on the Dream Machine, and could see also that Dr. Willow was within arm's reach. The experience felt similar to when she'd melded her mind with the bearded man's consciousness back in the hallway. Now that she'd successfully inhabited the white silhouette, the time for her grand escape had arrived.

Nora rewound through Dr. Edmonds' memories with ease. Visions of lonely breakfasts, late nights at the lab, and a secret attraction to Dr. Willow all flew by her field of vision. The experiments with Nora, as well as with other Defected youths, were likewise projected for her to view. She continued to dive deeper into his memories.

Finally, she found herself in what appeared to be a lecture hall within Obsidia. Dr. Secora stood at the front of the room, giving a disquisition. Exerting a high amount of energy and focus, Nora was able to take control of Dr. Edmonds' body. She used this control to stand him up, and walk him out of the auditorium and into the white hallway that lay beyond it.

Dr. Edmonds' body had such vastly different proportions from her own, that it felt very awkward to move him through the building. Nora was able to locate a stairwell and ascended the stairs at the fastest pace she could manage while navigating Dr. Edmonds' gangly body.

When she'd turned a corner at the top of the stairwell, she saw a sign indicating she had made it to the door which provided roof access for the building. She ushered Dr. Edmonds' body to it, heaved the heavy metal door open, and then burst outside into the warm sunshine. The view from the rooftop was incredible, and she walked towards the edge of the roof as she surveyed the surroundings through Dr. Edmonds' eyes.

From this vantage point, Nora could see the thick, dust-filled fog that perpetually hovered above Arrant, as well as the sun-drenched landscape and clear blue waters of the lake in Blear. A few pillars of burning smoke rose from the water sector, near the wall. Nora figured the smoke had some connection to the situation that had arisen, which required Dr. Secora and Brielle's presence.

To her left the golden fields of Fallow were visible in the far distance, though she was not close enough to see their wheat stalks gently sway in the wind. She savored the moment, knowing she'd never have a view like this again—all five sectors, so vastly different from each other, visible all at once.

When she turned 180 degrees she was able to see the Sonant sector. Its streets were a beautiful dull white that sparkled in the sunshine which poured down from above. The buildings were all made of a kind of marbleized stone. A strong emotion came over Nora as she surveyed the whole city of Constance for the first time in her short life. She knew that very few citizens would ever get to see anything beyond their own sectors, let alone the landscape of the entire city all at once.

The elation she felt quickly faded away, as Nora looked further to her left and saw the enormous, imposing prison of Jejung. There was a dull, gray dirt that covered the ground surrounding it, and a long, slate gray path that made its way from the center of Constance all the way to the prison. She found it difficult to keep her gaze on Jejung for very long, not wanting to focus on the idea of her ending up there if her plan wasn't executed correctly.

She turned Dr. Edmonds' body back around, and returned to the edge of the roof that faced Arrant. After one last, lingering gaze at the sector she'd called home for nearly her entire life, Nora inhaled deeply, closed her eyes, and then jumped. Dr. Edmonds' gangly body soared over the edge of the rooftop and began to hurtle towards the ground below.

Free falling proved to be an even more intense experience than she'd anticipated. Several yards of empty air rushed past her vision as she tried desperately to focus. She felt her gut rise up to her throat, and a wave of fear take over. She closed Dr. Edmonds' eyes, in an attempt to block out the reality of the treacherous fall she was currently in the midst of. As the world rushed past her at an alarming speed—or more accurately as she rushed past it—Nora was somehow able to center her mind enough to push herself out of Dr. Edmonds. She clung onto the atmosphere of the gray outlined world around her with all the focus and determination her brain could muster. After she had departed his consciousness in the new memory of his past, he was left alone again, hurtling towards an inescapable and brutal end. As Nora's mind floated up and back onto the rooftop, she saw Dr. Edmonds' white, silhouetted body plummet the rest of the way, before it impacted with the gray dirt.

When she re-entered Obsidia she was at such a vantage point that she could survey it as a whole from above. A group of red shadowed people came into view—they ran frantically up one of the stairwells until they reached the fifth floor, when they then burst out into the hallway. As she tracked their movements it seemed as though they were headed towards the test lab where her body was currently hooked up to the SIRT. Nora quickly found her way back to the room marked 504 herself, and then zoomed in towards the red shadow of her body, re-entering it.

Immediately she opened her eyes and sat up, turning to see Dr. Willow staring at her--horror and dread clearly present in her expression.

Dr. Willow's mouth was open and she was screaming at Nora. "What have you done?! What have you done!?" she repeated over and over as she shook her head violently.

Nora turned to look at the console Dr. Edmonds had been seated at when they had begun the test—the chair before the console was now empty.

Without warning the sliding door to the lab burst open from a loud explosion—the force from which was strong enough to detach the mechanism and send it flying. Startled, Dr. Willow jumped back. When Nora turned to look at what was happening, she saw a group of people pouring into the lab, and her heart skipped a beat when she recognized the faces of her fellow rebels.

CHAPTER 20

As the smoke cleared from the explosion, Nora's ears began to loudly ring. Peering through the lingering smoke and debris, she saw a few more rebels enter the lab, their guns held out in front of them and pointed in every direction.

She saw a male figure emerge from the group of rebels and make his way over to her. When she realized that it was Bray her eyes immediately welled up with tears. Their eyes met, and for a moment the hazy chaos around them ceased to exist. They savored the sight of each other, and even when Nora began to dismount the Dream Machine, she could not bear to take her eyes off him. Clumsily, she slipped forward, falling off the machine. With lightning-fast reflexes, Bray managed to reach her fast enough to catch her before she crashed into the cold, white floor. Allowing her body to go completely limp in his arms, she looked up at his face to see him break out into a huge smile.

The rest of the rebels cleared the room, while Jack and Cady restrained Dr. Willow and kept her near the back wall beside the large display screens. Nora glanced over at Dr. Willow, trying to give her an apologetic look, but as soon as she was able to catch her eye, Dr. Willow averted her gaze to the floor. Nora felt horrible for what she had just done to Dr. Edmonds. Seeing all of the other rebels, and of course Bray in particular, only affirmed in her heart that she'd made the wrong decision when planning her escape. Dr. Edmonds had been a needless casualty.

Otto and Phoenix came over to Nora, who was still being held up by Bray. Phoenix hugged her. "I'm so glad we found you!" Phoenix said into her ear as the two embraced. "I hate that we left you to enter Fallow all on your own. I'm so sorry Nora."

She nodded at Phoenix with understanding, and then looked over to Otto. "We need to get out of here right now," she informed him. "Dr. Secora and his daughter, Brielle, will be returning from the Blear wall soon. I'm sure they can't be too far away. Also, Dr. Secora has probably already been informed of what's just happened here."

"We know, Nora," Cady let out a high-pitched deliberate chuckle. "That was our explosion at the wall!"

Otto flashed Nora a smirk, and then motioned to the other rebels to get their attention. "Let's move out," he called out. "Trim and Bretta, you two are on the hallways, the rest of you fall in line behind us."

The rebels began to exit the lab, and Bray nudged Nora along to follow suit. Suddenly remembering something, she resisted, firmly standing her ground. "Wait," she began, her hand on his chest, "We can't go yet," she said. She pushed Bray aside and went over to the consoles. She searched the workspace frantically, shuffling through papers, and quickly grew frustrated when she was unable to locate what she was looking for.

She stomped over to Dr. Willow, who was still tied up in the back of the room, "Where is it? Which console is it in?!" Nora yelled so loudly —in an attempt to frighten the scientist into talking—that she even shocked herself somewhat. "Do you want to know what happened to him? I suggest you tell me where it is right now, or I'll show you exactly what I did to Dr. Edmonds!"

Dr. Willow motioned towards one of the three consoles, "In the portable drive, underneath the screen."

Racing back to the console, Nora reached out and pressed an eject button. A small, plastic disk with metal on one end popped out and Nora grabbed it, holding onto it tightly as she ran to exit the lab. She found Bray waiting for her outside, and handed it to him quickly before he shoved it into his pocket. "We have to get this to Lace and the other rebellion in Fallow. This little thing will change everything," she said.

Bray nodded in understanding, and then turned to head down the hallway. Nora grabbed his arm with force, causing him to turn back around and look at her inquisitively. She reached her hands up to grab his face and pull him down closer to her, as she stretched up onto the tips of her toes.

"Thank you for coming here and rescuing me," she whispered to him. Her heart began to race as he pressed his fingers firmly into the back of her neck, and leaned down towards her. Their lips were magnetically drawn towards each other, and just as they were about to kiss—when Bray's exhaled breaths were already filling her lungs—Obsidia's alarm bells began to blare.

Chaos instantly resumed, as Otto and the rest of the rebels flooded back into the hallways. Otto—with Trim and Bretta just behind him—led the entire pack as they navigated their way through the building. Each time they approached a corner, the trio would peer around it cautiously and inspect the path ahead, before waving the rest of the rebellion group through safely.

Nora was thankful to have Otto there, guiding all of them with such confidence. Bray held tightly onto her arm as they walked, and Phoenix was right in front of them. Jack and Cady were positioned behind her, actively making sure Nora was kept protected. Nora knew that it was imperative she make it out of the building alive. She possessed an ability that the whole rebellion had never seen before—the ability to control the world and the people around her.

Her capacity to enter other people's subconscious minds, have access to their memories, and be able to control the actions their bodies made, was hard for Nora to comprehend. The more she thought about her newfound abilities, the more regret she felt for what she had done to Dr. Edmonds. Nora had erased him from their existence when she projected him off the rooftop.

The sound of loud gunfire from up ahead startled her out of her contemplations. Trim shouted back towards her and Bray, "I've got a group of agents pinned down around the next corner, move across the hallway now!"

As she ran across the break in the hallway, she caught sight of Trim laying down on the floor, shooting at the oncoming agents. The agents had taken cover around a tight corner and were returning shots whenever Trim ceased firing. Nora made it to the other side of the hallway and leaned against the wall which sheltered her from the agents. Waiting for Bretta up ahead to give the all-clear signal for the rest of the rebels to move forward, Nora looked across and saw the window to her white cell. Chills ran down her back. She still wasn't quite sure how long she had been locked in there for, but it had been her home for a decent amount of time. She stared down at the floor, realizing that she felt like a completely different person from the one who had woken up inside the cell that first day in captivity.

Nora felt a hand on her shoulder and looked up. Bray didn't speak, he only looked into her eyes with understanding, as if he knew exactly what she'd just been thinking. Reaching his arm around her neck, Bray pulled her head in close to his chest. Nora closed her eyes and tried to forget about her experience in the small, white cell, locked away inside of Obsidia.

Bretta's voice rang out, disrupting their tender moment, "Okay, it's clear up here, a few more corners and we should be at the stairwell again," she called out to the rest of the group. Trim was still behind Nora with his rifle pointed around the last corner, shooting bullets into a group of agents every time they got the courage to poke their heads out in an attempt to fire.

Nora stood up to move, causing Bray to release his arm from around her neck. Trim ran past the two of them and the whole group started to move forward again.

"Let's move. Move, come on," Bretta urged them, "Get up here. Let's go!"

Nora kept up with the pace of the group, and things seemed to be fine until Bretta yelled out, with terror in her voice, "Nora, behind you!"

CHAPTER 21

Nora felt a pair of cold hands grab her from behind and begin to drag her away from the group. Squirming within the vice-like grip, she managed to turn her head enough to catch a glimpse of the agent who held her. The agent sneered as he surveyed the rest of the rebels. She desperately clawed at his hands and thrashed her body about. The fear of being shoved back into that white cell fueled her with a surprising amount of strength. Her incessant struggles to escape his grasp only resulted in him clutching one of his hands around her throat. He then pulled a gun out from a holster on his hip and aimed it directly at her head, pressing the cold steel barrel against her temple.

"Stop! All of you, stop right now or I'll shoot the girl," the agent screamed. Nora trembled at the idea of a bullet being shot point blank into her skull.

All of the rebels had, at this point, turned to see what was happening behind them. Bray and Phoenix turned around, and when they caught sight of the hostage situation their eyes opened wide with shock.

"Let her go," Bray yelled out. Both Phoenix and Bray were pointing their rifles at the agent, but there was no way they could get in a shot, since the agent held Nora's body directly in front of himself. Bretta and Otto poked their heads around the corner in the distance. Otto had a somewhat helpless expression across his face, which was terrifying for Nora to witness. Bretta came around the corner and brought her rifle up to eye level, keeping it fixed in the direction of the agent. Jack and Cady simply stood, and not being able to do anything to help, watched in silence. The sheer number of firearms being aimed at her, and knowing that any one of them could go off at any moment, made her palms turn clammy. A bead of sweat formed near her temple, and the agent pushed the gun's barrel into her even harder.

"Drop your guns now!" the agent ordered the rebels. His voice boomed so loudly that Nora could feel the vibrations of his words in her own body.

Despite the utter panic and chaos of the life-or-death situation, a realization occurred to Nora. Something about the way the agent had phrased his threats made it seem like he was unaware Nora was the rebel that had been held captive and tested on in the white lab. He doesn't know what I'm capable of, she realized with a start. She quickly devised a plan in her head, closed her eyes, and then dove into her subconsciousness. Suddenly, just like that, there they were, the agent and her—one red and one white shadow above a gray floor. Nora directed her mind to move backwards into the unknowing agent's consciousness.

Once she occupied him and had full control of his faculties, she was able to feel her own small frame inside of the unknowing agent's clutch, just as she'd been able to do when she entered the bearded man's mind. Nora moved backwards through his most recent recollections, until she arrived at the memory where he'd hidden behind the corner, dodging Trim's ammunition. Now that she'd brought him to the right memory, Nora made the agent reach down and remove the pistol from the holster on his hip. She had him raise the gun up to his own temple. Taking a deep breath, she guided the muscles in his fingers, squeezing them tighter until the trigger was pulled.

She flew quickly out of the agent's subconscious mind, and re-entered her own, returning to the present moment around the corner. When she opened her eyes she saw all of her fellow rebels staring at her in shock.

Whirling around to ensure the agent that had been holding her hostage was gone, she breathed a sigh of relief. She blinked her eyes in disbelief, still shocked at what she was capable of, and then raced over to the corner. When she peeked her head around it, she caught sight of the agent sprawled out in the middle of the white hallway, in a pool of his own dark red blood, the small pistol still being clutched in his hand. His face had been blown apart from the gunshot, and his blood had spattered in an arc across the formerly pristine white wall. One of his eyeballs had somehow remained intact, but had been blown off with the shot and projected halfway down the hallway. The lifeless and unblinking pupil stared up at the ceiling.

Nora returned to the rebels, too shocked to speak—she couldn't believe what she had just done. Her hair fell forward across her face and her knees began to tremble.

Phoenix was the first of anyone to speak. "I've never… how did… what was all…" she stuttered, unable to get a complete sentence out.

After another moment of shocked paralysis, Nora suddenly snapped back to reality. "I'll explain it to all of you later, but first, get me out of this damn building!" she yelled, her voice breaking with emotion as her fingernails dug into the back of her neck. They stared back at her in horrified confusion.

Otto cleared his throat and straightened his posture, resuming his position of authority, and called out, "Whatever Nora just did, it saved this mission. You heard her, we need to move! Let's go now!"

Nora and the rest of the rebels piled into the stairwell and descended the flights of stairs as quickly as possible. They flew down so fast it barely felt like her feet touched the ground.

"Make sure you keep Nora covered on all sides," Otto ordered as they made their way to the ground floor. "I don't want to risk a situation like that happening again!" Her fellow rebels stayed close to each side of her, surrounding her fully.

A few flights above their heads, a door opened with a loud screech that filled the entire white stairwell. The pounding footsteps of a group of agents thundered over them as they ran down to catch the rebels.

"Give me your pistol," Nora said breathlessly to Phoenix. "I don't want a repeat of the last time."

Phoenix reached into her waistline pocket and handed a pistol over to Nora. "Keep it pointed away from yourself and the rest of us," Phoenix reminded her. Nora nodded in response as she tucked the gun away under her arm.

Panic set in over the whole group when it became apparent that the agents were gaining on them, so they quickened their pace. Nora was surprised that she was able to keep up with everyone, considering she'd been immobile for close to a week being locked up in the cell. Somehow her body felt fresh and rejuvenated.

At last, they all made it to the ground floor of the white stairwell. Otto burst through the door at the end of the landing and held it open for the rest of them to pass through. Trim ran through first, but as soon as he'd disappeared from view gunshots immediately began to sound from outside. Otto ran after Trim to provide back up, and the rest of the rebels followed. As soon as each rebel ran through the door they began to yell and fire their guns. Nora and Bray waited to be the last ones through, hanging back enough to make sure that Nora would be exposed to the least amount of danger. Nora turned to look behind her, knowing there were even more agents that would be coming down the stairs at any second. Bray fired a few warning shots up the center of the large stairwell, and the sound of the descending agents' pounding footsteps came to an abrupt halt.

Nora and Bray darted out of the stairway and quickly found cover behind a desk on the opposite side of the grand room. The lobby of the building was full of gunfire, yelling rebels, and agents screaming in agony as they were shot. Phoenix had already made it to the desk. She nodded at the two of them before she stood up and shot a couple rounds towards the front doors of the building.

Otto, Trim, and Bretta were a few yards ahead of them, all taking cover behind large pillars. Most of the lobby was made from the same marble stone that Nora had seen when she looked out over the rooftop of the building towards Sonant, including the pillars. The marble was shiny and white, with thin gray veins running through it. The front wall was made entirely of glass and Nora could see the outside world through it. A path of pale marble steps lined with green grass led away from the building. Jack and Cady kept their weapons aimed back at the stairwell door, waiting for the descending agents to emerge.

Nora counted nine agents in total ducking behind various pieces of furniture in the bright lobby. A few hid behind pillars as well. Her heart started to race with anticipation, when the footsteps of the agents that had been trailing them became audible—they'd be there any moment.

Otto looked up and made eye contact with Bray, as he kept his body tightly pressed against the pillar he hid behind. He shot Bray a despairing, questioning look. Bray scanned the large, white room and then returned his gaze to Otto, shaking his head dishearteningly. Bray ducked back down behind the desk. "They have us completely surrounded," he said to Nora. "Got any fresh ideas on how we are going to get out of this place?"

At that moment Phoenix slid over to the two of them, "We aren't going to last much longer like this," she said. "We're like fish in a barrel."

They both stared at Nora, looking to her for a solution to their dire circumstance. Nora poked her head up from behind the desk to assess the situation herself. She caught Otto's eye, and he wordlessly communicated the same urging for her to help them as Bray and Phoenix had.

The first agent pushed open the doorway from the stairwell, and at the sight of him Nora decided on a haphazard plan. Jack and Cady's bullets pinged off the metal door frame in their attempt to gun him down. More agents were sure to protrude from the doorway as soon as they thought it was safe to enter the lobby.

Slowly, Nora stood up and raised her hands above her head, looking directly into Otto's eyes as she did so. "Don't shoot," she yelled out to the lobby at the top of her lungs. "I am unarmed," her voice echoed off the walls around her. "My name is Eleanor Rose, and I am the one you are all after. To kill me now would mean an end to the experiments and all the progress that Dr. Secora has made."

Otto looked at Nora stunned. She silently hoped he trusted her judgment.

The gunfire from agents and rebels alike ceased, and the remaining agents hidden in the stairwell emerged. Nora approached the closest one to her, trying not to make any sudden movements that might alarm him or anyone else. "I will surrender myself to you now, but my demand is that you must let the rest of my companions leave this place unharmed. They must be allowed to leave the center of Constance peacefully and return back to their homes."

She heard the voice of an agent speaking, who seemed to still be behind the stairwell door. The way the others shielded him from danger suggested he was some kind of commanding agent. "Constance stands firm that there will be no deals made with the Defected. Either surrender yourselves now and live out your days in Sector 1's prison, or die here in this room today."

Her heart sank with the agent's threat. She looked over at Bray who had made his way out from behind the desk and joined her. "If I pass out, do everything you can to get me out of here, I don't want to end up back in that cell again," she said to Bray, who looked at her quizzically. She then took a deep breath, shook her head, and closed her eyes. As her body stiffened and began to teeter over, he caught her, and held her up against his chest.

Nora's mind fluttered around the large, now gray room, until she was able to locate the commanding agent's white silhouette, sheltered by a small group of other white shadows—the agents protecting him. Nora focused on his flickering aura, and melded her mind into his consciousness.

Everyone in the room watched in awe as the commanding agent stepped out from the stairwell and into plain view in the lobby. "Stand down!" he called out. "All agents stand down now!" his voice boomed.

The rest of the agents looked around at each other confused. He walked confidently into the middle of the room, until he was in the midst of all the rebels and the wide-eyed agents. "All eyes on me.

Defected rebellion and agents of Constance, hear my voice. All agents stand down now! If you refuse my orders, then what you are about to witness will become your fate as well."

All the eyes in the large white lobby watched, transfixed, as the man that stood before them vanished.

The agents standing by the doorway to the stairwell looked at each other in confusion. After some debate one of the agents walked towards the center of the room where their commanding agent had just been standing. Carefully reaching out into the area that once contained his commander, the agent suddenly vanished too.

This sent the remaining agents into a confused panic. Screams filled the room as they ran in fear for their lives. Most of them exited out the front glass doors, and a few of the others ran back up the stairwell. Those who were not close enough to either exit remained huddled in fright, their bodies pressed up against the large white walls, unwilling to look back into the room for fear that they would meet the same fate as the two agents who had just vanished.

Feeling Nora's body suddenly go limp in his arms, Bray looked down at her. A small amount of blood trickled down from her nose, and spilled onto the white tile beneath her. He shook her slightly, in an attempt to wake her up, but there was no response. Leaning down to her nose and mouth, he affirmed that she was, at least, still breathing. Bray hoisted her body up off the floor, and carried her towards the large glass doors at the front of the lobby. The other rebels and remaining agents all watched in shock and horror, as Bray transported Nora's lifeless body past them.

The other rebels followed along behind Bray, as he lifted Nora out of the building and down the steps. The few agents that were left cowering against the walls turned and watched as the rebels exited.

Bray carried Nora all the way down the white marble steps, through the wide grassy area, and past numerous dilapidated buildings, until they reached the area where the wall that surrounded the center of Constance joined with the wall that enclosed Blear and Arrant.

At the wall, Bray laid Nora's limp body in the tall grass and sat down next to her. None of the rebels spoke. Nora's efforts had effectively bought the rebels their lives.

As nightfall descended, Jack and Cady leaned their backs up against the wall, still anxiously keeping watch for the possibility of agents coming after them. Otto, Phoenix, Trim, and Bretta all sat together in a small circle, forming a plan to get everyone safely out of the center of Constance. In hushed voices they conversed, and finally decided that the hole to their right—that they had already blown through, between Blear and the center of Constance—would be their best bet for escape.

Otto ordered them all to get some rest. They had made a strong stand against the oppression today, he reminded them, and Constance had definitely felt it.

CHAPTER 22

Night fell on Constance before Nora opened her eyes again. She was lying on her back in the tall grass, her face turned up to the star-scattered sky. Before electing to sit up and face the world around her, she took a deep breath and surveyed the night sky.

Bray was laying down next to her. Further off, Otto laid beside Phoenix, though the two were not quite touching. Nora smiled at the sight of them looking so peaceful with each other. Trim and Bretta laid together on the far side of Otto and Phoenix, barely visible to Nora. Jack and Cady were positioned the furthest from her, sitting with their backs to her, as they kept watch on Obsidia.

She felt a light touch on her back and was momentarily startled, before she realized it was only Bray. He sat up and scooted closer over to her, so that their legs were barely touching.

Bray cleared his throat, "How are you feeling?" he asked, making sure his voice was low enough not to disturb the other sleeping rebels. "I was starting to worry that you were never going to wake up."

"Completely worn out." Nora tried to chuckle and make light of the situation, but the reality of what she had been through in the last week was really weighing down on her spirits. "I suppose you are as curious as everyone else about what happened?" she asked him.

"Yes, of course I am," Bray responded calmly, "But only if you feel like sharing. All I know is that you saved a lot of people's lives today. Both agents and the rebels alike."

"Maybe..." Nora's head hung low and she shivered. "Then again, maybe not. I killed four people today."

"You killed them?" Bray asked, tilting his head down in an attempt to look Nora in her eyes. "What happens when you make them disappear like that?"

Nora sighed and looked off into the grass. She picked up a small stick and began to fidget with it, dragging it through the dirt around her. "Try and think of it like this," she said, and then drew a long line in the loose dirt. "This represents your life," she continued. "Now imagine that this point," she gestured to the far left end of the line, "Is the beginning of your life. And this point," she gestured to the far right end of the line, "Is the end. Everything between those two endpoints is the entirety of your existence—past, present, and future."

Bray looked pensive and nodded to confirm that he was following along with her dirt diagram. She drew a point near the middle of the line. "Now try and imagine what would happen if I selected this one single moment in your life, right here." She tapped the stick on the point she'd just drawn. "For some reason, after what they did to me in the lab, I can go back into your memory of this single event and alter how it unfolded."

Nora took the stick, and drew a new segment that branched off from the original line she'd drawn. "I can manipulate the outcome of your memory, and do it in a way where you would never notice the alteration I'd made." She continued to draw the new deviating segment, until it ran parallel with the original line. "In your new reality, the changed memory will seem as though it had always been that way. After I alter a memory, I essentially move your consciousness up and over to the deviating segment I just created, and you continue along on that new branch, running parallel to your original path. But for whatever reason, I'm different. I'm still trying to figure it all out, but it seems that essentially my mind exists in both realities simultaneously—the original line and the deviating segment."

Bray's eyes darted back and forth between the dirt lines as he tried to make sense of her explanation. "So you're saying that when we watch you do something—like what you did back with the agent in the lobby—you are rewriting one of his points on this original line, but from our perspectives as bystanders, we are unable to see the changes you have made, because the agent now exists on this secondary segment?" His fingers traced the space between the two paths. "And the rest of us remain on this original line without him."

Nora nodded in confirmation. She was pleased he was able to grasp the concept so quickly. "So because of this phenomenon," Bray continued, "Things around the rest of us will just disappear and we'll have no understanding of why that something no longer exists?"

"Maybe it would be easier to understand fully if I were to show you?" Nora asked him with a small smile.

"But how?" Bray replied hesitantly, "I already can't remember my life prior to joining the rebellion, and I really don't want you to make me disappear forever like you did to those agents!" he exclaimed.

Nora couldn't help but laugh at the look of fear that flashed in his eyes. "Don't be silly," she said, "I don't want to make you disappear forever either."

As he lifted his gaze from the ground, Bray met Nora's eyes and exhaled slowly, as though preparing himself for what was about to happen. "So, what do I have to do?"

"Just relax," Nora said in a soft voice, as she placed a hand on both his shoulders. "I'll do the rest." She then closed her eyes, and mentally sought out the gray world of the silhouetted people. Each time she navigated her consciousness to the shadow world, she was able to get herself there faster.

There they were—two small red shadows that held each other, curled up on the slate gray landscape, near a wall inside the center of Constance. The flickering silhouettes were of her and Bray. Nora watched her shadow as it lovingly raised its red, pulsing arms to hold Bray's face. His flowing shadow, in return, yielded to her touch—an act that exuded complete trust.

She continued to move her mind further from her isolated location in the lonely gray world, to be closer to Bray's red shadow. She took in a deep breath and then passed into his consciousness. Now her perception lined up with his, and she was able to see her own face as it stared back at her. Her flaming shadowed face was motionless, as if in deep concentration.

"Bray, can you hear me?" Nora called out from inside of his mind in a very loving tone. "Bray it's me."

"Yes, I can hear you," he replied, a touch of confusion in his voice. "How is any of this even possible?"

She paused as she considered the best way to explain their strange circumstances to him. "I have entered into your consciousness," she began. "We are existing inside of your mind at the same time, and we can feel each other's thoughts."

His confusion over this explanation was immediately palpable to her, so she continued, "Okay, I'm going to show you exactly what I mean. Try and direct your thoughts to a memory you have of the two of us— just the two of us. Close your eyes and focus on it."

As he thought hard and dug into the past, locked inside of his subconsciousness, Bray suddenly changed the world around them. The memory began to materialize in both of their views—the two of them were alone inside the Dream Machine room of the rebel base in Blear. Nora left Bray's mind and travelled over to her own subconsciousness locked inside of that specific time and place. She looked over to see Bray at his console, his eyes closed.

"Bray, you can open your eyes now," Nora said, with a hint of flirtation in her voice, as she walked over to him. Bray peeled his eyes open slowly and saw Nora right in front of him.

"Where are we?" he asked her. The room around them was dirty, and light blue paint was peeling off of the walls.

Nora sat down in the chair beside Bray. "Well," she started with a smile, "You tell me. You're the one that brought us here."

Bray peered around the room. The Dream Machine was lit only by a single bulb that hung from the ceiling. "Wow," he marveled, "We really are here. I brought us back to the day we first met."

Feeling a flush of happy warmth at the fact that this was the memory he'd chosen, she bent forward in her chair and kissed him firmly on the lips.

After a few tender moments, Bray finally pulled back from the embrace, "Are we not at the wall along the outer edge of the center of Constance anymore?" he asked her.

"We are," Nora began to explain patiently, "But right now, in this other moment, we are here, inside the base in Blear—back inside your memory of the first day we met each other. Right now we are changing the middle point on both of our life lines." Leaning in she kissed him again, this time deeper and more passionately than the first time. "Try to think of it as though we are rewriting history—the first time this experience occurred you and I never kissed in this Dream Machine room. But now when we leave here, and open our eyes again near the wall around the center of Constance, that kiss will be included in our memories of the day we first met. We could spend a lifetime recreating this moment here, meanwhile, not a single second of our lives would slip by back in our reality. Time seems to move differently inside of our memories," she said, shaking her head as though she herself did not quite understand it.

This time Bray sat up, and leaned forward in his chair, burying his face into Nora's neck. He began to kiss her softly. "I think I understand now," he said. "So when those people vanished in front of my eyes, you had gone back into their memories and changed the outcome of a specific moment?"

Sighing as she forced a weak smile, Nora again helped fill in the gaps for Bray. "Yes. I wanted to alter one of their memories in such a way that they could never have been inside the lobby with us. Unfortunately for them, I didn't completely understand how it worked until now, so my first reaction was to think that if they ceased to be alive before the day we all converged in the lobby, they wouldn't be able to be there in the first place. Now that I see how needless it was to take their lives, I feel terrible," she said as she hung her head. "But I've made a promise to myself now, that no matter what the circumstance is, I will always make the time to find a better option than what I chose with those poor agents, and Dr. Edmonds inside of the lab." She paused thoughtfully before continuing. "Death is never the answer," she said, as her eyes welled up with tears.

As a tear rolled down her cheek, it shone from the light of the bare bulb that hung above their heads. Bray wiped the tear from Nora's face, and placed both his hands on her shoulders. "Look," he began, his voice filled with compassion. "I understand why you did what you did. I'm having trouble though, understanding how you affected their stories so much just by viewing their memories."

"There's one last thing I could show you that might help," Nora said. She stood up and motioned for Bray to join her. She held out her hands and he rested his on top of hers. "Close your eyes again."

Nora left her body and entered Bray's subconscious mind once again. When Bray opened his eyes he saw her sitting motionless across from him in the Dream Machine room.

"Nora?" Bray asked hesitantly.

He heard her voice from within his own mind again, "I'm right here. I'm in your subconscious mind with you now, just as I had been before we came into this memory. Try and relax and stay calm," she instructed.

Bray watched in awe as his arm moved up and down on its own, without him directing it to do so. A ghostly chill ran through him—he had never felt anything like it before.

"See?" Nora asked, still from inside him. "I can move your body in just the same way that you can. This is how I was able to remove those agents from our present reality back inside of Obsidia." After she finished explaining, she retreated from his subconsciousness and returned to her lifeless body in the Dream Machine room.

Bray nodded again, finally able to understand how Nora had accomplished what she did inside of the lobby. "When I open my eyes and we are back in the center of Constance, will we remember this experience in my memory?" he asked her.

"Yes," she said, reaching out to hold his hand. "But you will remember it differently than I do. You will remember our first kiss as occurring inside this Dream Machine room. The first day we met. To you it will seem as real as any other memory you have." Nora was pleased with how easily Bray accepted all of this new information. "For me though, I will remember this memory in both ways—the original experience, and the altered edition we've created just now."

"It all makes sense now!" Bray exclaimed. "This is so incredible! I knew you were special from the moment we met."

His happy excitement gave her a sense of relief. She had been worried that people might be afraid of her, for what she was able to do. "If you knew that I was so special, then why didn't you kiss me that first day?" Nora asked him shyly.

Without missing a beat Bray replied, "Well... maybe I did." He leaned in and kissed Nora on the lips. It was such a light kiss, but a loving energy pulsed between their mouths. Nora felt the world around her melting away—the Blear rebel base faded and they passed into the dark, infinite room she knew so well. When Nora opened her eyes back by the wall inside the center of Constance, she saw Bray before her, his lips still positioned as if they were kissing hers.

"Whoa..." Bray said, speechless. "That was... that was..." he stopped talking altogether for several long moments. "How long were we sitting here like this?" he asked.

"Only for a second," Nora replied.

"Then," Bray paused, trying to formulate his question. "How long could we have stayed inside of my memories?"

"An entire lifetime," she answered earnestly. She then felt her body go limp—the exhaustion of her recent travels through Bray's memories was about to make her faint. Just before her eyes fell shut, she felt the warmth of Bray's forearms on her bare skin as he laid her gently onto the dewy grass, and saw the dizzying array of stars for a single, brief instant.

CHAPTER 23

Nora was startled awake by someone aggressively shaking her shoulder. When she cracked her eyes open, she saw the vague impression of a man's face hovering inches above her own. It was difficult to make out his features, because he blended in with the dark night sky, but she immediately recognized the dark hair that swung down near her eyes as Otto's.

Before she could gather her thoughts enough to form a sentence, Otto whispered, "Shh, you need to get up right now. We tried to let you sleep, in order to regain your strength, but a few agents have started heading in our direction. Bretta and Trim went to scout and found five of them walking towards us. They are probably only a hundred and fifty yards away at this point. It's time to move."

Rubbing the sleep from her eyes, Nora lifted her head closer to Otto's. "Why are they coming for us now?" she asked, sitting up so that Otto could relax and kneel beside her, instead of hovering over her in such an awkward position.

"Who knows. I'm guessing they had time to regroup and have built up the confidence to pursue us again," Otto replied without looking at Nora—he was peering off in the distance to keep an eye out for agents.

Tilting her head up to the dark sky above them, Nora asked Otto, "How long was I asleep for? Must not have been very long, the sun hasn't even started to rise yet."

"You've only been out for a couple hours," Otto replied, finally turning back to her. "I'm surprised the agents have regrouped so quickly. The ones that are coming towards us must have missed your little display in the lobby earlier. I can't imagine that any of the agents that were there would have the courage to try and take you away from us again." Otto smiled. He placed his palms together and then separated them, wiggling his fingers in the air towards the sky, "Poof!" he exclaimed.

Leaning forward onto her knees, Nora gathered her belongings, which were scattered throughout the tall green grass that surrounded her. The grass was grown so high that in her crouched position it reached far above her head. "I wish it were as simple as a new, ignorant group of agents, but I think it's more likely that they've figured out a way to counteract my ability, or at least figured out a way to protect themselves from it."

Otto gave Nora a puzzled look. "I can't imagine the agents being able to accomplish all that much over just the last few hours. Have you tried the thing where you close your eyes and save everyone's life again lately?" Otto mimicked what Nora's face looked like when she focused intently. "I'm thinking it's time to send the entire agency another message."

Closing her eyes while Otto sat by watching her, Nora focused her mind outward in the direction that he had indicated the agents were coming from. Nothing new appeared in the dark, gray outlined world of her mind, since the last time she accessed it with Bray. Nora could see the red shadows of her fellow rebels standing around her, but further out from where they sat in the tall grass, there was nothing. Dark gray lines ran all the way up to where the front entrance of Obsidia would be, and she could see the gray outline which represented all of the building's corners and edges.

Just as she was about to give up, Nora glimpsed what appeared to be a white shadow far off in one of the abandoned buildings, further into the center area of Constance. As soon as she saw the white flash, however, it disappeared.

Opening her eyes back in reality, Nora looked at Otto. "Something weird is definitely going on. I wasn't able to see any of the agents that Bretta and Trim said were approaching." Otto looked down at the ground in disappointment. "But," Nora continued, "At the last moment, when I was ready to give up looking, I finally caught the smallest peek of a white shadow far away from us, back inside one of the older buildings. Unfortunately, as soon as I attempted to focus on it, it vanished. That's the weird part. It was almost as if someone or something took the shadow away from my view."

Otto stood up and dusted off the front of his grass-covered pants. "Whatever is going on in that strange world inside your mind, it still sounds like it's time for us to leave this place. Enough messing around. Let's gather the rebels and get out of here." Otto reached down into his bag and pulled out some dark clothing, which he tossed to Nora. "Put this on," he instructed. "You've got to be freezing out here in that thin gown."

Nora grabbed the warm clothing gratefully. Otto really was a good leader, he always seemed to be thinking at least one step ahead of the rest of the group, and the fact that he'd brought an extra set of clothing was a good example of that.

"Thank you," Nora said, as Otto turned around to give her privacy to change.

As Nora attempted to keep her body concealed while she got dressed out in the open grass field, Otto continued to talk. At least, she reasoned, it was still dark out and this afforded her some seclusion from the rest of the group.

"There is still one slight problem we have now," Otto said calmly, his back still towards Nora. "The section of the wall that we blew through to get here is directly between our location and the agents that are currently walking towards us." He paused to let out a small sigh. "We exploded through the wall alongside the large water pipe that leaves Blear and runs directly into the center of Constance. Unfortunately it looks like going back that same way is not going to be possible. With the agents coming at us from the north, leaving here through either Blear or Jejung are no longer an option. The way I see it, we have only two choices left—we can keep running and try to get through the wall somewhere along Fallow or Sonant, or we can press forward right here and try to break back into Arrant."

Tapping Otto on the shoulder, Nora signaled to him that it was okay for him to turn around and face her again. Straightening out the dark shirt she now wore, Nora continued their conversation. "Any thoughts on how we get through this part of the wall and back into Arrant?" There were a few moments of silence as they both thought through their remaining viable options. "Do you have any more of those explosives with you?" she asked. "The ones you used to blow up the wall before, and the lab door earlier?"

Shaking his head in response to her question, Otto clenched his fists. "No, we only had enough time to make the two we needed to get into the center of the city and out. We didn't count on having to use one of them to rescue you inside of that lab, and we all figured that we could have just escaped the same way we came in, by that water pipe." Otto was visibly frustrated at himself as he looked around the tall green field, hoping the solution would magically appear.

Suddenly, an ominous, low rumble began to shake the ground below their feet. Otto and Nora exchanged nervous looks with each other, and the rest of the rebels all locked eyes in silence. As the sound grew louder, the rebels gathered closer together.

Trim was the first person to speak out over the noise. "Whatever's making that noise has got to be pretty powerful if it's shaking the ground below us," he speculated.

Otto surveyed the landscape, trying to locate the source of the commotion. "Everyone get into a low formation," he ordered. "No one moves until we know exactly what we are up against." They all obediently followed his instructions.

"There!" Bray shouted out, pointing ahead at the wall. He knelt down even lower, into a crouching position, as he made his way to join the rest of the rebels. He jabbed the air with his finger, pointing to the wall between the center of Constance and Arrant again, "Look at the wall, it's moving!" he exclaimed.

Nora turned and saw that the wall to the sector she used to call home had started to slide open, it had split apart in the middle. The edges where the separation had occurred were jagged, as the bricks had parted unevenly.

Otto motioned for everyone to huddle around him. "Okay, this is it. We don't have a whole lot of other options here. Anyone have a brilliant idea of how to approach this?"

Nora drew the groups attention to three agents who were walking into the center of Constance through the gap in the wall. Two of them were guiding the large hovering cart—which had been loaded up with building material from Arrant—while the third agent walked in front, and directed them through the opening. The two agents navigated the large cart with ease as its spinning exhaust ports expelled dust up around their feet.

Trim turned his attention away from the cart and looked at Otto. "If we let those three agents get a good distance away from the wall, we should be able to sneak through before that gap closes back up."

Otto nodded in agreement at the simple plan. "My guess is that we will most likely encounter a few more agents waiting on the other side of the opening. Let's hope that no one has ever been foolish enough to try something like this. If we are lucky, no one would expect a group of people to run directly through the wall during one of the deliveries and attempt such a blatant move."

Slowly they all walked in a single line towards the opening, and stopped to lean against the wall. As they edged closer to the widening gap, they stood near one another, waiting for Otto's next instruction. The three agents pulling the cart had now left a substantial amount of distance between them and the opening in the wall as they made their way towards Obsidia. Nora and the rest of the rebels knew it was only a matter of time before the wall was closed—their escape route could be sealed back up at any moment. Otto slowly raised his hand into the air, and the rest of the rebels waited with bated breath for him to drop his arm and signal everyone to take off. Nora dug her heels into the soft, moist dirt, and tensed the muscles in her calves and thighs, getting ready to run for her life.

CHAPTER 24

All eyes were on Otto. After a few moments of surveillance, he turned to signal the group that it was time to move ahead through the wall opening. His eyes widened suddenly though, and he quickly ducked back down from his standing position.

The rest of the group followed his lead and squatted lower against the wall. "Damn!" Otto yelled out. "Those five agents are right on top of us, maybe only fifteen yards out now. If they see us dip through the wall, we'll miss our chance to sneak away discreetly."

Nora watched as one of the agents bent down in the tall green grass and retrieved the dirty white lab gown she'd left behind. He lifted the garment high into the air and inspected it carefully with a flashlight. The fabric billowed in the evening breeze. Not sure what else to do, Nora tried to reach out to the agent with her mind.

Catching the look of concentration on Nora's face, Phoenix placed a hand on her shoulder. "Nora, what can you see? Are you able to get a better look at what is going on with those agents out there?"

Opening her eyes to look at her friend, Nora shook her head. "There is nothing. I can't see any of those agents anymore." She paused and sighed in disappointment. "They are right in front of my face, and I can see them in the real world so I know they are there right? But when I go into the gray world their shadows are nowhere to be found. Something weird is definitely going on."

Just then Otto cleared his throat and addressed the group, "I hate to say it, but right now, we need a new plan." He looked down at the ground and shook his head. "Someone has to volunteer to make a mad dash towards Obsidia," he said somberly. "We need something to distract the agents and take their attention away from the rest of us. Then when we are all clear on the other side of the wall, whoever volunteers to be the distraction will have to make a run for the opening on their own. Anyone want to throw their name into the hat on this one?"

Everyone looked around at each other anxiously, and for a long time no one spoke. Somewhere nearby a cricket began to chirp in the wild grass. Finally Bray spoke, breaking the awkward silence, "I'll do it," he said with resignation.

Nora desperately wanted to beg Bray not to go, but she bit her tongue. Despite how selfish it was, she didn't care if any of the other rebels took on the dangerous mission, as long as it wasn't Bray. She looked up at him with pleading eyes, but he only shrugged his shoulders at her.

"No, I'm the fastest of all of us. I'll do it," a small voice called out. Nora turned around to see that it was Cady who spoke the brave words.

Nora stared at the mousy, young girl as she continued to reason with the group in a hushed tone. "Look, it only makes sense for me to go. I can beat all of you in a foot race and you guys know it. And please stop looking at me with those sad eyes, okay? I've got this."

Nora made eye contact with Cady and mouthed the words, "Thank you" to her. Cady nodded firmly in response and smiled back at her.

"When the rumble starts again," Otto called out, his hand up in the air, "And the wall starts to close, we move out." Despite the tense situation, Otto's voice was calm. All of his movements were purposeful and exuded his confidence as a leader. Nora kept her eyes fixed on him as she waited for his next command. Even when Bray took her hand and intertwined her fingers with his, she didn't take her gaze off Otto.

Everything started to happen all at once. The rumble of the wall as it begun to close shook the ground so much that Nora could feel the vibration throughout her entire body. The rest of the rebels rose up from their squatted poses and took a runner's stance. Nora felt Bray's hand slip from hers as he got into position.

"Go!" Otto cried at the top of his lungs, deftly lowering his hand to signal everyone to move. He took off in a full sprint towards the opening in the wall.

Things began to move at lightning speed. All of the rebels began to run towards the closing wall. The voices of agents were audible behind them—they called out as Cady took off towards Obsidia.

Nora's feet pounded the ground, and she kept her focus on Phoenix, who was a few feet ahead of her. She thought back to the day she had met Phoenix, when they were running through the streets in Arrant. Now yet again, Nora was laser focused on her back. Phoenix's shoulder blades continually rose and fell in rhythm with her movements, and it nearly had a hypnotizing effect on Nora. In a way, Nora mused, Phoenix was kind of like her lighthouse—something that she could always rely on to guide her to safety. As much as her life had changed over the course of the last few weeks, here she was again, running at a full sprint away from pursuing agents. Nora was thankful that her path had crossed Phoenix's—she implicitly trusted her and knew she was safe in her hands. Additionally, she was happy to have someone like Phoenix around during such a difficult transitional period of her life.

Nora felt a hand on her back, pushing her further down the path towards the wall, which immediately snapped her out of her trip down memory lane. She was moving faster than she ever thought she could. Despite the fact that she couldn't see who was touching her, she knew instinctively that it was Bray.

She tried to focus on the rhythm of her breathing and the pulsing of her feet. Just then she saw the agents that had been pulling the floating material cart out of Arrant—they caught sight of her and yelled out. The agents dropped the ropes that had tethered them to the floating cart and raised their rifles, pointing them directly at the rebels.

Nora winced at the thought of the rifles being fired at them. She reached back and grabbed firmly onto Bray's arm, trying to signal to him that she needed his help to keep pushing her so she could get through the wall. Seeming to understand just what she meant, Bray put his other hand on her shoulder, and continued to urge her along.

Nora closed her eyes and focused her mind outwards, trying to reach the gray world as quickly as possible. It was a difficult task to perform while running at full speed with her eyes shut, but she was able to navigate her mind to where the three agents who had been pulling the cart stood. Surprisingly, Nora could see the three of them this time. Their three white shadows appeared as clear as the stars in the sky above them. She urged her mind to float forward, and then, straining her focus to its fullest potential, Nora entered into the nearest agents' consciousness.

Bray watched as Nora's body went limp before him. He immediately sprang to action and hoisted her body up, throwing her over his shoulder before continuing toward the opening in the wall. To his left he noticed that one of the three agents had turned away from the rebels and had his attention focused on his fellow agents. Bray heard him yell out something in an aggressive tone, but couldn't make out his words over the loud rumbling of the wall and the frantic footsteps of the rebels ahead of him.

In response to whatever the agent said, the other two agents proceeded to crouch down, and gingerly placed their weapons in the dirt. The agent then ordered them to lay down, and stood over the two of them, pointing his rifle at the back of their heads.

Bray raced through the opening in the wall and set Nora's limp body on the ground on the other side, safe from the view of the agents that were busy chasing Cady around the green field. The wall was only a few feet from being shut entirely. Otto and Trim had gone through and called back to let the rest of the rebels know that it was clear up ahead.

When Nora's eyes opened she saw Bray standing over her. She sat up slowly, and rubbed the back of her neck, while looking around and trying to figure out where she was.

Turning to look back, Nora saw that the agent she had controlled was still standing in the same position she had left him in— his gun still pointing at his fellow soldiers. Relieved that her actions had been successful, she then looked out to the green field to see if she could locate Cady.

Their plan had worked—Cady had been able to distract the other agents, and she now made her way towards the narrow opening that remained in the wall. The rest of the rebels sat, anxiously watching her. Run, Nora thought, Run! Cady only had a few yards left to travel before reaching the rest of the rebels. The smile on her face grew bigger with each step towards freedom. The agents pursued her from behind at their full speed, but were unable to keep up with her pace.

Without warning, Cady stopped dead in her tracks. The smile she had faded from her face, and a blank stare took over.

"Why did she stop?" Nora screamed.

Phoenix was the next to yell out, "Why are you stopping?! We are almost out of here, keep running!"

But Cady didn't move. She looked like a stone statue of her former self, and simply stood in place, staring at the rebels. The agents behind her caught up, but to everyone's surprise, they just stopped and lined up behind her. Nora turned and looked at Bray, her eyebrows furrowed in confusion.

"What is she doing?" she whispered to him. "Why won't she come to us?"

Bray shook his head, not knowing what to say.

"This is not the end for us, Eleanor!" Cady called out. Her voice was much louder than Nora had ever heard it before, and had a distinctly different speech pattern. "Be thankful for your escape this time. Know that because of you, we have been able to progress to an entirely new stage in our ongoing effort to eradicate this world of the

Defected. You can rest assured that when we meet again—and we will meet again—that day will be your last."

After uttering the threat, Cady fell to the ground. The agents swarmed on top of her small body. As Nora watched the agents restrain Cady's wrists and begin to drag her body off, Nora shut her eyes, deciding in a panic that she had to reach out to her. Just as she began to drift off Bray shook her.

"No," he commanded.

"We have to help her!" Nora protested. "Let me go!"

She continued to squirm and pull against him, trying to escape the tight grasp he had over her. Her lips curled and her teeth were slightly barred. Nora closed her eyes and focused again on reaching Cady. Despite Bray's intervening, she was able to make it into the shadow world and over to where Cady was in the field. She saw Cady's mousy red shadow, all alone in the expanse of gray landscape. The agents' shadows no longer appeared to Nora. Helplessly, she watched as Cady's red shadow slowly faded from the gray world. Nora shook her head and opened her eyes back in reality, just in time to see one of the agents placing a small, blue, shining light device inside of Cady's ear. Not knowing what else to do at that point, Nora called out to her, pleading for her to get up and run.

It was too late, and Bray knew it. All he could do now was drag Nora through the dirt with him as tears ran down her cheeks. He watched as the wall in front of them closed shut completely. Then, Nora fell limply to the ground.

CHAPTER 25

As she sat with her back against the wall and her knees pulled in to her chest, Nora looked up to see that the sun had begun to rise behind the gray, dust-covered sky of Arrant. The sight brought a little peace to Nora's aching heart, and the thick wall that separated her from the center of Constance brought comfort to her weary mind. She felt the desire to exact revenge on Dr. Secora and bring about justice in every last cell of her body.

Nora had told Otto and Bray how she had seen one of the agents place a small, blue, lighted device inside Cady's ear. She'd explained that once the device was in place, Nora could no longer see Cady's shadow in the gray world. The group had then contemplated what the device might be, and how it might work, as they walked away from the wall and further into Arrant. They felt safer with every step they took away from the evil that dwelled inside of Obsidia.

They had kept the wall to their left as they moved along, and finally stumbled upon a cluster of buildings that hid them from view. The buildings and the wall were situated closely to each other—there was only a few feet of space between them. They'd decided it was a good place to stop and rest.

Nora felt the cold bricks of the wall press against her back as she relaxed. She could hear the group's conversation about the device, but didn't participate. Visions of Cady came back to her in short, painful bursts, and she found it difficult to concentrate on anything else.

She figured that the test results from her time with Dr. Willow and Dr. Edmonds had given Dr. Secora enough data to combat Nora's newfound ability.

The small devices—which seemed to render people's shadows invisible to Nora—couldn't have been the only thing Dr. Secora gained from her numerous lab tests. She knew that he must have figured out a way to enter the minds of others, thereby using the gray world to his own advantage.

Dr. Secora had been able to block Nora out of the agents' subconsciousness, and she was certain those lighted blue devices had something to do with it. The rebels would have to get their hands on one of them somehow, so they could inspect it and try to make some sense of things.

As Nora tallied up all the deaths that she had been responsible for over the past few weeks, she wondered if the world wouldn't be a better place without her around. The weight of death rested on her shoulders and she felt a sudden burst of melancholy. Nora contemplated reaching back into her subconsciousness and ending her life, at a point in the past, to prevent any of this from even happening. She could find a warm, familiar memory of spending time with her family, so that her last few hours would be comforting. Then when the time came, she could excuse herself from the room, or wherever they were, and perform her execution.

As if he could sense what she was thinking, Bray came over and sat down next to her.

"Whatever it is you are contemplating in that pretty head of yours, don't even think about it," he said quietly, as he brushed the hair from her face and tucked the loose strands behind her ear.

With her shoulders slumped and her head hanging, Nora turned to look at him as a tear fell from her eye. "It could be for the better. All of this could just go away for the rest of you." She paused and placed her hand on Bray's cheek. "I could go back and change a single point in my life line. Just one alteration and I wouldn't be here messing things up for everyone."

Bray collected his thoughts for a moment before he spoke again. "If you, for one second, believe that any of this could possibly be better without you here, with us right now, then you must not have heard how this story turns out," he said.

This seemed to get Nora's attention, and she straightening her back, and leaned in closer to him.

"In the end, the world becomes a better, safer, happier place for us all." Bray placed his palms together and then fanned them open, pretending as though he was reading a book. "All of it was possible thanks to one brave girl. For if it wasn't for her," he added in a theatrical voice, "The rest of the world would have continued on as normal. Lives would have been lived in total oppression, never having questioned what was real and what wasn't. Never having imagined the true path life laid out before them. Thankfully, however, this brave girl showed the world just how free they all could be." He smiled and winked at Nora.

Seeing that she wasn't quite convinced yet, Bray mimed himself turning a page in his invisible book again. "The beautiful brave girl thanked everyone around her for pushing her to reach her full potential," he went on. "There was one boy in particular that she felt the most thankful towards, and this boy... well this boy was too selfish to let her leave his world, because he had learned how much better his world had become with her in it." Bray leaned in closer to Nora and then whispered, "The end," before he planted a playful kiss on her lips.

"I think your book needs a little work on the ending," Nora said in return. She playfully nudged him away. "The beautiful brave girl would never just stick around for the ending because of the love she had for a boy."

Just then Otto came up to the two of them. "As much as I really want to see how the rest of this love story plays out, we need to figure out what to do now," Otto said, a teasing smile on his face. Bray and Nora separated and straightened their postures, turning their full attention to Otto. "I think we should put our options to a vote."

The rest of the rebels had gathered around the three of them at that point. They all nodded in agreement with Otto's suggestion.

Trim was the first to speak up. "I vote for whatever you think is the right play here Otto. You haven't steered us wrong yet, and I don't anticipate you doing so anytime soon."

Otto gave a halfhearted laugh, "Yes, that may be so, but the real fight has yet to begin. I believe we have two options." He paused to scan the eyes of the rebels looking back at him. "Option one," he continued, "We could high tail it back to Blear, lay low for a while and wait for Dr. Secora to bring the fight to us."

Seeing several of the rebels wince in reaction to this idea Otto surmised that the majority of them were against it. "Or option two, we continue right here where we left off—head further into Arrant and quickly make our way over to Fallow, where we'll meet up with the other rebellion, and deliver our prized soldier, Nora, to Lace." He hesitated and glanced around again until his eyes landed on Nora. "So, Nora, what will it be? Run and hide and try to wait it out, or are you ready to see if you were meant to save this crumbling world?"

The rest of the rebels cheered and waited for Nora's response. She looked around at everyone's hopeful faces. Nora raised her hand to silence them so she could speak. She took in a deep breath. "Let's go meet with Lace in Fallow and then bring this fight right to Dr. Secora's front door step!"

Everyone clapped and cheered in response to her declaration. After a few minutes of celebration, Otto settled them down. Nora bit down on her lip to suppress the smile that had started to form, not wanting to seem too prideful.

"All right, towards Fallow it is," Otto declared. "There is no time to waste. Everyone do a bag check. Phoenix and Bretta, hopefully between the two of you, you packed enough clothes to lend Nora. We will need both Arrant and Fallow apparel. The rest of you get changed quickly—we head out in ten minutes."

CHAPTER 26

Phoenix and Bretta brought their bags over to where Nora was sitting. She stood up to join them and the three of them quickly ducked behind a wall, and then made their way into an alley, around the corner from where the boys were busy changing into their own Arrant clothing.

"I think it's important to maintain some mystery, and leave some things to their imaginations," Phoenix said as she gestured in the direction of the boys. They were all now safely hidden from view, and began to remove clothing from their bags. After rummaging through the clothes they had brought for Arrant, Bretta and Phoenix tossed several items over to Nora.

Finally the three of them agreed that they'd be able to put three outfits together from the contents of the two bags. Phoenix noticed Nora wrinkle her brow at the selection.

"Don't worry," Phoenix reassured her, "I know none of these would be your first choice to wear in public, but I'm pretty sure it'll beat walking around naked for the rest of the day."

Nora let out a light chuckle and smiled at her. "Hey now, don't you know that you are talking to a brand new girl? And besides, anything would beat that flimsy white gown they had me wearing at the lab—I was totally exposed the whole time!"

Bretta closed her eyes and let out a heavy sigh, as she pulled her sweater tighter around herself, covering up the exposed skin of her chest. Next to her, Phoenix clenched her jaw and squared her shoulders—they were both wondering how they would have reacted in Nora's vulnerable situation.

"Don't worry," Nora continued, "I didn't want to make a habit of walking around those brightly lit hallways, showing off my backside to everyone in the building. So I improvised and wore the gown backwards."

"No, you're right," Phoenix said, a hint of a smile on her lips. "You would NEVER want to expose your backside to an entire building full of people." She paused and a huge smile grew on her face. "Just to Bray!"

Nora threw one of the extra shirts at Phoenix playfully, but Phoenix dodged it. "You shut your mouth right now. I've seen the way you prance around here in front of Otto." Nora smiled and began to imitate Phoenix. "Oh no Otto! I dropped my knife on the ground again." Nora bent over suggestively in front of the two girls.

"Hey! I have never dropped my knife on purpose in front of him!" Phoenix yelled out. She had a serious expression on her face, but there was a hint of laughter in her voice.

Bretta glanced up from tying the laces on her shoes and chimed in. "What's wrong with that? I've pretended to drop something plenty of times—Trim likes it."

The three of them shared a hearty laugh. It felt nice for Nora to have a normal, goofy, non-important conversation for a change. By the time their giggling had died off they'd finished getting dressed in their Arrant clothing.

Unexpectedly, a voice sounded from around the corner, "Would you girls finish up already, we are all dressed and waiting for you," they heard Trim call out. "Also, we can hear every word you are saying, just so you know. Stop dropping things and get back out here."

The three of them looked at each other, their mouths falling open. Phoenix grabbed onto Bretta's shoulder as she let out an uncontrollable laugh, which only caused Nora to burst out laughing as well. Though the situation was a little embarrassing, it was also very funny. She grabbed one of the bags and walked around the corner, back to where the boys were waiting, bouncing on her toes along with the other now-giddy girls.

Otto hoisted himself off the ground where he had been sitting against the back wall of one of the buildings. He gave the three of them a glassy stare, one of his eyebrows raised, and with his arms folded across his chest. Clearly he was annoyed at how long it took them to get dressed.

Looking over at Trim, Otto elbowed him in the ribs lightly. "Some things will never change," he said, "Even if the fate of the whole world is at hand." The two boys exchanged a smirk. "Let's get going," Otto said.

This time Otto wanted to exercise extra caution, so he commanded all the rebels to stick together. No one would walk through the middle of Arrant this time. Thankfully for them all, they were already on the right side of Main Street and wouldn't have to cross through the center of town to get to Fallow—they could keep the wall at their left side the whole way through, and be shielded from view.

At every building and alleyway corner, the group would slow down and wait for someone to peek around the corner and give the go ahead. Carefully, a couple rebels at a time, they crossed each opening when the path was clear, and made their way to the corner of the large wall where Fallow, Arrant, and the center of Constance all met. Otto decided this would be as good of a point as any to regroup. They all rested, and refueled with food and drink, to prepare themselves for the final push. Their goal was to reach the point in the wall where Otto had blasted an opening through, the last time they were all in Arrant.

As they sat and recuperated from their taxing journey, Bray came over to Nora and offered her some of the food and water from his bag. Together they sat and ate in silence, saving their energy for whatever was to come next for them. Nora was thankful for the period of silence to rest her mind. It felt good to not have to focus on anything other than very basic human functions—eating, drinking, and breathing.

After a good amount of time had passed, Otto stood up, and signaled to the others that it was time to start moving again. When Nora looked up, however, she noticed something that she hadn't seen before. If she tilted her head just right, she could see through one of the windows in the back of the building, all the way through the interior, and out another window onto the front entrance's street. Nora stood up and walked closer to the window for a better view.

She gasped when she saw that a small group of agents were gathered on the other side of the building. Nora motioned for Bray to come over and take a look with her.

Seeing what was happening, Bray whispered to Nora. "Why do you think they are meeting here in Arrant?"

Nora didn't have an answer, "Whatever the reason is, we need to find a way to hear what they are saying. This might be our chance to get a step ahead and find out about any of Dr. Secora's new plans."

Bray motioned for Nora to quietly walk around the side of the building. Nora followed his lead, and the two of them pressed against the wall a small distance around the corner from where the agents were talking. Nora leaned her head in—she was close enough to hear that the commanding agent was speaking to the entire group.

Nora strained to hear his words, but everything was muffled. She looked back at Bray and shook her head. Bray only shrugged his shoulders in response.

Relaxing and closing her eyes, Nora reached out with her mind into the street around the corner from where they stood. She could see all of the agents standing there—all fuzzy, white shadows of people. The only one that Nora couldn't see in her gray world was the commanding agent. Nora allowed her mind to bounce from one white shadow to the next, listening to the commanding agent's words from inside the gathered agents' minds. Her mind crept closer and closer to the talking agent with ease until she found her consciousness landing inside of someone she hadn't thought about since being locked inside of her white cell.

At the front of the small group of agents, Deryn listened intently at what the commanding agent said to him. Nora hesitated, not quite sure if she should delve deeper into his mind or not—it felt like more of an intrusion than it usually did when she entered the thoughts of the other agents. Finally, she took a deep breath and went for it. Her view point shifted and suddenly she was looking directly at the commanding agent. Although she could clearly hear what he was saying now, she was overwhelmed with the rush of emotions within Deryn that she could now acutely feel. She floated for a while on the surface of his intense emotions, not able to will herself to delve in any deeper—it was painfully obvious that he was still consumed with love for her. The entire time the commanding agent spoke, Deryn thought about Nora non-stop. She felt a wave of guilt rush over her, as she remembered that in the past few weeks she had all but forgotten the man she had once loved so much.

Being this close to him—inside his thoughts no less—made Nora miss him that much more. During her time within the confines of his mind she felt her love for him returning with every breath he took. Nora tried her best to focus on her mission, and to ignore the distracting emotions.

"...effective immediately, all agents will be required to wear one of these Neural Feedback Inhibitors. Simply place the NFIs inside of your ear and wrap the small antenna around the back, just as mine is positioned now." The commanding agent turned his face towards the small crowd to exhibit the placement of the small, blue device.

"Please know that every effort is continually being made to keep us all safe from the rebels, and the great Dr. Secora has truly blessed us all with this new piece of technology. Allow yourselves to wear it with pride." The commanding agent ordered the rest of the agents to line up so that he could pass out the NFIs to each one of them.

Nora knew it was a bad idea to stay much longer inside of Deryn's mind, but she couldn't resist herself. As he waited in line to obtain his own NFI, she began to trace through his memories of her. At first she scrolled through the moments of their life together at rapid speed—entire weekends flew past her vision in mere seconds—but when she reached a particular period of time she began to slow things down. Once she located the exact evening she was looking for, she allowed the memory to play out in real time. It was the night the two of them had moved into their own home and had shared a romantic dinner together inside of their small house. Nora let her mind relax and watched the scene unfold before her eyes as the two of them laughed wholeheartedly, seeming to fill the entire room with a loving glow.

The table was spotlessly clean and gleamed in the glow of the small flame emitted by a single, white, tapered candle. An array of delectable dishes were spread out, and Deryn sat in the wooden chair across from her, his hands folded in his lap.

Nora felt a pang of longing for the dusty home she once called her own, and the simple, wholesome love she had shared with Deryn. She couldn't bear to leave the memory within his head as it had played out in reality—instead she decided to change it. Focusing in on the scene, she entered into her past self's consciousness. She directed herself to stand up from the table and walk over to where Deryn sat, at which point she kissed him passionately.

Reliving the memory, and editing it to include that kiss, brought a rush of feelings back to Nora, and she almost wished she could just stay in that dining room with him, eating a grand feast of seared meats and potatoes au gratin, for the rest of her life. Instead, she directed her former self back to her own seat, and then drifted out of her past consciousness and back into the tense reality of spying on the Agency.

Once Deryn had collected his Neural Feedback Inhibitor, Nora took control over his movements and walked him to the corner of the building, near where she currently stood. She had him kneel down and place the ear device on the ground, and then had him turn around and rejoin the agents. Once he was safely back with the group of unsuspecting agents, she removed herself from his consciousness and returned to her own. She dashed over to the spot she'd had him leave the NFI, grabbed it, and then went around the back of the building to meet up with the rebels.

Feeling flustered, and with her heart still racing, Nora instinctively lifted a hand up to touch her necklace, finding a strange comfort in its small, metal bends, as she always did. Turning the corner, she saw some of the rebels watching the agents through the dirty windows of the building. Bray looked up at Nora, sensing something was wrong.

"Did you hear anything?" he asked her.

Nora shook her head, her eyes dull and expressionless, and stared down at the small device in the palm of her hand.

"Not much. Only that every agent out there has been given one of these…" she paused, trying to remember the device's technical name. "Neural Feedback Inhibitors. I'm afraid now that the advantage I could have given all of you in this war is quickly fading away. When the agents put these devices in, I am no longer able to see into their minds," she exhaled sharply, and the disappointment in her voice was obvious.

"Don't worry about it," Bray said, as he moved closer and put his arm around her to offer solace. "We will find a way to finish all of this soon enough." He then leaned in for a kiss, but Nora turned her head away, and pushed him off gently. The feeling of Deryn's lips still lingered in her, and she wanted to hold onto it for just a little bit longer.

"Ready to move out now?" she asked Otto, ignoring Bray's inquisitive look.

"You've got it. You heard her, let's go." Otto rallied the rest of the rebels onto their feet, and they continued their journey towards the hole in the wall, albeit now with a noticeably lower level of confidence.

CHAPTER 27

As Nora and the other rebels walked along the wall, her mind began to wander. For the majority of their walk, the only view they had was that of the backs of the numerous tall buildings that lined Main Street. However, each time they dashed across an alleyway, they caught a brief glimpse of the bustling world within the city of Arrant.

Every time this happened Nora tried to take in as much as she could. During one dash she was able to see a family strolling through the town. At the next alleyway crossing she was able to catch sight of a couple young men in work clothes, who were heading towards the factory. At one point Nora even spotted a couple that Deryn and her used to double date with on occasion. The couple was seated at an outdoor cafe and laughing about something.

Each time she passed an alleyway, Nora felt a pang of nostalgia for her previous life. She longed to be out in the open, on the other side of the buildings, with her fellow Arrant citizens. But she reminded herself that they were no longer her fellow citizens. Her new fellow citizens were the very rebels she currently ran alongside of.

The rebels had graciously and quickly accepted Nora as one of their own. She was extremely relieved that she'd been able to find a new home for herself so fast. She was grateful that they had risked their lives in order to protect her. Nora wondered what they saw in her, and why she was so precious to them.

Nora shook her head, not wanting to get lost in her own thoughts. She picked up her pace and ended up keeping stride with Phoenix. Nora bit her lip, and kept moving along wordlessly.

Sensing that Nora could use a distraction, Phoenix struck up a conversation. "How are you doing?" she asked Nora, her eyes filled with compassion. "I know how hard it is to come back here to Arrant for you. All of your old memories must be tough to deal with. I can't say that I'm not nervous about when we get into Fallow myself."

Nora attempted to steer the focus off of herself and onto Phoenix for a change. "I'm okay," she began with an unconvincing smile.

"I'm excited to get back into Fallow—I'm jealous that you got to grow up in such a beautiful place."

"Unfortunately when you grow up there you tend to take it for granted, especially since you had no idea what the other sectors of Constance looked like, so you just imagined the grass was probably greener on the other side. But with my expanded perspective now, I can agree with you. I was lucky—just these Arrant clothes alone are pretty boring!" Phoenix said to Nora jokingly.

Mimicking Phoenix's words, Nora played along. "Well, we took it for granted just how boring our clothes were. Since we never saw any other sector's fashion, we just assumed the grass was more boring on the other side." They both laughed at each other for being so frivolous.

"What's new with you and Otto, since I left and got myself kidnapped?" Nora continued, trying to keep the mood light.

Phoenix smiled at Nora's attempt to initiate girl talk. "Well, the night before we came to rescue you was very intense. A few days before, we had received a message from a man that was inside of Obsidia with you—the bearded man. We didn't know much, just that he was once part of the rebellion, but had been captured and forced to work there. He was communicating with us through one of the Dream Machines inside of the building."

"After he told us you were being held captive, it was decided that we had to take the risk and do all we could to bring you back," Phoenix continued. "The boys planned extensively, until we figured out what had to be done."

"The night before the rescue mission, the whole group of us hung out together—packing up our bags and joking around. When it started to get late people went off to bed, one by one, until eventually it was just Otto and myself left..." Phoenix's voice trailed off.

"And, what?" Nora pressed, "Come on, you can't go that far into a story and end right before the good part!"

"I guess I thought that us planning to rescue you was the good part." Phoenix laughed, purposefully avoiding what Nora was hinting at.

"Well yeah, but I mean, what happened between the two of you?" Nora asked pointedly.

Phoenix pursed her lips. "We kissed. A lot," she said matter of factly. Nora laughed, and Phoenix smiled back at her. The two continued on walking, and Nora tenderly put her arm around Phoenix's shoulder.

"My little Phoenix is becoming a woman," Nora teased.

"It will be nice to have him with me when we go back into Fallow. I haven't been back there since the day the Agency took me away." Phoenix sighed. "Maybe I'll just take a page from your book, and if I get to feeling overwhelmed I'll stop everything I'm doing and kiss him."

"And if that doesn't work, I'll drop my knife so that you can bend over and pick it up in front of him again!" Nora quipped.

They both laughed hard, and it felt good to distract themselves from the reality of their situation. As they passed around the last corner, Nora glanced a few yards off and realized they'd made it to the hole in the wall.

Otto was already there, kneeling down by the wall and scanning the area around them. When Nora made her presence known, he asked if she could scan the area in her own special, mental way as well. Nora knew what the results would be, but humored his request anyway. Once she had entered into the gray, outlined world, there was nothing to be seen, just as she had expected. Not a single white flicker of an agent in sight. She saw the shadows of a few random citizens strewn out through the streets of the sector, but no sign of the Agency.

Pressing on the bricks, one by one, Otto felt around until he located the block that he'd blown free before—it was loose and pressed in easily. He forced it all the way through the wall, until it fell on the ground inside of Fallow. Bray crouched down next to Otto and the two of them pushed and kicked at the remaining blocks that surrounded the hole, while Jack used his knife to scratch away the material squished between the blocks, so they'd be easier to break off.

Trim and Bretta stood back from the rest of the rebel group, each standing guard at a spot where the opening of an alleyway was situated. They watched the pathway intently, and at one point Bretta motioned over to Trim. She made a series of hand gestures at him, to which Trim nodded. Trim then went over to Otto.

"Two agents approaching from the west street," Trim reported back to Otto. Trim kept his eye on Bretta, who continued to signal him with hand cues. "Walking slowly," he continued, deciphering her gesticulations. "I don't think they are aware of us—not yet anyways."

Grunting as he kicked out another brick, Otto struggled to reply through his clenched teeth. "Let me know if any of that changes. Keep your sights on them," he instructed, without taking his eyes off the wall.

Finally the last block began to loosen. Bray shoved his shoulder against it with all his weight, his feet planted firmly on the ground. With a dull thud, the remaining brick tumbled onto the heap of all the previous blocks that lay in the dirt on the other side of the wall.

Otto turned in the direction of Trim and Bretta, "We have a big enough gap for all of us," he called out. "Let's go. Trim and Bretta, you two come through last. Hold up the rear and keep your eyes glued to those agents."

Climbing through first, Bray reached his arm back into the opening to give Otto a hand. Jack was the next one through after him.

"We've been made!" Trim yelled suddenly. "Here they come!"

"Everyone into the tunnel!" Otto ordered. "Phoenix, Nora, move!"

Phoenix and Nora leapt into action and ran over to the wall. They both passed through the gap easily because of their smaller frames. Bretta entered afterwards, and close behind her was Trim. Being on the larger side, Trim's shoulders ended up getting wedged in the opening. Otto ran over to help him through, and began pulling on Trim's body, grabbing under his arms. As Bray joined in the effort, the sound of the oncoming agents' footsteps became audible amidst their grunts as they struggled to free Trim.

"Suck it in Trim!" Otto exclaimed. "Or we're going to end up ripping your arms off."

Finally, they were able to free Trim, and he tumbled onto the dirt. Bray and Otto fell back as well, but quickly leapt up and began replacing the bricks into the hole in the wall as quickly as they could. Just as Otto was lifting the last brick, Nora caught sight of two agents closing in on them from the other side. Otto pushed the brick back into place just in time, right as one of the agents had reached the opening and was bending down to peer through.

Both Bray and Otto were out of breath from the physical exertion, but they didn't have any time to recuperate—the large brick was being pushed out by the agent on the other side. Bray and Otto positioned their large bodies against the moveable blocks, trying to hold them in place while the agents on the other side continued to try and shove their way through.

"Run into the fields behind you!" Otto commanded the rebels who stood before him. "Bray, keep them safe, I won't be able to hold this thing together much longer."

The rebels ran off into the tall golden fields. The crops reached high above their heads, so they quickly disappeared from sight. Once Otto watched the last rebel vanish into the fields, he stood up and then lunged off the wall. The brick he'd been pressing back against immediately tumbled off onto the ground. Otto began to run at full speed, heading toward the crops.

As he dove into the safety of the thick wheat stalks, one of the agents popped his head through the gap. The agent turned his neck from side to side, searching for his target. It was inevitable that within minutes, more agents would be arriving as well. Otto took a deep breath to calm his nerves, then turned and made his way further into the dark, dense field of crops to join up with the rebels hidden within.

CHAPTER 28

Nobody spoke as the rebels sat in the golden field. The crops stretched up into the cloud-speckled blue sky above them. The only audible sound was the soft rustling of the wheat stalks as they gently swayed in the wind.

Once they'd all caught their breath, and their nerves had settled down from the recent excitement, they all began to change into their next disguise. Nora helped Bretta and Phoenix comb through their remaining clothing so that they could assemble Nora's Fallow outfit.

Sitting on a pile of broken stalks, Otto addressed the group, "I have no doubt that those agents have already sent word ahead to the Agency inside of Fallow. They will definitely be looking for us now."

The rebels murmured in agreement with Otto's statement. "As you all know, there has always been talk of a second rebel alliance base located here in Fallow. The only real problem is that none of us know for sure where it is, and of course it might not even exist at all." Nora detected a note of pessimism in Otto's voice as it trailed off.

"All we have to go on is a single name—Lace—but we don't know who she is. So the fact of the matter is that there is only a possibility that the rebellion is still strong here."

Nora had information she eagerly wanted to share with the group, but she patiently waited for Otto to finish.

"Phoenix, how much do you remember of Fallow?" He shifted his gaze in her direction. "Did you ever hear of another rebel group here when you were younger?"

Phoenix stretched out her legs and looked at the ground as she considered the question. "No. But I was so young when I lived here. Stuff like that probably just didn't reach a kid's ears," she said and shrugged.

"How about any old connections, like friends and family," Otto prodded her. "Is there anyone here that you would trust enough to contact again?"

"I haven't been back here in so long that I'm not sure any of my old friends would believe their eyes if they saw me." Phoenix sighed.

"And honestly," she continued, "I can't bear to put myself through the pain of having to lose them all over again."

"How about..." Otto hesitated. "Any family?" Otto could tell that Phoenix had purposely ignored this part of his previous question, but their dire circumstances did not afford them the luxury of skirting painful issues.

Phoenix shook her head. "Look, I'm sure you can all understand that I'm not in a big hurry to dive back into a world that I have spent the last few years trying to forget. When you guys took me in I let go of the hope of ever returning to my old life." She looked up from the ground and over to Otto. "You all are my family now."

Wiping his dirt-encrusted hands on his pants, Otto smiled. "I definitely can't argue with that," he said. "So does anyone have any ideas?"

Nora took a breath as she tried to word how she would share her news with the group. "Well," she began, "While we have been sitting here, resting, I reached out into Fallow with my mind." Suddenly everyone around her leaned in towards her intently. The sudden pressure of their collective attention made her stumble over her words.

"So far all I—all I've been able to see is a few white shadows—"

"Shades," Bretta interrupted. "Sorry, we have been calling the ones you see as white shadows Shades. I thought it would be easier for us all to have a common name for them. Please continue."

"Okay," Nora said agreeably. "These... Shades, seem to be the everyday citizens of Fallow, simply going on with their daily lives."

She took a moment to glance around the group, to make sure the rest of the rebels were following her. They all continued to stare at her. "There are a few red shadows..." Nora paused to see if Bretta would jump in again with a name for the red shadows, but she didn't so Nora went on. "I've simply been calling them the Defected. This is the term Dr. Secora and the rest of the center of Constance uses to refer to us anyway. I was able to see that there are only a few Defected currently here in Fallow."

Otto dropped his gaze to the ground, and opened his mouth to reply, but decided to wait and see if she had anything else to share with them.

"The thing that I've been trying to wrap my head around is that we know the agents are wearing their NFIs now, right? That would account for the lack of Shades here in Fallow. But what I don't get is why am I not seeing more of the Defected around us. It's as if they've evacuated or something."

Otto tried to grasp the point she was trying to make. "I think what you are confused about, is that if the other rebellion is indeed here in Fallow, you should be seeing a lot more of the Defected inside that gray world of yours right now."

Nora bit down on the inside of her cheek as she waited for someone else to chime in. She hoped one of the others could bring meaning to it all.

Bray was the first to speak up. "If Nora is right, then what she is telling us could mean only two things. One, the rebellion has ended here, and we are the last ones surviving. That would mean that the responsibility for the entire battle falls directly onto our shoulders." This statement visibly upset the entire group. He continued, "The second possibility is that maybe the other rebellion was able to technologically advance for security reasons. They may have found a way to hide themselves from Dr. Secora and the Agency."

Otto stood up. "Let's hope we aren't the last of the rebellion. We have asked a lot of good questions today, unfortunately none of us have the answers yet. I think our best chance is to discreetly survey what's going on around Fallow. If, by the end of the day, we still don't have any answers, we will abandon the plan and head back to Blear to regroup."

Phoenix pointed over Nora's shoulder. "From what I can remember, if we continue to head straight east, away from the wall, the fields will eventually end on the outskirts of the main processing plant. I'd estimate it's about a mile or two away from where we are."

The rest of the rebels stood up, including Nora. Otto faced all of them. "Sounds good, let's move out. Once we get near the processing plant, we will lay low near the edge of the crops and survey our surroundings."

The rebels began to head out. Nora quickly realized how difficult it was to walk through the tall crops. Each long stride she took had to be carefully calculated, and her muscles twitched from the exertion. As she made her way through she had to part the tall golden stems, and bend many of them back in order to allow for her passage.

Noticing a far-off look in Phoenix's eyes, Nora decided to ask her some questions about her young life in Fallow. "Did you ever walk through these fields when you were a kid? You don't seem to be having nearly as much trouble as I am!"

"Yes. All the time. We would always play this one game in particular. One of us would wait on the outskirts of the field, while the rest took off running into it. Everyone then found a hiding spot and waited, and the person who'd stayed on the outskirts would enter the field and try to find everyone," Phoenix gave a half smile as she recalled the memory.

Struck with a bolt of inspiration, Nora grabbed Phoenix's arm and pulled her towards the right, away from the line of forward-moving rebels.

"Let's play a little trick on the boys," Nora said as she pulled Phoenix deeper into the field, away from the rebel group.

Going forward with her antics, Nora could tell that Phoenix was welcoming the distraction, just by how willingly she was playing along. "Okay. I think we are far enough to the side of them now. Let's hurry up and get a ways out in front of them." Nora smiled towards Phoenix.

The two of them raced forward, trying to make the smallest amount of sound as possible. When they were sure they had gone far enough ahead of where Bray and Otto were leading the group, Phoenix grabbed Nora, and pulled her towards the ground.

"All right," Phoenix whispered to Nora, "Crouch down and we will wait until they get close. Then we will scare the life out of them!"

Hearing the glee in her voice, Nora couldn't help but latch onto her giddiness. It was like being next to the childhood version of the girl she had come to know over the last few weeks. Nora was swept up in the mischievous excitement.

As the two of them waited, Nora heard a soft, rustling noise coming from behind them. Her ears strained to focus on the source of the new sound.

"Shhh. Wait," Nora whispered to Phoenix. "I can hear something behind us. I saw a small animal in the fields the last time I was here, let's hope that's all it is."

Crawling very low to the ground, Nora went up ahead to survey the situation, and cleared an opening with her hands in the the crops so that she could peer through. As soon as she narrowed her eyes she saw a pair of tall, black boots walking a few feet ahead of her. Nora swallowed hard, knowing exactly who would be dressed in that style of footwear.

Scrambling back to where Phoenix was waiting—who was still hoping for a chance to scare the approaching boys—Nora pulled her back down onto the ground.

"Phoenix, there are agents in the field with us!" Nora hissed. "We have to find a way to warn the others."

Phoenix's expression immediately went from mischievous to serious, and the two began to make their way back to the others. They started a steady crawl back to the wall. As Nora saw a pair of familiar feet pass by, she reached out and grabbed onto the ankle of the shoe's owner. The person who had been walking stumbled and fell onto the ground—it was Bray. Nora leapt on top of him and put her hand over his mouth so that he couldn't speak. His eyes stared back at her in shock.

Phoenix, meanwhile, had done the same when she caught sight of Otto, and she motioned for the rest of the rebels to get low to the ground as well. Otto looked at her with as much confusion as Bray looked at Nora with.

"Agents," Nora whispered to the group. "A few yards to our right, walking into the field from the east."

"What do we do?" Phoenix asked Otto. His only response was to shake his head and shrug his shoulders.

Bretta joined in the conversation. "Let's wait it out. Let the agents go past us, back towards the wall, then we will make a break for it."

Otto knew it was a dangerous option, but huddling on the floor of the field waiting for one of those agents to stumble over them seemed like an even worse idea. He motioned for the group to stay low and follow his lead.

Slowly they all moved forward and curved to the left, in an attempt to create a little distance from the patrolling agents. The only way the rebels could tell how far they were from them was the sound of the agents' shoes crunching the crops below them.

Holding up his arm, Otto signaled the rebels to stop. "All right. When I give the signal, everyone fan out. Phoenix, Trim, and Bretta with me. Bray and Nora, you go with Jack and slide out toward the left, turn back towards the processing plant after you have made it about ten yards away. We will be doing the same, only towards the right. Let's meet at the clearing before the processing plant. If you three get there first, find cover and wait for us."

They all nodded. Nora felt her heart start to race. She took in deep breaths knowing she would have to run as hard as she could any second now.

As Otto dropped his arm the rebels split into two. Otto and his group went to the right and Nora, Bray, and Jack to the left.

The high stems of the crops whipped Nora's face and body as she ran. A sting occurred every time one of the plants swung back at her. She held her hands out in front of her to try and stop the onslaught, but it was useless.

One of the agents yelled out, and Nora could distinctly hear what was said. "Over there! Movement in the field!" She pushed herself to run faster as a gun shot went off behind her. It sounded like the gun had been shot straight up into the air.

Trying her best to not feel like a wild animal being hunted down, Nora kept her focus on Bray's shoulders, who ran in front of her. Jack brought up the rear of the small group, and continued to push her along from behind. She figured that they must have made it far enough to the left when she saw Bray turn and start running straight forward.

The agents continued yelling and Nora knew that they must be on the tail of one of the rebel groups. Nora followed close enough to Bray that she could touch him if she extended her arms out. She hoped that Otto and his group were able to get away. Together the three of them ran in sync, almost as if they were one single unit, as fast as they could.

"We are almost there," Nora heard Bray call out from in front of her. "I can see where the field clears up ahead. Hopefully the plant isn't too far after that. We can't afford to be out in the open for too long."

Nora didn't respond, too focused on keeping up the fast pace. More gun shots rang out, this time they sounded like they were directly in front of her. Suddenly a burst of shots resonated into the field. There were too many for her to count. So many shots were fired, that it became difficult to pin point what direction they were coming from— they seemed to be coming from all around her.

After a few more yards, Nora noticed that she could no longer hear the agents yelling and that the gun shots had stopped. As her mind scrambled to figure out why everything had suddenly become silent, Nora collided into Bray, who had stopped dead in his tracks. Jack smashed into the back of her soon after.

Regaining her balance, Nora peered through the edge of the field. She could see the small processing plant directly in front of them, only a short distance away. Nora scanned the area, and to the right she saw what had caused Bray to stop so abruptly.

Ahead of where the field ended and the brown dirt road resumed, in the space between the three of them and the processing plant, Nora saw Otto and the rest of the rebels laying face down in the dirt. A small group of men stood over them, pointing rifles at their heads. They were all yelling commands at the captured rebels, but Nora couldn't decipher what was being said.

Moving forward, Bray pulled Nora with him. Emerging from the field into the clearing, Nora stood up to run, but in that same moment she felt a sharp sting in the back of her head. The whole world around her turned black. The last thing she remembered was feeling the hand that Bray had been pulling her with let go of her body, and the lingering warmth of his touch fading away.

CHAPTER 29

Nora awoke with a start, and sat up gasping for air. The room around her was very dark, and she could not see much. Her head throbbed and she lifted a hand to touch the back of her skull. She discovered that there was a strip of cloth wrapped around her forehead. As she pressed her fingers into the painful spot, the cloth quickly became saturated with warm blood that gushed out of her wound. She brought her hand around to inspect the bright red residue.

It felt like deja vu, waking up for the second time in a strange room, having no idea what had happened to her. Remembering the last time she'd been in that situation, she felt for her necklace, and breathed a sigh of relief when she found that it was still securely clasped around her neck. A feeling of comfort washed over her.

As her eyes adjusted to her surroundings, Nora realized that she was laying on a cot. She swung her legs over the side of it. The air in the room hung around her—it was cold and damp. The walls were irregularly shaped, and brown. When she squinted she realized they were made of packed dirt. Multi-colored wires ran across the ceiling and connected to a few small lights which hung down from a dirt ceiling. Looking around herself, she saw a few more cots in the room, but they were all empty and had no linens covering them.

Suddenly a door behind her swung open. A metallic clank sounded loudly in the room as it closed shut again. Nora turned her head slowly towards the sound, dreading to see what lay in store for her. She saw that it was a woman who had entered the room. As the woman approached, Nora scooted towards the back of her cot.

"I'm glad to see you are finally awake," the woman said to Nora. To Nora's surprise, her voice was soft and welcoming.

The woman made her way to the other side of Nora's cot. She had dirty blonde hair that was well kept, and which loosely fell around her face. The large curls bounced as she sat down across from Nora. Her entire outfit was black, with the exception of a red tank top which peeked out from beneath a fitted jacket. All of her clothes were very form fitting, and her shoes reminded Nora of the kind Phoenix liked to wear. The jacket's high collar framed her slim face and pointed chin. Intimidated by the woman's beauty, Nora fidgeted with her hands. She reached up and felt the cloth bandage around her head again.

"Where am I?" Nora asked, her voice sounding somewhat dazed.

"First off, please know that you are safe here. In fact, safety is our number one priority," the woman replied, with the same warm tone.

"Where is Bray?" Nora blurted out without thinking.

The woman smiled knowingly in response. "All of your friends are safe here too. They are waiting for you in the cafeteria."

"Cafeteria?" Nora was struggling to put everything together.

"Don't worry Nora, in time all of your questions will be answered."

Nora immediately realized that the woman hadn't called her by her birth name—Eleanor. Another wave of relief came over her, and was evident in her body language.

Still smiling at Nora, the woman dropped her gaze to the floor before she continued. "First off, on behalf of myself and Tusk, the man who..." the woman paused and pointed to Nora's bandaged head. "The man who did that to you. We would like to apologize. You all had rushed out of those fields so suddenly, and what with the agents roaming around simultaneously, it just created pandemonium. Tusk felt absolutely horrible for hitting you with the end of his rifle."

It was clear to Nora that the woman was telling the truth. "So what happens now? Are you going to tell me where I am? And who you are?"

"I will show you where you are, through that door. As for who I am," the woman paused. "I have to say, I'm surprised you haven't figured that out yet. It didn't take the others very long to put it together." She grinned at Nora, still waiting for a response, as if it were some kind of test.

Nora's hands slowly drifted up to touch her necklace and she swallowed hard. "Are you...?"

The woman locked eyes with Nora. "My name is Lace. I am the leader of the Defected Rebellion, and you are safe with us inside of our underground base. Come with me now, I am sure you are hungry."

Nora got up gingerly, feeling the blood pulse in her wound when she stood up. She followed Lace out into a hallway that was similar in appearance to the room she'd been in—dirt walls, colored-wire cables, and small dim lights. They passed through the room and turned right, continuing down the long dirt path.

After they'd passed through a few more rooms, Nora caught a whiff of food being cooked. Her stomach rumbled and she realized just how hungry she was. She couldn't remember the last time she'd eaten. Silently she prayed that Lace was taking her to the source of the savory aroma.

Lace gave Nora a tour of the underground rebel base. "Over there, to your left, are the sleeping quarters. We have a few larger sized rooms that consist of several beds, and a couple, much smaller areas, which contain single sleeping cots. For now we have given your group one of the larger areas for you girls to share and another large room for two of the boys. Inside each large living area is a private bathroom. Since we have the room to spare for the time being, both the leader of your group and his second-in-command have been given their own private rooms. They seemed quite pleased when I gave them the news."

Lace continued with the tour as they turned another corner. "Behind this door is the electrical room where our entire base is powered by an independent generator. This not only allows us to stay off of Constance's grid, it also enables us to power our facilities after the city's curfew is in place.

Nora tried to take mental notes as they walked, to orient herself with the surroundings, but it was difficult to map the place out in her head since everything looked alike. Finally she gave up and just listened to Lace's tour.

"To your right, up ahead, is our Dream Machine room. I'm sure by now you are familiar with their inner workings. Regardless, after we meet in the cafeteria for some food, I would like for you to accompany me there before I set you loose to roam around on your own."

A weighted breath escaped from Lace's chest before she continued speaking. "Many years ago we were able to acquire a Dream Machine straight from Obsidia. We had a man on the inside who helped us smuggle it out. He installed it for us too." She paused, a thoughtful look in her eyes, "Ryden was a very helpful and brave man." The somber tone in her voice made it clear that whoever this man was, he was no longer with the rebellion, or possibly even dead.

Finally the two of them reached a door at the end of a long, narrow room. When Lace opened it, she revealed an even larger room. Inside were plenty of wooden bench tables, along with a buffet set up on the perimeter. There looked to be over fifty other people in the room, in various stages of eating dinner.

Turning to face Nora, Lace started to give her orders in a very matter-of-fact manner. "I want you to get in that food line and grab all the items you want to eat. After you are done, I'll be seated at that table towards the back," she gestured to one of the tables that already had several people seated at it. "There are a few other people I'd like for you to meet. Please come and join us when you are ready." Nora nodded in response. Lace tenderly took Nora's hand and shook it. "Happy to have you here with us."

With that, Lace walked over to the table she had pointed out, and Nora went over to the beginning of the long buffet. Since most of the people had already begun eating, she was able to leisurely survey her food options. She must have been one of the last rebels looking to feed herself.

The food being served was very similar to the meals she'd had back in Blear. Everything was set out in large metal trays, kept warm by a light above them. Nora grabbed a plate and commenced piling on whatever items caught her eye, or smelled enticing.

After she had stacked her plate high with as much food as it would hold, she began to weave her way through the tables and people to rejoin Lace. Nora noticed Phoenix, Jack, Trim, and Bretta all sitting at a table together out of the corner of her eye. Phoenix looked up from her plate and caught sight of her, and then motioned for Nora to come sit with them. Nora tilted her head in Lace's direction. Phoenix winked and nodded in understanding, then continued to eat her food.

Lace was already joined by Otto and Bray. As Nora put her plate down on the table she couldn't take her eyes off of the boy she had grown to care so deeply for. He smiled at her, and opened his eyes wide in amazement, shaking his head, as though he couldn't make sense of how they had all ended up there. Nora derived a small but distinct pleasure at being able to interpret Bray's facial expressions so easily.

"Welcome Nora," Lace greeted her. "We are all sure you have as many questions for us as we have for you. I'd like to keep this conversation light for now though, we have plenty of time to talk about the more important things later."

Nora felt relieved that she could eat her meal in leisure, rather than during a tense conversation, and started to shovel the warm food into her mouth. Lace began by introducing the others who sat at the table with her. Nora nodded a pleasant greeting to each of them as Lace made her way around the group.

"Starting at my left. Nora, I'd like to introduce you to Tusk. The two of you met briefly out in the fields. I assume that you would both rather forget about that. Tusk is our local mechanic. If anything breaks he is your guy to fix it," Lace said with a laugh.

Tusk was a very large man—Nora guessed he had grown up working in the fields of Fallow by his size. His short, cropped, light brown hair only made his head look larger. She instantly felt intimidated by him. But, she reasoned, that was probably just because he'd recently bashed her in the back of her head.

"Next to him is our resident brainiac, Grane. He has kept the Dream Machine running after all these years of abuse."

It surprised Nora to see such a frail-looking person at the underground base. His skin looked like it hadn't seen the sun in years. His glasses slipped off his nose when he bent forward, which caused him to constantly tilt his head up at an awkward angle in order to eat.

"I'm sure you know the next two gentlemen—Bray and Otto. They've told us great things about you Nora, and what they've shared has made us all very excited to get to know you better. Lastly, seated right beside you is Ailee. She is the one responsible for taking care of any patient concerns. You can thank her later for that beautiful head wrap of yours," Lace said with a teasing smile.

Suddenly remembering her bandage, Nora felt embarrassed to meet so many new people looking the way she did. As she touched the wrap self-consciously, she looked over to Bray for reassurance, instead he gave her a teasing wink.

Ailee was around the same age as Nora and Phoenix, but had the composure of a woman much older than that. She was slim and had light ash brown hair, which was kept pulled back to reveal the delicate bone structure of her face. Her most striking feature, however, was undoubtedly her intensely bright blue eyes. The sharpness of the color contrasted starkly with her otherwise soft and dainty features.

Nora swallowed hard, realizing it had come to the point in the conversation where she would have to speak up. "It is very nice to meet all of you. I look forward to getting to know each and everyone of you on a more personal level."

The composed way she responded to the situation surprised Nora. She didn't know she'd had that in her. Speaking like that made her feel more ladylike, and she felt as though she'd taken another step away from her young, naïve former self. As she went on, she made a concerted effort to maintain her dignified tone as she addressed the group.

"If you all don't mind, I will excuse myself, as I would love to have a second look at all of that food over there. I'm sure you can understand that it has been quite a while since I've had the chance to eat anything this good."

Lace nodded. "Take your time, and catch up with your friends over there. When you are done eating, please meet with Grane and myself back in the Dream Machine room."

After Nora had stood up from the table she bowed to the group. She took a few extra seconds to look at each new face one by one, and flashed a big smile at them before she walked off. Nora had to keep herself from running back to the food line, she was still that famished, and walked as briskly as she could without seeming improper.

After she helped herself to a second plate full of food, Nora turned and headed towards the table where Phoenix was seated. She slid over, making room for Nora to sit down and join her, Jack, Trim, and Bretta.

As Phoenix began to talk, Nora caught sight of Bray and Otto coming over to join them—Lace's dinner table had finished their meal and everyone seated there were heading their separate ways.

"Well aren't we lucky," Phoenix began as Nora shoveled the first bite of food into her mouth. "We get to have the second round of dinner with the Queen of the Underground herself!" The rest of the table broke out in a mocking round of applause.

Attempting to play along with their teasing, Nora raised her hands up and took a seated bow. She could see Bray laughing.

"How's the head, Miss Nora?" Jack asked her as he pointed to her bandage.

"It's fine now. Hurt like crazy when I first woke up though," Nora replied. The throbbing pain was still grueling, and she felt it every time her heart beat, but she wanted to put on a brave face. "I hope I never have to feel anything like that again."

Jack nodded respectfully, as though in approval of her tough attitude.

Just then, Otto addressed the group. "Well, it wasn't very pretty, but somehow we found the Fallow Rebellion. I really didn't think it'd be this easy." Nora had never heard Otto be so playful with regards to a potentially fatal error he'd made. It was nice to see him act that way.

"It sounds like they have been gearing up around here for something big to happen soon. They made it seem like we showed up here just in time. They said that by showing up with Nora, the last piece of the puzzle was finally here, and that we should be prepared to move out with them soon."

"Where are we going?" Nora asked Otto.

160

"From what I gathered, they are planning a massive strike against the center of Constance. Lace told me that they need our small group to join their forces." Otto looked around at all of the rebels at the table. "I didn't want to volunteer for us all, so I told them that I needed time for my team to decide. This mission would be our most dangerous one to date, and participating in it is a decision you all have to make for yourselves."

No one at the table seemed eager to speak up, and they sat in silence for a few moments, contemplating the situation at hand. "Did they tell you why they are striking back against the Agency and Dr. Secora now?" Nora questioned. "I would like to know exactly what their plan is, and I think we should compare notes with them."

"I told them I would talk with all of you first, and then discuss things further with them after that," Otto quickly replied.

All the Blear rebels seemed to agree with Otto. Many separate conversations branched off as the rebels discussed what to do amongst themselves. "There is one more thing," Otto interrupted. "If we agree to join them, a few of us will have to go back into Blear and gather the rest of the rebels we left behind. This all has to happen very quickly, so those going back to Blear will have to take off immediately."

Without missing a beat, Trim spoke up. "I'm in. Let's get back there, grab the rest of our gang and the remainder of our weapons. Then we can finish this mess once and for all. We have been living in the shadows way too long. I don't want to wait another minute to be free from the oppression of Constance. The faster we do this, the faster we get to have peace."

The rebels around the table cheered at Trim's comment. Otto smiled at their enthusiastic reaction, but then hushed them and settled everyone down. "So then, who wants to go back to Blear with Trim and who wants to stay here in Fallow?"

Nora kept her mouth shut. She knew that out of all of them, she had the biggest target on her head—every agent would be looking for her under Dr. Secora's orders. She remained quiet and watched the rest of the table.

Bretta was first to volunteer, which came as no surprise to Nora. "I'm in!" she chirped, in her typically cheerful tone. She looked up at Trim adoringly, and it was obvious there was no way she'd sit around in Fallow waiting for him to return, even if it mean risking her life.

"As am I." Jack announced, adding himself into the fold.

Otto nodded. "That makes four of us—I think five would be enough. So it comes down to the two of you now," he said to Phoenix and Bray. "Which one of you is it going to be?"

The two rebels looked down at their empty plates, as they contemplated the benefits and risks of heading back to Blear. The tense silence at the table was palpable. Finally, Phoenix cleared her throat.

"I'll—" Phoenix started, but was quickly interrupted.

"No. I'll go." Nora felt her heart drop when she heard Bray's voice. "It should be me."

Bray kept his head low, his eyes glued to the plate in front of him. He knew how Nora would feel about him leaving her alone at the rebel base, and knew that if he looked her in the eyes he wouldn't be able to go through with it.

"All right then, it's settled. Trim, Bretta, Jack, Bray and myself will head back to Blear. Phoenix and Nora, you will hold things down here. The Fallow rebels will be expecting your full cooperation while you are here," Otto said briskly. "Everyone else grab your bags, we will move out in twenty minutes."

Everyone seated at the table stood up and left, leaving Bray and Nora alone together for the first time since they arrived at the Fallow rebel base. Nora sighed, her hands folded across her butterfly-filled stomach. Bray reached out for her hand and finally raised his eyes to meet hers.

"It's not that I want to leave you here all alone Nora. I have to. We need to finish this war, and I'm the right person for the job," he said. He was trying to stay strong, but his voice wavered slightly in fear.

"I know," she replied softly. "I'm just not ready to lose you again so soon." Bray winced in response to her words. Nora could see that her attempt to reassure him was failing. She shook her head. "No, I'm fine. And you'll be fine. You'll be back here before we know it. Besides, I won't be completely alone—I'll still have Phoenix."

"I wish it wasn't so risky to bring you along. I hate the thought of being out there without you," Bray confessed.

"With those new devices the agents are wearing, I wouldn't be much use to you out there anyways," Nora sighed.

Taking a long, drawn-out breath, Bray gave her a half-smile. "I know it's in the best interest of the group, but that doesn't mean I have to like it."

"No, it doesn't," she agreed. "We just have to accept it, that's all. Get there fast, and stay with the group. I'm not worried about you guys out there, and you shouldn't worry about me in here." Nora leaned in and kissed Bray tenderly on the cheek.

Bray reached into his pocket and retrieved the small, plastic device containing the data of Program 7 that Nora had taken from the console inside Obsidia's lab.

"I should leave this here with you," Bray said as he handed it to Nora. "Maybe Grane can figure out a good use for this," he suggested.

Her heart sunk as the memories flooded back of Obsidia, Program 7, and the four deaths that now rested heavily on her shoulders. She placed the small object securely in her pocket.

"Let's get out of here," Bray said, standing up and reaching a hand down to help her up too. "You know, I have twenty minutes, and they gave me my own private room," he added, with a mischievous smile.

Nora felt a wave of heat rush over her body. "Oh, trust me, I've already thought about that. Unfortunately I have to meet with Lace and Grane inside the Dream Machine room." She could see the disappointment in Bray's eyes. "But I'll make you a deal. Go back to Blear and do what you need to do, then get back here as fast as possible. Then I promise you, you won't ever get that room alone to yourself again."

Bray laughed and they made their way over to the door.

"You know, you shouldn't make me a promise that you can't keep," Bray teased her.

Nora felt her cheeks grow warm as she laughed in response. "Just get back here in one piece and we can take it from there," she replied.

The two of them left the room holding each other's hands tighter than they ever had before.

CHAPTER 30

Nora opened the door to the Dream Machine room in the underground rebel base and was immediately surprised. She wasn't sure why, but she had expected it to look different than the rest of the place. It had the same dirt walls, the same messy web of colored wires running all over the room, and even the same kind of lamps hanging overhead.

The room was big and domed at the top. Lace and Grane were already there working. They both turned and looked at Nora as she came inside. Next to them were three consoles, just like the run-down ones in Blear, as well as top-of-the-line, brand new, white ones similar to what Nora had seen inside of Obsidia. Located in the middle of the room was another Dream Machine. It was similar to the one inside the center of Constance, but had obviously seen its share of abuse over the years. The padding was ripped in a few places and many spots were held together with tape.

After they all greeted each other, Lace and Grane watched as Nora walked around the room, circling the machine in the center thoughtfully. Her hand glided over the chair as she passed. Inside the test lab of Obsidia the chair had been well manufactured and meticulously maintained, and all of the wiring had been neatly gathered within a single tube. Here, in Fallow, there was no tubing keeping everything contained, so the wires ran in all kinds of directions. There was a thin layer of dirt over everything.

"We've had to keep up our own maintenance on it over the years," Lace said, noticing Nora's attention to the machine's condition. "Grane here has been a blessing to us. He's always managed to keep this machine alive."

Nora smiled at Grane. "They definitely could use your help in Blear. This is leaps above what they are working with over there."

Grane looked up from his console and smiled at the compliment. "I wish we could have procured a Dream Machine for the Blear base as well. We are lucky to even have such a machine down here. Building something like this from scratch would have been nearly impossible."

As the conversation dwindled, Nora thought back to her period of captivity inside of Obsidia. There was an unsettling resemblance between that experience and her current situation—both situations involved her being surrounded by people that wanted nothing more than to experiment with her inside of a Dream Machine. Even though Lace and Grane were on the side of the rebels, Nora still felt the need to protect herself—after all who knew what they might be willing to do for the rebels' cause.

Turning to look at the two of them, Nora reached out mentally into the gray world and entered into Lace's thoughts. As trustworthy as they both seemed, she wanted to make sure she could trust them completely. As her mind melded with Lace's consciousness, Nora felt her view shift. She could now see herself standing over the beaten down Dream Machine, deep in concentration.

Closing Lace's eyes, Nora started to drift backwards in her memories. She stopped the process a few moments before she had entered into the room, when Lace and Grane were alone. Nora wanted to hear what the two of them were talking about before she arrived.

Feeling Lace's vocal chords vibrate as she spoke, Nora listened without intruding into the memory. "Yes, and we have been waiting so many years for her to appear. I honestly didn't think that I would live long enough to see any of this come to fruition."

Responding to her while continuing to work on one of the consoles, Grane's voice filled the room. "How can you be so sure that Nora is the one from the stories? I remember when Ryden came here a few years ago and you had these same feelings." He gave her a look with his eyebrow raised, before returning his attention to the screen in front of him.

"There is something different about Nora, I just know it. I think we should bring a test subject in with her so we can witness her ability first hand," Lace said emphatically.

Standing up from the console, Grane looked directly at Lace. "I think it might be too soon, but what do I know? I just keep this ludicrous thing running. You make the decisions, I fix things, remember?"

"Yes I know I'm in charge. I was just looking for a second opinion, that's all," Lace replied. She seemed to relax a bit.

Feeling reassured that Lace and Grane had only good intentions, Nora returned to her own mind. Only a moment had passed back inside the Dream Machine room, and Nora's new spying technique had gone undetected. Lace blinked a couple of times as if she felt something was off, but couldn't explain it. Nora pretended not to notice her reaction.

Walking over to where Grane was working, Nora bent down next to him. He looked up at her curiously as she reached down into her pocket.

"Grane, I have something that I think you will be very interested in." Nora revealed the small plastic disk in her hand. "There is a very special program on here that I need you to figure out how to run inside of your Dream Machine. Do you think you could design something to make it work that way?"

"I can definitely try. I always love a new challenge!" He paused, and his excitement seemed to momentarily recede. "Can I ask you what it is?"

"Don't worry. Once you have figured out how to implement it into your system, I will show the both of you exactly what it is."

Handing over the disk, Grane took it immediately from her. He rushed over to one of the other consoles and started pushing the small buttons like a crazed man. Nora admired his willingness and determination. She could hear him grunting and talking quietly to himself as he worked.

Lace walked over to where Nora was standing and cleared her throat, which startled Nora and drew her out of her thoughts.

"I have a request for you Nora. That is, if you wouldn't mind humoring me for a moment."

"You would like to see my abilities in action, right?" Nora asked bluntly. She began to feel a sense of power over Lace, since she had the capability to secretly know what Lace wanted, and could stay a step ahead of her.

Lace stumbled on her words, taken aback by Nora's insightfulness. "Well, yes. That's exactly what I was going to ask of you. Would this be something you'd be willing to participate in for us?"

"Yes. What would you like me to do?" Nora smiled as she replied, trying to seem agreeable.

Lace turned away from Nora and made her way to the opposite side of the room, where she opened the door to the hallway. "Yes, now," she heard Lace say to someone on the other side of the door. "We are ready for them. Please bring them in." Lace shut the door and returned to Nora.

"We have two children—soon to be Defected—with us at the base. We were going to remove their subconscious impressions this afternoon, helping them to escape the death fates that have recently been revealed to them. Now that you are here, we were hoping you would give us a demonstration," Lace said in a questioning tone. "Would it be possible for you to join me inside of their subconsciousness while they are hooked up to the Dream Machine?"

Nora agreed, purposefully smiling as she did so, despite the fact that she felt weary of the situation. She wasn't ready to reveal the extent of her power to them yet. Nora thought back to the moment she had spent with Bray by the wall inside the center of Constance. Her ability was not something she could share with just anybody. Suddenly feeling unsure of what to do, she found herself wishing Bray was in the room with her.

Two girls entered the room, and Nora's heart dropped as she saw just how young they were.

"This is Gemi and Lynn," Lace said, introducing the girls to Nora. "They are sisters as it turns out. The case for the two of them is a bit different than normal. They both share the same time line of events in their death visions. I figured if we were going to see what you could really accomplish, we shouldn't start off with a situation that Grane and myself could easily handle on our own."

It seemed as though Lace wanted to test Nora'a capabilities, and while this was somewhat expected, she felt frustrated at the thought of having to prove herself. Nora swallowed hard. Trying to release two Defected at the same time was not going to be easy.

"Hello, my name is Nora," she said pleasantly to the two girls. "You two are just about the prettiest sisters I've ever seen."

The girls blushed at her comment. The older of the two, Gemi, spoke up. "Thank you ma'am. Lace told us that you would be able to help us," she said. "That you would be able to make the nightmares go away," she added, in a softer voice.

"Of course. I will help you as best as I can," Nora reassured them. "Lynn is it?" she asked the younger girl. When the girl nodded she continued. "Can you close your eyes for me?"

"Yes, ma'am," the girl said softly.

"Can you tell me what happens in your nightmare?" Nora asked her.

Lynn took a deep breath before speaking, and it was clear that she needed to gather up her courage before continuing. "We are playing together in the room when the angry man comes to the door. Mom is crying and she tells us we need to run away."

Lace interrupted them. "Why don't we get one of them on the machine now Nora. You and I can guide them from there."

A plan started to come together in Nora's mind. The last thing she wanted to do was to completely reveal everything she was capable of while inside of the Dream Machine with Lace watching. Lace seemed trustworthy enough to her, but Nora was starting to wonder if keeping most of her ability to herself would be the best plan from now on.

"I think we will be fine right here," Nora said, nodding toward where the girls sat. She didn't turn to look at Lace, but instead kept her focus entirely on Gemi.

"Now, Gemi, if you would please close your eyes too." Once Gemi had followed her instructions Nora continued. "The two of you relax your thoughts as much as you can. Focus on breathing in and out slowly. Imagine your lungs are like balloons filling up and then deflating. Do you think you can do that?"

"Yes, ma'am," the two girls answered in unison.

Lace's eyebrows furrowed, clearly confused over what was going on. Nora ignored her and continued to focus on the girls.

The three of them—Nora, Gemi, and Lynn, sat huddled together, in total silence, as Lace watched, trying desperately to make sense of things. Grane, still busy working on his console in the background, had his focus fixed on the screen in front of him.

Once her mind had left her body and entered into the lonely gray world, Nora could see two small red shadows positioned in front of her own. She mentally reached out to the younger of the two girls—Lynn—and then proceeded to slide into her subconsciousness.

A wave of emotions came over Nora as she delved into Lynn's thoughts. She continued to dig through until she reached the specific memory that took place in the girls' home. The two girls were playing in a room together, and looked so carefree and innocent. Nora couldn't help but stay in the early moments of the memory for a while longer, and revel in the joyfulness of the childhood scene.

The room was small and colorful. The walls were painted the color of lemon buttercream frosting, and there were windows across three walls of the room. The windows—framed with a dark brown wood—seemed as if they had just been cleaned, and sparkled in the mid-day sun. The hardwood floor was made of the same wood, and had toys strewn across it. In the distance, there was music playing, and a woman singing.

Nora could feel the intensity of Lynn's love towards her older sister Gemi. Lynn was playing with several dolls, and having them act out various scenes, while her sister, Gemi, had all of her stuffed animals spread out before her. Watching the girls play, Nora wondered how differently her life would have turned out, had her long-lost sister been a part of it. She reached up instinctively to touch her necklace, as she always did when she thought of her sister, but then remembered that she was in Lynn's subconsciousness, not her own.

Nora knew she would have to leave the memory eventually, but couldn't resist staying a little longer. It felt so comforting to be around a loving family once again.

The smell of food being prepared wafted up from the kitchen into the play room. Nora allowed the scene to unfold without her interference—she released control over Lynn's movements and let the child move on her own. As Lynn skipped to the far end of the play room and stopped to inspect a wandering ant, Nora felt grateful for getting to view how magical life seemed through the eyes of a child.

Suddenly, Nora heard a door in another room of the house burst open with a loud bang. A man a few rooms over began to shout. Lynn craned her head as a blur of movement passed along the outside of the wooden framed windows. As this happened, Nora felt a wave of panic overcome the young girl's mind. The girls' mother ran into the play room at that moment, and grabbed them by the arms, dragging them over to one of the windows.

As the girls burst out crying, their mother began to give them instructions.

"As soon as you reach the ground you run away, okay? As fast and as far as you can," the mother said, fighting against the tears that were forming in her own eyes.

The mother then grabbed hold of Gemi's face, and held her daughter's cheeks in her palms. "You need to take care of your little sister okay?" Gemi nodded, without saying a word. The mother picked Gemi up first and lowered her out of the window, down to the ground below. She turned and did the same with Lynn.

As she lowered Lynn out of the window to Gemi's waiting, outstretched hands, the mother kept repeating how much she loved both of them. "Listen to your big sister," she whispered into Lynn's ear before letting her go. Gemi grabbed Lynn's arm and the two girls started to run towards the back of the house.

At this point, Nora stepped in and controlled Lynn's movement so that the girl would turn her head back to the house to see what was transpiring. She saw a small group of agents standing at the front door, talking with who she assumed to be the girls' father.

Nora knew that now was the time for her to intervene. The heartbreaking scene brought back painful memories from her own experience a few weeks ago, but she pushed the feelings aside and focused on what she had to do. Taking control over Lynn's young body,

Nora made her little legs run as fast as they could. She reached back and grabbed Gemi's hand, pulling her along.

Voices sounded from behind the girls as an agent that had been surveying the perimeter of the home caught a glimpse of them. Nora pushed the girl's little body to its limits as she headed towards the neighbor's backyard. Suddenly Gemi's hand jerked in her grasp. Nora turned to see that another agent had gotten a hold of Gemi and was trying to pull her away, but Gemi held on resiliently.

Thinking on her feet, Nora made the abrupt decision to close Lynn's eyes, and tried to relax herself despite the sounds of Gemi screaming. Nora let her mind drift away from Lynn and dive into the agent's consciousness instead. Once she gained control over his movements she released his grasp on Gemi's body. This would buy the girls time, but Nora knew it wouldn't be enough to ensure their safe escape, so she began to sift through the agent's memories.

She stopped once she'd reached the vision of him getting ready that morning, in the bathroom of his home. Raising the agent's arm high into the air, Nora took a deep breath and then slammed his arm down onto the corner of the sink. As his forearm made contact with the hard porcelain, pain seared through his body. She raised his shoulder and smashed the injured arm down again. This time a loud cracking sound pierced the air—his bones had started to break. Wincing internally, Nora willed herself to finish the job. Knowing full well of the massive bruise that was sure to appear on her own forearm once she left the subconscious world, Nora smashed his arm down a third time. When she was able to look down at her handiwork she saw the unnatural way his arm was bent and the huge, dark blemish of pooling blood that had already begun to form under his skin.

Nora removed herself from the agent's memory and drifted back to Lynn. As she opened the little girl's eyes, she saw they were back behind the neighbor's house. The agent was no longer with them. The girls continued to run, far away from their home, and Nora pressed them to keep moving until she found an old worn-down wooden home in Fallow. There was a well in the backyard, where the girls could safely hide.

Opening her own eyes back in the Fallow rebel base, Nora saw the two girls still stood facing her with their eyes closed. Lace was hovering above them.

"Okay. Let's get Gemi onto the Dream Machine. Are you ready Nora?" Lace asked when she saw that Nora's eyes were open again.

Nora ignored the question and reached over to tenderly touch Lynn on the cheek.

"It's okay to open your eyes now girls, you may leave us." Nora said softly.

"Nora?" Lace asked impatiently as the girls turned away, toward the door.

Nora finally looked up at her. "I'm done," she replied simply, and began to stand up.

"Done?! What do you mean you're done, don't you want to help those poor girls?" Lace asked accusingly.

"I already did," Nora replied, trying to think of the best way to explain the situation to Lace. "You wanted a demonstration of my abilities, well, now you have one. To answer your next question, I don't need a Dream Machine to help the Defected anymore."

"How is that even possible? No one has ever been able to redirect some one else's fate line without the help of a Dream Machine," Lace shook her head in disbelief.

"I can't explain it to you right now. You just have to trust me. I have one last demonstration for you." Nora called over to Grane who was still plugging away on the console. "Are you ready for me yet, Grane?" she asked him.

"Yes, any second now. I'm not sure what this thing is that you brought us, but it looks incredible," Grane replied, as he frantically typed.

"This…" Nora started, and then paused, wanting to make sure she had their full attention. "This is Program 7. Dr. Secora has been developing this in an attempt to gain the upper hand over the Defected."

"And what exactly does this Program 7 do?" Lace asked her.

"I will demonstrate as soon as Grane and the consoles are ready," Nora said as she looked over to Grane. He looked up and locked eyes with her before dropping his gaze to the screen in front of him. His hand hovered over a large button on the console, and he looked up at Lace.

She nodded her head at him, "Run it."

CHAPTER 31

Nora climbed up onto the Dream Machine inside the underground rebel base in Fallow. The chair's padding was cold against her skin, and when she lifted her shirt up the chilly metal disk on the seat made her shiver.

Over at the consoles, Grane worked quickly to make the final preparations, so they could run the contents of the disk that Nora had brought. She sat patiently and waited, not wanting to interfere with the set-up. Lace, however, briskly paced back and forth across the room, anxiously trying to comprehend what she had just witnessed Nora accomplish without the help of a Dream Machine. She chewed her nails thoughtfully as she paced. Finally Grane broke the tense silence in the room.

"Okay," he called out. "The console has accepted the new input parameters you brought. It seems to be running stable now. I believe we are ready to go live." He looked up from his console and over to Nora. "Are you sure about this code you've given me, because whatever it is, it is untested and we have no idea what it will do to you or the Dream Machine."

"Don't worry about it, Grane. I've done this before. You just make sure all of that new coding remains stable and I'll take care of the rest." Nora craned her neck up so she could meet Grane's eyes and give him a reassuring smile.

When Nora turned to Lace she saw that Lace was still anxiously biting her fingernails. "Lace, would you hop on the other console and join me inside of my dream state? You are going to want to see this too."

Lace nodded excitedly in response, and went over to one of the free consoles, hooking herself up to it. She had a hopeful yet slightly fearful look in her eyes.

"Ready Nora?" Grane called out from beside Lace. "Everything is a go on our end."

Nora had her eyes fixed on the light hanging above her. She answered without averting her gaze. "As ready as I'll ever be."

Grane began the countdown. "Going live in 3...2...1—"

Nora immediately plummeted into complete darkness within her mind. She was starting to grow familiar with the sensation of nothingness that occurred when she travelled between mental states like this, but it was still unnerving, and slightly terrifying. It was definitely her least favorite part of the whole Dream Machine experience.

When the small white light appeared, Nora braced herself for the impending rush of sensory overload that would soon follow. The white glow began to expand and then the orbs of colorful light began to swirl around her. Once the multi-colored orbs ceased their whirlwind, a black room appeared.

Nora spotted Lace a few yards away. She sensed Lace's confusion and made her way over to her. Nora attempted to break Lace out of her shell-shocked state.

"Is everything okay, Lace?" she asked.

Lace mumbled something incomprehensible, but then her eyes seemed to suddenly focus when she saw Nora standing before her. She cleared her throat and attempted to straighten out her already perfectly straight clothing.

"Yes. Yes. I'm sorry. It's just that my whole life I have been told that one day one of the Defected would bring unimaginable talents into the world. The story has been told for so long now that most of us think of it as an old wive's tale—a story created perhaps to help us cope with our situations, and motivate us to continue our fight. I just never thought I would be the one standing here..." Lace took a breath, "...with you."

Placing her hand on Lace's shoulder, Nora tried her best to comfort her. "Don't worry about any of that, we'll figure it all out. For now, just try and relax and allow me to demonstrate my abilities. Then we can take a break and meet again later after you have had time to process all of this. I was just as confused as you are now when I was first introduced to this new coding."

Lace nodded and Nora felt her shoulders relax a bit under her hand. "Are you ready?" Nora asked her.

"Yes. Please enlighten me."

"Okay, try not to get disoriented at first. It'll help if you keep your eyes focused on the ground," Nora said.

As Nora gazed at the dark ground below her and Lace's feet, she began to feel Program 7 starting up.

"What are those dots that are moving around down there?" Lace asked.

"Well Lace, they are us. All of us." Slowly the gray outlined shapes that represented the five sectors and the center of Constance became visible. "This is the whole city of Constance, and all five sectors surrounding it," Nora explained.

"Where did you get this program?" Lace asked incredulously.

"When I was held captive in Obsidia, they tested this new coding program on me. They told me that they had been waiting for a long time for someone with as much promise as I had to come along. They needed a mind capable enough to test it out," Nora paused, allowing Lace to digest the new information. "It's called Program 7, and the scientists wanted me to help them locate all of the Defected hiding inside of the city."

"All of those dots are Defected people?" Lace asked, as she looked up at Nora in confusion.

"Just the red ones. The white ones are the rest of the population. As far as I can tell, even most of the red dots don't know they are Defected yet. Program 7 has a way to identify them before their death visions start," Nora replied.

"So this all means that we could finally..." Lace began, her voice trailing off in awe.

"Yes," Nora confirmed. "We can get to the Defected before their death dreams begin. It will help us grow the rebellion much faster and minimize casualties. This could be the advantage we need to finally win this war."

"Since we have the Program 7 disk now, can Dr. Secora still use the technology?" Lace asked.

"Well," Nora hesitated. "Yes and no. The coding we are using right now came directly out of the Dream Machine console inside one of Obsidia's test labs. This appeared to be their only working copy, and I stole it during my escape," Nora answered. She saw a hint of a smile emerge on Lace's face. "But it is only a matter of time before the scientists there are able to analyze the data from my sessions inside Program 7. With that they'll be able to figure out how to reconstruct it." The smile on Lace's face faded away.

"Fortunately for us, and not so fortunate for them, you still need a mind capable of understanding how to operate Program 7 while inside it. The center of Constance doesn't have a very high Defected population like we do here in Fallow, so it could take them years to find another one like me."

"Can any Defected run Program 7?" Lace inquired.

"I'm not sure. As far as I know, I'm the only one who has tested it. There was an instance outside of Obsidia, where Dr. Secora had taken over the mind of one of our own—Cady. I'm assuming he had found a way to run Program 7 himself, or with some kind of outside help. I haven't witnessed that since though, which leads me to believe that whoever is helping him doesn't quite have the mental ability to reach the whole city—their range is likely a lot more limited than mine."

"Well, we should assume Dr. Secora will soon find a way to expand his reach with Program 7. We need to stay a step ahead of him," Lace said with determination.

"Dr. Secora has found a way to block me from getting to his agents—they've all started wearing devices in their ears that somehow make them invisible to me. We should ask Grane if he can come up with something similar for the Defected to wear, so we can even out the playing field. While we were in Arrant, I was able to grab one of these Neural Feedback Inhibitors from an agent, so maybe Grane will be able to replicate the devices for us," Nora said.

"So with Lynn and Gemi, you were able to run Program 7 in your mind without being hooked up to a Dream Machine that had been embedded with the coding?" Lace asked, trying to put everything together.

"Yes. Although to me it's not Program 7, it's just something inside of me that I can feel. When they hooked me up to the Dream Machine with Program 7 running, I think it unlocked a part of my mind that I didn't know existed before," Nora answered.

Lace turned her eyes away and appeared to be deep in thought.

"I knew you'd come to save us all," Lace said, after a few moments of contemplation. "You are the key to all of this. We now have a chance—a fighting chance—to end Constance's reign over us, once and for all," she added, her eyes lighting up.

"Let's keep this between you and I for now, if that's all right. I don't want anyone treating me any different because of it," Nora said hesitantly.

"Okay," Lace agreed. "I just have one more request." Lace paused and locked eyes with Nora. "Show me how Program 7 works."

Nora focused on the ground below them as it grew and expanded. "We'll be looking for a Defected. As soon as we are done here, send a crew out to rescue them."

Red dots slowly grew into red shadows as Nora focused her attention on the sector of Fallow. The shadows of a dozen or so Defected grew larger against the gray background. Nora set her sights on one in particular—a young boy, traveling the dirt roads of Fallow alone. His light, wavy hair gave into the slight breeze that passed over him. She then used her mental powers to transport her and Lace so that they were right beside the boy's shadow. Nora peered into the eyes that hid behind the flickering red flames, feeling magnetically drawn to their familiar innocence.

Nora then pulled both her and Lace into the young boy's mind. She immediately began to sort through his subconscious.

"Can you access the memories of his entire life?" Lace asked.

"Yes, from the moment he came into this world. But, more interestingly, I can also move forward through his memories, into his future," Nora replied.

"You can go into the future events of his life?" Lace asked incredulously.

"Yes, if I have to in order to locate his death vision," Nora answered. "But it looks like this boy's visions have already started."

Nora had found a memory of the boy laying in bed about to fall asleep. The death dream came quickly as he drifted off. In the vision, the boy didn't look much different physically, so whenever they were, it couldn't have been too far off from the present day. It was dark outside and the boy was in what appeared to be a prison cell—there were concrete walls on three sides of him and a set of thick metal bars in front.

Suddenly an explosion sounded in the distance and the boy leapt out of bed. He darted over to the bars and wedged his head between them, trying to get a glimpse into the concrete hallway of what was going on. He was unable to see much of anything, but the sound of gun fire filled the air, and started to grow louder.

As the boy leaned his weight even more against the cold bars they gave out and the gate swung open. The boy looked at the opening suspiciously—it made no sense that it would simply unlock just like that. He cautiously made his way out into the hallway.

All the while, Nora and Lace watched, without interfering. They saw a group of people appear down the hallway to the left. They started yelling at the boy, urging him to run towards them.

As the boy began to sprint, new voices started to call out from the opposite direction—a group of agents had appeared. When the gunshots started, Nora decided it was time to intervene.

She let herself drift out of the young boy's mind, leaving Lace alone inside of the boy's subconsciousness. She mentally made her way into the nearest member of the group that was encouraging the boy to run, and a strange sensation rushed over her. She'd never felt this way in any of her experiences diving into other people's minds. It was an oddly intimate, almost comforting feeling—like how it feels to return home after a long period of absence.

She shook her head when she realized what had happened. She had managed to merge with her own, future self. Apparently, in this version of the future, she was a part of the young boy's death. Memories of her future flooded her vision all at once, and the hallway full of gun fire narrowed into a small pinhole of light. Her knees buckled, and she nearly collapsed.

As the light tunnel moved further and further from her vision she sensed someone grabbing hold of her. She used every ounce of strength to keep herself anchored to that reality and within her future self.

"Nora, you are okay," she heard an older woman's voice say. "You knew this was going to happen and asked me to comfort you when it did. Allow the new memories to fill your mind. I know it's overwhelming, but it's fine. It will pass."

Nora realized she was squeezing her hands so tightly that her fingernails were cutting into her clammy palms. Additionally, she was barely breathing. She took as deep of a breath as she could manage into her tight chest, and tried to relax her body.

When she started to regain her senses, she looked around to see what was happening in the hallway. The boy was running at a full sprint towards her, as bullets shot dangerously close to him. He called out for her by name, panic filling his voice. Nora struggled to her feet, as her mind raced with thoughts of what she should do.

"Now, Nora. You have to act now," the woman said softly, but urgently into her ear.

Still wobbling, Nora planted her feet firmly onto the ground and squared her shoulders before lunging towards the boy.

"Pith, get down!" Nora yelled out the moment before their bodies collided and they both tumbled onto the concrete ground—a swarm of bullets passing thru the empty space the boy had just occupied. The impact was so hard that it knocked the wind out of Nora for a moment, and the boy seemed similarly dazed.

As more gun fire passed above their heads, Pith screamed in fear. Nora kept him pinned to the ground, her weight pressing on top of him, to shield him from the bullets that continued to hurtle past. They huddled on the cold floor, almost too afraid to breathe.

Finally the shots died down, and the hallway grew quiet. At this point Nora decided it was time to leave her future body and return to Lace inside of Pith's subconsciousness.

"You did that, didn't you? You were able to control her," Lace said, referring to the older version of Nora who currently still sat beside them.

"Yes. I can easily move from one mind to the next," Nora confirmed.

"She looks so much like you—you two could be sisters!" Lace exclaimed, as she peered at the future Nora more intently.

"She is me," Nora said quietly, shaking her head. Even she could barely believe it herself. "She's a future version of me. I'm not sure why I am a part of this boy's death vision. All I know is that we just saved his life, and that back in our current time and reality, he is now Defected. You will immediately need to send out a group to get him and bring him back to the rebel base before the Agency finds him," Nora said urgently.

With that, Nora mentally removed her and Lace from Pith's subconsciousness, and left him there on the floor of the concrete hallway. Lace and Nora re-entered the blackness, back inside the Dream Machine. Below them, the gray shadow of the city became visible once again, and they watched as thousands of red and white dots pulsed and moved throughout it. Nora placed a hand on Lace's shoulder.

"Give yourself some time to process all of this. Send out a crew to grab the young boy, and we will talk again later. I need to rest," Nora said authoritatively.

"Thank you Nora. Thank you for sharing this with me," Lace's voice broke with emotion as she spoke.

Nora then opened her eyes, and the florescent bulb overhead shone so brightly that it made her squint. They were safely back in the Dream Machine room at Fallow's rebel base. She turned to look at Lace, who caught her eye and flashed her a smile.

As Nora struggled to undo the machine's restraints and stand up, Lace leapt out of her seat and ran out into the hallway. Nora could hear Lace calling out for a group of rebels to suit up and be ready to head out. Nora tuned their voices out and thought back to the scene in the concrete hallway. She couldn't believe that she'd just been in her future self's body.

As images of Pith's death vision lingered in her thoughts, Nora couldn't stop thinking about the merging of her present mind with her future mind. The voice that had spoken to her sounded so familiar, yet Nora couldn't place where she had heard it before. As she struggled to dig through her memories in an attempt to locate the source of the voice, she felt an odd sensation—it was as if her consciousness was expanding and collapsing all at once. Breathing in deeply, she tried to keep her mental state steady.

Despite her attempts, she began to see visions of her future—flashes of scenes, conversations and even emotions that were yet to come. She saw faces of people that she'd never met, but were somehow familiar. As all these things rushed into her mind, she felt the weight of her future self's added memories and became somewhat disoriented. There was an abundance of new experiences that she absorbed all at once, and though the quantity was too vast to sift through she was somehow certain about one thing which she felt in her gut, almost as instinct—Bray was not a part of any of them.

CHAPTER 32

Nora got up and walked over to the console where Grane was seated. His eyes were wide as he reviewed the data from Nora's recent trip inside of the Dream Machine. He raised his head up to look at her when she approached.

"You know, what you have brought us here is nothing short of a miracle. The implications Program 7 could have in our favor are astronomical," he paused thoughtfully. "This is truly a game changer for us all."

"In time, we will use this as a tool for the war. For now, all of your focus needs to be on building something similar to this Neural Feedback Inhibitor. We need to even the playing field."

Nora handed him the small, blue device and stood to leave the room. Before shutting the door behind her she glanced back at Grane, who was staring at his console. Analyzing all the new information available to him would take some time. Nora knew Grane couldn't resist having a new challenge, and she hoped he would be able to come up with something soon that would protect the rebels against Dr. Secora and Program 7.

A little further down the hallway Nora caught sight of Phoenix leaning against a wall. Phoenix lifted her head when she noticed Nora approaching and smirked.

"There you are! I started to think you snuck off with Bray," Phoenix teased Nora.

"Not yet," Nora replied with a smile. "I was busy catching Lace up on all of our new discoveries since we left the center of Constance. What have you been up to?" Nora asked. Phoenix stopped leaning against the wall and put her hands on her hips.

"I gave myself a little tour of this place. You know, once you get past all the dirt and wires tangled up everywhere, this underground base is pretty cool. It's much bigger than I thought," Phoenix replied.

"Well, since you are an expert now, why don't you show me around some more? I haven't been anywhere." Nora had barely finished her sentence when Phoenix grabbed her hand and started to pull her down the hall.

"Let's go," Phoenix urged.

Phoenix guided Nora to a split in the corridors, where she paused. There were three doors down the passageway—two on the right and one on the left. Without deliberating, Phoenix made her way over to the door on the left, still pulling Nora along.

As they entered the room Nora thought about how nice it was to be led on a little tour by her friend, and to let someone else be responsible for making decisions—as inconsequential as they might be.

"This room is great," Phoenix said excitedly. "You will love this one."

The room, though similar in construction to all the others, had something different inside of it—metal racks full of clothing. The racks stretched the entire length of the room.

"What is this place?" Nora asked.

"This, my dear friend, is our own personal closet. These guys have been stocking up on clothing from around the entire city for years. It's divided into boys and girls' clothes, and then further divided by sector. Every sector gets its own rack," Phoenix informed her as she began to browse through the girls' clothing.

Wandering around the room, Nora stopping to look at the Arrant rack. She pulled a few articles from their hangers and held them out in front of her, one by one, so that she could admire them. The clothes appeared to be unworn.

"I was never able to afford anything this fancy back home. I would have to work for a whole year to afford some of these outfits," Nora exclaimed when Phoenix came over to see what she was looking at.

"Same here," Phoenix said, shaking her head. "And besides that, these clothes would never have lasted a whole day of running through all the fields and wet crops outside."

At that moment something caught Nora's attention out of the corner of her eye. She walked over to a rack near the back of the room.

A beautiful shirt was hung on the stand, and Nora felt magnetically drawn to it. The material of the garment was soft, yet still looked crisp. It was all white, except for a small hint of green along the seams. Nora grabbed it and held it up to her body, turning to model it for Phoenix.

"What sector do you think this one is from?" Nora asked.

"From what I can guess, it has to be Sonant apparel. It sure is beautiful isn't it?" Phoenix answered. Nora continued to grab more articles of clothing from the rack.

"Yes, very," she murmured as she continued to inspect the fabrics. "Have you ever been to Sonant?"

"Not yet. None of us have, in fact. We never had a reason to," Phoenix replied. Suddenly Nora remembered something.

"You know, the day we escaped from the center of Constance, I thought I had to remove the scientists from the lab, so I took one of their body's up to the roof of Obsidia. While I was there I was so high up that I could see everything," Nora said. Phoenix stopped browsing the clothing and gave Nora her full attention.

"Could you see Sonant and Jejung from up there?" Phoenix asked.

"Yes. All the sectors, and even a little beyond our walls. It was amazing," Nora replied.

"Jejung looked pretty much how I imagined—mostly dull gray with a ton of dirt on the ground. Towards the back of the sector was a huge building—it took up almost half of the entire area. I could only assume that was the prison," Nora said. Phoenix looked down at her feet.

"A lot of the Defected have been sent to Jejung over the years. I'm happy not to be stuck in there myself, but I feel guilty for not being able to help the ones who are," Phoenix said somberly.

"I felt bad too," Nora said. "I couldn't look at it for too long. I did take a look at Sonant however," Nora added.

"It was so beautiful from above. The streets were all lined with shiny glittering white stone—I could see the reflection of the sun off them. Most of the buildings were made from the same beautiful material. The buildings there were pretty tall too—most were four-or-five stories high. From where I stood, I couldn't see one inch of empty space left in the whole sector," Nora said. While Nora had been speaking, Phoenix's eyes grew wide.

"I wish I could have been there with you," Phoenix said. "Sounds like a once-in-a-lifetime kind of view. I doubt most Constance citizens would ever get a chance to see something like that," she continued, a note of sadness in her voice.

Nora held an expensive-looking blouse up to her chest. "So, what do you think?" she began, changing the subject. "I bet no one in Sonant would ever guess I was a poor, dust-covered girl from Arrant if I showed up wearing this, huh?" Phoenix laughed.

"And I could be your fancy friend on my way to meet you for brunch," Phoenix said in return.

The girls continued to laugh as they put all the clothing back on the racks. Suddenly Phoenix's eyes lit up.

"I say, tomorrow, we come with our bags. We should stock our supply of clothing so we can be prepared, just in case we happen to wind up in Sonant," Phoenix said with a wink.

"Yes we should," Nora agreed. "You can never be too prepared. And we may need to infiltrate the fancier parts of town in Arrant and Blear too, so we might as well prepare for that while we're at it," Nora tried her best to keep a straight face.

She lasted until they had made it out of the clothing room before she burst out laughing. As they walked down the hallway, they decided to go get something to eat—browsing through all that clothing had left them hungry—so they made their way over to the cafeteria.

They got in line and piled their plates high with food from various serving trays around the room. Once they'd gotten everything they wanted, they found an empty table to sit at. Both of them were too hungry to talk at first, so only the sound of their chewing filled the air. Phoenix, with a mouth full of food, was the first to speak.

"How far do you think the boys and Bretta have made it? Do you think they got through Arrant yet?"

Nora shook her head. "It's a long walk, and Otto, Trim and Bretta can't just waltz though the center of town with wildly colored hair and a face full of metal. My guess is that they made it back through the fields and to the hole in the wall. Hopefully they wait until the sun goes down before they move again. Once it's dark outside they can quickly move throughout Arrant and cut right through the middle—otherwise they'd have to take the long route, all the way around the wall."

Phoenix chuckled, using her fork to swirl her food around the plate, and then looked up and grinned at Nora.

"What's with that, do you think they are doing something else right now?" Nora asked her.

"It's nothing really," Phoenix replied with a grin. "I was just thinking about how far you've come from that scared girl I found in Arrant just a few weeks ago. You've really made a place for yourself here with the rest of us."

"Thanks. I guess you guys are not too bad yourselves," Nora teased in response. "Anyway," she continued, her tone serious again, "I hope they are all okay."

"I'm sure our gang will be back in no time," Phoenix said in a reassuring tone.

After they finished eating they placed their plates in the dirty dish bin and went back out into the hallway.

"I think after all that food, I'm ready to check out the sleeping accommodations," Phoenix said with a slight yawn. Nora nodded in agreement.

"Lace showed me earlier where we all would be staying. I'll take you there."

Nora led the way, and as they made turn after turn in the labyrinth of hallways, she realized again how massive the underground base really was. When they turned the corner on a particularly long corridor, Nora felt completely disoriented and began to think she'd gotten them lost—everything was starting to blur together and look the same. But when they made the next turn she breathed a sigh of relief—she'd found it.

"Here we go, these are the doors to the sleeping areas—our beds are through the ones on the left," Nora informed Phoenix.

When they went inside they saw the usual dirt walls and mess of wires. There were four cots—two on each side—and a walking path in the middle. A small closet and sink were located at the back of the room. The whole set-up was pretty similar to the base in Blear.

"We should save one of the beds for Bretta," Phoenix suggested. "I'm sure she'll be pretty tired when she gets back." Nora nodded in response as she made her way to the cot at the back of the room on the left side. Along the way she placed her bag on a bed on the right, to reserve it for Bretta.

She put the rest of her belongings down on the cot she'd chosen for herself. Phoenix took the bed beside it. It comforted Nora to know that Phoenix would be sleeping right beside her—she wasn't quite ready to be alone at night in such an unfamiliar place yet.

The two of them took turns at the sink, washing the grit from the last few days off their faces. Nora hadn't realized how dirty she was until she felt the cool water splash on her face. She could feel all the bad memories of Obsidia washing away.

Inside the small closet, the girls found comfortable clothing to sleep in. Phoenix picked up a very small, revealing top and held it up.

"This must be for when Bray comes back from Blear," she teased Nora.

Nora blushed slightly in response. She wasn't as used to talking about boys and relationships as the other girls seemed to be.

Sensing her uneasiness on the subject, Phoenix tried to ease her mind. "It's okay Nora. At least the two of you know where you stand. Otto is too focused on the rebel's cause to think about any romance between him and I. It makes it pretty confusing for me, but I guess I'll just have to wait for you to save the world before my love life can be taken off hold!"

They laid down in their bunks and continued to chat as they let their bodies relax and their minds wind down. The underground room was chilly and Nora wished she had another blanket to cover herself with.

"I don't think we will stay here long." Nora said sleepily, her eyes already closed.

Phoenix took a moment to respond, feeling groggy herself. "I hope not. I mean, I like it here, but I would rather be out there—helping the other Defected to end all this."

"I wish I could just wander around for a few hours, and feel like I had a normal life again," Nora confessed.

"Hopefully one day, when this is all over, we can enjoy the world again like we used to," Phoenix said.

Phoenix's comment made Nora think about her childhood in Arrant. She'd grown up without a care in the world. The world was simple back then—you ate, played, and slept. It really didn't get much better than that. No one was worried about becoming Defected. No one worried about having to fight to survive, or winding up in Jejung for the rest of their life.

The thought of prison life brought chills to Nora's already cold back. She contemplated what a day in the life of a prisoner would be like. Thinking back to the young boy's death vision from her Program 7 experiment with Lace, the sight of the cold gray walls and metal bars filled her mind.

As her mind concentrated further into the boy's death dream, she realized that herself and the rebels must have broken into the prison. Nora wondered how far into the future the boy's path had led her.

Trying not to think too hard about what it all could have meant, her mind began to drift off into a twilight state of consciousness—the world that existed somewhere between awake and asleep. She hoped that the rebels presence inside the prison was a sign of Constance losing its powerful hold over the city. Whatever the reason was for her being there, Nora knew that soon enough she would find out. In the end things would make sense.

Through the haze of impending sleep, she could hear the heavy breathing of Phoenix next to her. The sound of her breath was comforting after all those lonely nights inside that small white cell in Obsidia.

Visions of an idyllic scene filled her mind as she slept. A tall field of green grass—its blades dancing in the wind—lay below white clouds that were suspended in the blue sky above. Nora felt lighter than air. The grass was up to her waist and she ran effortlessly through the field. Her family was there too, all laughing and running along with her. She felt a supreme sense of peace.

Suddenly she woke up from her happy dream and found herself back in the sleeping unit beside Phoenix. As her heavy lids struggled to open, the green fields and blue skies faded away. Staying completely still, Nora darted her eyes around to survey the room—there had been a jarring noise that had woken her, and she tried to locate the source of it.

The unit was dark, but a small light near the sink created enough illumination for Nora to make out the vague shapes of everything in the room. The other two beds remained empty. Phoenix still lay on the cot next to her. Her back was turned to Nora and her only motions were the heavy, rhythmic breathing of someone fast asleep.

Nora shook her head. It was probably just a noise from the hallway or her imagination. She shut her eyes again and tried to fall back asleep, but then she heard the faint sound again. This time it was unmistakeable. Suddenly extremely alert and awake, she opened her eyes and tried to stay still as she strained to hear where the noise was coming from.

At that moment Phoenix's breath became labored, as though she were struggling for air. Panicking, Nora thought her friend might be choking in her sleep. She turned to look at Phoenix's back, and the deep gasps turned into a quiet moaning.

Phoenix's silhouette was visible from the faint light in the room, and Nora watched as her friend convulsed, as though she had a bad case of the hiccups. Sudden sharp movements shook Phoenix's whole body, interspersed with a dull, pain-induced moan.

Nora reached over to Phoenix in hopes of comforting her friend. She reasoned that Phoenix was probably having a nightmare. As her hand neared her body, Phoenix shifted. First she rolled onto her back and gasped for air, and then she proceeded to wail in pain as she convulsed. Nora shot up in her bed and went to grab for Phoenix's shoulder.

Again Phoenix moved in response to Nora's attempt to reach out to her. This time she turned to her right side and faced Nora. Her eyes remained closed, and the sharp movements continued. Nora gingerly stroked the hair out of Phoenix's face.

As she did this, Phoenix took a deep gulp of air, as though she were about to dive underwater. Phoenix's eyes suddenly opened and startled Nora. Her gaze was unsettling—glazed and empty. Nora, feeling frightened, jumped back into her own bed.

"Phoenix?" she asked timidly. Phoenix said nothing in response, and continued staring right at Nora with the same blank gaze.

"Are you okay?" Nora asked, trying desperately to slow her racing heart.

"Hello? Phoenix?" This time she waved her hand around in front of her friend, hoping to break through to her.

Phoenix's mouth opened slightly. Her eyes were still fixed on Nora in the same glossy, trance-like manner. She heard a slight hiss of air escape Phoenix's mouth.

Nora's eyes widened in fear and disbelief. She began to stand up, in an attempt to run to the door and get help.

"Please, sit," Phoenix's booming voice filled the room and Nora, stunned, fell back into her bed. Her friend's voice sounded different somehow, the intonations and pacing were not the same.

CHAPTER 33

After a few stunned moments of silence, it suddenly dawned on Nora that this was not her friend speaking. Somehow, someone had been able to use Phoenix's body as a vessel to communicate to Nora. Remaining seated on her bed, she bent forward at her waist and leaned in towards her friend.

A small hiss of air escaped from behind Phoenix's lips, causing Nora to sit up straight with a loud gasp. Nora reached out for her friend, her fingers trembling, hesitant to make contact with Phoenix's now motionless body. A moment before Nora's finger made contact with Phoenix's shoulder, her eyes finally closed. Pausing and withdrawing her hand briefly, Nora repositioned herself on the cot so that she was more stable and then reached out to her friend once again.

Making contact with the bare skin of Phoenix's shoulder at last, Nora heard a low growl escape from between her teeth. Nora sat back, frustrated and unsure of what to do next.

"Phoenix, wake up!" Nora yelled. "Wake up!" she repeated insistently. When she yelled out the second time she clapped her hands together forcefully.

Beads of sweat had formed on her temple as adrenaline pumped through her body. With a sudden burst of courage, she leapt up and lunged at her friend—both arms extended outwards so that she could physically shake Phoenix out of whatever was happening to her.

As she landed on her friend—her fingers clenched around both of Phoenix's shoulders—Phoenix let out a growl so loud it seemed to fill the entire room.

It was at that point that Phoenix's eyes flashed open. Feeling vulnerable, Nora crossed her arms protectively around her chest. She watched as Phoenix's lips parted slightly. "Eleanor," a raspy voice sounded from behind her clenched jaw.

"Whoever is doing this, reveal yourself now!" Nora yelled out. "What do you want from me?"

Another slight hiss of air escaped Phoenix's mouth before the voice spoke again. The voice that emerged sounded faint, as though it were coming from far away.

"You are a smart girl, Eleanor. I don't think I need to introduce myself to you," the voice said. Phoenix's eyes were still staring off blankly past Nora.

"Maybe I shouldn't give you as much credit as I thought you deserved."

Closing her eyes, Nora tried to recognize who was speaking. She knew she'd heard that person's voice before, the intonations were eerily familiar. Finally she realized who it was.

"Dr. Secora?" Nora asked. "Is that you?"

Another hiss of air came out of Phoenix's mouth. "Let's skip the formalities—I'm not sure how long I can hold on to your friend's mind, and I have much to say to you." His voice struck a nerve in Nora, and she began to grow agitated.

"Fine then," she said forcefully, gritting her teeth. "Program 7. You were able to reconstruct the data from my test."

"Finally. Now that's the Eleanor I wanted to speak with," Dr. Secora continued. "Dr. Willow worked around the clock with my daughter, Brielle. The two of them were able to piece back together Dr. Edmonds' work. You do remember him don't you—the innocent man whose life you so callously took away?"

Ignoring his rhetorical question, she squared her shoulders. "Why have you come for me now, why here?" she demanded.

"You haven't made it easy for us to locate you. Once your friend fell asleep, we were able to locate her subconsciousness and find you as a result. I have a surprise for you, Eleanor. Something I think you will take very seriously when you consider your response to my next question."

"I'm listening," she replied.

"Good. Pay close attention now," Dr. Secora said. "While you were busy running away from me, hiding in Fallow somewhere, I had my agents pick up a security package of sorts for me."

Nora's heart raced as she tried to think of what he could be talking about.

"You will now be faced with a difficult decision," Dr. Secora continued. "Come to Obsidia within the next thirty-six hours, or I will take the life of your dear brother, Will."

Bolting up out of her cot, all of the muscles in Nora's body grew tense. She felt her heartbeat pulse in her temples as fear flooded her thoughts. She admonished herself for being so stupid as to not have protected against this obvious way of manipulating her—by threatening her family.

"He's an innocent child!" Nora yelled angrily.

"The choice whether or not any harm will come to your brother is yours alone Eleanor," Dr. Secora replied, his voice devoid of any emotion. "In thirty-six hours the wall between Sector 5 and the center of Constance will open. If you are there, we can discuss the terms of your surrender. If you are not there, your brother will be executed. After him, we will continue to move up your family tree, until nobody is left. This is a promise, not a threat. The choice is yours Eleanor." With those final words Phoenix's eyes shut, and the hissing ceased. It seemed as though the conversation were over.

Nora fell back onto her cot, stunned, and reached out for Phoenix's shoulder. As soon as she grazed her friend's arm, Phoenix's eyes shot open. Phoenix blinked repeatedly, and then focused her gaze on Nora.

"Nora, what's wrong," she asked, noticing the terrified expression on her friend's face. "Did you have a bad dream again?"

Nora breathed a sigh of relief—she had never been so happy to hear Phoenix's voice before. Nora leaned in closer to her, and stared at the floor for a moment, trying to figure out the best way to explain what had just happened.

"Don't freak out," Nora cautioned. "But Dr. Secora was just talking to me..." she paused and Phoenix sat up straight, a quizzical look on her face. "...through you," she finished. Phoenix was silent for a moment.

"Um, what do you mean he was talking through me?" Phoenix asked. Nora took a deep breath.

"Dr. Secora was able to use Program 7 to locate your subconscious mind once you fell asleep. He was trying to get through to me, and he must have somehow known that you'd be the one most likely to be sleeping next to me, so he took control over you," Nora explained.

"How could he have known something like that?" Phoenix asked as images of Cady flowed into Nora's mind.

"It gets worse," Nora continued, her voice softening. "He has my brother, Will."

"He didn't make me do anything to hurt you, did he?" Phoenix asked, sounding anxious.

"No," Nora assured her. "We were only talking."

"Okay, well that's good at least. So what did Dr. Secora want from you? Why does he have your brother?" Phoenix asked.

"He wants me to surrender myself to him," Nora said carefully.

"But we need you!" Phoenix exclaimed. She jumped up out of bed, "We need to go tell Lace about this right now," she ordered.

Nora waved her hands dismissively at the idea. "We will tell Lace, but not just yet. Dr. Secora gave me thirty-six hours to make my decision. When Bray and the rest of the rebels get back I'll talk it over with them first, then we can tell Lace, but for now, please keep this between us. I have an idea, but I don't want too many people to know about it just yet. The more people that know about the plan, the more opportunities Dr. Secora has to find out about it. Since he can enter dream states he can retrieve any information stored in a person's mind," Nora explained. Phoenix nodded in agreement with her logic.

"Okay," Phoenix sighed. "That makes sense. So what do we do now?" she asked, hugging her knees into her chest. "I don't think I can go back to sleep again after what just happened."

"Me either. Let's just hope the boys come back soon."

They both sat at the edge of their beds quietly in thought.

"What should we do while we wait?" Phoenix asked, breaking the silence. "I'd rather do something to stay busy and keep my mind off things."

"Well I'm too upset to eat," Nora replied. Since no sunlight infiltrated the underground base, it was impossible to tell what time of day it was. She glanced over to the clock that hung on the wall opposite their beds and saw that it was almost four o'clock in the morning. Walking over to the entrance of their sleeping unit, Nora pressed her ear against the door and listened for signs of other rebels moving about. Everything was silent.

"Maybe we should start getting our things together," Nora suggested to Phoenix when she got back to their beds. "I'm not sure what will be decided once the group returns, but it couldn't hurt to get our bags packed just in case—we might have to leave right away depending on our plan of attack."

Phoenix nodded. At the very least, it was something to do other than sitting around worrying. She got up and walked over with Nora to the back of the room.

They grabbed bags out of the closet and sorted through the clothes. Selecting what they wanted to pack, they placed the unwanted clothing on the empty bed beside them.

"I feel bad saying it," Phoenix started. "But it's hard for me to choose amongst this clothing, knowing how much nicer the clothes in the base's main closet are."

"I agree," Nora said. "So why don't we go see if that room is still open?"

They both smiled, and the mood instantly lightened with their new plan. Nora knew that the more they kept themselves occupied, the sooner Bray and Otto would be back.

Outside in the hallway there was no noise besides the sound of their feet. It seemed everyone else in the underground base was fast asleep. Phoenix lead the way back to the base's main closet. Nora was impressed with how easily Phoenix seemed to familiarize herself with the surroundings after such a short period of time.

They arrived at the clothing room, clutching their empty bags in hand. The door opened easily and they both breathed a sigh of relief that it was unlocked. Feeling her way along the wall beside the door, Nora located the light switch and illuminated the dark room. The shiny buttons and zippers on all the clothing seemed to sparkle in the florescent light.

As they went through the clothing from all the different sectors, they kept mainly to themselves. Neither spoke much at all—they were both lost deep in thought. It was impossible for Nora to keep herself from worrying about her brother all together, but she knew that there was nothing she could do at the moment, so she tried to keep her mind on other things. Certain styles of the clothing reminded Nora of her mother, and a long gray jacket with purple trim reminded her of the cold seasons from her childhood.

Beside her, Phoenix was starting to relax. Rummaging through the Fallow clothing racks was proving to be a great distraction. As she tucked several items into her bag, she also came across a few things she knew Nora would like and held onto those as well.

Nora had developed a particular affinity to the vibrant shade of red that was favored amongst Fallow citizens. Every time Phoenix found something she thought Nora might like she would hold the item up for judgement. Nora would give her either a nod of approval or a shake of the head. On a few occasions she was undecided after glancing over, so Phoenix would toss the item to Nora for her to inspect it closer. Nora did the same whenever she found something she thought Phoenix might like.

After they'd thoroughly combed through all the items in the Arrant and Fallow section, they moved onto the Blear rack at the back of the closet. As Phoenix made swift and decisive choices over all the Blear items, Nora thought about how long Phoenix had been living in Blear as a Defected, away from her friends and family.

Nora selected several blouses and pants from the Blear clothing. The most noticeably different thing about Blear's apparel was that hints of varying shades of blue were incorporated into the designs. This aspect paired the clothing especially well with Phoenix's appearance, since the blue tones made her green eyes stand out more.

"Okay, we've got Arrant, Fallow and Blear," Phoenix announced as she looked in her bag. "Do you think we should check the other racks just in case?" As Phoenix spoke Nora looked at the clock on the wall, noting that only an hour had passed.

"I don't think we'll end up on the other side of Constance, but the boys still aren't here, so we some have time to kill. It couldn't hurt to take a look."

First they went to the Jejung rack. There weren't many options there. The prison of Jejung had a pretty strict dress code. The clothes were all gray, and girls had the option of either pants and a shirt, or a long dress. There was only one style for shoes that came in different sizes. They too were in the same dull gray shade. Nora glanced over at Phoenix and laughed incredulously.

"I guess Jejung doesn't like anyone to think for themselves," she commented as she held up one of the many nearly identical long dresses.

"Let's just hope we don't ever have to wear one of those," Phoenix replied, tossing a bleak gray top over her shoulder. As she continued to reject item after item of the Jejung clothing, a little gray pile began to form behind her.

Finally they worked their way over to the last rack—the Sonant clothing. Nora loved the beautiful green hues woven into the apparel. Since growing up the only color she'd had exposure to was purple, she'd never been able to choose a "favorite" color. But now that she was exposed to so much variety, she could. In that moment she decided that green was her official favorite.

They stuffed their bags until they could barely zip them closed, then strapped them onto their backs. Though the bags were filled to the brim, the clothing was so lightweight that they weren't too heavy.

On the way out of the closet Nora flicked the light switch off, and the room was again swallowed by darkness. Out in the hallway, Nora turned to Phoenix.

"I can't believe they still aren't here. I'm running out of ideas of how to keep us awake."

"Maybe it would be okay if we went outside. I'm not sure what the rules are and if that's allowed, but I'm thinking the fresh air would give us a burst of energy," Phoenix suggested.

"Well, I was unconscious when they brought us down here." Nora thought back to the moment she collapsed in the field after Tusk had knocked her out. "Do you remember how we came in?"

"You really should try and pay more attention," Phoenix teased. "Luckily for us, I wasn't napping when we were brought here." Phoenix smiled. She never missed an opportunity to tease her new friend.

Phoenix led the way and they took a few turns before arriving at a wooden wall. Phoenix twisted and yanked at the knobs until the large wood door clicked and swung open. Together they walked through it and into another dark room.

The air immediately felt more refreshing to Nora as she passed over the threshold. It was too dark to see, but she felt sheets of cloth hanging around her. She parted them with her arms to make way for her and Phoenix.

Nora wasn't entirely sure of where they were located, but it appeared to be some kind of abandoned store in Fallow's market area.

When she was near one of the windows, something caught Nora's eye. A dark mass flashed by far off in the distance. Nora squinted her eyes to try and make out what it was, but whatever it had been was too far away and had disappeared behind a nearby building.

Grabbing Phoenix's arm, Nora motioned with her eyes towards where she saw the unknown object. The two of them stared out the window, waiting to see if the movement would occur again. After a while Phoenix sighed and gave up. "Maybe we should go back," Nora said uneasily.

"Let's go outside for a moment. I want to feel the air of Fallow around me. I can't stand the thought of going back underground so quickly. It was probably just a wild animal," Phoenix pleaded.

Nora thought about it. The sun hadn't come up yet and the citywide curfew was still in place, most of Fallow was sure to still be asleep. The work day was still several hours away from beginning. "All right," she conceded, and slowly creaked open the door leading out from the abandoned shop.

They stepped out into the world and the slight breeze felt good on Nora's bare skin. There was a pleasant warmth in the air that made Nora realize just how chilly it was back inside the base. She closed her eyes and inhaled deeply. She started to stretch all her stiff muscles, and paid particular attention to her neck. Quickly she began to relax.

Feeling the stress drift away from her, Nora opened her eyes. Immediately another quick movement caught her attention. She squinted in the direction of unknown object, and continued to watch as the moving blur came into view. It was moving right towards them. When she realized this she drew a sharp breath in, but then quickly released it when she saw that it was Bray and the rest of the rebels. They were running at full speed in their direction. As they got closer, Nora could see Bray waving his arms at her. He was yelling something, but Nora couldn't make out what he was saying.

Without hesitating Nora began to run towards them in case they needed assistance. Once she'd closed some of the distance between them she was able to make out the words he was shouting.

"Turn back, they found us!" Bray gasped for air as he continued to yell.

"Get back inside! Hurry, they are right behind us!" Bray continued.

Nora spun around and ran back towards the doorway that Phoenix and her had just exited from. The two of them went in and watched through the window located at the front of the abandoned store. Nora counted each rebel as they came into view—there were 8 in addition to Otto, Bray, Jack, Trim, and Bretta.

They all came crashing into the abandoned store one after the other, until Jack shut the door behind all of them. Most of the rebels collapsed onto the floor, gasping for air. Nora immediately ran over to Bray.

"What happened out there, what took you guys so long to get back?" she asked, overcome with worry.

"Somehow the Agency found us," Bray managed to get out as he continued to gasp for air. "We were coming back through the wall between Blear and Arrant. They were right there waiting for us so we had to split up." As he spoke Nora helped him sit down against the wall.

"Where are the agents now?" she asked him, turning to look back out the window.

As if in answer to her own question, Nora saw the group of agents appear at the top of the hill towards the center of Constance. They paused for a moment as they looked around for any sign of movement. Otto turned from the window towards the rest of the group.

"Everyone stay quiet. The agents are just up ahead. Try and slow your breathing, we need to get back into the base without any of them seeing us."

Not yet having recuperated from their exhausting sprint, the group struggled to their feet. Phoenix led them through all the hanging cloths to the wooden door at the base's entrance. They quietly filed inside, careful to make as little sound as possible. Otto remained at the window keeping watch as the agents got nearer to their location. When all the other rebels had safely gotten into the base, he turned and headed through the wooden door himself, closing it shut behind him.

Nora helped Bray walk down the hallway—he was limping slightly so she let him lean up against her.

Inside, Otto leaned against the brown wall. He looked around the packed dirt hallway, counting under his breath.

"We lost three," he informed the others, his voice nearly breaking. "Three of our own. Gone. They are probably being escorted off to Jejung as we speak." His fist pounded the dirt wall behind him. "How could the agents have known we would be at the wall? We have been using that exit for years without any interference from the them." Otto looked over to Nora, as if seeking an answer from her.

"I think I know," she said. Everyone turned to look at her. "While you were gone, Dr. Secora took control of Phoenix's mind." Otto cast an immediate look of concern over to Phoenix, who nodded to confirm what Nora was saying. "It seems that he was able to reinstate Program 7 from the leftover data they collected while testing me in that lab. I'm guessing he used the concept to locate you guys coming out of Blear too," she said. Otto sighed loudly in exasperation.

"Great. Now we have to worry about that bastard spying on us and knowing our every move too?" The frustration in Otto's voice was unmistakeable. Nora hung her head, feeling dejected as well.

"What else is bothering you?" Bray asked. "I can tell that there is more to this story than that."

"They have my brother captive inside Obsidia. Dr. Secora gave me an ultimatum. Either I surrender myself or he will kill my brother Will." Everyone looked at Nora with shock and sympathy as she continued.

"The deadline for me to turn myself over to the Agency is in about thirty-four hours from now. If I decide not to, he will continue the executions with my parents."

As the reality of the situation sank in to the Blear rebel group, she hoped someone would speak up and tell her exactly what to do, but nobody spoke for a very long while. Finally Otto broke the silence in the dirt hallway.

"So, here is what we know. We have thirty-four hours to figure out our next move. I think we all can agree that there is no way we are giving up Nora to Dr. Secora. It's still early in the morning. Let's head to the sleeping units and get some rest while we have the chance—"

"We can't," Nora interrupted.

"What do you mean we can't?" Otto asked, confused.

"I mean, we can't fall asleep. That's how Dr. Secora located Phoenix's subconsciousness before. As soon as she fell asleep he was able to find her," Nora explained.

"Okay..." Otto said in response. Nora could hear the frustration in his voice. "So we won't all sleep at once. Everyone pair up. One of you will sleep and the other will stand guard. If there are any signs of someone being taken over by Dr. Secora, or anyone else from the center of Constance, you grab them and shake them until they wake up. If you can't wake them up, bring them to me—I've got a few things I wouldn't mind saying to that old bastard."

The group followed his orders and began to pair off. Nora started towards Phoenix, but saw that her friend was pairing up with Otto instead. Just as she was starting to blush with embarrassment, she felt a hand on her shoulder.

"I guess it's you and me," Bray said coyly. Nora could feel a smile creeping onto her face.

"Well then, I hope you don't snore too loudly," Nora teased.

CHAPTER 34

Bray stepped aside as he opened the door to his sleeping unit, and allowed Nora to enter first—the room was significantly smaller than the one Nora shared with the other girls. Inside was a small bed, with a chair against the opposite wall, and a wooden dresser in the corner. The floor, walls, and ceiling were all made of the same compressed dirt that made up the rest of the underground base, and the room was lit by a single hanging bulb.

As Bray followed in after her, Nora lingered by the door, unsure of what to do. He made his way over to the chair and sat down, sighing deeply as he did—clearly happy to finally be off his feet. Nora was relieved he didn't head straight to the cot. She was a little nervous about being alone in a bedroom with him, and not sure how much self control either of them would have. Purposefully avoiding the bed, which at the moment felt like the elephant in the room—Nora made her way over to the dresser in the back of the space and began to rummage through the contents of the top drawer.

She absentmindedly examined the various items of Bray's clothing, but her thoughts weren't really on men's fashion at the moment. It helped somewhat to keep her mind distracted, and it was good to keep her hands busy. After a few minutes of awkward silence Bray cleared his throat.

"Are you looking for a new style of clothing to wear?" he joked.

Nora didn't respond, and didn't turn to face him—she could feel tears welling up in her eyes. She forced herself to continue focusing on the dresser, and ran her hands along the edges, picking out chips in the paint. Despite her best efforts, she felt her emotions continue to bubble up inside of her. Her cheeks grew hot with embarrassment at the thought of Bray seeing her cry. All she had wanted from when they'd first met was a night alone with him, and here she was, about to bawl her eyes out.

Her shoulders rose and fell as she took in a deep breath, but then her breathing became shuttered and erratic. A few moments later the tears began to spill helplessly down her cheeks. Without saying a word, Bray walked over to her and wrapped his arms around her from behind.

As he cradled Nora in his arms, she reached up to grab his wrists. His skin was warm and comforting. She could feel his chest rising and falling against her back. Wriggling to loosen herself from his grasp somewhat, she turned around in his arms to face him. She tried to laugh, but instead more tears rolled down her cheeks.

"It's all too much," she said as she gently pushed him away. He winced at her rejection of his touch. "I never knew I could be happy, and sad, and so full of hate and love all at once like this," she continued, trying to explain her feelings to him.

Bray reached up and wiped a tear from Nora's cheek. He still did not speak, but instead waited patiently to hear what else she wanted to say. Appreciating his kindness, Nora took his hands in hers.

"Dr. Secora has Will," Nora finally blurted out. Her forehead furrowed and her eyes squinted in pain. "If I don't turn myself in, he will kill my entire family." Feeling somewhat relieved at having confided the truth of her feelings to Bray, her face relaxed, and a fresh batch of tears streamed out of her eyes. She watched as a single teardrop landed on the dirt ground between them.

"If I turn myself in, I will spend my life in Jejung," she paused and inhaled sharply as another thought occurred to her. "Or worse—I'll spend the rest of my life inside of Obsidia in a test lab until they are done with me."

Placing a hand on the back of Nora's neck, Bray tilted her head up to force her to look him in the eyes. He then brushed aside a few damp strands of hair that had stuck to her tear-soaked cheek.

"I'm sorry," Nora said, letting her head fall back down to stare at the now tear-splattered dirt floor. "We finally have a chance to be alone, and all I can do is break down and cry in front of you."

"I'm glad you feel comfortable enough with me to let me see this side of you," Bray said, finally speaking. "We all put up some kind of a wall around people. It's nice to find someone who is willing to let you inside those walls once in awhile." Nora looked up at him as he continued to talk.

"You can access the few scattered memories I have left at any time and see for yourself what lays within my walls, but I don't have it so easy with you. If this is what it takes to get a glimpse inside of Nora, then I welcome it."

Bray wrapped an arm around Nora and pulled her in closer, before whispering into her ear.

"You don't have to put on a tough act around me. I can be strong enough for the both of us, until you get through this. And you will get through this," he said with a smile.

He turned around and tugged at her arm to follow him. Together they made their way over to the bed. Bray sat down on the starchy white blanket and invitingly patted the cot next to him. Nora obliged and sat gingerly down as well.

They stared off straight ahead at the dirt wall across from them, without saying a word. Bray wrapped an arm around Nora's delicate frame, his palm cradling her hip. In return she leaned in and rested her head against his chest.

"Thank you," she said softly, her eyes closed. Since her crying had ceased, the skin on her cheeks began to dry out. Her eyelashes were weighed down, heavy with a few remaining tears that were yet to spill out.

Bray raised his hand from her hip and began to caress her back through her shirt with his fingertips. Chills ran down her spine as he continued to touch her, and the hair on the back of her neck rose. His hand drifted upward to her hairline, and he gently stroked the area behind her ear. He then brushed the hair out of her face, which Nora instinctively knew meant that he wanted her to look up at him. She lifted her head and locked eyes with him.

They stared at each other for a few moments, trying to interpret what they saw in each other's eyes. Nora blinked several times in rapid succession, and she felt butterflies in her stomach. Bray placed a strong grip around her waist—his palm pressed tightly against her stomach and his fingers curved around to her back. In a moment of shyness she bit her lip and dropped her gaze.

"Bray," she began, but then paused. "Thank you for being so nice to me. I've wanted to be alone with you for what seems like forever now," she paused again, trying to think of the right words to say. Bray's expression didn't change as he waited for her to speak.

"I didn't want it to be like this though. Not under these circumstances, I mean—with me being so distracted and weighted down by fear and sadness."

"I'd never want you to do something you weren't completely comfortable with. You have shared something with me just now that I could have only dreamed of—something so pure and real. This has only made me feel closer to you," he said tenderly.

"I always thought things would be different when I was ready for something like this," Nora said, but then instantly regretted her words.

She wrinkled her nose in frustration, hoping that Bray hadn't picked up on the meaning behind her slip of the tongue. She tried to cover it all up quickly.

"What I mean is I thought the circumstances would be different," she said hastily, trying to promptly bury her error. "That we wouldn't be stuck in some underground cave worried that the world was about to end," she managed to get out.

"We have plenty of time to figure all of that stuff out. No sense in spending the next few hours talking about what should have or could have been," he said kindly. "Anyway, I think you should be the first to rest. I'll keep watch over you," he continued in a comforting tone. Nora looked up, thankful that he hadn't pushed the subject any more.

"Well, if worse comes to worst, I could always sneak into your mind and implant a memory of tonight as being the best night of your life," she teased, a smile forming on her lips.

"Trust me. I'll be waiting in this cold dark room for eternity if that ever becomes the case," he joked back. Nora's smile widened and they both fell quiet.

Getting off the bed, Bray knelt down on the floor in front of Nora, placing his hand on her foot. She looked down at him quizzically, trying to figure out what he was doing.

"You need at least a few hours of sleep so that you can tackle the day tomorrow," he said. As he spoke, Nora felt her shoelaces being untied. "You, of course, are welcome to sleep in my bed, but these dirty shoes are not invited," he said with a smirk.

Bray lifted off one of her shoes, set it to the side, and proceeded to loosen the laces on the remaining one. Once both her shoes were off he lifted her legs up and swung her around onto the bed. He lifted the blankets and folded them over her body, tucking her in loosely.

He was just about to rise up off his knees and stand when Nora reached out and wrapped her arms around his neck and forcefully pulled him in closer. They shared a long, hard, passionate kiss that left them both slightly out of breath.

"I've been wanting to do that since you came back from Blear," she said, a huge smile on her face. "I'm going to try and rest for a little while now," she added. "I'll see you in my dreams," she said with a wink.

Nora shut her eyes, and she could feel Bray move away from her. She heard him walk across the floor and sit in the chair. She felt safe knowing that he would stay there, watching over her. Sleep came quickly to her.

* * *

When Nora opened her eyes, it felt as though she had slept much longer than she had wanted to. Immediately she noticed that Bray was laying next to her in the bed, his arm wrapped around her chest. As she relished in the warmth of his body pressed up so close against her own she wondered at what point Bray had given up his watch duty and gotten into bed with her. She must have been really out of it for her not to have noticed him joining her.

Though she wanted badly to stay on the cot with him, Nora knew that she had to get up. There was too much to accomplish now, and laying in bed, hiding from the world, wouldn't solve any of her problems.

Being careful not to wake Bray, she inched her way toward the edge of the cot and slipped out of his embrace. She then carefully got out from under the blanket and placed her bare feet on the cold dirt floor. As she maneuvered away from Bray she thought back to the day she'd left her old life behind, when she had snuck out and left Deryn still sleeping in their bed.

She squeezed her eyes shut, trying to push away the memories of that day. Standing up, she retrieved her shoes, finding them under her pants which lay in a heap on the floor.

Nora stood still, momentarily confused—she didn't recall taking her pants off before going to bed. Shrugging, she figured she'd woken up in the middle of the night and removed them while still half asleep, and she simply didn't remember. She put her pants on as quickly as she could, not wanting to risk Bray waking up in time to see her half naked.

She sat in the chair opposite the cot as she tied her shoelaces, and lovingly observed Bray as he slept, remarking on how peaceful and vulnerable he looked in that state. He really was quite handsome, she marveled. Normally she could not stare at him for such an extended period of time, for fear of him catching her in the act.

Nora left the room, shutting the door gently behind her, and headed back towards the sleeping unit she shared with Phoenix. Once she had reached the girls' quarters she was surprised to find that all of the beds were still made. There were no signs that anyone had slept there. Nora snickered to herself as she guessed where Phoenix was most likely sleeping. She was happy for the two of them. Otto was a very gentle, but serious man, and someone like Phoenix was good for him—she was able to bring out a joyful and more playful side of him.

202

She removed a few pieces of clothing from the closet so that she could get changed into something clean. As she walked over to the sink to wash up she caught a glimpse of herself in the mirror. She was suddenly very thankful she had left Bray's room without waking him.

Her hair was a tangled mess and her eyes were still swollen from crying the night before. She splashed some cold water on her face and immediately felt refreshed. In an attempt to get her hair situation under control she wetted her hands and tried to smooth it down. Still not satisfied with the results, she decided to dunk her whole head under the running water. As her hair grew thoroughly soaked she contemplated how else she could improve her appearance that morning.

Nora felt a pang of guilt at using such valuable time on something as superficial as what she looked like. There was so much at stake, and the clock was running out. But, she reasoned, if she could at least feel somewhat presentable and halfway human, she'd be in a much better emotional state and better equipped to handle the situation.

She found a couple makeup brushes and eyeliner pencils that Phoenix had left on her bedside table. Trying to recall the instructions Phoenix had given her back in Blear when she taught her how to apply the makeup, she pressed one of the pencils to the corner of her eyelid. A few carefully placed strokes of the dark pigment made her look remarkably different.

After running a brush through her wet hair she let it air dry and then dug around Phoenix's bag until she found a small hair tie which she used to hold her hair back and out of her face. Now that her physical transformation was complete, she observed herself in the mirror again. If she was going to give into Dr. Secora's demands, she reasoned, she would do so as the tough, rebel girl she had become, not the fresh-faced, innocent girl she once was.

She replaced Phoenix's pencils and brushes where she'd found them and left the room, deciding to make her way over to the cafeteria. As she walked down the dirt hallway she could already smell the food that was there waiting for her.

Wasting no time, Nora got in the food line, and when it was her turn she made her way around the room, piling her tray just as high as she'd done each time before. Once she felt satisfied that she had enough, she walked around the room towards the table Lace and Grane sat at.

Grane looked like he hadn't gotten any sleep at all—his hair was greasy and disheveled, and there were dark bags under his eyes.

Grane and Lace greeted her with a tired smile, and Lace complimented her on her new look.

"You look different," Lace began, "In a good way. In fact, I would say you were glowing with a brand new radiance," she continued with a smile.

"Thank you Lace," Nora said pleasantly, already uneasy about the bomb she was about to drop on the two of them. "It looks like someone has been up all night," Nora commented, tilting her head over to Grane.

Grane looked up from his food. "Once I started making progress, I couldn't stop," he said between bites. "I was able to build a similar device to the NFIs Dr. Secora has been using for the agent's mental protection from you. It was quite simple really. Once I figured out which frequencies the Neural Feedback Inhibitors were using to block out the theta waves produced by the user's subconsciousness, all the other components easily fell into place."

"That's great Grane! This is fantastic news," Nora exclaimed, attempting to absorb the large amount of technical information he had just given her. She grew excited over the progress he'd made, but Grane's somber expression remained unchanged.

"Well, don't get too excited yet. I was only able to make five of them before I ran out of supplies. We should be able to get more as soon as—"

"Sorry to interrupt," Nora interjected, unable to contain her news any longer. "But Dr. Secora visited me last night." Lace and Grane looked at her in shock. Their eyes widened and they both stopped eating.

Nora went on to fill Lace and Grane in with the disheartening details of the recent developments. She explained how she could see no other option than to yield to Dr. Secora's demands, and that she had woken up that morning prepared to march alone to the center of Constance and give herself up.

She also told them about how Phoenix and herself had snuck outside the night before and found Bray and Otto and the rest of the rebels returning from Blear, that they had been followed by the Agency and Nora was certain it was only a mater of time before they discovered the Fallow base. Lace and Grane's faces sank as they digested the news.

"However," Nora added brightly, "Thanks to Grane's efforts from last night, I think I have a new idea that might work in our favor. Dr. Secora doesn't know we have our own NFIs yet," she said.

"We only have five though," Grane said dejectedly. "I won't be able to make any more until we make a supply run. The next one isn't scheduled for a few days from now."

"Let her finish, Grane. Let's hear about this plan," Lace said, urging Nora to continue.

"Okay," Nora began, her mind working quickly. "You were only able to build five of the Program 7 blocking devices. This means we can form a small team of rebels to escort me to the center of Constance. I don't think Dr. Secora would find anything suspicious about me wanting to protect myself along the way."

The two of them continued to listen as Nora laid out her entire plan. She spoke decisively and gesticulated often as she explained her thought process. Lace and Grane listened intently and nodded along as Nora talked.

"Yes! I do believe this could actually work!" Grane exclaimed once they'd heard the whole thing.

"Who do you want to escort you then?" Lace asked.

Nora felt a surge of pride over the fact that Lace was treating her like such an adult—consulting her for who would best be suited to accompany her on the journey.

"Honestly, I think it's best to ask my fellow rebels from Blear— Otto, Bray, Phoenix, Jack, Trim, and Bretta," Nora replied.

"Okay," Lace said. "Though I think you should include one or two members from the Fallow base on your team."

"My fellow Blear rebels have all been inside of Obsidia before. Is there anyone here at the Fallow base that has that experience as well?" Nora questioned.

"Well, no," Lace admitted. "Okay, you have made your point. You can have your team as you wish," she conceded. "I have to ask though, with only 5 NFIs, how will that work with your team? By my count, there would be 7 of you."

"Don't worry," Nora started, "I have that part figured out. All that matters is that now I'll have a proper security team to escort me right up to Dr. Secora's front door."

Lace nodded. "Okay then. So—what can we do for support?"

"I think the most important thing you guys can do is to remain here and protect the rebellion. You've worked so hard, and no matter what happens to me, the fight will have to continue," Nora said. She reached across the table and placed her palm on top of Lace's hand, squeezing it slightly. "I want the two of you to hold onto the disk containing Program 7. Please use it wisely to find more of the Defected amongst the rest of the citizens. Bring them in and keep the rebellion growing, even if I never return."

As Nora got up, ready to find her team members and inform them of the plan, the entire base suddenly shook. Dirt began to come loose from the ceiling and fill the air. Large clods of dirt tumbled onto the floor and the lights flickered. Lace shot up out of her seat, her chin trembling. Another loud boom sounded, and the ceiling and walls crumbled even more around them. The lights flickered again and then went out, leaving them all in darkness for several long seconds before flashing back on.

"The Agency must have found us!" Lace yelled.

Nora ran for the door and into the hallway. Behind her she could hear Lace shouting orders to the other rebels that remained in the cafeteria. Nora didn't turn around to listen, she had one goal on her mind—to get to her Blear rebels.

She deftly navigated the hallways and sped around each corner. The base continued to shake and crumble as the loud booms sounded from overhead. Finally she had made it to Bray's room. She flung the door open and saw that Bray still laid in the bed asleep. Without thinking, Nora leapt onto him and violently shook him, in an effort to rouse him from whatever comatose state he appeared to be in.

Bray awoke with a start and shot up straight, nearly flinging Nora off the bed. He blinked repeatedly as he tried to comprehend what was happening. As another loud explosion went off above their heads, Bray jumped out of bed and frantically began to throw on some clothes.

"What is going on?" he yelled, his voice nearly drowned out from the noise of another loud boom.

Reaching down, Nora grabbed the bag that she had left in his room the night before.

"The agents from last night must have found out where we were all hiding! Go find Otto, Jack, and Trim," she ordered him. "Then meet me by the Dream Machine room."

With that Nora ran out of the room and down the hallway to her sleeping unit. As she grabbed the doorknob the whole wall vibrated and threatened to crash down on her. She braced herself against the door as she swung it open.

Phoenix and Bretta were inside, frantically packing.

"What in the world?!" Phoenix exclaimed, her eyes filled with panic.

Nora grabbed a hold of them both, and began to drag them out of the room.

"Forget about the rest of the clothes, we need to move, now!" Nora ordered them. Just as they were exiting the room a massive piece of the ceiling plummeted to the ground, right where the girls had been standing as they packed.

The three of them ran down the hallway, with their heads ducked to protect from the falling debris. When a small chunk of dirt landed on Bretta's head she let out a loud, startled shriek.

Finally they turned the corner that led to the Dream Machine room. Otto, Trim, Jack and Bray were already there waiting for them outside of the door. All three were backed against the wall, bracing themselves in anticipation of the next ground-shaking explosion.

"We need to get out of here!" Otto yelled out over the noise.

Ignoring him, Nora opened the door and went inside the Dream Machine room.

"What are you doing Nora?!" Trim yelled out. "We need to move now!" A large piece of dirt landed on the ground next to him causing Trim to jump to the side.

Knowing that they only had few moments left, Nora raced over and scanned the consoles. Reacting quickly, she grabbed the five NFIs Grane had left sitting nearby on one of the tables. As she turned to leave the room, the door frame gave out under the pressure and crashed down to the dirt floor.

"Nora!" Bray called out worriedly from the other side of the wall.

"I'm okay!" she called back. Her voice was muffled behind the barricade of dirt and debris that was getting larger by the second.

Thinking fast, Nora ran at the falling dirt pile as hard as she could. The loose soil gave into her efforts somewhat, but not enough for her to make her escape. One of her arms had managed to penetrate the forming dirt mound and stuck out on the other side of it. She felt someone's hands on her arm, as they began to pull her through. Once more of her body was through the dirt pile, more people grabbed ahold of her. At a certain point she began to get nervous that her next breath would be a mouthful of soil, but suddenly her body was pulled free.

Bray held her up with his arms as Phoenix slapped piles of dirt off of her shoulders.

Nora saw Lace at the end of the long hallway, running towards them at full speed and waving her arms.

"This way!" Lace called out. "There is another way out of here that only Grane and I know about." The rebels immediately started to follow her, and Nora recovered quickly, leaping to her feet and making her way up to run alongside Lace.

"Have any of your rebels been able to get out?" Nora asked her.

"We have lost a couple to the falling rubble, so far," Lace replied breathlessly. "The rest are on their way out of here through the storefront. I have no doubt that the Agency will be waiting for them there. I ordered them to stand their ground and fight back before heading towards Blear, so that they could distract the agents long enough for you guys to sneak out the back, and ideally lead the agents off your trail entirely. Let's hope their weapon supply will be sufficient to allow them to complete their mission safely."

"We will head towards the center of Constance," Nora informed her. "I still have faith that this plan will work. Hopefully we will see each other again on the other side of all of this," Nora said as Lace stopped at a door.

"Up this hill you will find a way to the surface," Lace instructed them. "Look for the old wooden shed and run towards it. We will do our best to keep the agents at bay. Hopefully that will give you enough time to get back into Arrant. From there you should be safe heading towards the center of Constance," she stopped to look Nora and the other six Blear rebels in their adrenaline-fueled eyes. "Good luck," she said sincerely. "Whatever happens here today, do not come back for us. Now go!" she urged. The rebels all fled, following the directions she had laid out. Lace grabbed a hold of Nora before she ran off.

"Let's hope this plan of yours works," Lace said. "We all need the chance to live long and happy lives. Hopefully that day will come. Until then Nora, we are all counting on you."

Nora nodded and then turned to run up the hill of dirt after the rest of the rebels. She spun around in an effort to get one last look at Lace, but saw that the doorway had caved in. All that was left was a large pile of dirt. Her throat tightened, and she hoped Lace had gotten away in time before the collapse.

As she continued to make her way out of the underground base, gun shots rang in the distance. There was a small beam of light pouring in up ahead, so she knew they were almost to the surface. Nora braced herself as she continued to run at full speed, having no choice but to go straight towards the deafening sound of gunfire and explosions that lay on the other side.

CHAPTER 35

Otto began to push open a hatch door at the top of the dirt ramp—the above ground world of Fallow lay on the other side of it. Sunlight started to fill the corners of the hatch's opening as the muscles in Otto's arm twitched from the weight of the heavy, cast iron door. Once he'd gotten it up a little higher more light appeared along the seams. With a loud grunt Otto was able to heave the door open completely and the sunlight flooded in, illuminating the face of each rebel.

Otto raised himself up and climbed out of the hatch, disappearing from view. Nora's heart began to race—unsure if she should follow him or remain hidden. Thankfully, Otto peeked his head back into the opening after only a few moments had passed. His head was a dark silhouette in front of the bright sky behind him.

"It's all clear up here," Otto whispered down to the rest of the group. He motioned with his arm for them to follow.

Phoenix climbed out first. Otto extended a hand to help her out, and though at first she stubbornly refused—believing she could do it on her own—she ended up taking his hand. Nora followed after, and then the rest of the rebels climbed out one by one, with Bray hanging back until everyone else had gone through. They all backed away from the opening and Bray shut the hatch behind him.

Once the door was shut, the hatch blended in seamlessly with its surroundings. The top of the trap door was covered with the same crops that grew around it. Nora blinked a few times, it seemed almost like an optical illusion—she no longer could see where the entrance was.

Trim lifted Otto onto his shoulders so that he could see over the tall, golden crops and get a better view. He made a full 360-degree turn, moving slowly, and all the while asking Otto if he could see anything. When gunshots began to ring out in the sky above them, Otto quickly hopped off Trim's shoulders.

"The wood shed Lace told us about is only a few yards to the left. If we stay on this path the field will hide us until we reach the wall." Otto motioned with his hands as he laid out the plan to the rebels.

The group took off at a swift pace—wanting to ensure they had a good head start on the Fallow rebels, just in case the Agency was on their tails.

Once they had made it to the edge of the field, Otto stopped, parting the dense crops with his hands and gestured to a wall a little bit away from where they stood.

"Okay, we're here. I need to get a better look at what is going on out there," Otto called out, motioning for Trim to come over and boost him up again.

Just as he had done before, Trim turned slowly to allow Otto to survey the entire surrounding landscape. Once Otto had inspected the scene thoroughly he jumped down, landing hard in the dirt. He recovered quickly from the dismount and put a finger over his lips, signaling everyone to stay quiet.

"There are two agents walking the path between this field and the next one. We should be okay, but I still want to play it safe. Bray and I will go out to the wall and remove the bricks. The rest of you wait here. Don't come out until we signal for you," Otto said in a hushed voice. He looked around at the rest of the rebels and they all nodded in response.

Bray and Otto took off for the wall, leaving the safety of the crop hideout behind. They dashed quickly and covertly towards it—Otto arriving first, with Bray following soon after. They then began to push on various bricks, as they tried to find the removable ones.

Though Nora was somewhat nervous at the tense situation, her breathing began to slow to normal—there was no need to get worked up over anything, as it seemed they'd made their escape. She watched as one of the bricks Bray leaned into gave way slightly. Bray waved Otto over to come help him push it all the way through. Once it had fallen onto the other side of the wall, they continued on to the next brick— they were able to push this one through much more easily.

Otto turned to the watching rebels and signaled them to join him at at the wall. The rebels dashed over, keeping their heads low as they ran.

Otto pointed at them one by one, signaling the order that they were to go through the wall in. Trim was first followed by Nora. As he positioned himself to squeeze back through the wall into Arrant, Otto whispered to him.

"Once you are through, find a place for us to hide. We don't know what's on the other side waiting for us. If anything happens, you get Nora to the center of Constance."

Trim nodded without responding and climbed up into the opening in the wall. Once he'd gotten through, he crouched near the hole and surveyed the surroundings, hunting for a hiding spot, as he waited to help Nora out. Nora got through easily, and grabbed his hand to steady herself as she jumped onto the ground in Arrant.

He led Nora to a building on their right—which he'd deemed the safest option to hide out in. Once there, the two of them sat, waiting anxiously for the rest of the group to catch up.

As each rebel appeared one by one, Nora thought about how surprising it was that they'd gotten through the wall without any trouble from the Agency. The battle currently underway at the Fallow rebel base must have been doing a good job of keeping the agents preoccupied.

Once they had all regrouped, Otto looked off in every direction, scanning the roads meticulously to ensure the coast was clear. He then waved them across the alleyway. Otto was the last to cross over, and they repeated this procedure at each subsequent stopping place.

As they moved from building to building there were no signs of agents anywhere. Even on a normal day in Arrant you could expect a few of them to be patrolling the streets. Nora ran a hand through her hair and bit her lip, deep in thought. Something felt off to her—it all seemed far too easy.

While Otto was crouched down, doing his inspections before another alley dash, Nora approached him, tapping him on the shoulder. Otto, startled at the unexpected touch, whirled around.

"Aren't you a little confused as to why we haven't seen one single agent yet?" she asked him. Otto turned back to look down the alley before responding.

"Of course I am. I'll take an easy exit over a barrage of agents any day though. So even though it's a little suspicious, I'm still grateful we haven't encountered any," he replied, his eyes still fixed on the alley.

Nora had to agree with him, what else could they do but thank their good fortune and continue along the perimeter of Arrant until they reached the place in the wall where the building material shipments passed through.

The group continued on at a cautious pace, and Nora let the others get ahead of her until she was beside Phoenix.

"So, where did you sleep last night?" Nora asked, trying anything to break up the tenseness of the situation. "I noticed you weren't in our sleeping unit this morning when I went in there." Her blunt question caused Phoenix to blush.

"Hey now! You told me not to go back to sleep. I had to do something to stay awake," she responded with a smile.

"And?" Nora investigated further.

"And..." Phoenix shifted her eyes towards the ground. She sighed before looking up again.

"We decided that there were more important things going on that we had to take care of first," Phoenix gave a wide smile, clearly masking a bit of hurt feelings. "Besides, one day this will all be over and we can start pretending like we were meant to be together like the two of you do," she continued, gesturing up ahead to where Bray was. Nora knew she was teasing, but she felt a little insulted at the suggestion that her and Bray's romantic situation caused them not to take things as seriously as Phoenix and Otto did.

"Well just so you know, I fell asleep and was out of the room before Bray even woke up," Nora said, somewhat defensively. Phoenix looked at her quizzically.

"I guess I just thought because of that goofy smile on Bray's face and the way you fancied up your appearance today that something more had happened. I didn't mean anything by it," Phoenix said apologetically. "I'm glad you two found each other. It just makes me wish this whole thing would be over already."

Phoenix squeezed her hand and Nora instantly felt silly for getting defensive.

"It looks like we are almost at the wall opening," Nora said, pointing up ahead.

The breathless, sweat-soaked group of rebels lingered behind the building in Arrant that was closest to the spot where the walls would eventually open. As Nora waited, she tried to keep a patient and calm expression on her face, even though her throat continued to tighten.

At any moment, those walls would slide open. What would happen after that was unknown. Nora had led her team of rebels—people whom she had already begun to care very deeply for—right into the heart of the beast. If anything went wrong with her plan, she knew she'd carry that guilt with her for the rest of her life—however long that was.

She took a moment to admire the faces of everyone around her. Otto was focused intently on the wall ahead, his hair in his face. He stood with his back against the wall of the building, with both of his arms placed firmly on his rifle. He took a deep breath, never averting his gaze and barely even blinking. Even the pace of his breathing was consistently measured—he was the epitome of strength and self control.

Nora felt a rush of gratitude as she observed him. Her newfound abilities had propelled her into a leadership position that she was in no way prepared for, but luckily Otto stepped in every time the pressure of it was too overwhelming for her. She hoped that one day she'd be able to see the softer, more relaxed side to him that she was convinced existed.

She then turned her gaze towards Jack, who faced away from the wall, back into the sector to keep watch. He reached up to wipe away a bead of sweat that had formed along his hairline. His face had very rugged lines, and his thick brown hair was matted down with sweat. Nora felt bad for not making time to get to know him better. Jack glanced over and flashed her a big smile, exposing all of his teeth.

"Thank you for coming along, Jack," Nora said, giving him a big smile in return.

"I wouldn't have it any other way, Miss Nora," he replied with a wink, his voice as calm and friendly as always.

As the weight and reality of their situation continued to sink in, Nora fiddled with her hands. "I just realized that I'm sitting here, expecting you to risk your life for me, and I don't know a single thing about you," she said, her voice nearly cracking with emotion. She slapped a hand against her thigh in frustration.

Jack simply smiled at her again. "I'm exactly where I am supposed to be, Miss Nora."

"No, that's not enough," Nora said, raising her voice so much that the rest of the rebels glanced over. "I need to know something about you. How long have you been Defected?" she asked him bluntly.

Jack sat up straighter and shook his head. Nora began to worry that she had offended him. As Jack's glance fell and he leaned in to speak she saw an expression on his face that she'd never seen before.

"Miss Nora," he paused and let out a sigh. "I am not like you."

"Apparently no one is, Jack," Nora said, trying to reassure him.

"No, Miss Nora, you have misinterpreted my meaning." He raised his eyes to meet hers. "I'm not Defected."

There was a long pause as Jack and Nora stared at each other. "When Dr. Secora began administering the brain scans 10 years ago," Jack continued, "I lived in the center sector."

Nora glanced around her and saw all of the rebels were now listening to Jack's story. When she returned her attention to him, Jack continued.

"My..." he began, and then looked up into the sky and squinted. "My daughter, Davina, was among the first to be examined. She was nearly the same age as all of you at the time. I couldn't bear to just let them take her away from us, so I decided to pack our things and run away from the center of Constance. I begged and pleaded with my wife to come with us, but she refused to believe the severity of the situation—thought I was over reacting. So, my daughter and I left. Just the two of us."

Without thinking, Nora spoke out, "Where is your dau-" she cut herself off just as Jack began shaking his head as he let his stare fall back into the dirt again.

As Nora's heart sank lower, Jack turned to her again. "As I said Miss Nora, I'm exactly where I am supposed to be." He smiled at her one last time before returning his gaze back into the sector to keep watch.

Phoenix was knelt down beside Jack, now keeping her hands busy by dragging a small twig methodically across the ground, carving out lines in the earth repeatedly. Nora wondered what was weighing so heavily on Phoenix's mind. She could only guess that it had to do with Otto telling her that they needed to wait until the war was over to fully commit to each other emotionally.

Phoenix's bubbly personality had helped Nora's transition into her new life in ways that she was sure Phoenix would never fully understand. The mystery girl that had pulled her from the alley so long ago, had turned out to be the best friend Nora had made in her short life. Nora wished that the day would eventually come when the two of them could sit in the sun-soaked fields of Fallow without a care in the world. Hopefully, Bray and Otto would be right there with them. The thought of going out on double dates like a normal young adult made Nora smile.

Trim and Bretta were huddled near each other, whispering and smiling, despite the nerve-wrecking situation they were in. Nora was envious at how easy they made love seem. They wanted to be together, so they were. And they always had smiles on their faces, as if their love trumped everything else. Nora found herself jealous and respectful of the two of them at the same time. They were never afraid to be who they wanted to be, and they didn't care what the rest of this walled-off world thought of them. Nora smiled as her gaze drifted away from them and onto the last member of her rebel group.

Bray was hunched right behind them, observing the wall as well, but also turning every once in a while to check on Nora. This time when he looked back and saw her watching him he flashed her a crooked grin. Nora began to reminisce about when she'd been laying beside him in bed, her head still filled with dreams, that morning before the bombs started going off. It had been so peaceful and comforting to be in his arms, and she longed to be back there. Ever since the explosions had begun things had moved at a frantic pace.

It was in this moment that Nora realized the extent of the changes Bray had caused in her heart. He had shown her that no matter where things in her life would take her, she would still have a place to belong. At a turning point in her life, when she assumed the worst, he was there to pick her up and remind her that people would always care about her. As she had shifted from the innocent girl from Arrant to the enemy of the entire city, he had been there to hold her up and protect her. To continue pushing her forward and reminding her that, while the loved ones from her past would always have a special place in her heart, there were possibilities in the future, and plenty of space inside her heart for new love and friendships.

Nora sat quietly, alone on the ground, unable to stop the stream of thoughts in her head. She contemplated what she should say to her brother when she eventually saw him. She wanted to be able to comfort him—to be a good older sister. More than anything, she prayed he was not too frightened. At such a young age, he would certainly have trouble understanding what was going on.

Dr. Secora would undoubtedly be there. She wondered if he'd be the one personally holding Will hostage, or if he'd have one of his agents doing it. As she imagined a gun being held to her little brother's head she shuddered, and decided to stop thinking about the different possible scenarios.

Nora determined that now would be a good time to lay out her plan to her fellow rebels. Quietly approaching each one, she gestured for them to gather around her.

Carefully she told them why she had brought them all to the center of Constance with her, that they were there to be more than just her escort. Once those walls opened, she explained, they would all be going through the opening together.

They stared at her as she finished detailing her plan—they appeared half confused and half excited. Though it was a somewhat complex plan, they all seemed to understand it. Bray asked the first, and most obvious question.

"Do you think it will work?"

Nora looked him directly in his eyes. "It has to. Otherwise this will be the end of the line for us. Do you guys understand that?"

They all nodded their heads. Nora was shocked by how calm and agreeable they were all being. Not only were their own lives at stake now, but the fate of the entire city of Constance was placed in their hands. They all knew that this could only end one of three ways—a life filled with freedom, imprisonment, or death—and yet somehow they were still on board.

At that point Otto chimed in, "Nora, we know what the situation is. The fact remains, no one can be forced into this. We all must make our decisions separately. If anyone wants out, now is the time to speak up. You can find your way back to the wall between Arrant and Blear and wait for the Fallow rebels there—they are heading into Blear, where they will be setting up a new base." As he spoke the expression on his face was dead serious. "No judgements will be placed on you if you leave. Every one of us knows exactly what is at stake here, today. I would not blame you if you decide to take the safer road out of here. Just know that whether you stay here and fight with Nora right now, or choose to go off and fight your own battle another day—eventually the real war will begin and come looking for you. We have a chance right now, right here, to end this. A chance to move forward and protect our futures."

Everyone looked at each other, but no one spoke or got up to leave.

"Okay then," Nora said after taking a deep breath. "You all know your places. For this to work, we have to execute this plan perfectly."

Reaching into her pocket, Nora handed out the five Neural Feedback Inhibitors that Grane had manufactured. She handed one to everyone but Bray. "Put these in your ears. They will stop Dr. Secora from being able to access your subconsciousness."

As if on cue, a slight rumble sounded, signaling that the wall was about to slide open. The rebels stared as the wall split and the opening slowly began to widen.

"Ready or not, this is it. There is no turning back now," Nora said, speaking as much to everyone else as she was to herself.

Otto ran over to the opening and peered through the small space that had formed. He only looked for a moment before he turned back to the group.

"Agents!" he whispered loudly. "I counted three of them so far, and they're all armed."

They all nodded, and Bray and Jack dashed over to the other side of the opening. As the walls moved further apart, the guys stepped back along with it so that they would remain out of sight.

Trim looked over at Bretta, his eyebrows raised questioningly, and she nodded in response. He then turned to Nora. "You need to stay behind us no matter what. We will get you in to the center of Constance so you can finish this damn thing."

Nora smiled weakly in response, wanting to appear courageous, even though inside she was terrified. The remaining rebels went over to the wall opening—Trim and Bretta standing in front, with Phoenix and Nora behind them. Nora had to strain to see anything, and craned her neck to get a glimpse of what was going on over Bretta's shoulder.

As the wall opened wider, a group of agents became visible. There were six in total, in staggered rows—one in the front, two behind him, and three bringing up the rear. All were armed with rifles.

Once the wall had opened as far as it would go, the rumbling ceased. Both the rebels and the agents froze for a moment—no one daring to move. When Nora was able to get a better view of the agents she began scanning through the area hoping to see her brother, Will. She frantically searched for her younger brother's innocent eyes amongst the hardened gazes of the agents. As all hope began to fade away, her gaze finally landed on a familiar face in the back row of their line-up—Deryn's. She let out a small gasp, but he didn't flinch at the sight of her.

Instantly she felt guilty, especially with Bray being right there as well. She had not considered the possibility that Deryn would be amongst the agents they would have to battle. As she continued to observe Deryn, it seemed as though there was something different about him. He stared straight ahead along with the rest of the agents, not once averting his gaze. There was no emotion in his eyes, and his posture was nearly identical to the men beside him.

Just then, the agent in the forefront sprung to life. He directed his words at Nora, who was safely hidden behind Trim and Bretta.

"You were instructed to come here alone. This is not what was agreed upon," the agent said.

"Where is Will?!" Nora demanded, her voice both angry and pleading.

"He is safe, for now. If you surrender you'll get to see him all you like, Eleanor."

It only took Nora hearing the agent use her birth given name to recognize that it was Dr. Secora, speaking through the agent. Clearly, Dr.

Secora was in a remote hiding spot to stay out of harm's way, and had taken control of his agent's consciousness so that he could still be present for the meeting. She wondered if Dr. Secora had informed all of the agents that stood before Nora to remove their NFIs so that he could access their consciousness if needed. Suddenly, her heart raced with excitement as she realized that there was a very good chance of this being the case, and if Dr. Secora could control them, she could too. As her confidence rose, Nora called out—her voice clear and strong.

"You have your security measures. I have mine," she said defiantly.

"You were given the luxury of safe passage through the sectors on my orders. Now you stand here with three of your fellow Defected," Dr. Secora replied through the agent's body, clucking his tongue in disapproval.

Relief filled Nora as she realized from his words that he hadn't caught sight of Jack, Bray or Otto. She made sure not to accidentally glance over towards where they remained hidden—the last thing she wanted to do was give them away. With their presence unknown, the rebels had the upper hand.

"Eleanor, you will be granted safe passage to my office if your Defected companions turn around and leave. If not, we will have no choice but to open fire on all of you," Dr. Secora declared. "You have been warned," he added flippantly.

Dr. Secora wouldn't do anything to risk harming her, Nora rationalized. Taking a deep breath, she edged her way past Bretta and Trim and stood in front of them—fully vulnerable, with her head held high.

"Shoot if you like. But don't neglect the fact that if your bullets hit me by accident, you'll lose the chance to experiment on me in your precious lab—I doubt my corpse would be of much use to you," she said with a shrug. She spread her stance wide and placed her hands on her hips, trying to shield the rebels behind her as best as she could.

Dr. Secora was quiet for a moment. Nora watched as the agent he was controlling dropped his gaze and began to blink repeatedly—as if his eyes were adjusting to sudden bright sunlight. Then, Deryn made his way to the front of the group of agents, and continued on right towards the opening of the wall.

Nora quickly lunged forward, desperate to stop him from taking the final step into the Arrant side of the wall and catching sight of Jack, Bray and Otto. The three guys pressed up against the cold bricks as best they could to remain hidden from view. They each held their rifles cocked and ready to shoot if necessary.

Nora held her hands open and out to the side as Deryn's movements came to a halt, to show that she was unarmed. Deryn was the first to speak. Fully expecting it to be Dr. Secora controlling him, Nora was shocked when she recognized the unmistakeable intonations of her former love.

"Eleanor, you need to end all of this now," Deryn said calmly. There was a tinge of sadness in his voice. "You need to give yourself up and live the life you were meant to live. Quit this crazy rebellion and come back to us. Come back to me."

"Come back to you? Think about it Deryn, where would I go? Things between us will never be like it was before. You understand that, right? If I give myself up I'll spend the rest of my life in Jejung, or in a test lab with Dr. Secora," she said with exasperation.

Deryn shook his head, and at that point she was able to see that he wasn't wearing the NFI in his ear. "You don't understand how your actions affect the rest of us. We aren't like you Eleanor. The more you change your own life, the more it affects us all."

The sadness in his voice was unmistakeable now. Nora locked eyes with him and placed her hand gently on his cheek. "I'm so sorry Deryn," she whispered. She didn't know what else to say.

"Don't be sorry, just end this," Deryn replied adamantly. "You never should have let it get this far out of your control."

"No Deryn, you don't understand. There is no going back for me."

"Of course there is. We could leave this all behind us, right now and have the life together that we were meant to have. We could—"

"No," Nora interrupted, her voice firm. "There's no going back. I can only move forward, and that means leaving the past behind where it is meant to be," she paused, thinking of what to say. "I'm sorry," she repeated softly.

As the apology left her lips, Nora closed her eyes and quickly latched onto Deryn's mind in the gray shadow world. She flashed through his memories like flipping through a scrapbook. As she watched the last few weeks of his life in reverse, Nora saw the pain and determination Deryn had used to push himself towards his ultimate goal—to bring her home. All the sleepless nights he had spent, angry, hurt, and confused, while training to join the Agency swept passed her vision. Nora could feel every drop of passion and despair Deryn had gone through since the day she had left him, all wrapped up into a single, tight ball of emotion.

The crashing waves of his passion began to subside as Nora continued to rewind through Deryn's memories. When she arrived at a particular one—which she knew held a special place in his heart—everything became calm. She had chosen the day the two of them had started living together, when they had finally moved into a place of their own.

Deryn had held the old wooden door open for Nora to step through, allowing her to enter their new home first. Her face lit up as she realized he had clearly gotten to the house earlier and set it up in an effort to surprise her. As she peered around the room, the smell of food cooking in the oven wafted over. The table was cleaned and set with dishes, and a single, white tapered candle gleamed, dancing in the slight breeze which drifted in through an open window. Deryn pulled out a chair for Nora to sit, and moved himself into the wooden chair across from her.

Nora then pulled Deryn's mind into the sweet memory with her as well. Once his consciousness was firmly lodged in the past—in that day when the two of them had been so happy and in love—she stood up and walked over to him, slowly kissing him as she left his mind and returned to her own. She had effectively trapped him in the past, and he would continue to exist amongst their memories of that day.

Back in the present moment, Nora opened her eyes to see that Deryn was indeed gone, and there was only empty space before her. The whole transference of Deryn had happened so quickly that the other agents stared in shock—to them Deryn had vanished in the blink of an eye.

The remaining agents proceeded to raise their rifles back up again—confused and fearful of what might happen next. Nora darted back behind the wall beside Jack and Bray. Phoenix, Trim and Bretta all dove to the other side of the opening—where Otto hid. The agents then made a beeline for the wall opening after them.

Otto handed Trim and Bretta their rifles just as the agents ran through the open wall. When the first agent came through, Trim shot him without hesitation. The wounded agent fell instantly to the ground. When she saw the copious amount of blood soak the ground surrounding him, and the stillness of his body, Nora realized he was dead. She winced, her heart stopping for a moment—this was not her plan at all. Now another life was gone because of her.

After that, gunfire erupted. Otto angled his rifle around the corner of the wall, and Bray did likewise. The two of them fired their weapons in a sweeping formation, going from side to side so that they could obliterate everything within reach. When they ceased fire and withdrew their weapons, everything was silent. Otto peeked around the corner.

"We got all of them," he confirmed aloud. "But there's certain to be more agents on their way. We shouldn't stick around and wait for them."

Otto turned and ran inside the center of Constance, headed for the grassy area they had all slept in a few nights earlier after breaking Nora out. The rest of the rebels followed his lead and headed in the same direction. Once they arrived, they huddled together and waited for Nora to tell them what to do next.

Nora, still emotionally shaken up from the recent events, stood silently, her eyes welling up with tears. Otto, seeing that she was too distraught to give further instructions, spoke up instead.

"There is no one between us and Obsidia now. I can see a few of them standing guard at the entrance. I think we should move."

Closing her eyes, Nora tried to focus her mind so that she could scope out the scene of Obsidia's perimeter, but she was unable to locate any other souls in the subconscious gray world. It seemed that any remaining agents were wearing the Neural Feedback Inhibitors.

"Let's head towards Obsidia," she said in agreement. As the rebels started to stand up, Nora stuck her hands out, stopping them. With her palms towards the ground, she lowered her shoulders. "First, everyone reload their weapons, take a moment and gather your energy. Dr. Secora isn't going anywhere. This is going to take everything we have." The rebels gave her their full attention as her thoughts drifted back to the agent laying in a pool of his own blood near the wall. The painful vision of his dead body lingered in her mind as she spoke again. "This war has begun."

CHAPTER 36

Nora took a moment to admire the center of Constance. The time she spent in the middle sector had either been when she was locked up, or after she'd been broken out and it was already dark. For the first time, she was able to really see the surroundings—the area was much bigger than she realized.

There were many other smaller buildings around Obsidia. Most of them looked like they had been neglected for many years. Several had broken windows and nearly all were in dire need of a paint job. It was difficult to tell if anyone actually resided in the surrounding buildings.

She turned her sights on to Obsidia—it dominated the city's skyline. The rebels were currently in a grassy area that led straight to the tall building's entrance. Leading up to the structure were additional roads, all made of concrete and containing numerous large cracks through which grass had grown.

There didn't appear to be any agents traveling the roads, and Nora had not caught sight of any movement through the windows. The only visible agents were scattered directly in front of Obsidia's main entrance, none of whom seemed to be paying any attention to the grassy area the rebels were currently hiding in.

She'd been convinced they'd catch on to their hiding spot in no time, but they gave no signs of it. Nora took another thoughtful glance and visually swept over the city. She thought back to her childhood. Obsidia had always been in the north, and she'd used this as a point of reference to navigate herself when going places. It was like a beacon, unreachable and idealized by her and the rest of the children. They'd all grown up coming up with stories about the center of Constance. As kids, the light that emanated from the top floor of Obsidia—late in the night after the citywide curfew had darkened everything else—was an emblem of freedom and hope. A symbol that there was more to their isolated, walled-in lives.

But now as an adult, Nora saw what the tall building truly was— in reality it was a dark and dangerous place. She winced as the horrific memory of her lonely imprisonment in the white cell flashed in her thoughts again. Her fists reflexively clenched as she recalled the hours that had been spent beating against those white padded walls.

Bray interrupted her thoughts, and informed her that it was time for them to move. Together the rebels crept through the field of grass towards Obsidia. They hid behind anything that would provide shelter from the agents up ahead. Otto motioned for the group to stop when they were still fairly far from the tall building.

"Something isn't right," he said. "I mean, why would they let us just walk up to the building after we have killed six of their own?"

"Five," Nora corrected defensively.

"Right," Otto nodded. He cast Nora an understanding look. She was clearly guilt stricken over each life she felt responsible for taking. "Still, if we were in their position, we'd have guards patrolling every possible entryway, to prevent any further casualties."

"Does anyone else think it could all be a trap?" Jack questioned the group.

All of them looked towards Nora, waiting for her to have some kind of insight on the situation. She, however, had no idea how to ease their worries.

"Give me a moment. I'll try to look around."

Nora closed her eyes and slipped into the gray world that Program 7 had allowed her to find so easily now. She felt her mind float upwards until she was looking down over the whole center of Constance. Nora saw nothing in the surrounding buildings. Checking each one, she finally found a small group of white shadows within the main building. She opened her eyes to report her findings to her fellow rebels.

"It's just a bunch of Shades inside of Obsidia. If there are more agents around, they must be wearing the NFIs," she said.

"I think it would be in our best interest to wait," Phoenix interjected. "I mean, if they are waiting to ambush us, then what is the last thing they would expect us to do? I don't think we should go walking off into traps just because we are in a hurry to get this thing over with."

Nora could hear the uncertainty in Phoenix's voice—she was clearly still rattled from the recent battle near the opening of the wall. As she observed Phoenix wiping her clammy hands on her dress, and saw how her eyes darted around to constantly survey the surrounding area for any incoming danger, it was obvious that her plan had been constructed largely motivated by her current state of intense fear.

Nora surveyed the rest of the rebels, whom she now felt responsible for. Bretta's hands gripped around the barrel of her rifle so tightly that her knuckles had turned white. A bead of sweat formed on Jack's forehead, and even Bray's movements were erratic and nervous. Nora sighed as she came to terms with the reality of the situation—they were all too afraid to continue pressing onwards.

Even Trim—the only one of them besides Otto who maintained a confident demeanor—seemed to like Phoenix's idea. "Phoenix has a good point. We know they are expecting us, so let's mix it up on them. I say we sit tight—that'll throw 'em off."

"That can't be the best option for us," Nora blurted out. "I think we are all a bit scared of what is to come, but if we stay here, we are leaving ourselves vulnerable to any agents that might come looking for us."

"And if we just walk right up to Obsidia's front doors without any idea of what could be waiting for us," Bretta interjected, "We are just as exposed."

"Bretta is right," Trim agreed again with a nod, "If we are patient, the Agency is sure to slip up and give us some kind of clue as to what we are going to be dealing with. I still say we wait it out."

Everyone nodded in approval. Nora knew it was foolish to sit and wait, but she tried to look agreeable with the new plan, not wanting to force her will on the scared rebel group. She didn't want them doing anything they weren't comfortable with. They were all there, after all, risking their lives for her.

Otto started to think out loud. "Okay. So we wait. How long do we just sit here, waiting for them to react?" The tone in his voice suggested that he found the group's idea as foolish as Nora did. When he turned to Nora for an answer the rest of the rebels did as well.

"Well I..." she began, not yet sure how to finish the sentence. "I'm not sure how long I can remain inside the shadow world at a given time, but I can go in and keep surveillance for as long as possible. If luck's on our side, an NFI might accidentally fall out of an agent's ear, or they could carelessly remove it for a moment. Even if it's just for a split second, it should allow me to locate their positioning."

Everyone seemed to be on board with this suggestion. "That sounds like our best move for now," Bretta chimed in.

"Good," Otto said matter-of-factly. "Then it's settled. Nora, do your shadow world surveillance. If that proves to be too draining for you to keep up for too long, we can figure out a different plan of action. The rest of you get comfortable—we may be here for a while."

The rebels all relaxed and leaned back onto the overgrown ground in order to remain hidden behind the tall grass. Trim and Bretta curled up together, and Bray came over to Nora.

"I'll be right here, next to you," Bray reassured her. "If anything happens out here, I'll pull you out of your shadow world state. And if for some reason I can't bring you back I'll just throw you over my shoulder and carry you to safety," he said playfully, puffing his chest out in an exaggerated show of machismo.

"Okay, let's keep that as a last resort—I can only take so much of waking up in strange places," she winked at him in return.

Bray relaxed beside her as she knelt on the ground and folded her hands in her lap. Nora then closed her eyes and drifted off, back into the gray world, positioning her mind high above the city. She located the same group of Shades inside of Obsidia—nothing had changed since her last visit. Nora tried to relax and settle in, knowing she would be there for a while.

As Bray sat—his gaze alternating from Nora to the ground and then back to Nora—a light sound startled him from above. At first he thought it was just his imagination, so he looked to Otto to see if he'd heard it too. Otto, however, was deep in conversation with Phoenix. The two of them lay on their backs in the grass, propped up by their elbows.

Looking around at the remaining rebels, no one else seemed to have noticed anything. He shook his head, convinced it was just his nerves playing tricks on him. Turning back to Nora, she was as still as a statue, and remained bent on her knees in the grass. Her breathing was rhythmic. Bray felt a strong urge to reach out and touch her, but instead returned his gaze to the ground ahead of him.

A few moments later the sound came again. This time it was unmistakeable, the same high-pitched noise as before. Bray went over and tapped Otto on the leg, startling him.

"What is it?" Otto inquired.

"Maybe nothing," Bray looked up toward where he thought he'd heard the noise come from. "Twice now, I have heard a weird sound coming from above our heads. The first time was so faint, I wasn't sure if I'd just imagined it. But after the second time, I had to come tell you. I think something is up there."

"Okay, stay low. I'm going to take a look," Otto stood up so that he could survey their surroundings. He lifted his head up above the tall grass, just enough so he had a clear view, and looked towards Obsidia. After a moment he settled back into the grass. "There is nothing there.

The agents we saw before are gone though. Maybe we were right, they must have gotten antsy waiting around for us all day."

"Makes sense," Bray agreed. "Anything else?"

Otto shook his head and raised his eyebrows questioningly. Just as Otto had opened his mouth and was about to speak the sound appeared. This time Otto, Phoenix, and Bray all heard it. Phoenix sat up quickly, her eyes darting around.

"What was that?" she asked nervously. "I definitely heard something."

Bray looked over at Nora, her face was now scrunched into a look of concentration. "It looks like Nora might have caught on to something over there. I'm guessing that whatever it is, can't be a good thing."

Trim looked over with a startled expression—clearly he and Bretta had heard it too. He nodded at Otto and then attempted to stand up, most of his body remained hidden behind the large cement boulder that Jack had positioned himself next to.

Together, Trim and Jack peeked their heads out above the large rock and looked towards Obsidia. As Trim was lowering himself back down, another sound occurred. This one, though, was different.

The other noises had seemed to fly past them overhead, disappearing off towards the wall behind them, but this one grew louder and seemed to be approaching them. The noise seemed to land at the large rock. A high-pitched swirling sound immediately filled the air. Bray's eyes widened with terror.

"Everyone get down!" he screamed.

* * *

Inside her mind, Nora continued to look down on the city center. She could see the Shades moving around on various floors of Obsidia. Presumably, they were all working hard on lab tests for the day. Focusing her efforts, she saw the slightest hint of red, way down underneath all of the other Shades.

Nora's mind strained as she tried to move closer to the red dots—they were so faint she could barely see them. As her mind drifted down into the building and passed through floor after floor of Shades, the red dots grew bigger. A few floors underground, dozens of the Defected had appeared, most of them huddled together in groups of three or four.

After a few moments of observing them, she realized that the Defected were not moving. Fighting the urge to return immediately to the rebels and tell them what she'd just witnessed, she forced herself to continue on with her surveillance—it was more important now than ever that she uncover just exactly what was going on.

Letting her consciousness exit up and out of the building and drift even higher above the city center to get a better view, she scanned the surrounding buildings. Not seeing any activity, she was about to give up and return to reality to give the rebels a report, but something suddenly caught her eye. Focusing intently on the area it had occurred, she waited until it happened again.

Small bits of white swam into her vision, but just as quickly disappeared again. She remained focused and alert, her mind trying to put the pieces of the puzzle together. What could all of this mean?

Nora decided it might be best to expand her perspective and get a comprehensive view of the whole city at once. Pinpointing the location where her fellow rebels were located in the grass, she saw white dots swarming around their huddled, red silhouetted bodies. They would appear and then disappear, just as the others had. There was a small group of Shades in an abandoned building to the right of the rebels, as well as in a building to their left, and a larger group right in front of them. At the rate that the white shadows flickered into her view and back out, Nora surmised that something was causing the agent's Neural Feedback Inhibitors to malfunction. Seeing this, she knew she had to get back to her rebel companions immediately, so she pulled her consciousness back down to their location as quickly as she could, and opened her eyes back in the real world.

Struggling to stand up, her eyes slowly regained focus. Just as her vision cleared she saw Bray rushing towards her with outstretched arms. Unable to react fast enough, he collided with her, tackling her to the ground. He kept her pinned down even as she yelled out in pain.

"Get off me!" she yelled. Her mind raced in panic—what if this wasn't even Bray? What if Dr. Secora had somehow taken over control of Bray's mind?

"Stay down!" he demanded, continuing to press her shoulders into the dirt.

She tried to push him off of her with all her strength, but it was useless. "Bray, get off me now!" she repeated, this time in a much more aggressive tone.

Nora's heart raced as she tried to break free. Finally Bray rolled off of her, remaining close at her side. He placed his hand over her lips before she was able to yell again. Squirming, she managed to partially pull his hand off.

"You don't understand," she said to Bray, twisting to look him in the eyes.

Bray lowered his hand from her mouth. "We know already Nora. Please, you have to stay down!"

Upon hearing him call her "Nora" her anxiety over Dr. Secora having took over his mind disappeared. "But the agents," Nora stammered, trying to wriggle out of his grasp. "They are all around us. Bretta was right—it was all a trap. They were going to ambush us."

When Nora tried to sit up and see what was going on Bray pressed her back onto the ground again. "You need to stay down, they are shooting right at us. From what we can tell, they don't know exactly where we are. Most of the shots are just flying over our heads. We have to stay low—otherwise we'll give our position away."

"Can you tell where the shots are coming from?" she asked, taking a deep breath, finally settling herself down.

"No. For some reason we can't hear the shots being fired. We can only hear the bullets when they fly over our heads," he replied. "It's the strangest thing," he added.

"Right before I came back I saw two small groups in the buildings to our left and right, and a larger group right in front of us at the main entrance," she informed him.

"Okay, that helps. I'll tell Otto—"

"Wait," Nora interrupted. "There's more. I think they are holding some of the other Defected as prisoners under the main building. The Defected I saw weren't moving around though, so they must be restrained somehow. Maybe they're being used as some sort of a test, I don't know, I couldn't see enough," she said. "Bray," she added, in a more somber tone, "There were dozens of them."

Bray nodded silently, flipped over onto his stomach, and then began to crawl his way over to Otto and Trim.

"Whatever is happening to those Defected, we can't help them if we don't stop these bullets first," he said, without turning back to look at her. "Keep your head down."

When Bray got to Otto, Trim, and Jack he informed them that Nora had been able to locate some of the hidden agents surrounding them, and that they were waiting to strike. With hushed voices, the four of them came up with a new stratigy, and then Bray crawled back to Nora. He informed her of the plan they had devised, and she listened intently as bullets continued to fly overhead.

"Here is what's happening," Bray began. "Otto and Bretta are going to move towards the building on our left. Trim, Jack and I will head to the one on our right. Maybe, just maybe, if we're able to sneak up on them before they've realized we split up, we might be able to take down their flanking units."

Nora stared down at the ground, worried about the huge danger they'd be putting themselves in. Seeing her pensive expression, Bray took her hand in his own.

"What are Phoenix and I supposed to do?" she asked after an extended period of silence.

"We need the two of you to stay here. Once we have been gone for five minutes, fire a shot towards Obsidia. Continue to fire every couple of minutes, and move around to different positions for each one. Hopefully that will trick them into thinking the lot of us are all still here firing from this location," he explained. "Try and keep cover behind a rock after every shot, so you're shielded from any return fire. Do you think you can handle that?"

Unable to resist, Nora sat up and kissed him. "Yes. I'll be fine. Just promise me you will be safe. Don't do anything stupid over there, okay?"

At her approval of the plan, Bray turned to Otto and gave him a thumbs up signal. Otto nodded in understanding. Otto and Bretta then went off through the grass towards their designated spot, slowly disappearing from view. Bray, Trim, and Jack did likewise in the opposite direction. Shortly after the two groups were gone from sight, Phoenix approached her and handed Nora a long rifle.

"Let's get into our positions," Phoenix started. "I'll go over there behind that small square of concrete, you go over there behind that big rock," she instructed, pointing at the two spots. "I'll shoot first in about five minutes and then you count to five and then fire too. After you shoot, move to your next location immediately. And remember Nora—try and stay low."

Nora hoped that Phoenix couldn't see the fear in her eyes. She wanted to stay as calm and collected as the rest of the rebels, but it was hard. Once she'd safely positioned herself behind the large rock, she sat and waited, looking over in Phoenix's direction. She took a deep breath as she anticipated the chaos that was about to ensue in just a few minutes.

After the five minutes was up, Phoenix raised her rifle high above the tall grass, aimed straight ahead and then squeezed the trigger. The gunshot was loud and echoed throughout the field. Nora readied herself as Phoenix lowered her rifle, already dashing off to her next location.

Counting in her head, Nora had reached five and was just about to raise her rifle when the sound of gunfire erupted in the field—it was coming from all sides. Bullets lodged themselves into the concrete block Phoenix had recently been hiding behind, chipping off pieces of it with each shot.

Once the onslaught of gunfire died down, Phoenix motioned to Nora to shoot. Nora raised the rifle above her head, blindly shooting at Obsidia. Immediately, a hail of bullets descended upon the large rock in front of her. She knew she had to move, but stood frozen in fear.

Nora looked over at Phoenix, who was pressed up against a stone in her second position. The two girls looked at each other, and Phoenix widened her eyes expressively, trying to urge Nora to move away from the rock. Taking a deep breath, Nora scrambled over to her next position, right before Phoenix's second shot rang out. Again, this was met with nearly immediate returning gunfire from the surrounding agents.

As Nora readied herself, prepped to lift her rifle again, she heard Phoenix call out. "It's working! You're doing great Nora. Keep their attention focused on us."

Her friend's optimistic encouragement was all Nora needed to hear, and she was filled with a sudden burst of bravery. The thought of protecting Bray by making herself the target instead was the motivating force in her head. She jumped up purposefully and fired multiple shots at the front entrance of Obsidia. Her vantage point allowed her to see that the agents had crept out from behind the walls they'd been hidden behind. Nora was able to duck back down and move out of the way before the pounding of return fire hit her location. Phoenix called out to her again.

"Any second now, we are going to have to make ourselves more vulnerable. We need to look at where we are firing. Are you ready?"

"Ready!" Nora yelled back, her voice filled with determination.

She got into her next position—back behind the large rock from before. Phoenix was back in her first spot behind the smaller stone as well. Just as Phoenix was about to fire, new shots rang out in the field—this time the bullets weren't directed at the two of them however.

Otto, Bretta, Bray, Trim, and Jack had begun their attack on the flanking agents. Catching them off guard had left the agents vulnerable and exposed. Screams from the agents as they were hit filled the air.

Phoenix took the opportunity to fire off a few shots towards Obsidia. This time only a couple bullets were shot back at her.

As Nora looked down the sights of her rifle, setting up her next shot, she saw a young agent directly ahead of her. His slender body was turned towards her left, firing at where Otto and Bretta would be. Nora aimed carefully at the unsuspecting agent, took a deep breath and pulled the trigger. She watched as he collapsed from the instant bullet wound.

Nora dropped onto the ground, her heart racing. Her throat tightened, as she thought about what she'd just done—enemy or not, it tore her apart to have just killed a human being. She looked over at Phoenix who was currently firing multiple shots and swaying the barrel of the rifle before pulling the trigger again. As the gunfire continued to surround her, Nora felt like she was in a haze. She pounded the ground in an attempt to shake herself out of it, and stood up, rifle pointed towards Obsidia yet again.

Turning her head and the gun barrel back and forth, Nora pulled the trigger each time an agent came into her sights. Her aim—especially for such an inexperienced shooter—was impeccable. The agents fell to the ground one by one as she continued firing off shots. Even once the barrel was empty of bullets, she squeezed the trigger several more times—the rifle only clicking uselessly. Her veins were filled with adrenaline and her nostrils flared as tears formed in her eyes.

Slumping back down onto the ground, Nora tossed the rifle to her side. She placed her face in her hands and released a muffled scream—the emotions inside her having reached their boiling point. Just then, she felt a hand on her shoulder.

She raised her head with a start, relieved to see that it was Otto. He had made his way back, and seemed to be in one piece. Feeling emotionally depleted, Nora reached up and hugged him, unable to control her tears from spilling out and soaking the sleeve of his jacket. Otto stood stoically, remaining calm and trying to soothe her as she continued to sob and pound the ground in frustration.

"Shh," he said softly into her ear. "It's over now. We got them all."

"I want to take it all back!" Nora yelled into his shoulder, her voice muffled against his jacket. She pulled herself away and then blinked her watery eyes rapidly. "I can do it," she said, as though just realizing it. "I can go into my memories and take everything back!"

Just then Bray approached. Otto let Nora go and allowed Bray to take over comforting her.

"It didn't have to be like this," she screamed, too distraught to even acknowledge Bray's arrival. "There must have been another way! I want to go back. Back to my life before any of this madness."

Bray held her tight as he rocked her shaking body back and forth. "It's okay Nora. We had to do it. Yes it was awful, but it's over now."

Slowly, her anger began to fade. She looked around to see that the other rebels were all staring at her. It was almost as though she could feel their confidence in her fading. "I know I had to do it. That's not what I'm upset about." She paused, looking up from Bray's chest and addressed everyone in their small group. "The thing is, I can change all of it."

The group stared at her trying to comprehend her words. "I can go back," Nora explained. "Back to a time before all of this started. Maybe I could find another way. Maybe I could change something in the past that would be better than all of this—" she gestured around the grassy field, "this death."

Bretta approached Nora and placed a firm hand on her shoulder. "Look, I understand what you can do, but that doesn't mean you should do it." Nora looked up at her expectantly. "What could you change really? None of this could play out any differently. We would all eventually be here, right now. The only difference you might be able to make is to take yourself out of the picture. I would hate to think of the situation we would be in without you here, helping us."

Nora wiped the tears from her eyes. "It's frustrating. For some reason I have been given the ability to change the whole world in an instant." She looked down at her feet. "But the only way for me to make a real difference in this world is to be here, right now, in this moment with all of you. If I go back, the only thing that I know for sure will change is me. I don't have enough knowledge about the situation to know what to manipulate to make any of this better. I need to understand the whole story fully before I can make any changes that would help."

Nora took a deep breath, and decided in that moment to divulge to her fellow rebels what she had been keeping so secretively to herself. "When I hooked into Fallow's Dream Machine, I somehow melded my memories with another version of myself—a future version."

Phoenix tilted her head, somewhat confused, and Otto furrowed his brow in an effort to understand what Nora was saying.

"A flood of consciousness washed over my mind, forming new thoughts and memories that I have never had, but which now seem so real to me. What stood out the most to me..." Nora's voice trailed off as she swallowed hard, not wanting to finish her sentence, "...is that none of you were there with me."

The rebels let out a collective gasp, and began to whisper amongst themselves.

"This war is going to happen, with or without me. So for now, I need to stay here and fight with all of you," she said, attempting to stabilize the situation. She locked eyes with each rebel, one by one, trying to express a sense of comfort to them.

"Don't worry Miss Nora," Jack said reassuringly, placing his hand over hers. "You will get your chance to make this whole world a better place. I promise you."

The rebels all helped Nora stand up and she dusted the dirt off of her pants and looked up at them—her fellow rebels, her friends. "Well we better get moving then," she said, a faint smile on her lips. As she wiped the last tear from her face she added, "There is no time like the present."

CHAPTER 37

As the rebels approached Obsidia's front doors, the fading rays of sunlight reflected off the shiny white marble from within the lobby. Despite the absence of any guards, they couldn't help but look over their shoulders in paranoia.

At the base of the entrance, the bodies of many agents were littered across the ground. The rebels quickly went to work removing weapons, rounds of ammunition, and protective gear off of the dead agents. Everyone, that is, except Nora.

She bent down over a few of the bodies and looked closely at their faces. Most of them were hardened from age and experience, but she found the one face that still had soft features—a young boy.

Nora knelt down closer to him and inspected his scrawny body. The NFI he had been wearing in his ear let off a small spark. At that point, she felt something very odd occur. It was hard to comprehend, but it was almost as though the boy's mind began to drift around her.

"Did you find something?" Bray asked, approaching Nora.

"This one was too young. He never should have been here," she replied.

Before Bray could stop her, Nora closed her eyes, drifted into the boy's mind and found one of his memories. In the vision, the boy—even younger than he was now—was with his father.

The boy's father had just come home from a long day, wearing an agent's uniform. He walked into the room to find his son drawing a picture. As his father approached, the young boy turned and looked up at him.

"This again?" the father asked. "How many times do I have to tell you, you need to give up on this dream of yours. No one in the history of Constance has grown up to be an artist," he said exasperatedly. "No," he continued, shaking his head. "You will join the Agency, like I did. Just like your grandfather before me."

Nora could feel the sadness in the boy as he listened to his father cut down his aspirations with a disapproving tone. She decided to take over control of the boy's movements, and forced him to stand up and walk towards his father. She then spoke through the boy.

"This is who I am dad." His father's eyes widened in shock, never having heard his young son speak to him with such a forceful tone. "This is who I am, and this is who I am going to be. You can choose to support my decision or not, but it won't change what I do." Nora walked the boy's body back over to his drawings, picked up the pencil he'd been using, and resumed his artwork.

Hoping a change so small was enough to have an impacting effect, Nora drifted out of the boy's subconsciousness and back into her own mind. As she opened her eyes, leaving the gray world behind, she saw that the boy's body had vanished. She breathed a sigh of relief, stunned that it had worked. Any sign that he had ever been there was gone—the pavement that had once been soaked with his young blood was now bone dry. Nora turned and looked at Bray.

"I'm sorry. I couldn't allow him to end up like this. He was fighting in a war that he didn't want any part of," she explained as Bray helped her up.

"I understand. Hopefully one day everyone can live the life they want to instead of getting caught up in all of this like he did."

Together, they walked towards the front door of Obsidia where the others were standing and waiting. No one said anything to Nora, although they all had seen what she did. They nodded at her and smiled with understanding.

Bretta placed a hand on her shoulder. "I think one day, the whole world will be thankful to have more people like you in it, Nora."

Nora leaned into Bretta, embracing her from the side. "Hopefully, one day, the world won't need someone like me in it."

As Bretta released Nora's shoulder, Otto pushed open the glass door that led into the main lobby. The rebels filed in and went immediately towards their pre-determined hiding spots behind the furniture and columns located nearest to the entrance.

Bray craned his head out from his hiding place behind a large marble column—there were no signs of agents anywhere. He motioned to the group to move forward, and everyone got in place in their second-round hiding spots. Nora positioned herself behind a desk at the center of the large marble room. It was the same desk she'd hidden behind before, however this time she was running into the building rather than out.

Bray cracked open the door to the stairwell and peered inside. Finding nothing, he turned and flashed an "all-clear" signal to the rest of them. Just as he was turning back towards the doorway, an agent appeared from out of nowhere and tackled him, knocking him to the ground.

The large agent crushed Bray onto the hard stone flooring, and Bray let out a yell in pain. Every rebel had their rifle focused on the scuffle, but no one took a shot, too fearful they'd hit Bray by mistake.

"We can't get a clear shot!" Otto yelled at Bray.

Bray continued to struggle under the weight of the large agent on top of him as Nora walked over. The agent paused for a split second to look up, and when he saw who was looking back at him fear filled his eyes. Taking advantage of the moment of distraction, Bray reached up and ripped the NFI from the agent's ear.

"Now Nora! Now!" Bray yelled, his voice strained from the crushing weight on top of his rib cage.

Instead of closing her eyes and going into the shadow world, as everyone around her had expected her to do, Nora extended a hand towards the agent. As soon as her fingers made contact with his body, the man vanished. The rebels stared on in shock.

"Nora! What did you do? How did you make him disappear so quickly?" Otto asked.

Turning from Bray, who remained on the floor still catching his breath, Nora looked at Otto, her lips pursed anxiously. "I panicked. When I saw him hurting Bray I got scared and didn't have time to think. Sometimes it's just quicker to go straight to the source," she said. Her response caused Otto to rub his head in confusion.

"Straight to the source?" he repeated.

Nora bit her lip and tried to think of a simpler way to explain what she meant. She instantly felt like she had gone too far. Instead of simply ending the agent's life, she had erased his existence in all realities. She didn't need to go to that extreme, but what was done was done, and besides—she knew that Dr. Secora wouldn't hesitate to do the same to her if he had the chance. Suddenly, remembering the surveillance system set up in the building, a thought occurred to her. Dr. Secora was most likely watching her right at that moment. She decided to use that to her advantage, and as an opportunity to show him that she had more malevolence in heart than she could ever bear to have in reality.

"Well," she began, squaring her shoulders confidently. "I just erased him from the world. If he was never born then he never existed," she snapped her fingers, as if to show how casually she took it. "And if anyone else gets in our way, I won't hesitate to do the same to them.

236

This is war after all, so all's fair, isn't that the saying?" She tried to speak as cold-heartedly as possible, and narrowed her eyes for extra emphasis.

Otto appeared taken aback by Nora's sudden shift in personality, but Phoenix seemed to catch on to exactly what Nora was doing. Phoenix came over to her side. "You did what you had to do," she said, patting Nora on the back. She flashed Nora a wink, to show she understood that it was all an act.

Feeling relieved at Phoenix's support, Nora straightened her posture and dusted off the front of her clothing. "Here we are. This is it. This will either be the end of the war, or the end of us."

Otto led the group into the stone stairwell. Nora felt horrible inside for what she had recently done to the large agent that had attacked Bray, but did her best to hide it. All she hoped for was that Dr. Secora had somehow been able to witness the event and that she'd been able to instill a little fear in him.

As they continued up the stairs, Nora looked over at the rest of the group, but no one met her eyes. She consoled herself, saying that when everything was over, she'd be forgiven.

The stairs seemed to go on forever—their journey up feeling infinitely longer than when they'd descended them not so long ago. Otto was in the lead, with Bray rounding everyone up, directly behind Nora to ensure her safety. Their main goal was to keep her safe, at least until she could meet with Dr. Secora.

The group continued to climb, higher and higher, floor after floor. Nora's breath grew labored, and her head began to pound. She tried to shake it off, but with each step she took she felt worse and worse.

When the group had reached a landing between two floors and she was able to get their attention, she motioned for everyone to wait a minute. She then held up her hands and closed her eyes—her temples continuing to throb.

As Nora closed her eyes, she drifted into the gray world. Her consciousness floated up and when she looked down she was able to see a white shadow hovering directly above her red silhouetted body. With a start, she realized why she'd suddenly begun to feel so awful.

She opened her eyes back in reality and addressed the group in a hushed voice.

"He's here. Dr. Secora is trying to get into my mind right now."

The rebels nodded in understanding, all looking in fear at the air around them. "Are you all ready for this?" she asked. Again they all simply nodded in response, trying to keep the conversation to a minimum.

"Good. Get ready to remove your NFIs on my mark. Let's finish this," she said assertively.

Nora pointed at Otto first, and he reached up and pulled his Program 7 blocking device out of his ear. His hands shook, anticipating what was about to occur. As she watched the expression on Otto's face, Nora realized this was the first time she had seen him noticeably afraid. Every rebel kept their gaze fixed on him.

He tried to resume his composure in an effort to calm his rebel group. They all watched in silence as Otto's eyes widened, and then suddenly he was gone. Everyone gasped. As the heart of every rebel began to pound, the pressure in the air seemed to raise.

One by one, Phoenix, Trim, Jack, and Bretta followed suit and removed their own NFIs upon Nora's cue. They each proceeded to vanish, just as Otto had. After Bretta was gone, Nora grabbed Bray's arm and pulled him along with her—it was time to run.

Nora ran at lightning speed, the heels of her shoes only touching the floor for an instant. She ascended the staircases with the measured discipline of an athlete, as though moving to the beat of a metronome. Everything—her heartbeat, footstep, and breath—all maintained a perfectly rhythmic beat.

Bray followed close behind her, his breathing steady as well. Nora knew he must be as terrified as she was, if not more so. She reached back and grabbed his arm, giving it a quick squeeze.

As they found themselves in front of the door that led to the top floor of the building, she turned to look at him. Though his eyes were clearly filled with dread, his jaw was set in determination.

"No matter what happens in there, I just want you to know how much our time together has meant to me. I need you to trust me now though—I've thought this through and if it comes down to it, I'm going to sacrifice myself to keep you safe," she said tenderly. Bray shook his head in disapproval.

"No. No matter what happens, you finish this. If things get too intense for me in there, let me go. There is only one thing that truly matters now and that is bringing all this to an end. Do whatever is necessary—don't let your feelings for me cloud your judgment. We may never get another chance like this one."

A tear began to form in Nora's eye. Bray did have a purpose there in the room with Dr. Secora, but Nora didn't have the heart to tell him her true plan. She stood for a moment looking at him.

"I just…" she paused, at a loss for words. "If you or I end up…" she stopped again, this time deciding to abandon language and express herself differently. She placed her hands around his neck—his skin slippery from sweat—and pulled him towards herself with both shyness and urgency. Allowing her lips to be magnetically drawn to his, she enjoyed the slow moment—there would be nothing less than sheer pandemonium beyond that door. As they kissed, both knowing it very well could be for the last time, they explored the cavernous worlds of each other's mouths, not willing to let any soft, pink crevice remain untouched.

Nora broke the embrace, and craned her neck up so that she could whisper directly into his ear. "I will always love you," she said. As her words hung in the air, Nora's heart stopped. She watched Bray's face, unsure of how he would respond.

Bray leaned his forehead against her's. "I've loved you since the day we met. And it doesn't feel like an ordinary kind of love either. I'm sure I'll love you in the dream world, in the shadow world, and in whatever world exists beyond all this," he said, gesturing around the empty stairwell. Nora smiled in response, her heart swelling with hope—it was crazy how much bravery and optimism love gave her.

Bray and Nora reached for the door to exit the stairwell at the same time. Their fingers intertwined as they turned the knob and pushed the door to Dr. Secora's lair wide open.

CHAPTER 38

Nora and Bray exited the stairwell and found themselves in a narrow room. The area was completely empty, except for a small white table and a coat—also white, but trimmed with a vibrant green—that was hanging up on a hook beside the table. The floor was a glossy white marble that had pale gray veins streaked throughout it, and was polished to a high shine. They crossed the room as quietly as they could, making their way over to the opening on the other side, through which a much larger room was visible.

The second room was considerably bigger, and featured windows taller than Nora herself, that went from one end of the room to the next. Consequentially the room was flooded with sunlight. There were a few pillars that reached from the floor to the ceiling, which added a dramatic and ornate touch to the room's appearance.

To their right was a wall covered entirely in screens that displayed scrolling data. Taking a quick glimpse at them, Nora recognized that the information from her time spent inside Test Lab 504 was visible. As she watched the data on the screens change constantly, she wondered just how many tests were being conducted simultaneously.

To the left was a large white desk, upon which were additional smaller screens. As she approached the desk a booming voice sounded from behind her.

"That's far enough," a male voice bellowed. Nora instantly recognized it.

Dr. Secora stood in the back of the room, near the wall of screens. His all-white outfit made him blend in seamlessly with the room. Nora's throat tightened at the sight of him, and she saw Bray fidget beside her.

"You have made quite a mess of things, Eleanor," Dr. Secora scolded her. "First of all, you broke the terms of our agreement. Then, you murdered several of my agents. Not only have you arrived in my city, set on destroying our very fabric of life, you've invaded my home—my sanctuary—and shown me exactly how cruel your little rebellion's recruiting powers can be. However, all of your undoing may have a redeeming quality." He paused as he cast his eyes in Bray's direction, then scratched his jaw as he continued to speak. "In an ironic twist of fate, you have brought a very special gift directly to me," he moistened his dry lips and continued to squint at the two of them.

Bray raised an eyebrow, confused over the last part of what Dr. Secora said. The dark eyed man dressed in all white took a step towards Bray and Nora.

"How nobel of him," Dr. Secora said to Nora, his voice dripping with sarcasm. "He didn't tell you did he?"

"Tell her what? Cut to the chase!" Bray replied. He was quickly getting annoyed with Dr. Secora's little mind games.

"The boy that you have brought here, is not who you once assumed him to be," Dr. Secora announced smugly to Nora before he shot Bray a triumphant look.

"Nora, I have no idea what he is talking about. This is just another one of his games. He is trying to turn us on each other," Bray said, shaking his head. He took a step back away from Dr. Secora.

Dr. Secora refused to back down, and took another step in their direction. "Your lying is the reason we were separated in the first place, Braiden."

"Braiden?" Bray turned to Nora in shock. "Was that my name?" he muttered quietly to himself before looking back into Nora's sympathetic eyes.

"I still don't remember," Bray tried to explain to her. "I think the Agency did something to me before. I have never been able to remember my past—if they bring you here, you leave without any remembrance of this place. It's happened to a few of us." He turned to Dr. Secora. "Did you do something to my memories?" he asked in an accusing tone.

A low growl of displeasure escaped Dr. Secora's mouth. "Of course not. What does the rebellion think of me? So callous that I would harm a child? She really must have done a number on you though," Dr. Secora said, shaking his head in disbelief. "That is, if you are telling the truth about not remembering the past," he added pointedly.

"She?" Bray asked through clenched teeth.

"Your mother, Braiden—who else? She ran away from here, and took you with her, many years ago. Our ability to detect the Defected disease had just begun. The first round of brain scans were administered right here in my office. When your results came back positive, she fled." As Dr. Secora recalled the story his cheeks began to turn red with anger. "I tried everything I could to stop her. To stop her from taking you away,"

Dr. Secora paused, and a hint of sorrow appeared in his face. It was the first time Nora had seen him look halfway human. "Braiden," he continued. "You are my son."

Bray recoiled in disgust, as if he had been slapped in the face. "You're a liar!" he exclaimed. "I could never be the son of a man as cruel as you," he said, his voice shaking with emotion. Nora placed a hand softly on his shoulder in an effort to calm him down.

"I suspect your mother was able to eradicate any memories you may have possessed from this place," Dr. Secora continued calmly, ignoring Bray's emotional outburst. "I sent out multiple search teams, unfortunately none of them were able to locate the two of you after your mother's little stand off in Sector 3. Now, in a surprising sequence of events, you have delivered yourself to me willingly. Trust me, every effort will be made to cure you from the evil mutation that your brain has been cursed with. Our scientists have been working on finding a cure for years—your sister, Brielle, leads the research team in fact."

"I have a sister?!" Bray asked in shock. His legs were beginning to shake and he felt dizzy—as though he could collapse at any moment.

Nora stood beside him as he processed all of the new information, her hand placed firmly against his back to support Bray's swaying body.

"Even if everything you're saying is true," Bray said, finally gathering the courage to speak. "I am not your son anymore—that perfect life you have been fighting so hard for is long gone. I'm an entirely different person now."

Dr. Secora let out a condescending sigh. "You've been a totally different person since the day your mother stole you away. It seems that the possibility of us having a happy reunion has been nothing more than a fabrication inside of my own thoughts. I did not want things to come to this between you and I, Braiden, but you have left me no choice. You will accompany me down to the lab to start your memory reconstruction. As for you Eleanor, I'm afraid I'll have to take care of you in the same way I handled your little friends inside of the stairwell."

Feeling like her heart was about to break as she thought of her fellow rebels, Nora continued to stand in silence.

"What you are doing is wrong!" Bray yelled in anger. "The Defected have just as much right to exist in this world as you do."

"Of course they do, and I have found it in my heart to allow your fellow remaining Defected to live out their days in Jejung, safely tucked away from the rest of us. You should be thanking me for sparing their lives after my agents have captured them. Once you are cured of this horrific disease Braiden, you will take your place next to Brielle at my side."

"A life in a cage is not a life worth living," Nora shot back, finally speaking up. "We deserve our freedom too."

"Freedom?!" Dr. Secora retorted incredulously. "The freedom to manipulate and distort reality for the rest of us?! No, no, I don't think so." He shook his head. "Why should we have to live in constant fear that our entire life's history could just be a lie that you manufactured in that little head of yours? Simply because you feel entitled to a better existence?" he scoffed. "I've seen what you can do Eleanor, and you are the reason we have been working so hard over the years to put an end to this awful curse the world has plagued us with. I watched what you did to that poor man down in the lobby of the building," Dr. Secora gestured to the screens on his desk. "And I am to let you loose to reign, and perform acts of thoughtless cruelty at your every whim? What a naïve little girl you are Eleanor," he said, clucking his tongue.

"I only did what I had to do to keep my rebels and I alive. Nothing different than what you and your agents are doing to us. We have been given a gift—the possibility to change the world around us for the better. You sit here in this building, running experiments on innocent people, and tell your citizens that you are protecting them from the Defected. If they knew what was really going on, the people of Constance would never stand for it."

Dr. Secora laughed at Nora's theory. "Stand for it? The city of Constance could never rise up and rebel. This place has been meticulously structured to prevent information from traveling between sectors. All of this does not end with you, Eleanor. And for your information, it didn't begin with you either. Humanity has entrusted their faith to us. Faith that one day, the power to control our futures will shift from the Defected into proper, responsible hands," Dr. Secora said, extending his hands for emphasis.

"How could one single person know what is best for an entire population?" Nora challenged. "No one should ever have that much control. We should be free to control our own fate. No one should have to die just based off your opinion."

"A path has been laid out in front of all of us. You don't get to choose when to follow and when to stray from it. A power beyond human understanding has determined our passage through this life. It would do you well to respect that," he said.

243

"Enough is enough, Dr. Secora," Nora said with a scowl. She'd had just about all she could take. "You know the reason I'm here. Where is my brother, Will?"

Dr. Secora hesitated for a moment, as if trying to assess the situation, and then reached into his pocket and pulled out a small transmitting device. He pushed a round button and the white wall behind him slid open.

Nora saw her brother run out towards her. There were tears in his eyes and his wavy brown hair bounced in his face as he moved. He went straight to Nora and threw his arms around her waist, squeezing her so tightly she could barely breathe. She bent down and stroked her brother's hair.

"You're safe now." she whispered in his ear.

Will sobbed as he tried to talk. "They hooked me up to these big machines. All day long. I didn't like it. It scared me. They scared me!"

Nora turned to Dr. Secora. "You experimented on him?! How dare you? He is only a child!"

"Yes, yes," Dr. Secora agreed, emotionless. "A child who is a direct relative to the strongest Defected we have ever seen. We had to know if genetics played a part in this awful mutation."

As Nora moved her little brother behind her—in an effort to shield him with her body—Bray positioned himself in front of Will as well.

Her blood began to boil as she imagined her innocent little brother being tested on inside one of the labs by Dr. Secora's scientists—she knew firsthand what it was like to be locked up and examined by them. She wondered just how far they had taken the experiments.

"Where do we go from here Dr. Secora?" Nora asked, as calmly as she could manage. "How can we end this peacefully, so that everyone can return to their normal life?"

"You were fully aware of the agreement and terms of your surrender when you entered this building." Dr. Secora drew a sharp breath. "Why you decided to sacrifice so many lives in an attempt to give yourself freedom is so asinine, I—" he chuckled, "I don't know what you were thinking my dear, deluded Eleanor."

Nora felt Will squirm behind her. Bray reached back and put a firm hand on the boy's shoulder. "It's okay Will," Bray whispered to him. A tear spilled from Nora's eye as she witnessed Bray's small act of kindness towards her brother. She took a deep, ragged breath and tried to fill her lungs, trying to come to terms with the series of events that would soon take place.

"By my count," Dr. Secora continued, "Your side is nearing two dozen casualties—all in an effort to continue on with your own life," he shook his head disapprovingly. "Selfish, selfish. How many more of your friends must meet their end because of you? And you just added another five to that estimate, because of your little stunt in the stairwell."

Nora's body tensed up. His words were starting to get to her and she began to worry about whether or not she'd done the right thing.

"There is no longer any choice for you to make," Dr. Secora said dismissively, staring Nora and Bray down. "This will be the end of the line for the both of you. Braiden, you will follow me down to the Memory Reconstruction Lab. Eleanor, you have served your purpose to Constance, and have made us stronger and more efficient than we ever thought possible. Without you, we never would have gotten Program 7 stable enough to run—of course we never would have needed Program 7 in the first place without the Defected! So, even though you've turned our whole world upside down and created chaos, cost numerous agents their lives, inflicted heartache and torment on innocent families torn apart, and forced us to spend years upon years and countless resources trying to restore the peaceful land we once had—" Dr. Secora's voice rose in anger as he ticked off each item on his fingers. He paused, interrupting his rant, and regained his composure before continuing. "Despite all this," he went on, his voice resumed its usual emotionless tone. "I must thank you, really I must."

Nora fumed silently, her mind racing with a million questions. She shook her head—there was no point in asking, and he'd probably never tell her the truth anyhow.

"If you let us go right now, we will leave your building and never look back." Nora felt a lump in her throat as she formed her next sentence. "Let us go beyond the walls of Constance, and you'll never have to deal with us again."

"Beyond the walls of Constance?! No one has been outside of the city since it was constructed! Do you think that is by choice?"

Nora desperately tried to think of any other scenario that would end with Bray and her life being spared. "Then let Bray and I live out our days together in Jejung, among the other captured Defected."

"Not a chance," Dr. Secora replied instantly, clearly not taking any time to consider the suggestion. "If you think I would allow someone like you, Eleanor, to exist in this world at all, then you must take me for a fool."

As she came to terms with the reality of the situation, Nora's heart felt as though it were weighted down with a brick. This was the end—for her, for Bray, for the rebellion, and for any hope of a good future for the city of Constance.

"What will it be then, a public execution for the whole city to see?" she asked, wincing.

"And risk the likelihood of the rest of the rebellion turning you into a martyr?! Not a chance." A smirk grew across his dry lips, and he laughed menacingly, showing off his yellowed teeth. "Oh, Eleanor. There is much worse in store for you."

As Dr. Secora took a few steps towards his desk, the pile of red Defected shadows underneath the building flashed into Nora's mind. Their motionless bodies all piled on top of one another down beneath the marbled main floor. Swallowing hard, she realized that there was a very real possibility that Dr. Secora was about to end her life—that her heart would no longer beat or race or be thrilled or love anyone, and that laying amongst the pile of red shadows buried under the lobby might be where she was destined to reside for all eternity.

CHAPTER 39

Dr. Secora retrieved a small helmet from his desk, and then turned towards Nora and Bray. There were colored wires dangling from the headgear—the thin cables swung around as he adjusted something and then placed it on his head.

"No more testing!" Nora yelled when she caught sight of the helmet. "I'm not a puppet!"

"Oh, Eleanor, this is not for you," Dr. Secora said as he fastened the leather strap securing the device in place. "This is because of you. And as a result, we no longer require your Defected abilities for us to win this war."

There were small disks attached to the helmet that he placed firmly on each of his temples. Almost immediately, the small metal circles lit up. "Because of the data from your testing, we have found a way to run Program 7 without having to rely on only one single Defected mind."

As he spoke, Nora's thoughts went back to the dozens of red dots she'd seen under the building, yet again. Suddenly her eyes widened when it dawned on her what she had observed.

"So, you've seen them?" Dr. Secora had a smug smile on his face as he spoke. "Yes, what you are thinking is correct. Why should we force ourselves to be dependent on the cooperation of a more powerful Defected such as yourself Eleanor? We can achieve the same goal using the minds of a group of Defected, forcibly under our control."

Dr. Secora moved in closer to Nora, and then out of nowhere struck her in the face with his tightened fist. Nora—caught off guard completely—stumbled back and fell onto the ground. Still dazed, and with her jaw aching, she watched as Bray lunged towards Dr. Secora. Bray lost any sense of self control and exploded on Dr. Secora, swinging his arms back in wide sweeps before bringing his fists down with as much force as he could muster. He hit Dr. Secora over and over again. Dr. Secora tried to grab ahold of Bray's arms, but Bray moved with too much speed.

After one particularly hard hit, Dr. Secora lost his footing and stumbled backwards a few steps. Bray tried to take advantage of his wobble, and lunged forward, aiming straight for Dr. Secora's face. He wasn't quite quick enough however—Dr. Secora managed to duck down far enough so that Bray's fist impacted the helmet instead.

Bray screamed out in pain as his hand collided with the hard shell of the thick headgear, and staggered back towards where Nora still was. The two of them watched as Dr. Secora regained his composure and as his eyes narrowed in rage. His breath grew labored as he stood up straight and closed his eyes.

It only took Nora a moment to figure out what was happening. She reached over to her brother and grabbed his shoulder.

"I would think twice about what you are doing if I were you, Dr. Secora," Nora shouted.

Dr. Secora opened his eyes. "Our discussion is over Eleanor—your fate has been decided. This all ends right now, right here in this room."

Nora flashed Dr. Secora a smirk, which took him aback. "I think you have been distracted long enough," she said confidently.

"What?" Dr. Secora asked in confusion.

"Why don't you check those monitors on your desk and have a look for yourself," she replied.

Nora hoped that he would take the bait. He stared at her long and hard before finally turning to his desk. When he looked at the surveillance monitors his eyes widened in horror.

Nora took advantage of his moment of distraction to quickly occupy Will's mind. She sped through his memories, and went back to a time before she'd even found out she was going to become Defected—when they were all still a happy little family without a care in the world—and left his consciousness to remain inside of that memory.

"Wait here Will, I promise I will come back for you," Nora instructed his conscious mind, and then left her brother's existence behind inside his past.

When she opened her eyes, Will was gone. She breathed a sigh of relief. Seeing what had happened, Dr. Secora threw a fit, and began to violently thrash around.

"How can this be!?" he yelled as he hurled one of his surveillance monitors onto the marble floor. "I removed your friends from the stairwell. I took them all the way back to their memories of the night that they stole you from my lab. I placed them into the fields outside of this building, took their weapons, and left them there, completely defenseless. My agents should have captured them in plenty of time."

Nora smiled at him. "I knew there would be one thing you wouldn't be able to count on Dr. Secora," she paused for dramatic effect. "I was there, inside of their minds, with them." As Nora continued talking Dr. Secora began to move out from behind his desk.

"Once I was sure you had moved on and left their minds back in that field, I stepped in and moved them forward. I didn't bring them right back into the stairwell, but rather into their own futures." Dr. Secora said nothing in response, and simply stared at her in stifled rage. "I moved them right into your precious Test Lab 504—the one that holds all the data you've collected on Program 7."

Dr. Secora yelled out in fury, spit flying out of his mouth as he screamed. Pleased that she was achieving the desired reaction, Nora smiled once more and then continued.

"This little conversation we've all had in this room just now was done with the sole intention of distracting you long enough so that our fellow rebels had time to destroy all the data you've gathered," she finished.

"You have proven even more to me now, how much of an inconvenience a problematic Defected like you is to the rest of us," Dr. Secora said through gritted teeth.

Dr. Secora then lunged at Nora, moving towards her with his eyes closed. When his body impacted hers, he fell on top of her, and remained there, motionless and pinning her to the cold floor. The air was taken out of her lungs as his dead weight pressed down on her. Nora looked over to see Bray standing perfectly still, a blank stare in his eyes, as he stared out the window behind Dr. Secora's white desk.

When she was finally able to free herself from under Dr. Secora, she left his motionless body on the floor. During her struggle she was able to sense that he was inside the gray world around her mind, attempting to invade her thoughts.

Now, however, the feeling of his presence had vanished, and seeing Bray's odd demeanor she could only guess that he had already begun attacking Bray's subconsciousness.

She looked down at Dr. Secora's body on the ground and briefly considered executing him right then and there. But she immediately dismissed that idea—if she killed him while he was inhabiting another person's mind, who knows what would happen. For all she knew, Dr. Secora would end up permanently trapped inside of Bray's mind. Nora shuddered at the thought of that.

She picked herself up and went over to Bray, taking his hand. Nora then closed her eyes and let her mind drift out of her body and find Bray's. Seamlessly, she melded her consciousness with his.

When she gazed around the black landscape of his subconsciousness, she saw that the three of them inhabited Bray's mind together. They all stared at each other.

Dr. Secora was focusing intensely to allow his own mind to function within Bray's black mental world.

As Nora was trying to plot out her next move, the atmosphere shifted without warning. She glanced around, trying to understand what had happened, and saw Bray as a small boy, sitting on the floor of his white bedroom.

The room was small and only had enough space for a child-sized bed and a small dresser.

Hearing a noise behind her, Nora whirled around to see Dr. Secora holding up a desk lamp over his head threateningly. Nora quickly hoisted up the child version of Bray and moved him to the tight space between the bed and the wall, so that he would be shielded from whatever was about to occur. She wasn't quick enough to get herself out of the line of fire though, and Dr. Secora swung the lamp at her, hitting her square in the temple. The massive blow shattered the lamp instantly and Nora remained there, not moving, blood beginning to spill out from the wound on her head.

The pain was somehow different than what Nora had felt before, when Dr. Secora had physically struck her in the face back in his office. This was a pain that occupied her mind, rather than her body. Her skin and bones didn't hurt, but her vision faltered. She shook her head, hoping to clear the haze that had filled it. Just then, the sound of Dr. Secora's voice became audible to her intermittently.

"Now you will see exactly how damaging your actions can be Eleanor." His voice faded out and the sentence he spoke afterwards was inaudible to Nora's ears. "Every step you take here," he continued, his booming voice resuming its volume, "—every single breath—will eat away at the very fabric of Braiden's mind. Therefore, the more you move and try to fight back, the more you will destroy his psyche."

"You would destroy your own son's memories?" Nora asked in disbelief.

"Dismantling Braiden's memories is the only way I will be able to place him into the future he truly belongs in," Dr. Secora said matter-of-factly.

250

Nora squinted in pain. "The future of a person is something that should be decided by the individual themselves, not by some insane, city leader like you. We each have the right to live our lives as we see fit."

"Eleanor, how you see fit affects everyone around you. How can you even question whether it's right or wrong to interfere in other people's lives?" Dr. Secora replied incredulously.

"Us rebels have been given a gift," Nora began. "One that we were meant to share with the rest of the world, so that we could make it a better place for everyone."

Nora scooted her body back towards Bray's white childhood dresser. Her fingers blindly grazed the surface of it, hoping to find something to defend herself with. Feeling something hard and metallic, she grabbed it and flung it right at Dr. Secora. As it flew through the air she saw that what she'd picked up was a metal cube. Just before it made contact with Dr. Secora's head, he vanished from the room.

The child version of Bray began to cry. Scanning the room to make sure that Dr. Secora was indeed gone, she went and sat down beside Bray and put a comforting arm around his young shoulders.

"You will do great things one day, little Braiden. Never forget that," she said affectionately as she gave him a squeeze. After that she closed her eyes and left the memory.

She sent her consciousness to Bray's memory bank, and began to shuffle through hastily. There was no telling the amount of damage Dr. Secora could incur to Bray's future mental state if she didn't stop him in time. The images of Bray's life flew by, and she began to grow impatient as she passed year after year with no luck. Finally though, she discovered where Dr. Secora was hiding.

Dr. Secora was in the hallway of what appeared to be Bray's school. Bray seemed to be significantly older than he'd been in the bedroom memory. Dr. Secora had him in a chokehold, as dozens of students watched on in horror, screaming.

Nora knew she had to act fast. She ran over to them, and saw that Bray's eyes were starting to roll back into his head. She could feel his mind getting weaker with each movement she made. The vision of the white school hallway flickered, and Nora knew this was an indication that Bray was dangerously close to fading away entirely.

She grabbed a fire extinguisher off the wall and made a beeline for Dr. Secora. Repeatedly, she whacked him with the heavy extinguisher, as she simultaneously yelled at him to release Bray. Nora was relentless in her attack, and though some physical damage appeared on Dr. Secora's body, she was able to sense that she was doing more damage to his mental state. Mustering all the strength she had left, she focused it into one final blow, hoping to knock him completely unconscious.

As her last swing made contact with him, Dr. Secora stumbled backwards a few steps, losing his hold on Bray, and then vanished. Nora dropped the fire extinguisher noisily on the floor, and reached out to catch Bray from collapsing. Bray took in a huge gasp of air and reached his hand up to clutch at his throat where Dr. Secora had been holding him. Nora bent down to his ear, so that she could impart a few words to this version of Bray before leaving him behind.

"Your mother loves you very much," she said softly. "You will end up in a world surrounded by people that love you more than you will ever know."

Knowing the coast still wasn't clear, Nora quickly left the memory and resumed her hunt. Scanning through Bray's subconscious, going further into the future from the scene at the school, she located the two of them standing in a dimly lit room.

When she noticed the blue chipped paint on the walls and the old wooden chair beneath a single hanging bulb, she knew they were back inside the rebel base in Blear.

Dr. Secora looked around frantically, before running over to the Dream Machine and ripping two metal rods from its frame. He plowed straight through all the delicate equipment, tackling Bray and pinning him against one of the consoles.

Bray's mind had slowed down, due to all the alterations taking effect in his memories, therefore his reaction time was delayed. Dr. Secora wielded one of the metal rods and bashed him over the head.

Nora ran over and tried to pull Dr. Secora off of Bray, but it was useless—he was much larger and stronger than she was. She kicked and punched at him, but nothing stopped his attack.

Nora felt helpless—nothing was working. Suddenly an idea occurred to her. She wasn't sure if it would work, but she had to try something.

Every blow that hit Bray's head sent waves of pain to Nora, and made her vision of the scene begin to fragment and flicker. She could tell instinctively, just as before, that he was reaching the brink of his mental limits.

Nora decided to enter Bray's mind and co-exist there with him in the Dream Machine room as he endured the blows. Once she had successfully done so she was able to feel each hit with much more intensity.

Nora spoke out to Bray from inside of his mind. "We have to do this together!" she urged him. She wasn't able to feel any response from him, so she prayed he was able to at least hear her instructions. "Right arm—get it underneath his chest!" Nora used all of her focus and energy to move Bray's arm and wedge it under Dr. Secora. "Good, now on the count of three we are going to push him back as hard as we can. 1... 2... 3!"

The combination of Nora and Bray's joint efforts at shoving Dr. Secora back was thankfully enough to do the trick. Dr. Secora flew backwards, landing in a pile of equipment on the floor. Nora felt Bray's brain pounding as she mentally forced him to stand upright. It took an excruciating amount of effort to perform even this simple task.

Dr. Secora peeled himself off of the floor and looked at Bray before glancing wildly around the room. Nora's body stood idle near one of the consoles.

"What is going on here, how were you able to overpower me?"

Nora responded using Bray's voice. "There are still a few things you don't understand about the Defected world, Dr. Secora. The collective mind is stronger than any single person could ever hope to be," Nora moved Bray's body towards where Dr. Secora stood.

She yelled out another instruction within Bray's mind. Nora could feel their joint strength as the directed blow squarely landed on Dr. Secora's skull. Nora and Bray began to move in more sync and she no longer had to call out instructions.

Dr. Secora's eyes started to glaze over and roll back in his head as they leapt Bray's body onto him. They sat pinning him down and began to pummel him with Bray's fists. With each punch Bray and Nora felt more and more as though they were one unit, rather than two people moving independently.

Just as Nora was beginning to feel triumphant, Dr. Secora's body vanished, yet again. Nora turned Bray's head so that she could survey the room, just to make sure. It was then that Nora realized she couldn't feel Dr. Secora's presence inside of Bray's mind whatsoever any longer.

Nora drifted out of Bray's mind and returned to her body a few feet away in the Dream Machine room. The two stood side by side within his memory of the room where they'd shared their first kiss.

Bray's brow was furrowed—he was clearly still enduring a lot of pain from all the alterations. Nora desperately wanted to keep this as a happy memory for him, even though she knew the damage that was caused would be extensive.

Bray looked down at Nora. She was pressed up against his chest and looked up at him. Too weak to even angle his head down, he began to choke out a few words. "That was..."

"...intense," Nora supplied.

A tear rolled down Bray's cheek. "I have never felt that close to anyone before. It was as if we were one person—as though our minds and souls had merged."

Nora looked at him with love and devotion in her eyes. "I'm so sorry for all of this Bray, I had to try something. Thinking that you needed to come here with me was a mistake. I was worried he was going to obliterate all of your memories again and I wanted to protect you. Bray, can you promise me something?" she asked, her eyes filled with a sudden intensity.

"Anything Nora, what is it?"

"Promise me that no matter what happens, you'll never forget me," she said, and then raised herself onto the tips of her toes in order to kiss him before he even had a chance to reply. Bray closed his eyes in anticipation. After a moment, no longer feeling her against his chest, he opened his eyes in confusion. Nora was gone.

Before Bray could comprehend what had just happened, Dr. Secora appeared in front of him in the Dream Machine room of Blear. Bray looked at him confused.

"What have you done?!" he yelled out. "Where is Nora?!"

"Eleanor exposed a weakness to me," Dr. Secora began to walk a slow circle around Bray in a predator-like way. "She was so focused on protecting your memories, my son, that she left the one thing she depended on completely vulnerable for me to take. I took full advantage of that fact. Thus her blinding love for you is, in the end, her undoing."

Bray's blood boiled, "Where is she?" he demanded.

"It's over," Dr. Secora replied calmly, ignoring his question. "Constance has prevailed. However, there is still one more task for me to complete. Don't worry Braiden, what I'm going to do to you will spare your mind from having to experience the heartache of losing your precious Eleanor, since I shall be removing all of your memories of her, amongst everything else."

The room started to flicker as Dr. Secora began to attempt his infiltration of Bray's mind. Bray blinked rapidly as he desperately tried to maintain control, but Program 7 was too strong for his unprotected mentality.

He was losing the battle for control over his mind, and as his consciousness began to crumble he tried to focus on a specific memory that he couldn't bear to lose. He narrowed all his efforts on recalling the night he'd spent alone with Nora, watching her as she slept inside the dirt-walled room in the Fallow base. The memory materialized around him, but his vision was strobing in and out and he was quickly losing his grasp on his mind. Using his final reserve of strength, he lifted himself up onto the cot where Nora lay soundly asleep. He managed to settle in beside her and then took one, last, ragged breath, before his whole world went dark.

CHAPTER 40

Otto, Trim, Bretta, Jack and Phoenix ran at full speed to Dr. Secora's office, flinging the door to the entrance wide open. They rushed inside and Trim yelled out excitedly.

"We did it!" he cheered, "We shut down Program 7!"

They sped through the entry room and into the main office, where each rebel proceeded to stop dead in their tracks. They looked around in shock, trying to make sense of the scene. Bretta and Phoenix ran over to Bray's crumpled body, laying motionless on the floor.

Otto and Trim ran over to where Dr. Secora was laying on the ground. He too was not moving. Otto placed a hand on Dr. Secora's neck, trying to find a heart beat. Feeling nothing, he turned his head to the side to listen for breathing. Otto looked up at Trim.

"Nothing," Otto reported. "No pulse. No breath." Otto shook his head. "One of two things must of happened—either Bray and Nora managed to take him down, or Dr. Secora was still inside Program 7 when we destroyed it," he said.

Otto turned as Phoenix yelled out. "He's alive! Bray is alive!" Otto ran over to join them. "His heartbeat is slow and faint, but it's still there." Phoenix shook Bray's shoulder gently in an effort to revive him.

"Bray, wake up, what happened to Nora?" Phoenix asked.

Bray didn't reply, and remained unresponsive despite her attempts. "Where's Nora?" she asked again tearfully.

Letting go of Bray, Phoenix turned to Otto and buried her face in his chest. Otto wrapped his arms around her and held her tightly. Meanwhile, Jack searched around the room for any signs of what might have happened. He headed back over to Dr. Secora's uninhabited body. He bent down and removed the helmet from Dr. Secora's head and placed it in his bag.

Otto, still holding Phoenix, locked eyes with the other rebels. "Bray's alive," he informed them. "If we can manage to wake him up, maybe we can get some answers."

Nobody moved, the shock of the situation seemed to have rendered them catatonic. "We have to get him back to Blear," Otto urged. "Maybe Lace can get inside of his head somehow and pull him back out."

The rebels agreed that this was the best course of action, and they seemed grateful for Otto having the discipline to maintain his leadership role even in the midst such a traumatic scene. Trim, being the strongest physically of the remaining rebels, hoisted Bray up and began to carry him towards the door.

The door to the top floor swung open in front of them without warning. Otto, letting go of Phoenix, pulled out his rifle, and when the first agent appeared in the doorway, Otto shot him without hesitation.

The rebels joined in the effort and began to shoot agent after agent that appeared, until there was a heap of bodies piled on the ground, their bright red blood spilling out onto the pristine white marble floor.

CHAPTER 41

Bray sat alone in an empty room. Although there was no apparent light source, he was easily able to see his body. Everything besides his own flesh however, was completely dark. It was difficult for him to sense the passing of time in a place that consisted entirely of nothingness, so he had no idea how long he'd been sitting there. As the moments continued to creep by, time became a useless concept to him.

With no external stimuli whatsoever, Bray had no choice but to turn inwards, and soon got lost within his own mind. As he searched through the remaining fragments of his various memories and ideas, every once in a while the face of a beautiful girl would flash across his vision. He was certain he'd never met this girl before, but there was an odd sense of recognition within him each time her face appeared—the way her lips curled up into a half-smile, the irrepressible light in her eyes, and the dark hair that fell across her face—all seemed familiar.

The first few times the girl materialized in front of him, Bray instinctively tried to run towards her, but she'd always vanish before he could get too close. There was a certain magnetism in her presence, and the pull was difficult to resist, but after many failed attempts he abandoned his efforts, and instead simply gazed at her face whenever she appeared.

Despite the fact that he could not pinpoint any memory within which this girl existed, he could not shake the emotions that arose from seeing her. Each time he tried to examine why he felt such a connection to this nameless stranger, a wave of sadness rose up within him. He turned his attention away from those feelings, always fearful that they would grow so strong as to wash over and consume him entirely.

Bray continued to struggle in the dark room for what felt like an eternity, and for all he knew, could have been. The darkness in the room was so vast that it almost dizzied him. As he peered out into the nothingness that surrounded him, he tried to focus on a single point of his life—something, anything, with which to ground himself to. Everything felt disorganized though, and nothing made any sense despite his efforts to connect with his memories. The only thing that felt tangible and real was the mysterious girl that kept reappearing, and so he focused completely on her.

Suddenly, a voice cut through the silence. At that point the isolation of being in that room had reached a stifling level for Bray, so the voice—which was that of a young girl—felt like a beacon of light piercing a heavy fog. Unsure at first if it could possibly just be his desperate imagination, he sat in stunned silence. But when the voice sounded again, it was unmistakably real.

"Bray?" the young girl asked. "Are you in here, Bray?"

He leapt up and turned his head wildly around to survey the room, but there was nothing. It was unyielding in its emptiness. "I'm here!" he yelled out hoarsely. He cleared his throat as his heartbeat quickened. "Hello? I'm here!"

"I've never done this before," the girl said. "I'm not sure how to find you."

Bray blindly fumbled his way around the room, hoping to reach whomever was speaking. He waved his arms out ahead of him, moving his hands to feel for anything that could be there, but the effort was futile. "Where are you?" he called out.

There was a pause before the girl answered. "I am here with you, Bray. We are both here."

"If you are here, then why can't I see you?" Bray asked.

"I don't know. Maybe if you try to focus on a memory you have, we'd be able to find each other using that as a point of reference. Can you think of any memory in particular?" she asked.

"No," he replied. "I don't seem to have a firm grasp on anything—there are glimpses of things, or little flickers of emotions, but when I concentrate on them they go out of focus," he said, his voice filled with frustration.

"Bray, I need you to tell me where to find you," she said urgently.

"I don't understand what you mean by find me," Bray responded, feeling frustrated by his own uselessness. "I'm in a dark room, alone, and I can't see or feel or smell or taste anything. There are no clues as to where I am. The sound of your voice is the only thing I can even sense outside of my own existence."

"You are locked inside of your own subconsciousness, Bray," the girl said quietly. "Right now you're at the rebel base in Blear, where you were brought back in an attempt to recover your mind."

"How are you talking to me?" he asked.

"You have been hooked up to the Dream Machine. It took Grane a while to fix it up so that it would be stable enough to run Program 7. During that time it was decided by Lace that I was the strongest candidate to come in and try to rescue you. But I can't do it alone—I need you to help me," she pleaded.

"I'm not sure I can. What am I supposed to do?" he asked.

There was another pause before she continued. "We have discussed it. Your data on the consoles shows that your mind is still full of memories. They haven't been destroyed, only blocked from you. It's as if another force is keeping your mind from accessing most of them. We think that you need to try and focus on a memory that doesn't include Nora."

"Nora?" Bray said slowly, almost as if to himself. "Is that her name?" he asked the girl.

"Grane has promised to do all he can to restore you to your previous self if we can get you out of here. We need you to focus on that right now."

Still silently repeating the name Nora to himself, Bray felt a surge of hope fill him. "Why does she continue to appear inside of my memories?"

Skirting around his direct question, the young girl spoke carefully. "I have been told that the rest of your group was able to shut down Program 7 entirely. Once disabled however, it left you trapped inside of your own mind. When the group came into Dr. Secora's office they found you unconscious on the floor. They then brought you back here to the Blear base. Their rescue was met with excess force from the Agency. Luckily, everyone was able to return here with only minor injuries, including you."

"And what about Nora?" he pressed.

There was a very long pause before the young girl answered. The silence went on for such an extended period of time that Bray felt the completely void room empty itself even further. His heart stilled as he waited for her to speak. The longer it took for her to respond the clearer it became to Bray that her answer would not be anything he wanted to hear.

"I'm so sorry, Bray," she said finally, her voice filled with emotion. "I'm so, so sorry."

Bray collapsed in the empty room at the realization that whoever Nora had been and whatever she had meant to him, was gone now. The only thing he had any connection to in his memories no longer existed. The image of that lovely face each time it flashed before his eyes was all that had kept him tethered to reality in that interminable blackness. As the apologetic words of the young girl speaking to him rang in his ears, he felt the tether snap.

* * *

After sitting in silence for a very long while, Bray inhaled deeply, hoping to tap into a reserve of strength. He had to make an effort to get himself out of what he now understood to be an imprisonment within his mind. Breaking down and giving up would not pave the road to his freedom—as the young girl said, he had to help.

He began to hunt for any memory that his fragile mind could hold on to. To his surprise, the world around him changed almost instantly. Pure, white light and a wide spectrum of colors flooded his vision. As his eyes recovered from the shock of the blinding glow, he found himself sitting in a chair, a few feet away from a small cot upon which the enticing Nora lay sleeping. After watching her for only a few seconds, he could already feel the memory beginning to slip away. Focusing his attention like a laser beam, he began to meditate on one single spot within the scene—a tear that clung to Nora's bottom lashes on her left eye. Immediately he felt greater mental balance, and his hold on the memory started to stabilize. He continued to stare at that small, round teardrop. From his earlier scan of the surroundings he knew there were no windows within the room that led to the outside world, but Bray could swear he saw just the tiniest hint of moonlight, or perhaps starlight, refracted in the iridescent sheen of the teardrop's surface. Wherever that light was coming from, it was unmistakably a celestial source.

As his teardrop-meditation continued, he tried to shut out any invading thoughts and focus entirely on the world of that single bead of moisture. He imagined the sadness that had willed it into existence. It appeared to have a slippery texture, and it most likely had the slightest briny taste to it. Less tangibly, there must of been something special about this teardrop. Nora was fast asleep and must have long since ceased crying, but this particular droplet clung on and stayed with her, after all the rest had fallen to the ground.

"I can see you have regained some of your ability," the young girl said, startling Bray out of his self-induced trance. "Where are you? If I can get to the same memory I should be able to pull you out of here."

"I'm..." Bray began to answer her, but then changed his mind. If this young girl was able to free him, then he'd be traveling to a reality within which Nora didn't exist.

Bray had developed a very strong grasp on the memory now, and felt rooted in it enough so that he could focus on the whole scene at once again. He stood up from the chair, tentatively at first, just to make sure it wouldn't cause any problems. He then walked over to the cot and sat down beside Nora. Instinctively, he bent down to kiss her.

As he neared her face, Nora's eyes suddenly opened and she locked her gaze on him. The teardrop he had been so lovingly observing spilled off her lashes from the movement.

"Please Bray, you have to come find me."

Bray jumped back, startled. Nora's eyes immediately re-shut and she continued to sleep peacefully, as if nothing had happened. It was as if she had left Bray a message in his memory of that moment for him to find. As if she knew he would be lost without her and needed a sign to continue to try and find her. For the first time since he'd found out Nora was gone, he felt a glimmer of happiness.

"Bray, you need to get out of there now!" the young girl yelled in a panic-stricken voice.

The dirt walls around him had begun to shake—he stared at them in confusion. "What is happening out there?" he asked. "I need to stay here and find her."

"There is no time, the Agency found us and they're attacking the Blear base. Get out now, Bray!" she pleaded.

He scrambled to come up with a plan, but the surrounding chaos made it impossible to concentrate. As the dirt walls and floor continued to violently shake, the scene of the memory began to flicker in his mind until it disappeared completely and he returned to the empty, dark room.

Back in his isolation everything suddenly became clear to Bray. "Are you still there?" he called out to the girl. "I need you to do something for me."

"There is no time Bray," she screamed back. "You have to come back to us now!"

"Please don't go just yet. I need someone out there to load Program 7 into my subconsciousness." He waited but no response came. "Please," he begged.

The young girl's voice never did return. After waiting a very long time in hopes of her coming back, Bray finally gave up. He decided to return to the memory with Nora on the cot.

As he gazed at her, affection rose up within him, and he went over and laid down beside Nora. Bray watched as she slept, enjoying the simple pleasure of observing her at peace. They remained like that, side-by-side on the cot together, for a very long time, until the memory began to flicker and fade away as it had before.

Back in the solitude of the empty room, Bray fought repeatedly to return to the memory, but it was no use. No matter how urgently he willed the vision of her to re-appear, he saw only the black space in front of him.

Emotionally depleted, Bray sat down on the ground and curled himself up, hugging his knees to his chest. As tears welled up in his eyes he didn't bother to wipe them away. Staring down at the ground, he watched as the tears rolled off his chin and fell, one by one, onto the dark ground. As the last tear collided with the black surface he sat upon, a sudden flash of red and white lights illuminated it.

Stunned, Bray quickly moved so that he was kneeling above the area where the flash had occurred. Staring intently down at the ground, he discovered he was able to will the lights to return with enough focus.

Bray looked up into the darkness. "Thank you," he whispered. He knew that this meant someone had heard his plea before when the Blear base was being attacked. Someone—before evacuating and making a run for their lives—had loaded Program 7.

There was no telling how much time he would have inside of the shadow world though. If the rebels weren't triumphant against the Agency's attack, the agents would most certainly head straight for the Dream Machine room and find him there. Bray prayed that at the very least the rebels would be able to keep them at bay for a long enough period of time for him to find Nora in the gray outlined world below him.

He began to scan through the red shadows underneath his knees. As he spotted each one, he would narrow in his focus to get a better look at who they were. Again and again he was filled with disappointment as each face did not belong to Nora.

As time wore on, his mind began to grow weak from the exertion—it seemed as though he had inspected a thousand red shadows. Finally he inspected what he believed to be the final red shadow, who turned out to be yet another stranger.

Making a second pass through the city, he decided to take it one sector at a time, starting with Arrant. Bray carefully inspected the area where Nora had grown up, but there was no sign of her. Next, he went over to Blear, followed by Fallow, Sonant, and then even attempted to

263

hunt through the overwhelming number of red shadows in the Jejung prison. He was beginning to lose hope.

Last, he checked the center sector of the city of Constance. As he surveyed Obsidia he saw a group of red silhouettes located a few floors below the building's ground level. After relentlessly checking through the dozens of Defected there, his throat tightened up as the bleakness of the situation set in.

He needed to take a break from the hunt, the level of intense focus was unsustainable for too long and he feared he would burn himself out. Allowing his focus to widen, he floated up until the entire city was visible. Bray watched as the countless red and white dots traveled throughout it. The presence of so many flickering red shadows—Defected just like him—comforted him somewhat. Though Nora was gone, every single one of those red souls could continue to fight for the chance to live a life worth living, all because of her sacrifice.

As he made a final sweep of the landscape and was just about to give up, something caught his eye.

His heart raced as he tried to focus in on the faint red dot that hovered just beyond the walls of Constance. Despite how hard he strained his mind, he couldn't get close enough to the shadow to confirm his suspicions. He didn't care that he couldn't validate it though, he knew in his gut that the red shadow belonged to her.

As he gazed lovingly at the red pinprick in the distance, everything that surrounded him began to shake. The gray world began to flicker in and out within his mental cell, and it felt as though he was going through an earthquake. Bray inhaled sharply as he prepared his weakened mentality to dedicate every thought towards setting his imprisoned mind free.

* * *

The door that led to the Dream Machine room exploded open and the small area filled with a heavy smoke. A few agents filed in, kicking aside the remaining fragments of the door as they entered.

One of the agents ran over immediately to Bray, who was still hooked up to the Dream Machine. The agent inspected his thin, malnourished body. A trickle of blood ran out of Bray's nose. As the agent moved in closer to see if he was breathing, Bray's torso began to convulse.

The agent pressed down on top of Bray to keep his body from jolting off of the Dream Machine. As Bray continued to writhe under the